Buffy
the Vampire Slayer

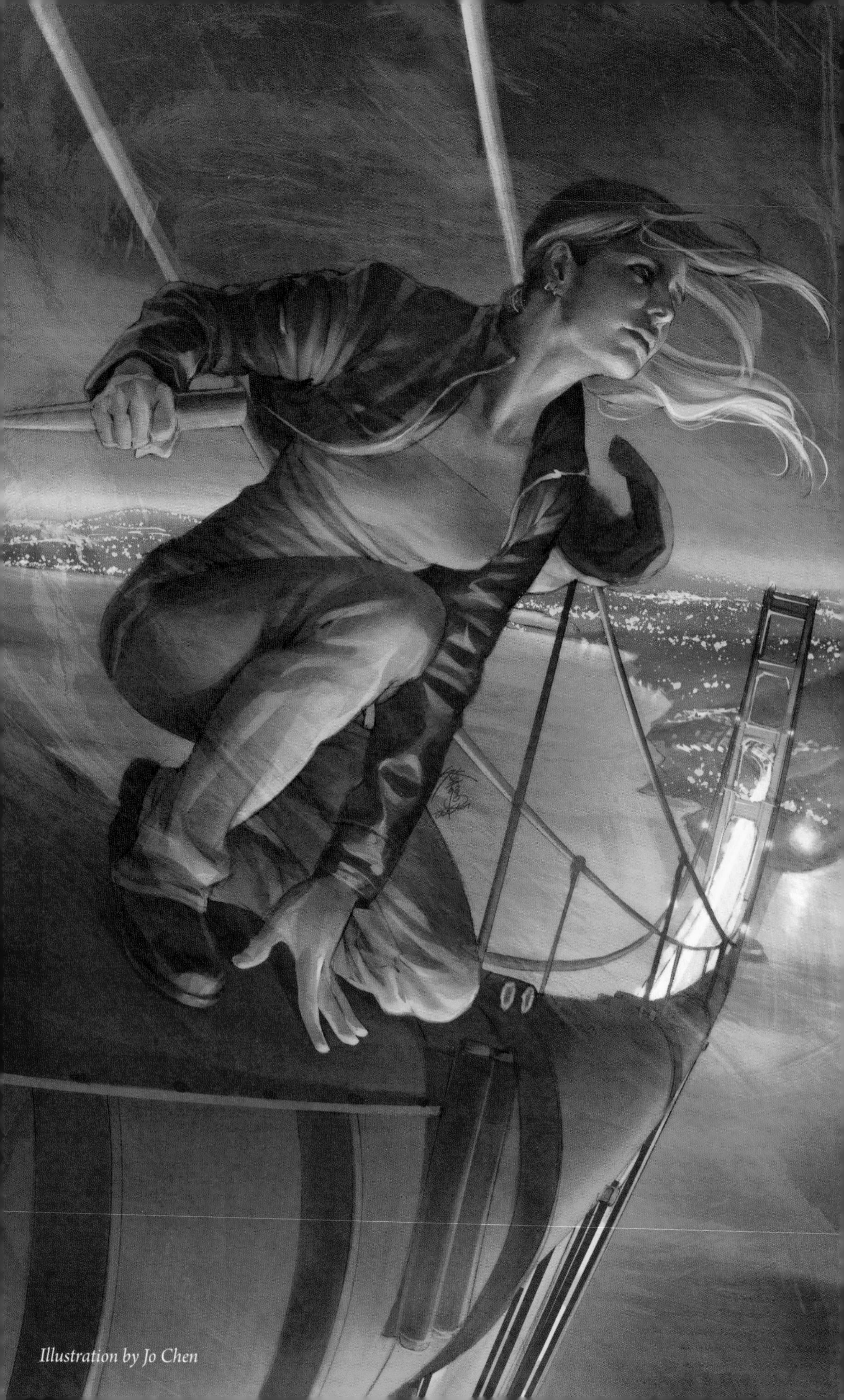

Illustration by Jo Chen

Buffy the Vampire Slayer™

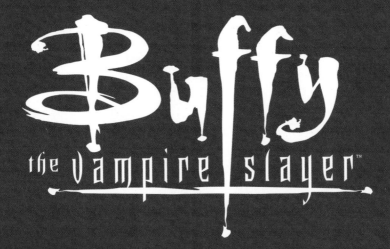

SEASON 9 · VOLUME 1

FREEFALL

SCRIPT
JOSS WHEDON & ANDREW CHAMBLISS

PENCILS
GEORGES JEANTY

INKS
DEXTER VINES

SLAYER, INTERRUPTED

SCRIPT
ANDREW CHAMBLISS

PENCILS
KARL MOLINE

INKS
ANDY OWENS

MAGICAL MYSTERY TOUR

SCRIPT
JANE ESPENSON

PENCILS
GEORGES JEANTY

INKS
DEXTER VINES

COLORS
MICHELLE MADSEN

LETTERS
RICHARD STARKINGS
& Comicraft's JIMMY BETANCOURT

CHAPTER BREAK ART
STEVE MORRIS

FRONT COVER ART
JO CHEN

EXECUTIVE PRODUCER
JOSS WHEDON

DARK HORSE BOOKS

President & Publisher
MIKE RICHARDSON

Editors
SCOTT ALLIE & SIERRA HAHN

Assistant Editor
FREDDYE LINS

Collection Designer
JUSTIN COUCH

Published by Dark Horse Books
A division of Dark Horse Comics, Inc.
10956 SE Main Street
Milwaukie, OR 97222

DarkHorse.com

To find a comics shop in your area, call the
Comic Shop Locator Service toll-free at
(888) 266-4226.

First edition: July 2012
ISBN 978-1-59582-922-1

10 9 8 7 6 5 4 3 2 1

This story takes place after the events of *Buffy the Vampire Slayer* Season 8, created by Joss Whedon.

Special thanks to Debbie Olshan at Twentieth Century Fox and Daniel Kaminsky.

NEIL HANKERSON Executive Vice President • TOM WEDDLE Chief Financial Officer • RANDY STRADLEY Vice President of Publishing
MICHAEL MARTENS Vice President of Book Trade Sales • ANITA NELSON Vice President of Business Affairs • DAVID SCROGGY Vice
President of Product Development • DALE LAFOUNTAIN Vice President of Information Technology • DARLENE VOGEL Senior Direc-
tor of Print, Design, and Production • KEN LIZZI General Counsel • MATT PARKINSON Senior Director of Marketing • DAVEY ESTRADA
Editorial Director • SCOTT ALLIE Senior Managing Editor • CHRIS WARNER Senior Books Editor • DIANA SCHUTZ Executive Editor •
CARY GRAZZINI Director of Print and Development • LIA RIBACCHI Art Director • CARA NIECE Director of Scheduling

BUFFY THE VAMPIRE SLAYER™ SEASON 9 VOLUME 1: FREEFALL

This volume reprints the comic-book series *Buffy the Vampire Slayer* Season 9 #1–#5 from Dark Horse Comics, and the short story
"Buffy the Vampire Slayer: Magical Mystery Tour Featuring the Beetles" from Dark Horse Digital.

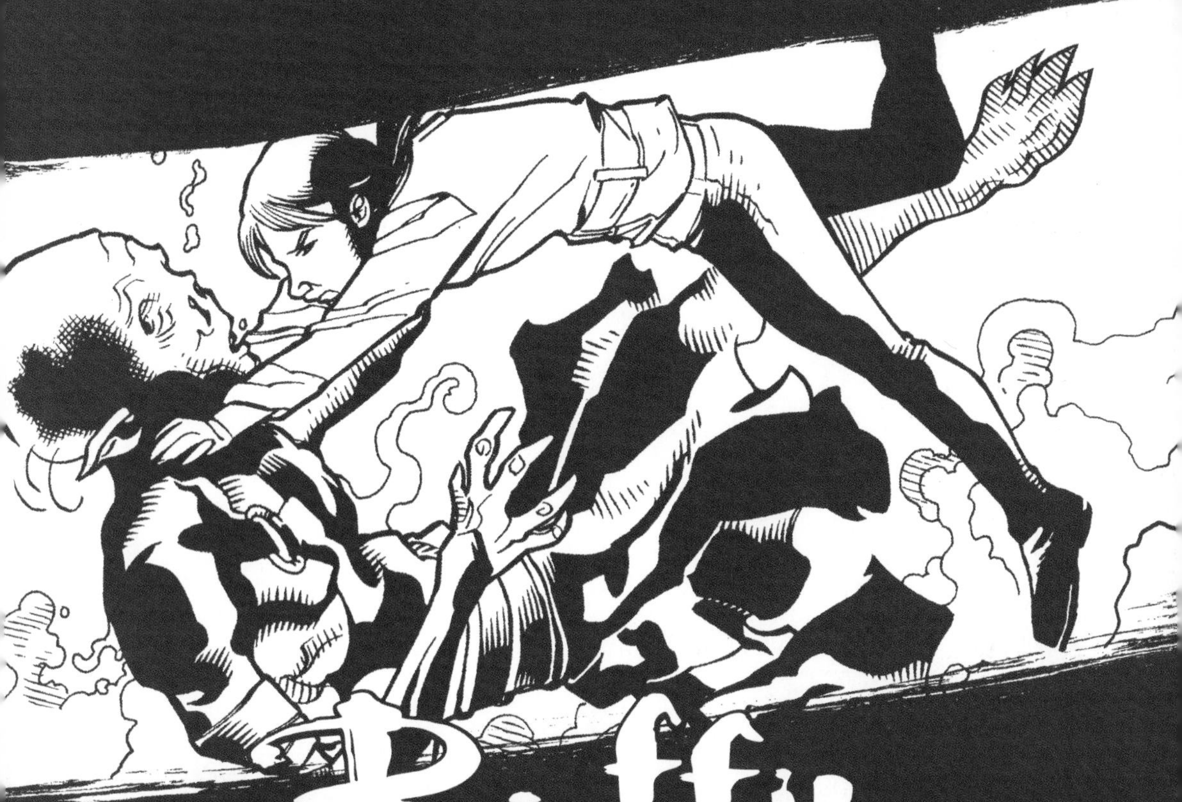

Buffy the Vampire Slayer™

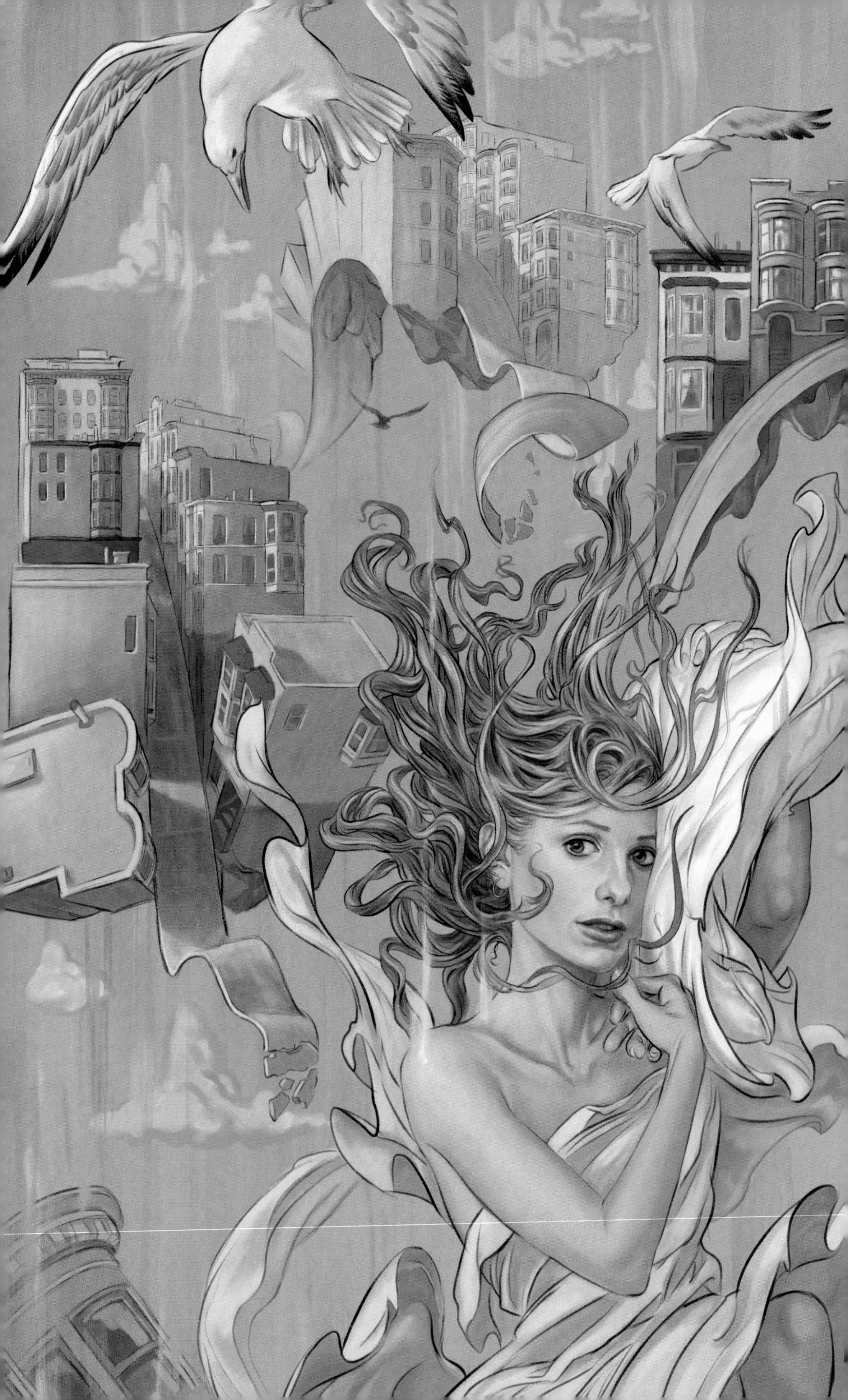

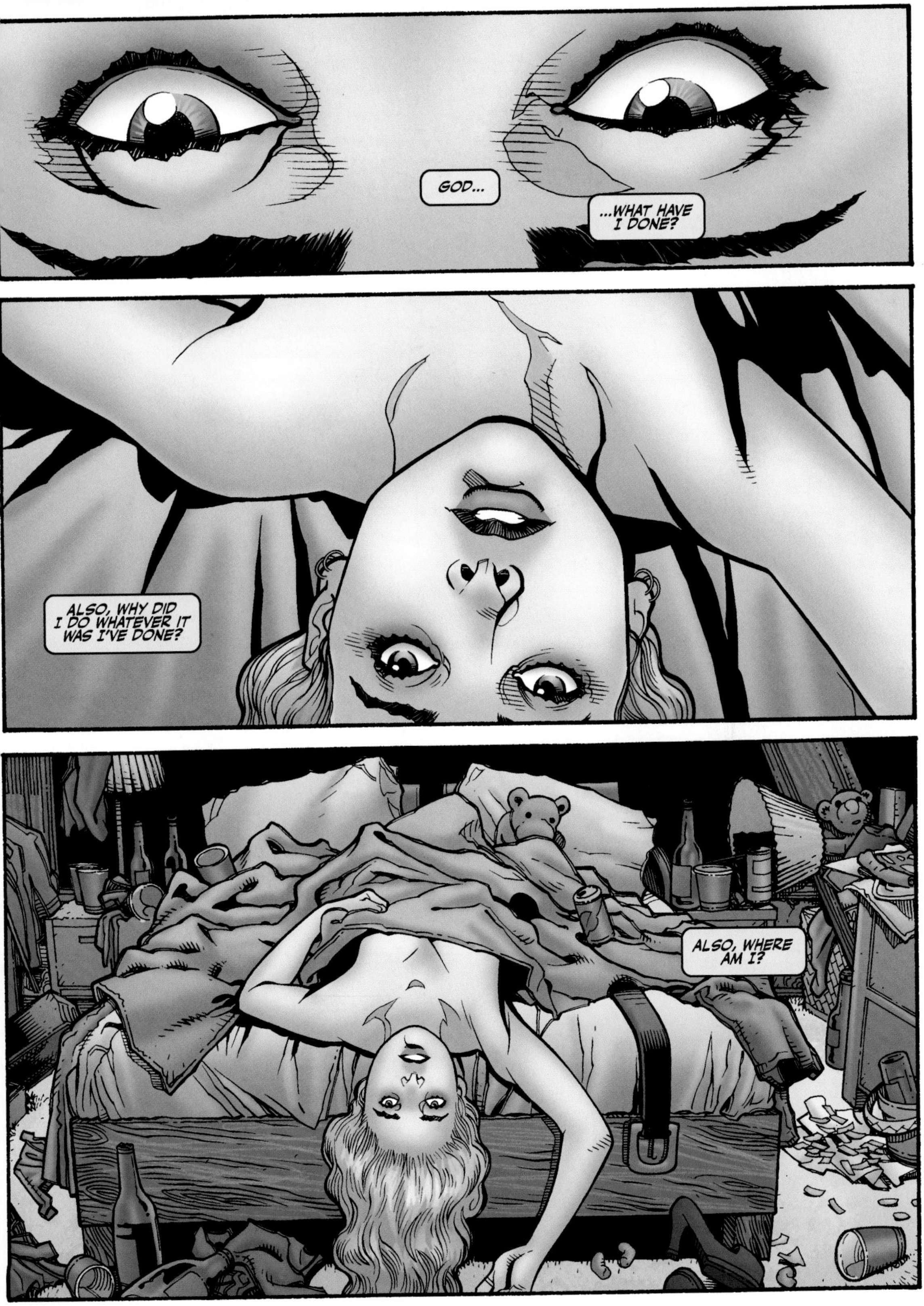
GOD...
...WHAT HAVE I DONE?
ALSO, WHY DID I DO WHATEVER IT WAS I'VE DONE?
ALSO, WHERE AM I?

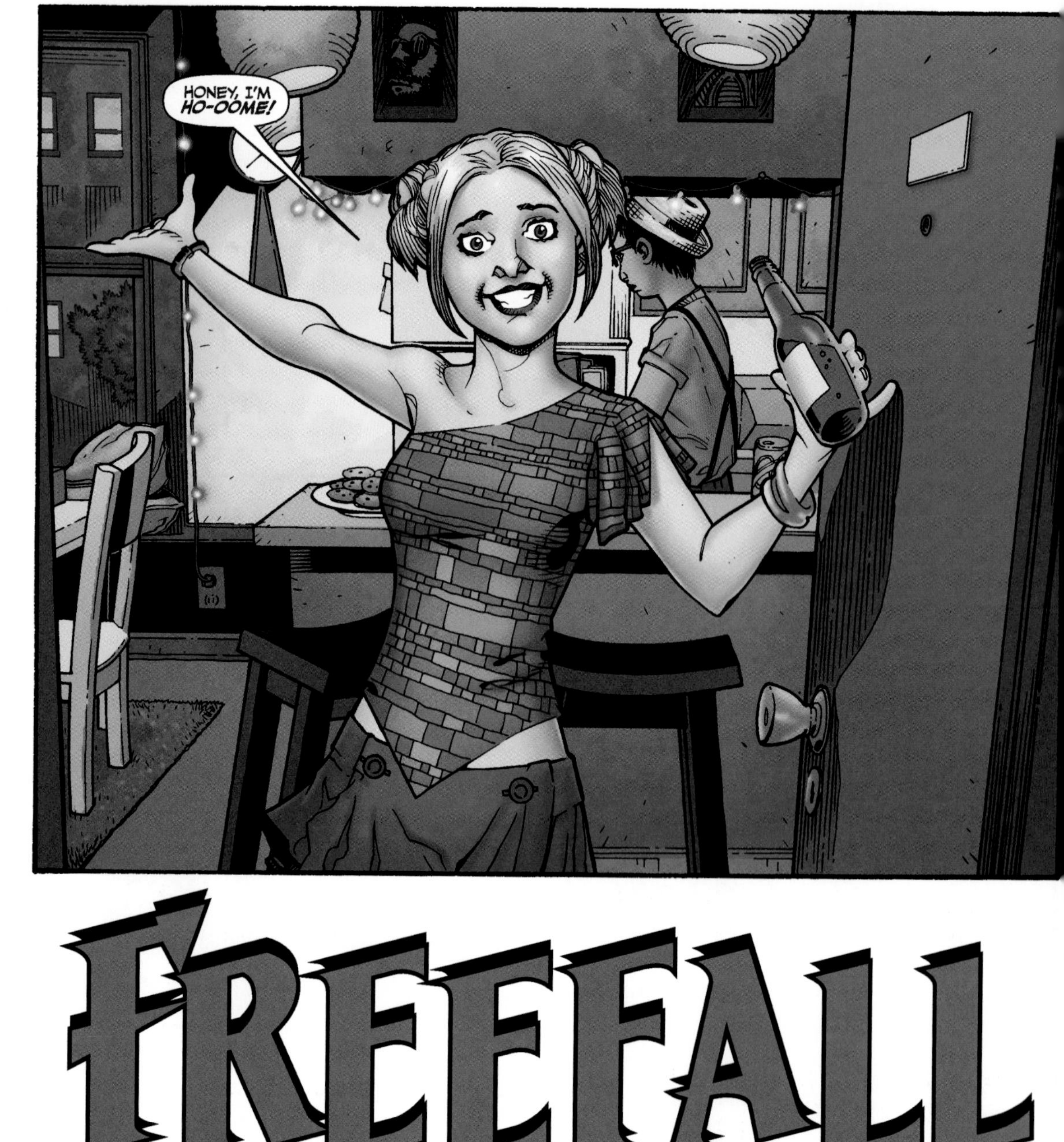
HONEY, I'M HO-OOME!

FREEFALL

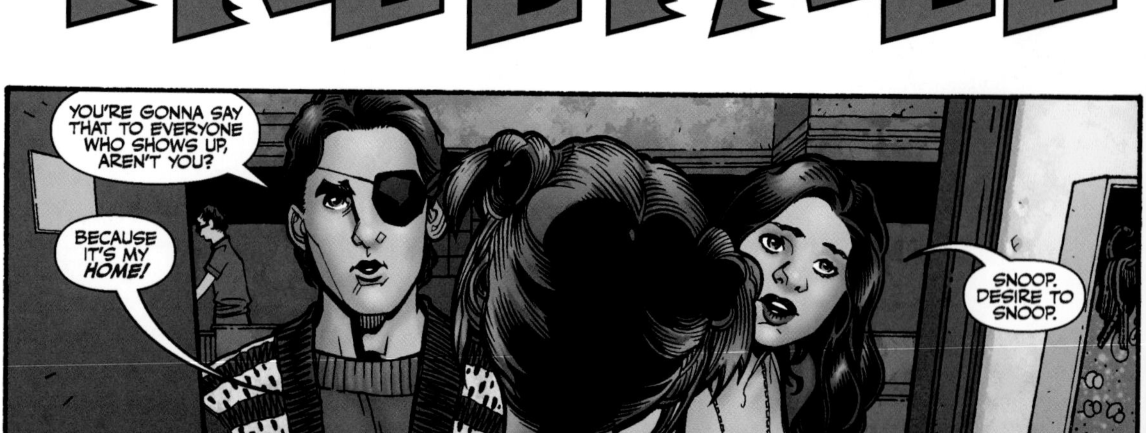
YOU'RE GONNA SAY THAT TO EVERYONE WHO SHOWS UP, AREN'T YOU?
BECAUSE IT'S MY HOME!
SNOOP. DESIRE TO SNOOP.

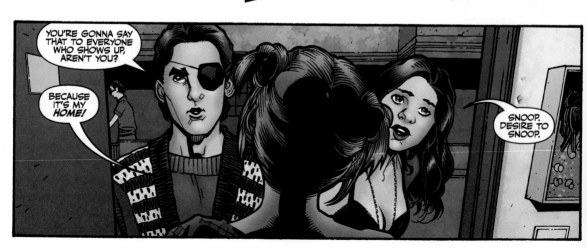

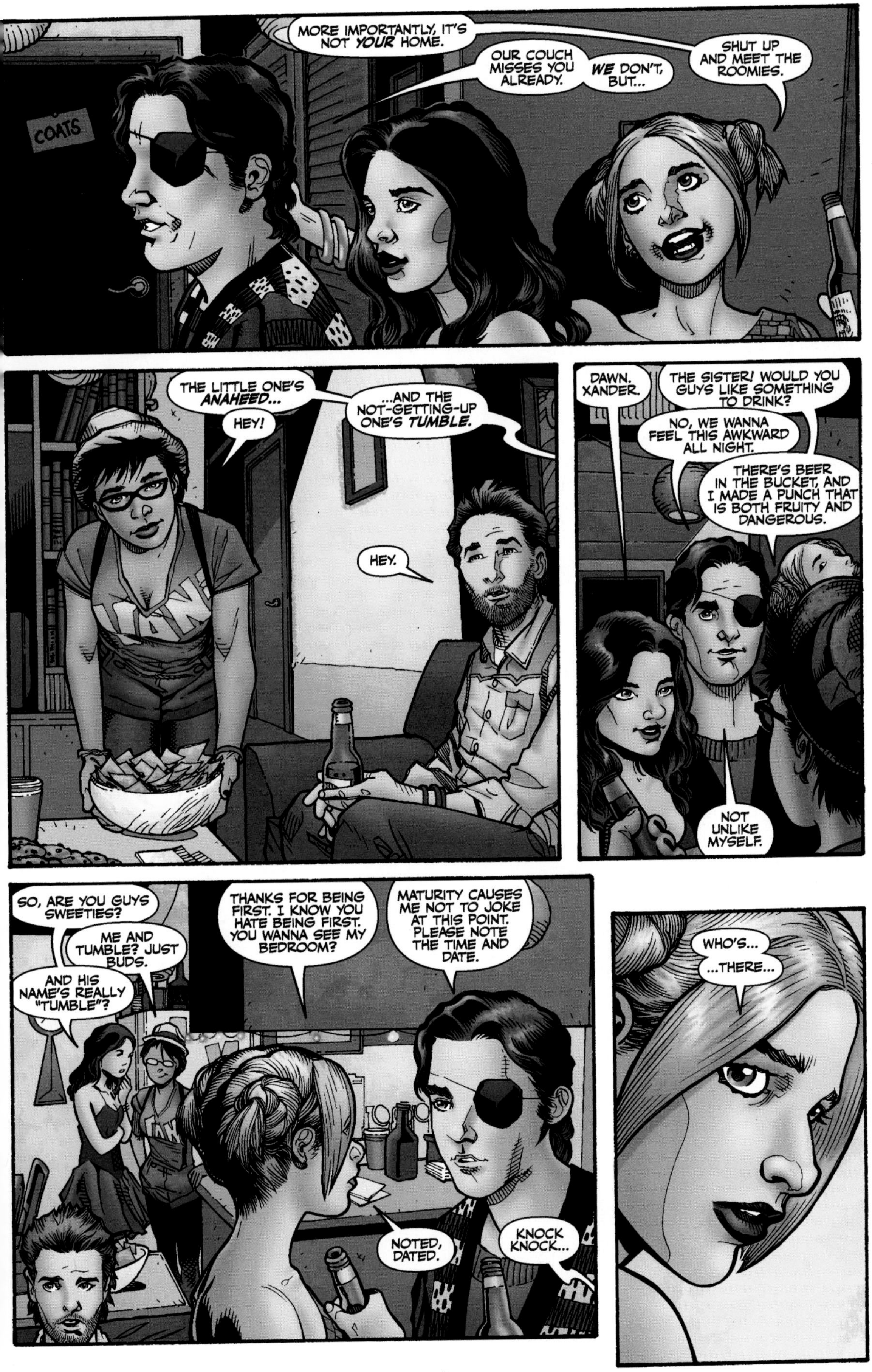

MORE IMPORTANTLY, IT'S NOT *YOUR* HOME.
OUR COUCH MISSES YOU ALREADY.
WE DON'T, BUT...
SHUT UP AND MEET THE ROOMIES.
THE LITTLE ONE'S *ANAHEED...*
HEY!
...AND THE NOT-GETTING-UP ONE'S *TUMBLE.*
HEY.
DAWN. XANDER.
THE SISTER! WOULD YOU GUYS LIKE SOMETHING TO DRINK?
NO, WE WANNA FEEL THIS AWKWARD ALL NIGHT.
THERE'S BEER IN THE BUCKET, AND I MADE A PUNCH THAT IS BOTH FRUITY AND DANGEROUS.
NOT UNLIKE MYSELF.
SO, ARE YOU GUYS SWEETIES?
ME AND TUMBLE? JUST BUDS.
AND HIS NAME'S REALLY "TUMBLE"?
THANKS FOR BEING FIRST. I KNOW YOU HATE BEING FIRST. YOU WANNA SEE MY BEDROOM?
MATURITY CAUSES ME NOT TO JOKE AT THIS POINT. PLEASE NOTE THE TIME AND DATE.
NOTED, DATED.
KNOCK KNOCK...
WHO'S...
...THERE...
COATS

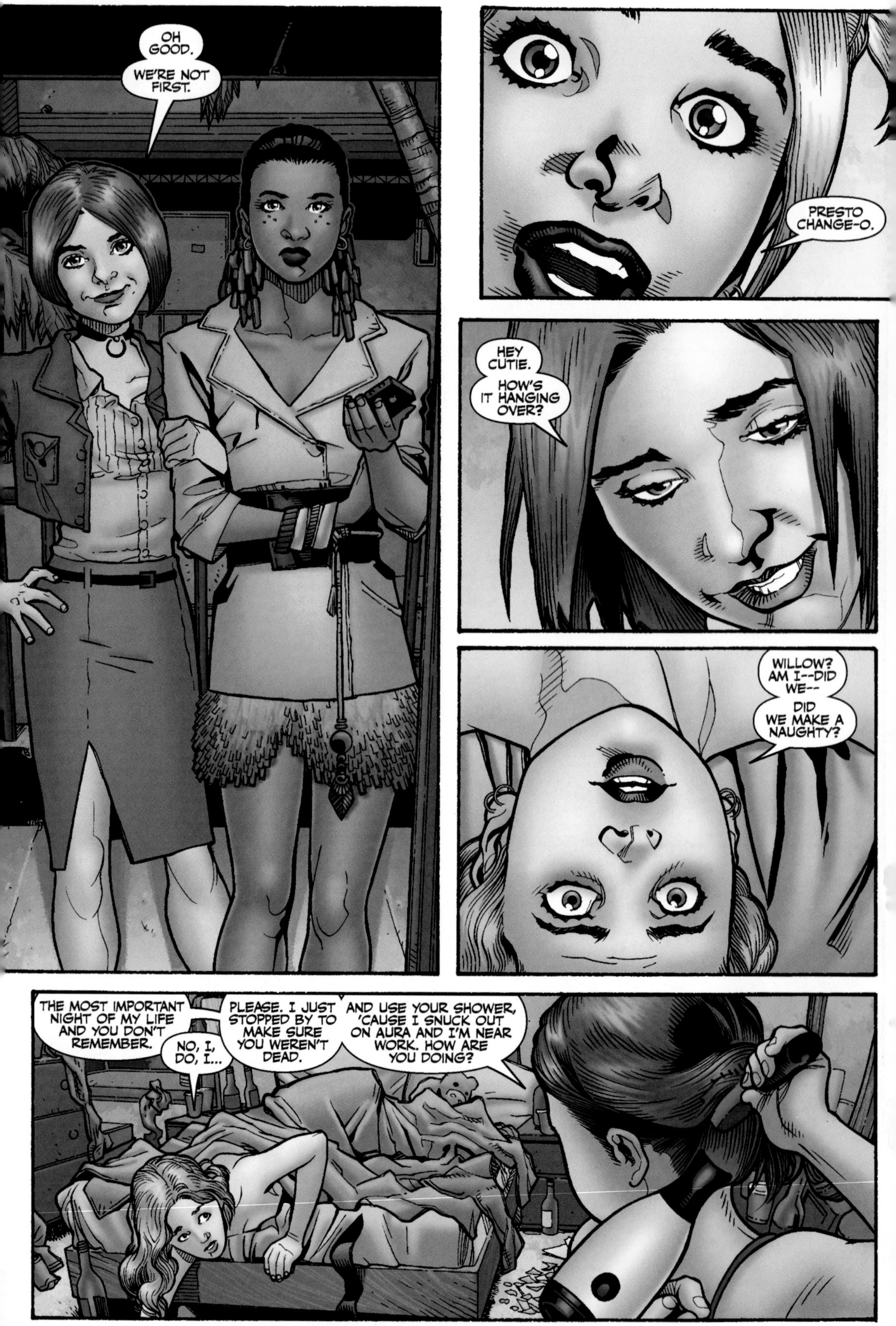
OH GOOD.
WE'RE NOT FIRST.
PRESTO CHANGE-O.
HEY CUTIE.
HOW'S IT HANGING OVER?
WILLOW? AM I--DID WE--
DID WE MAKE A NAUGHTY?
THE MOST IMPORTANT NIGHT OF MY LIFE AND YOU DON'T REMEMBER.
NO, I, DO, I...
PLEASE. I JUST STOPPED BY TO MAKE SURE YOU WEREN'T DEAD.
AND USE YOUR SHOWER, 'CAUSE I SNUCK OUT ON AURA AND I'M NEAR WORK. HOW ARE YOU DOING?

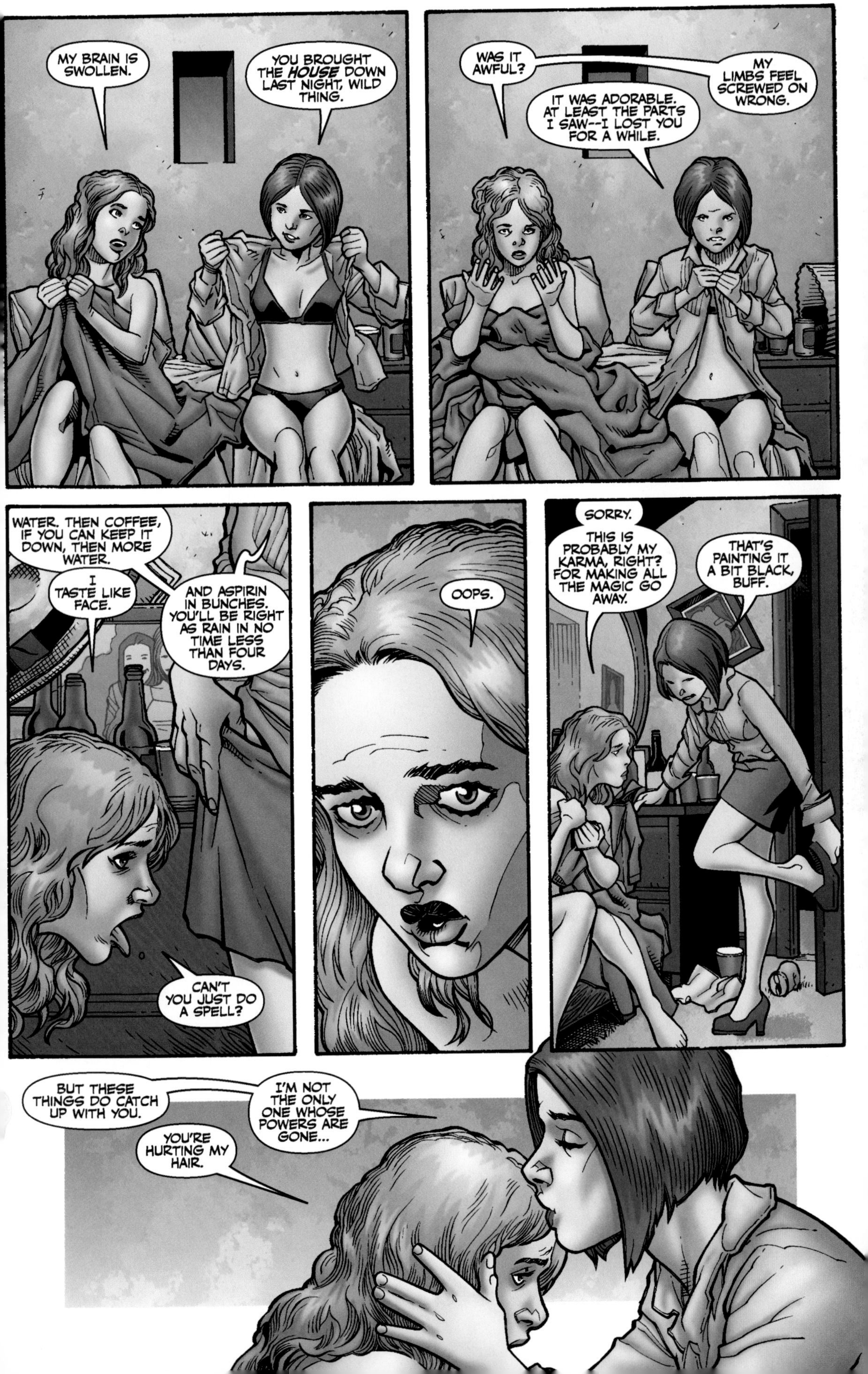
MY BRAIN IS SWOLLEN.
YOU BROUGHT THE *HOUSE* DOWN LAST NIGHT, WILD THING.
WAS IT AWFUL?
MY LIMBS FEEL SCREWED ON WRONG.
IT WAS ADORABLE. AT LEAST THE PARTS I SAW--I LOST YOU FOR A WHILE.
WATER. THEN COFFEE, IF YOU CAN KEEP IT DOWN, THEN MORE WATER.
I TASTE LIKE FACE.
AND ASPIRIN IN BUNCHES. YOU'LL BE RIGHT AS RAIN IN NO TIME LESS THAN FOUR DAYS.
CAN'T YOU JUST DO A SPELL?
OOPS.
SORRY.
THIS IS PROBABLY MY KARMA, RIGHT? FOR MAKING ALL THE MAGIC GO AWAY.
THAT'S PAINTING IT A BIT BLACK, BUFF.
BUT THESE THINGS DO CATCH UP WITH YOU.
I'M NOT THE ONLY ONE WHOSE POWERS ARE GONE...
YOU'RE HURTING MY HAIR.

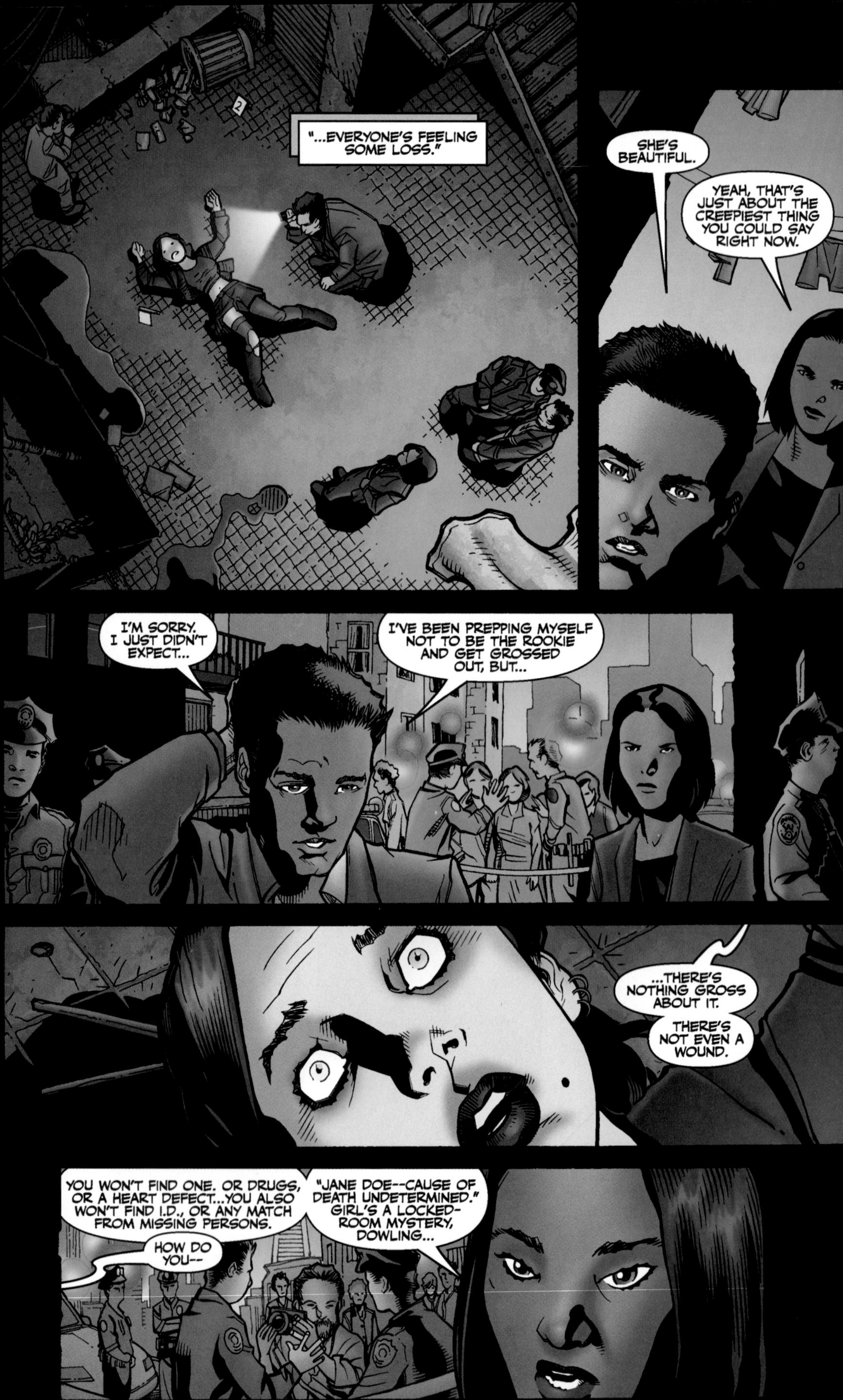
"...EVERYONE'S FEELING SOME LOSS."
SHE'S BEAUTIFUL.
YEAH, THAT'S JUST ABOUT THE CREEPIEST THING YOU COULD SAY RIGHT NOW.
I'M SORRY. I JUST DIDN'T EXPECT...
I'VE BEEN PREPPING MYSELF NOT TO BE THE ROOKIE AND GET GROSSED OUT, BUT...
...THERE'S NOTHING GROSS ABOUT IT.
THERE'S NOT EVEN A WOUND.
YOU WON'T FIND ONE. OR DRUGS, OR A HEART DEFECT...YOU ALSO WON'T FIND I.D., OR ANY MATCH FROM MISSING PERSONS.
HOW DO YOU--
"JANE DOE--CAUSE OF DEATH UNDETERMINED." GIRL'S A LOCKED-ROOM MYSTERY, DOWLING...

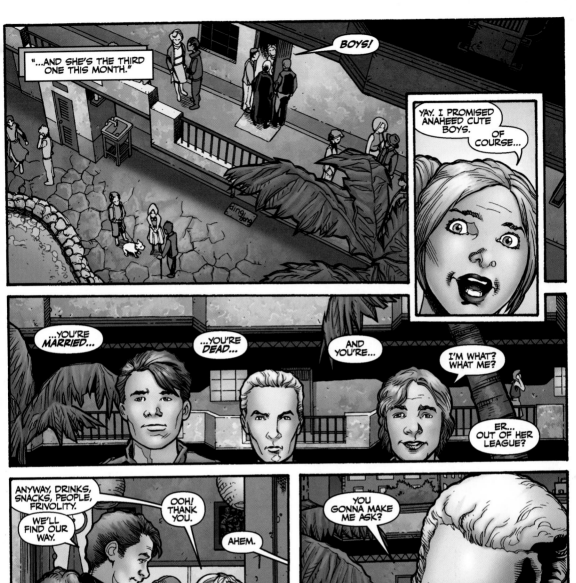

"...AND SHE'S THE THIRD ONE THIS MONTH."

BOYS!

YAY. I PROMISED ANAHEED CUTE BOYS. OF COURSE...

...YOU'RE MARRIED...

...YOU'RE DEAD...

AND YOU'RE...

I'M WHAT? WHAT ME?

ER... OUT OF HER LEAGUE?

ANYWAY, DRINKS, SNACKS, PEOPLE, FRIVOLITY.

WE'LL FIND OUR WAY.

OOH! THANK YOU.

AHEM.

YOU GONNA MAKE ME ASK?

HMMM...ANY CHANCE I CAN MAKE YOU BEG?

NOT THIS YEAR.

WAIT--DIDN'T THE INVITATION--

YOUR TEXT JUST SAID "PARTY." ACTUALLY, IT SAID "PRATTY," BUT I TOOK A CHANCE.

ENTER FREELY AND OF YOUR OWN WILL.

AND NO BUMPY FACE-- MY ROOMIES AREN'T IN THE KNOW.

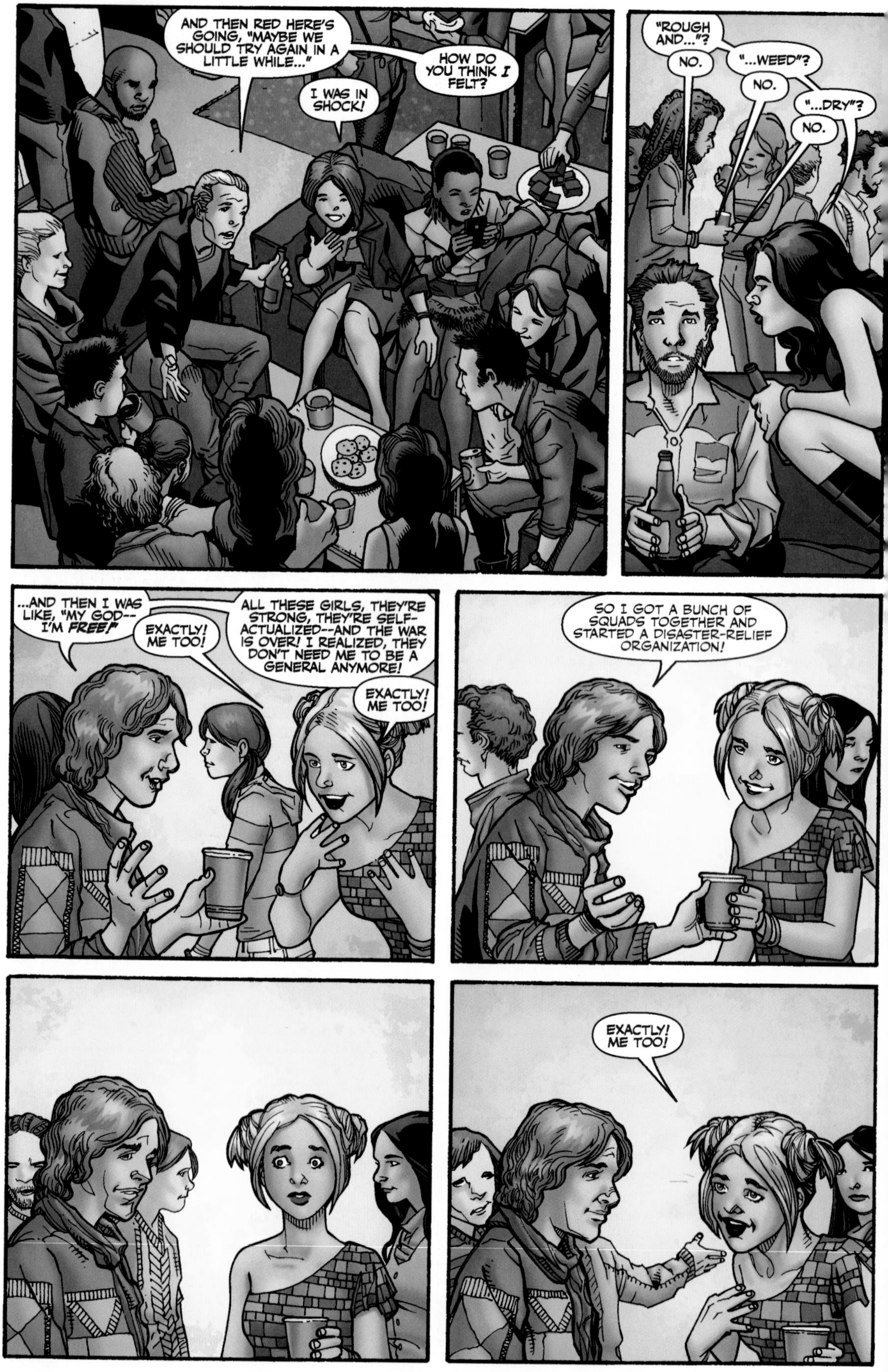
AND THEN RED HERE'S GOING, "MAYBE WE SHOULD TRY AGAIN IN A LITTLE WHILE..."
I WAS IN SHOCK!
HOW DO YOU THINK I FELT?
"ROUGH AND..."?
NO.
"...WEED"?
NO.
"...DRY"?
NO.
...AND THEN I WAS LIKE, "MY GOD-- I'M FREE!"
EXACTLY! ME TOO!
ALL THESE GIRLS, THEY'RE STRONG, THEY'RE SELF-ACTUALIZED--AND THE WAR IS OVER! I REALIZED, THEY DON'T NEED ME TO BE A GENERAL ANYMORE!
EXACTLY! ME TOO!
SO I GOT A BUNCH OF SQUADS TOGETHER AND STARTED A DISASTER-RELIEF ORGANIZATION!
EXACTLY! ME TOO!

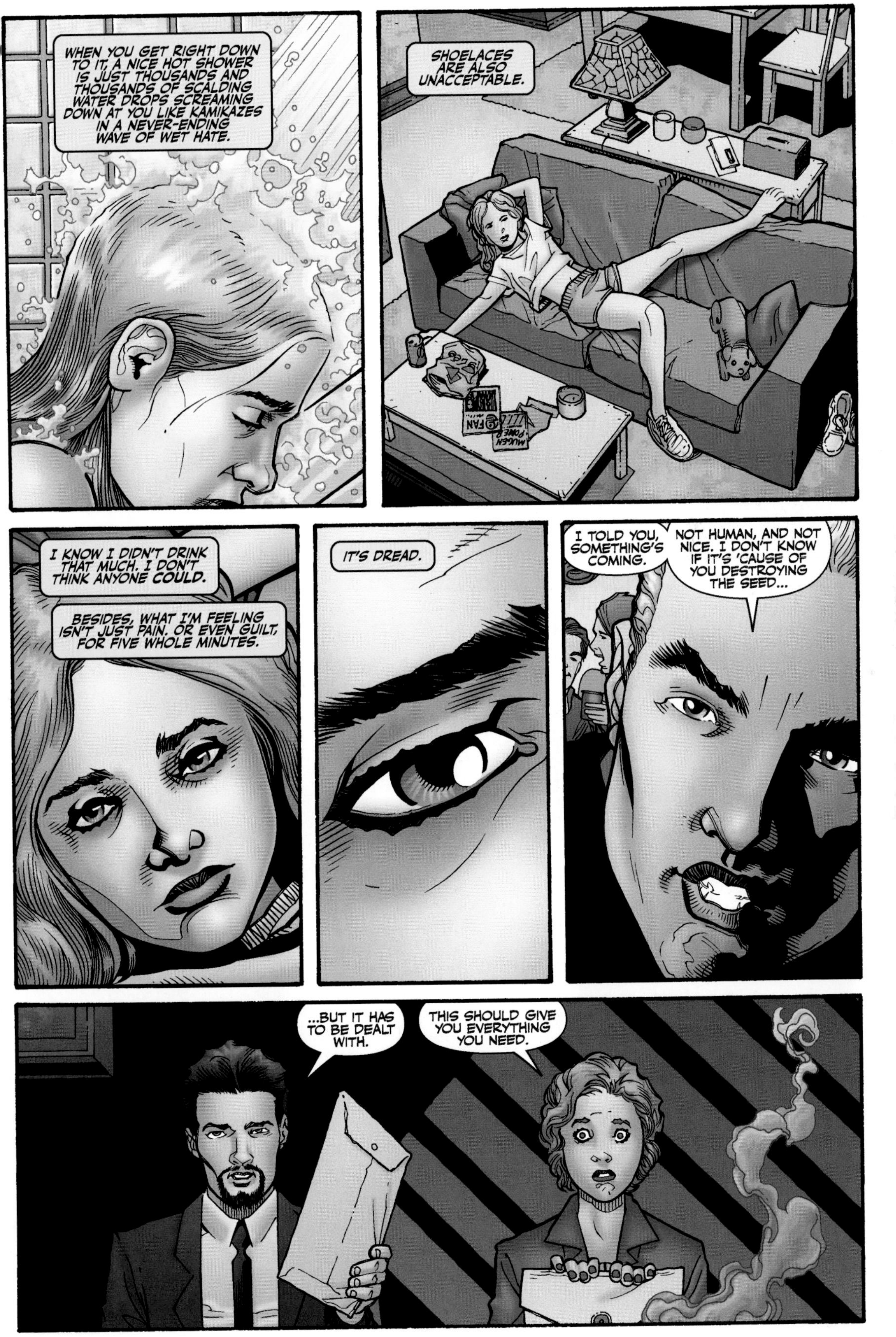

WHEN YOU GET RIGHT DOWN TO IT, A NICE HOT SHOWER IS JUST THOUSANDS AND THOUSANDS OF SCALDING WATER DROPS SCREAMING DOWN AT YOU LIKE KAMIKAZES IN A NEVER-ENDING WAVE OF WET HATE.
SHOELACES ARE ALSO UNACCEPTABLE.
I KNOW I DIDN'T DRINK THAT MUCH. I DON'T THINK ANYONE COULD.
BESIDES, WHAT I'M FEELING ISN'T JUST PAIN. OR EVEN GUILT, FOR FIVE WHOLE MINUTES.
IT'S DREAD.
I TOLD YOU, SOMETHING'S COMING.
NOT HUMAN, AND NOT NICE. I DON'T KNOW IF IT'S 'CAUSE OF YOU DESTROYING THE SEED...
...BUT IT HAS TO BE DEALT WITH.
THIS SHOULD GIVE YOU EVERYTHING YOU NEED.

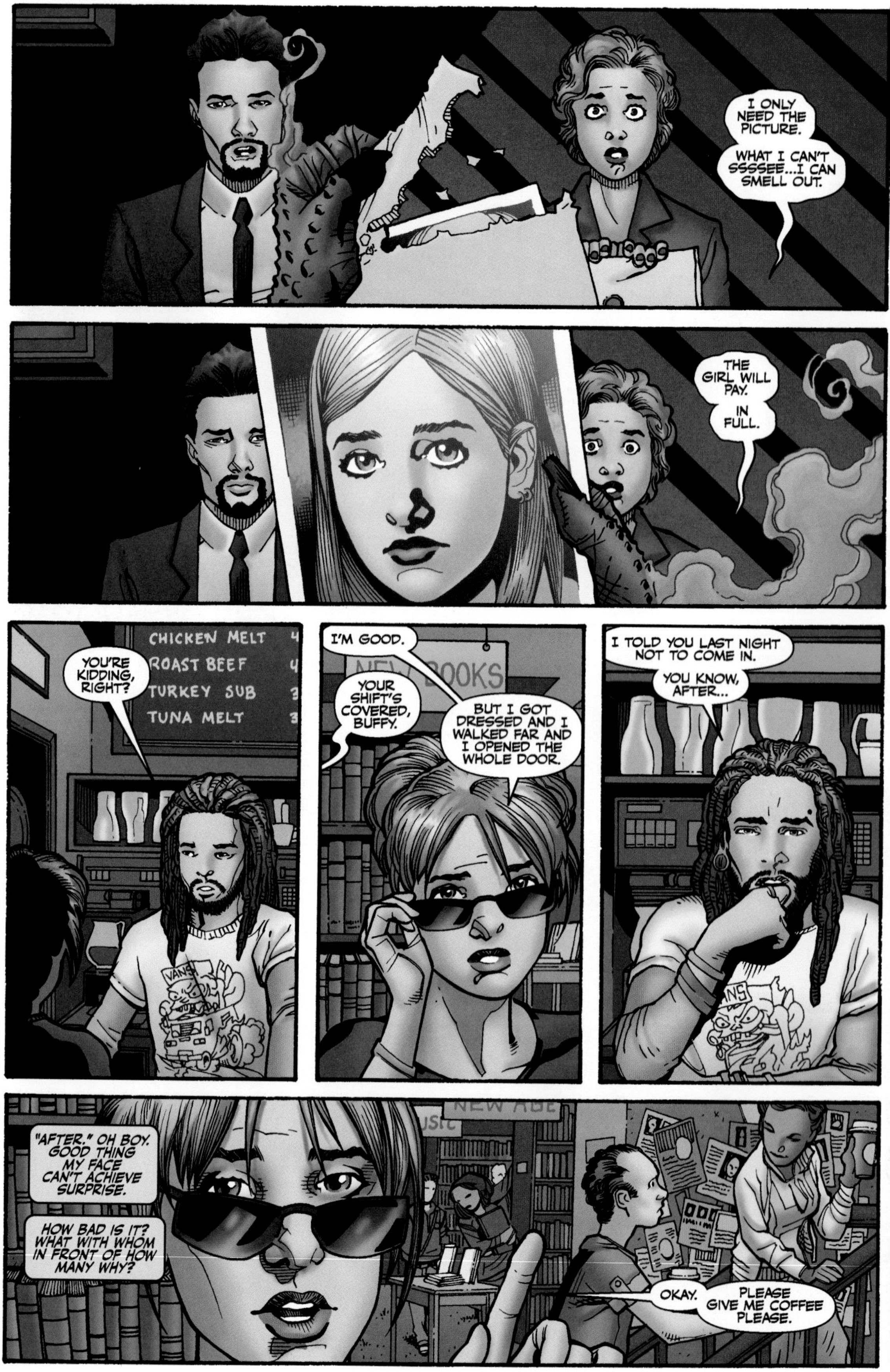

I ONLY NEED THE PICTURE.
WHAT I CAN'T SSSSEE...I CAN SMELL OUT.
THE GIRL WILL PAY.
IN FULL.
CHICKEN MELT
ROAST BEEF
TURKEY SUB
TUNA MELT
YOU'RE KIDDING, RIGHT?
I'M GOOD.
YOUR SHIFT'S COVERED, BUFFY.
BUT I GOT DRESSED AND I WALKED FAR AND I OPENED THE WHOLE DOOR.
I TOLD YOU LAST NIGHT NOT TO COME IN.
YOU KNOW, AFTER...
"AFTER." OH BOY. GOOD THING MY FACE CAN'T ACHIEVE SURPRISE.
HOW BAD IS IT? WHAT WITH WHOM IN FRONT OF HOW MANY WHY?
OKAY.
PLEASE GIVE ME COFFEE PLEASE.

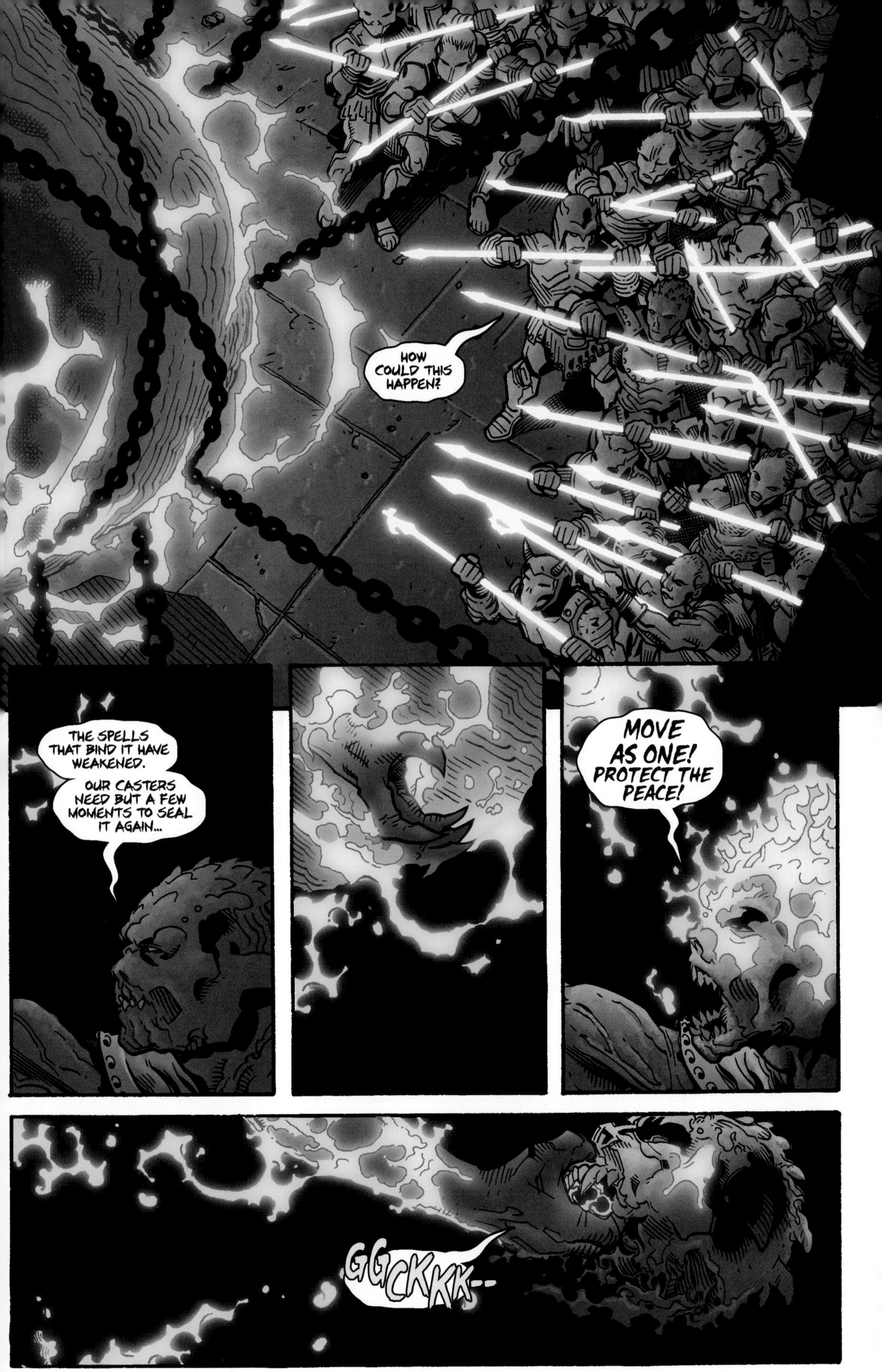
HOW COULD THIS HAPPEN?
THE SPELLS THAT BIND IT HAVE WEAKENED.
OUR CASTERS NEED BUT A FEW MOMENTS TO SEAL IT AGAIN...
MOVE AS ONE! PROTECT THE PEACE!
GGCKKK--

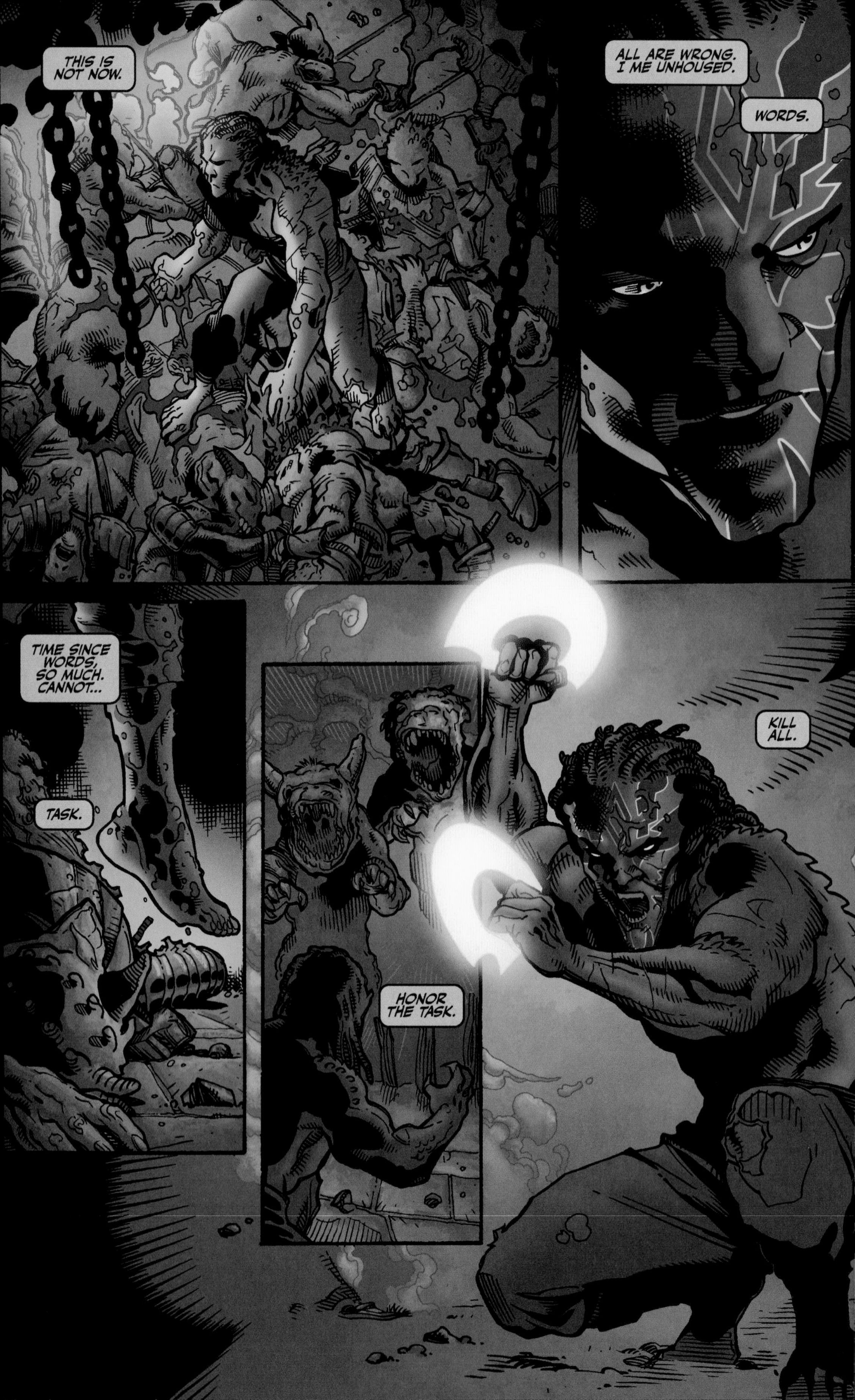
THIS IS NOT NOW.
ALL ARE WRONG. I ME UNHOUSED.
WORDS.
TIME SINCE WORDS, SO MUCH. CANNOT...
TASK.
HONOR THE TASK.
KILL ALL.

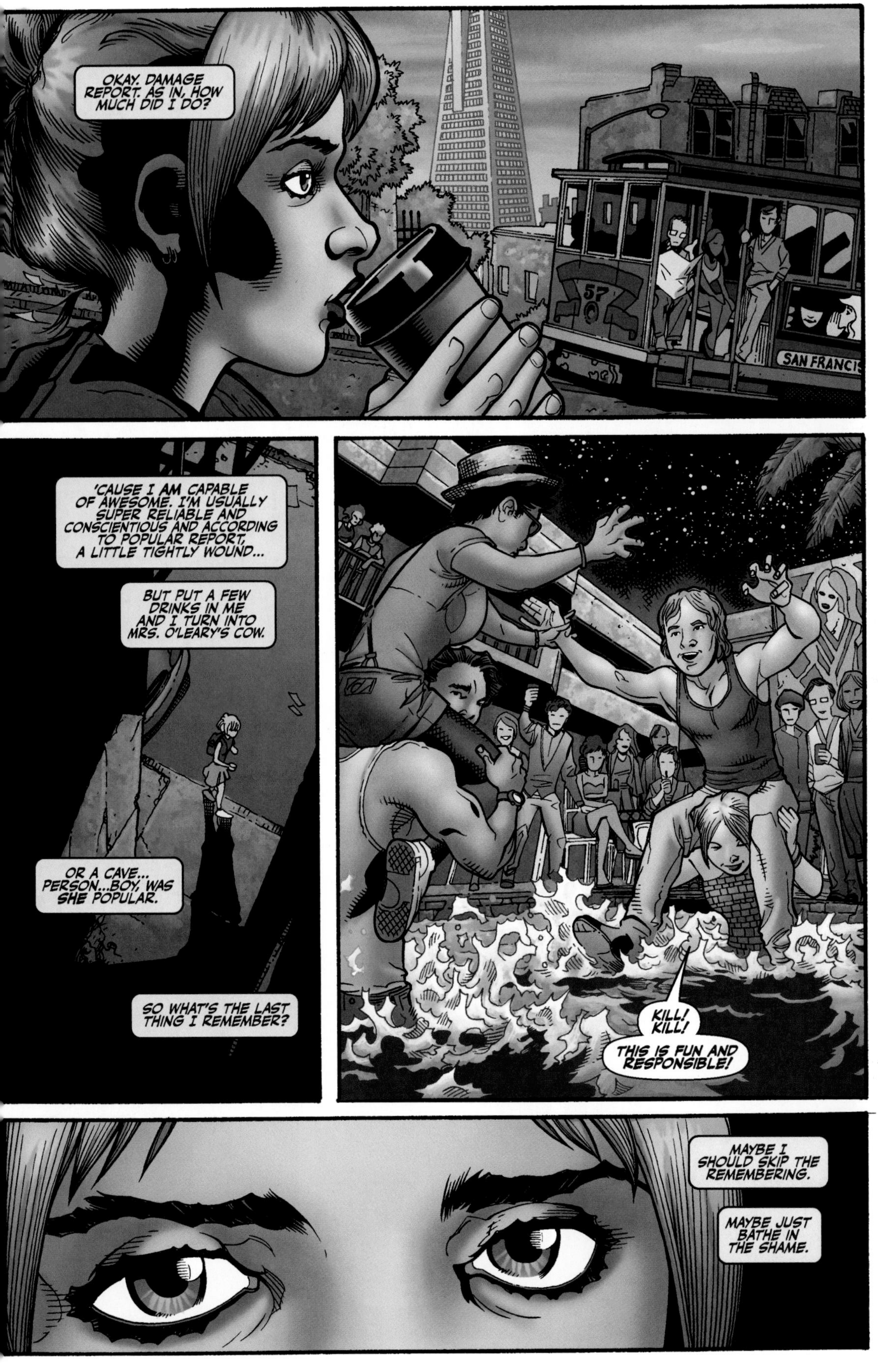
OKAY. DAMAGE REPORT. AS IN, HOW MUCH DID I DO?
SAN FRANCIS
'CAUSE I AM CAPABLE OF AWESOME. I'M USUALLY SUPER RELIABLE AND CONSCIENTIOUS AND ACCORDING TO POPULAR REPORT, A LITTLE TIGHTLY WOUND...
BUT PUT A FEW DRINKS IN ME AND I TURN INTO MRS. O'LEARY'S COW.
OR A CAVE... PERSON...BOY, WAS SHE POPULAR.
SO WHAT'S THE LAST THING I REMEMBER?
KILL! KILL!
THIS IS FUN AND RESPONSIBLE!
MAYBE I SHOULD SKIP THE REMEMBERING.
MAYBE JUST BATHE IN THE SHAME.

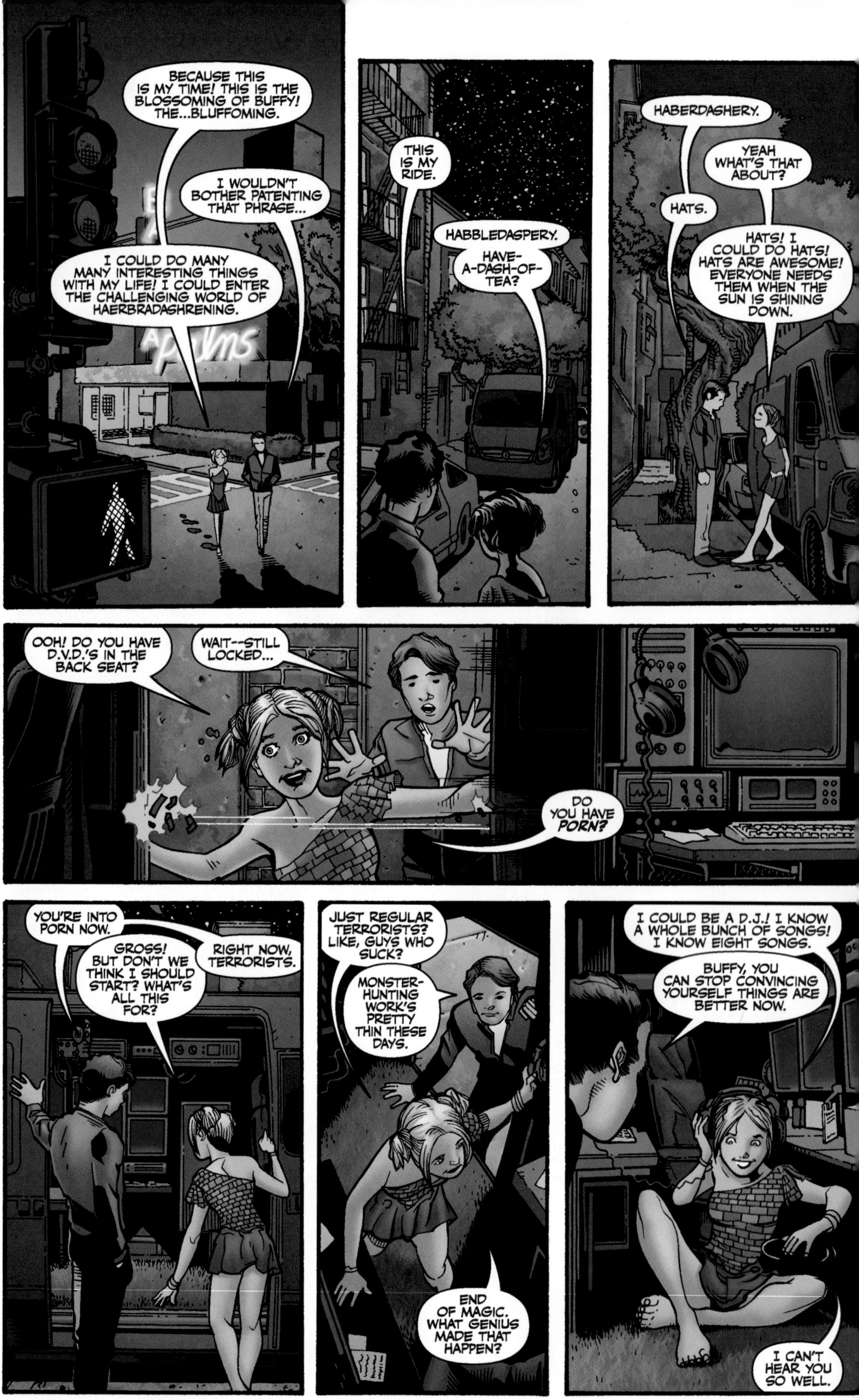
BECAUSE THIS IS MY TIME! THIS IS THE BLOSSOMING OF BUFFY! THE...BLUFFOMING.
I WOULDN'T BOTHER PATENTING THAT PHRASE...
I COULD DO MANY MANY INTERESTING THINGS WITH MY LIFE! I COULD ENTER THE CHALLENGING WORLD OF HAERBRADASHRENING.
THIS IS MY RIDE.
HABBLEDASPERY.
HAVE-A-DASH-OF-TEA?
HABERDASHERY.
YEAH WHAT'S THAT ABOUT?
HATS.
HATS! I COULD DO HATS! HATS ARE AWESOME! EVERYONE NEEDS THEM WHEN THE SUN IS SHINING DOWN.
OOH! DO YOU HAVE D.V.D.'S IN THE BACK SEAT?
WAIT--STILL LOCKED...
DO YOU HAVE PORN?
YOU'RE INTO PORN NOW.
RIGHT NOW, TERRORISTS.
GROSS! BUT DON'T WE THINK I SHOULD START? WHAT'S ALL THIS FOR?
JUST REGULAR TERRORISTS? LIKE, GUYS WHO SUCK?
MONSTER-HUNTING WORK'S PRETTY THIN THESE DAYS.
END OF MAGIC. WHAT GENIUS MADE THAT HAPPEN?
I COULD BE A D.J.! I KNOW A WHOLE BUNCH OF SONGS! I KNOW EIGHT SONGS.
BUFFY, YOU CAN STOP CONVINCING YOURSELF THINGS ARE BETTER NOW.
I CAN'T HEAR YOU SO WELL.

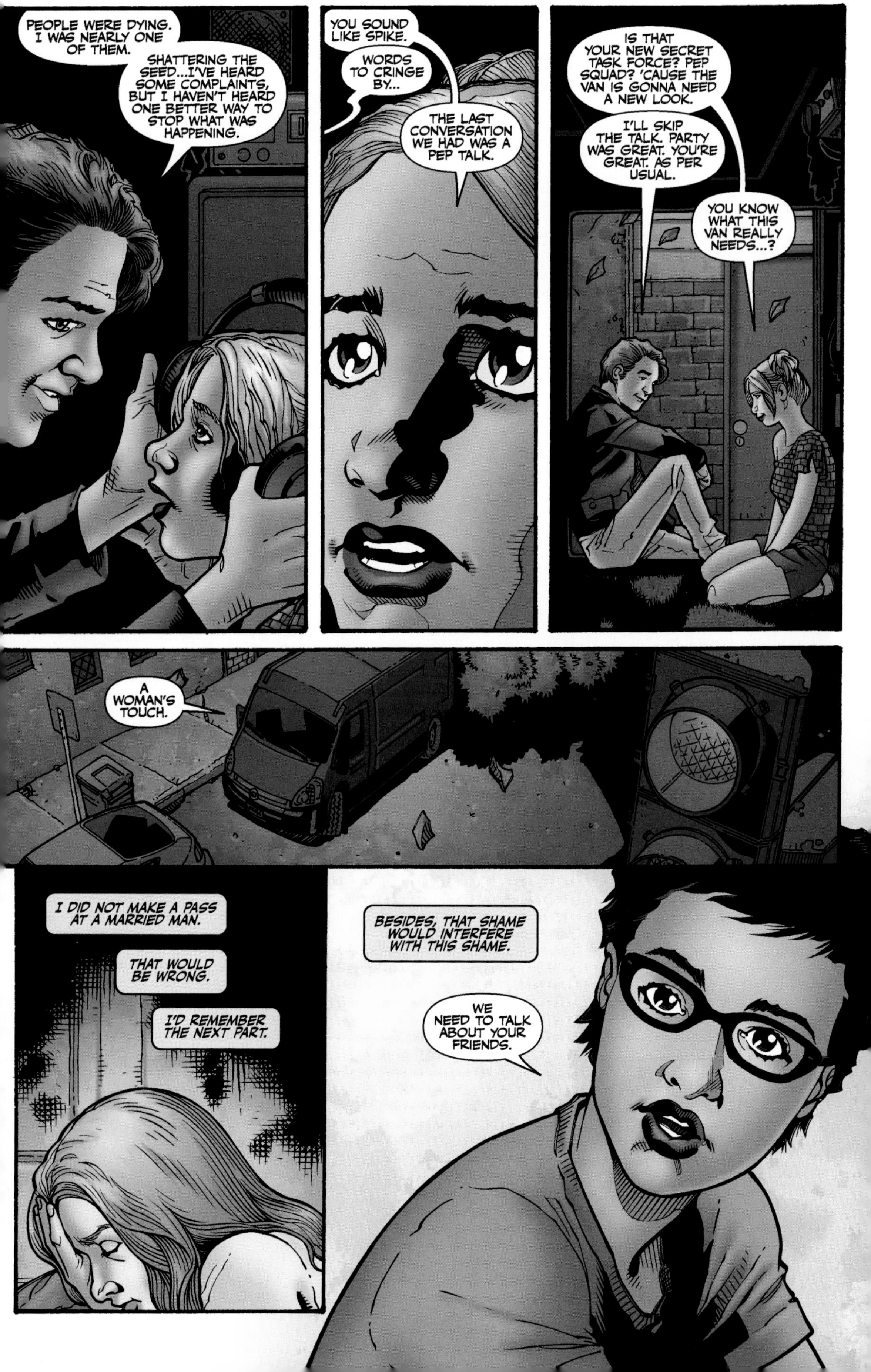
PEOPLE WERE DYING. I WAS NEARLY ONE OF THEM.
SHATTERING THE SEED...I'VE HEARD SOME COMPLAINTS, BUT I HAVEN'T HEARD ONE BETTER WAY TO STOP WHAT WAS HAPPENING.
YOU SOUND LIKE SPIKE.
WORDS TO CRINGE BY...
THE LAST CONVERSATION WE HAD WAS A PEP TALK.
IS THAT YOUR NEW SECRET TASK FORCE? PEP SQUAD? 'CAUSE THE VAN IS GONNA NEED A NEW LOOK.
I'LL SKIP THE TALK. PARTY WAS GREAT. YOU'RE GREAT. AS PER USUAL.
YOU KNOW WHAT THIS VAN REALLY NEEDS...?
A WOMAN'S TOUCH.
I DID NOT MAKE A PASS AT A MARRIED MAN.
THAT WOULD BE WRONG.
I'D REMEMBER THE NEXT PART.
BESIDES, THAT SHAME WOULD INTERFERE WITH THIS SHAME.
WE NEED TO TALK ABOUT YOUR FRIENDS.

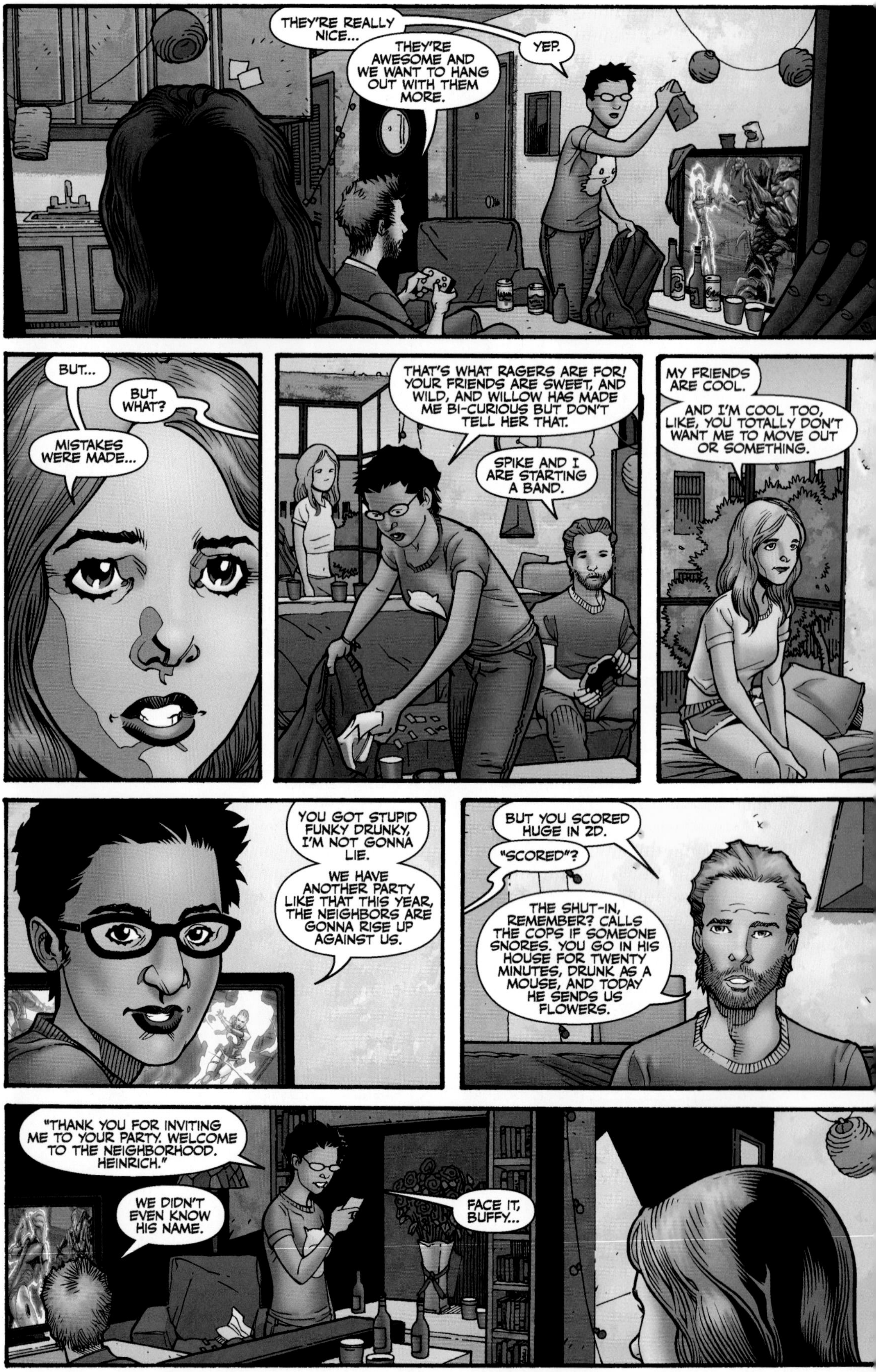
THEY'RE REALLY NICE...
THEY'RE AWESOME AND WE WANT TO HANG OUT WITH THEM MORE.
YEP.
BUT...
BUT WHAT?
MISTAKES WERE MADE...
THAT'S WHAT RAGERS ARE FOR! YOUR FRIENDS ARE SWEET, AND WILD, AND WILLOW HAS MADE ME BI-CURIOUS BUT DON'T TELL HER THAT.
SPIKE AND I ARE STARTING A BAND.
MY FRIENDS ARE COOL.
AND I'M COOL TOO, LIKE, YOU TOTALLY DON'T WANT ME TO MOVE OUT OR SOMETHING.
YOU GOT STUPID FUNKY DRUNKY, I'M NOT GONNA LIE.
WE HAVE ANOTHER PARTY LIKE THAT THIS YEAR, THE NEIGHBORS ARE GONNA RISE UP AGAINST US.
BUT YOU SCORED HUGE IN 2D.
"SCORED"?
THE SHUT-IN, REMEMBER? CALLS THE COPS IF SOMEONE SNORES. YOU GO IN HIS HOUSE FOR TWENTY MINUTES, DRUNK AS A MOUSE, AND TODAY HE SENDS US FLOWERS.
"THANK YOU FOR INVITING ME TO YOUR PARTY. WELCOME TO THE NEIGHBORHOOD. HEINRICH."
WE DIDN'T EVEN KNOW HIS NAME.
FACE IT, BUFFY...

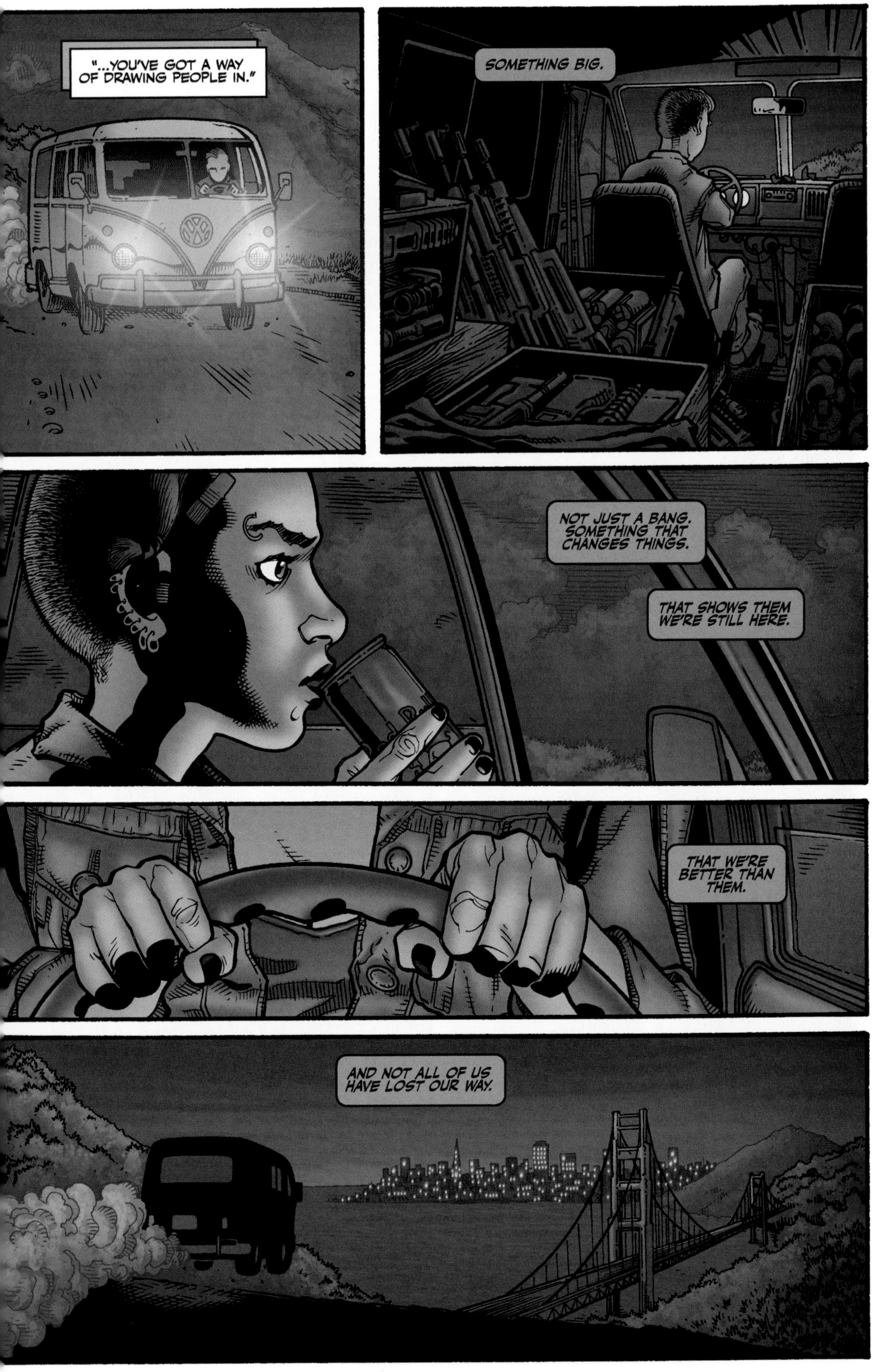
"...YOU'VE GOT A WAY OF DRAWING PEOPLE IN."
SOMETHING BIG.
NOT JUST A BANG. SOMETHING THAT CHANGES THINGS.
THAT SHOWS THEM WE'RE STILL HERE.
THAT WE'RE BETTER THAN THEM.
AND NOT ALL OF US HAVE LOST OUR WAY.

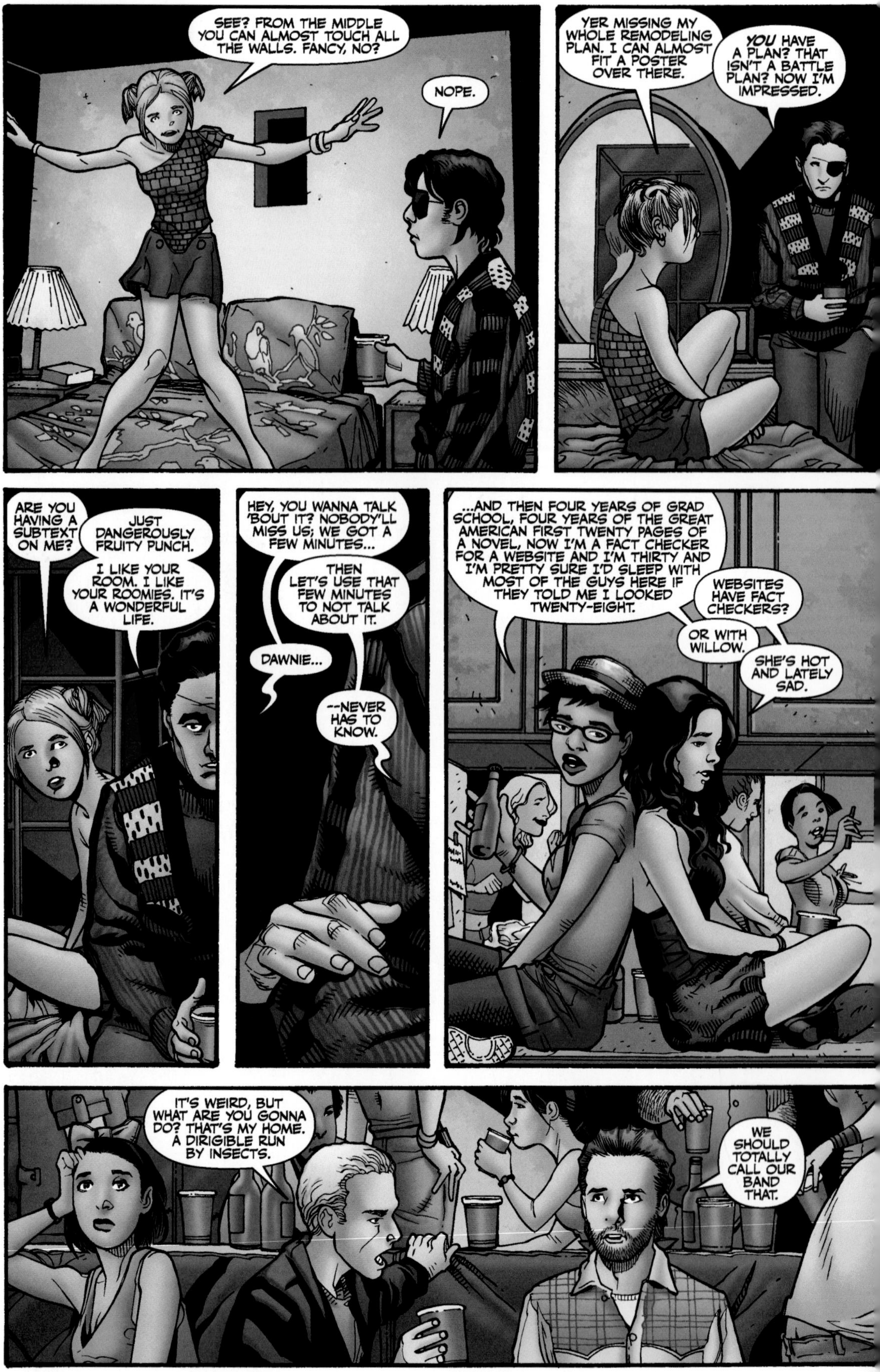
SEE? FROM THE MIDDLE YOU CAN ALMOST TOUCH ALL THE WALLS. FANCY, NO?
NOPE.
YER MISSING MY WHOLE REMODELING PLAN. I CAN ALMOST FIT A POSTER OVER THERE.
YOU HAVE A PLAN? THAT ISN'T A BATTLE PLAN? NOW I'M IMPRESSED.
ARE YOU HAVING A SUBTEXT ON ME?
JUST DANGEROUSLY FRUITY PUNCH.
I LIKE YOUR ROOM. I LIKE YOUR ROOMIES. IT'S A WONDERFUL LIFE.
HEY, YOU WANNA TALK 'BOUT IT? NOBODY'LL MISS US; WE GOT A FEW MINUTES...
THEN LET'S USE THAT FEW MINUTES TO NOT TALK ABOUT IT.
DAWNIE...
--NEVER HAS TO KNOW.
...AND THEN FOUR YEARS OF GRAD SCHOOL, FOUR YEARS OF THE GREAT AMERICAN FIRST TWENTY PAGES OF A NOVEL, NOW I'M A FACT CHECKER FOR A WEBSITE AND I'M THIRTY AND I'M PRETTY SURE I'D SLEEP WITH MOST OF THE GUYS HERE IF THEY TOLD ME I LOOKED TWENTY-EIGHT.
WEBSITES HAVE FACT CHECKERS?
OR WITH WILLOW.
SHE'S HOT AND LATELY SAD.
IT'S WEIRD, BUT WHAT ARE YOU GONNA DO? THAT'S MY HOME. A DIRIGIBLE RUN BY INSECTS.
WE SHOULD TOTALLY CALL OUR BAND THAT.

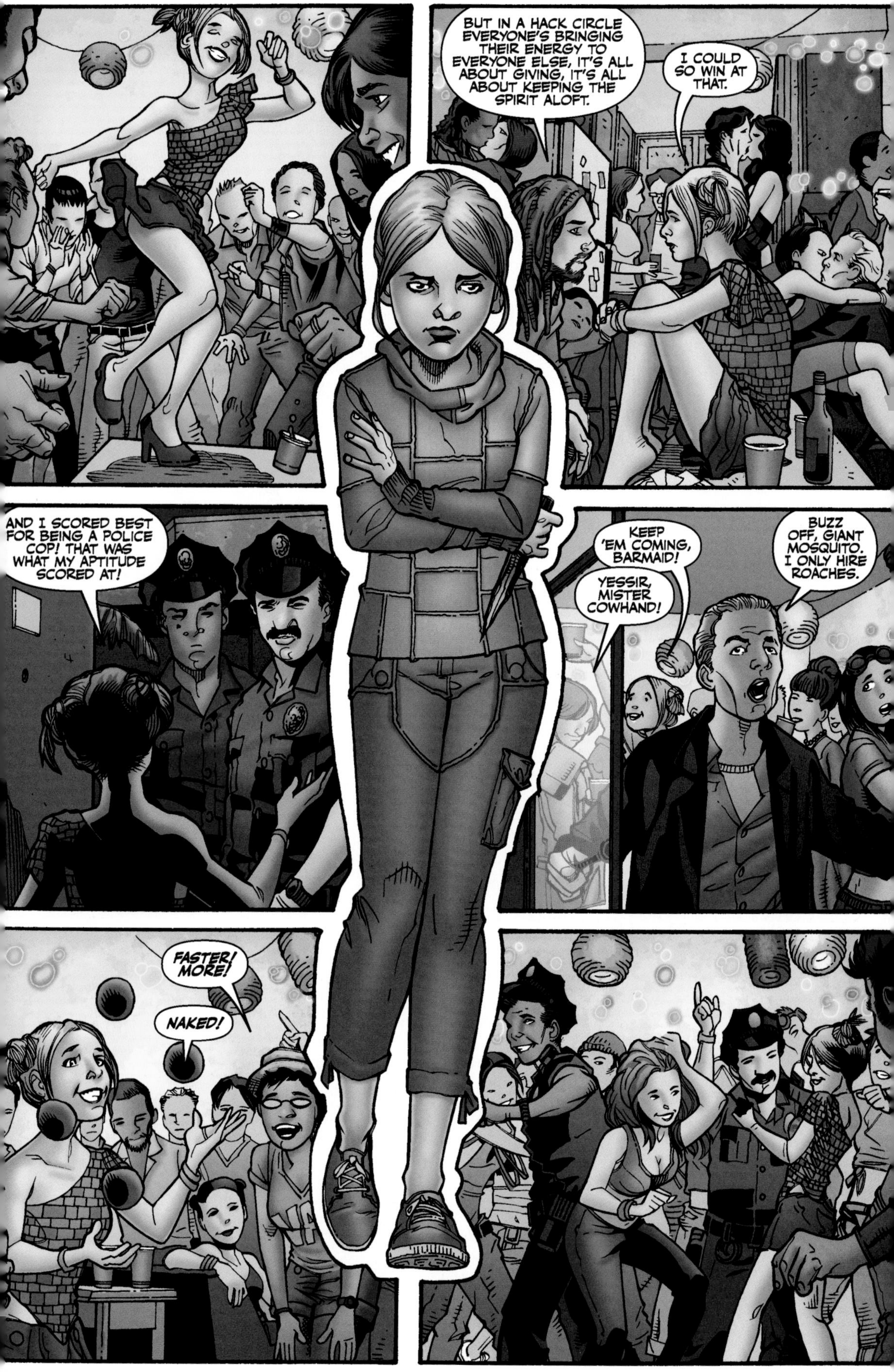
BUT IN A HACK CIRCLE EVERYONE'S BRINGING THEIR ENERGY TO EVERYONE ELSE, IT'S ALL ABOUT GIVING, IT'S ALL ABOUT KEEPING THE SPIRIT ALOFT.
I COULD SO WIN AT THAT.
AND I SCORED BEST FOR BEING A POLICE COP! THAT WAS WHAT MY APTITUDE SCORED AT!
KEEP 'EM COMING, BARMAID!
YESSIR, MISTER COWHAND!
BUZZ OFF, GIANT MOSQUITO. I ONLY HIRE ROACHES.
FASTER! MORE!
NAKED!

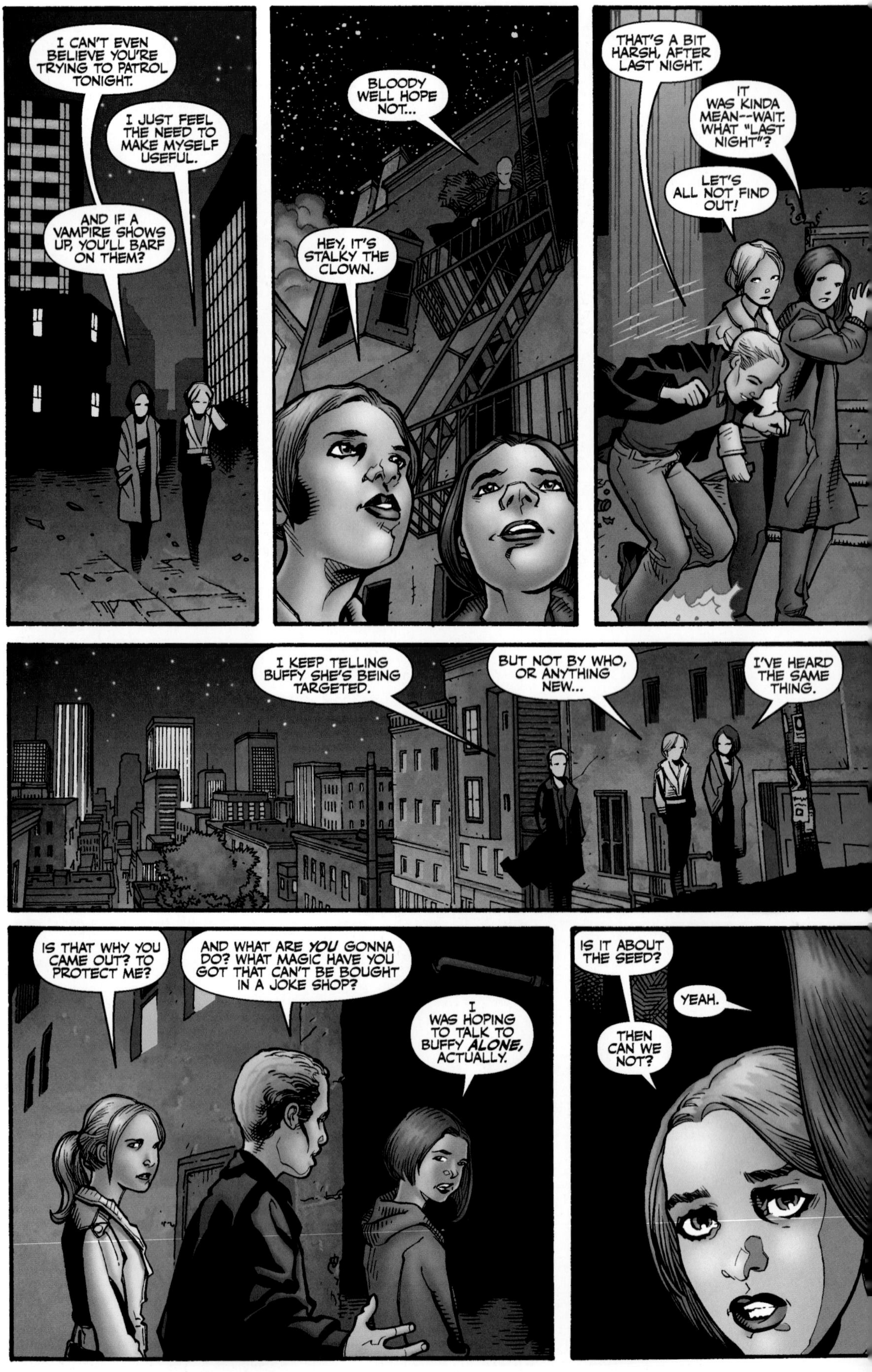
I CAN'T EVEN BELIEVE YOU'RE TRYING TO PATROL TONIGHT.
I JUST FEEL THE NEED TO MAKE MYSELF USEFUL.
AND IF A VAMPIRE SHOWS UP, YOU'LL BARF ON THEM?
BLOODY WELL HOPE NOT...
HEY, IT'S STALKY THE CLOWN.
THAT'S A BIT HARSH, AFTER LAST NIGHT.
IT WAS KINDA MEAN--WAIT. WHAT "LAST NIGHT"?
LET'S ALL NOT FIND OUT!
I KEEP TELLING BUFFY SHE'S BEING TARGETED.
BUT NOT BY WHO, OR ANYTHING NEW...
I'VE HEARD THE SAME THING.
IS THAT WHY YOU CAME OUT? TO PROTECT ME?
AND WHAT ARE *YOU* GONNA DO? WHAT MAGIC HAVE YOU GOT THAT CAN'T BE BOUGHT IN A JOKE SHOP?
I WAS HOPING TO TALK TO BUFFY *ALONE,* ACTUALLY.
IS IT ABOUT THE SEED?
YEAH.
THEN CAN WE NOT?

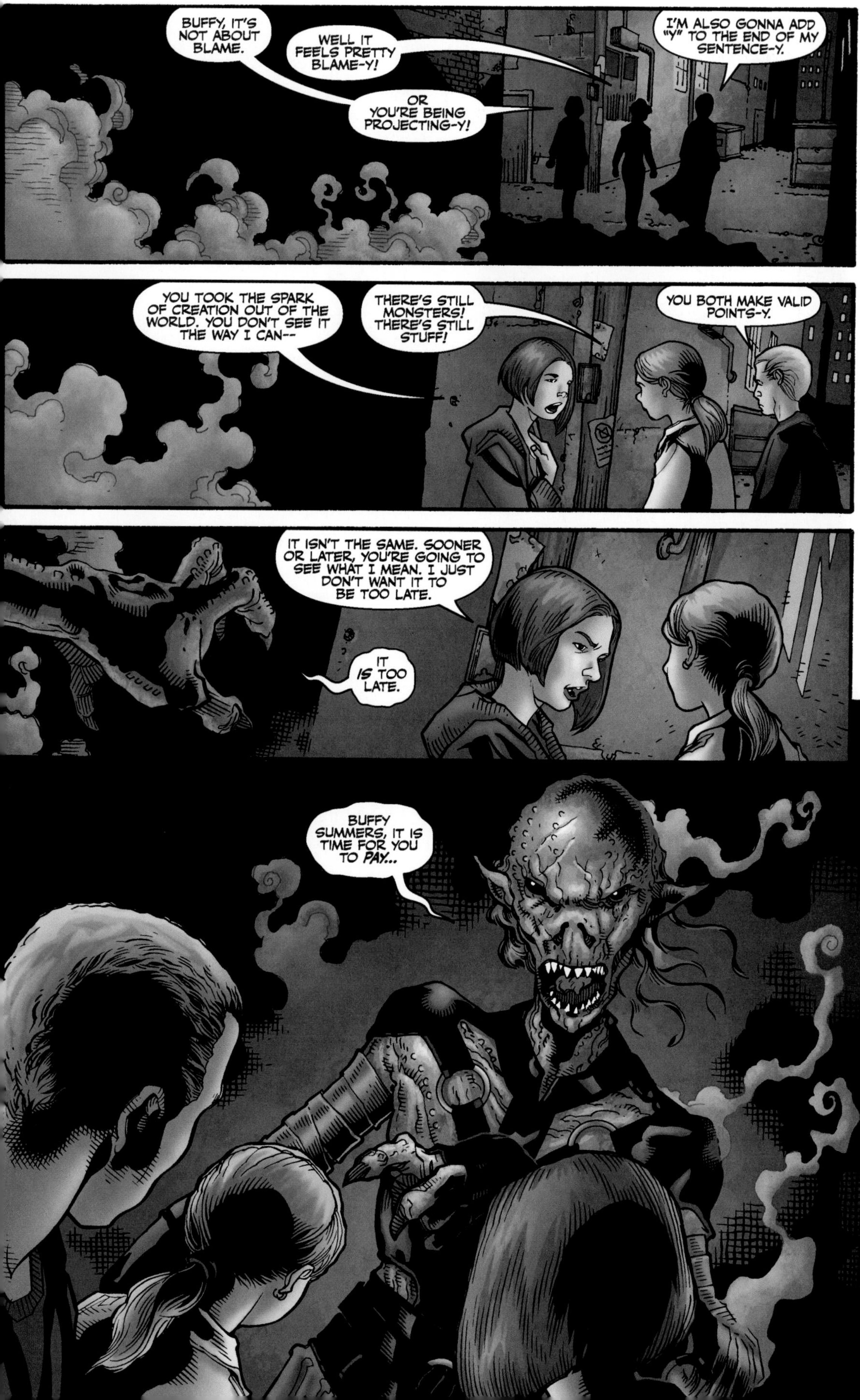
BUFFY, IT'S NOT ABOUT BLAME.
WELL IT FEELS PRETTY BLAME-Y!
I'M ALSO GONNA ADD "Y" TO THE END OF MY SENTENCE-Y.
OR YOU'RE BEING PROJECTING-Y!
YOU TOOK THE SPARK OF CREATION OUT OF THE WORLD. YOU DON'T SEE IT THE WAY I CAN--
THERE'S STILL MONSTERS! THERE'S STILL STUFF!
YOU BOTH MAKE VALID POINTS-Y.
IT ISN'T THE SAME. SOONER OR LATER, YOU'RE GOING TO SEE WHAT I MEAN. I JUST DON'T WANT IT TO BE TOO LATE.
IT *IS* TOO LATE.
BUFFY SUMMERS, IT IS TIME FOR YOU TO *PAY*...

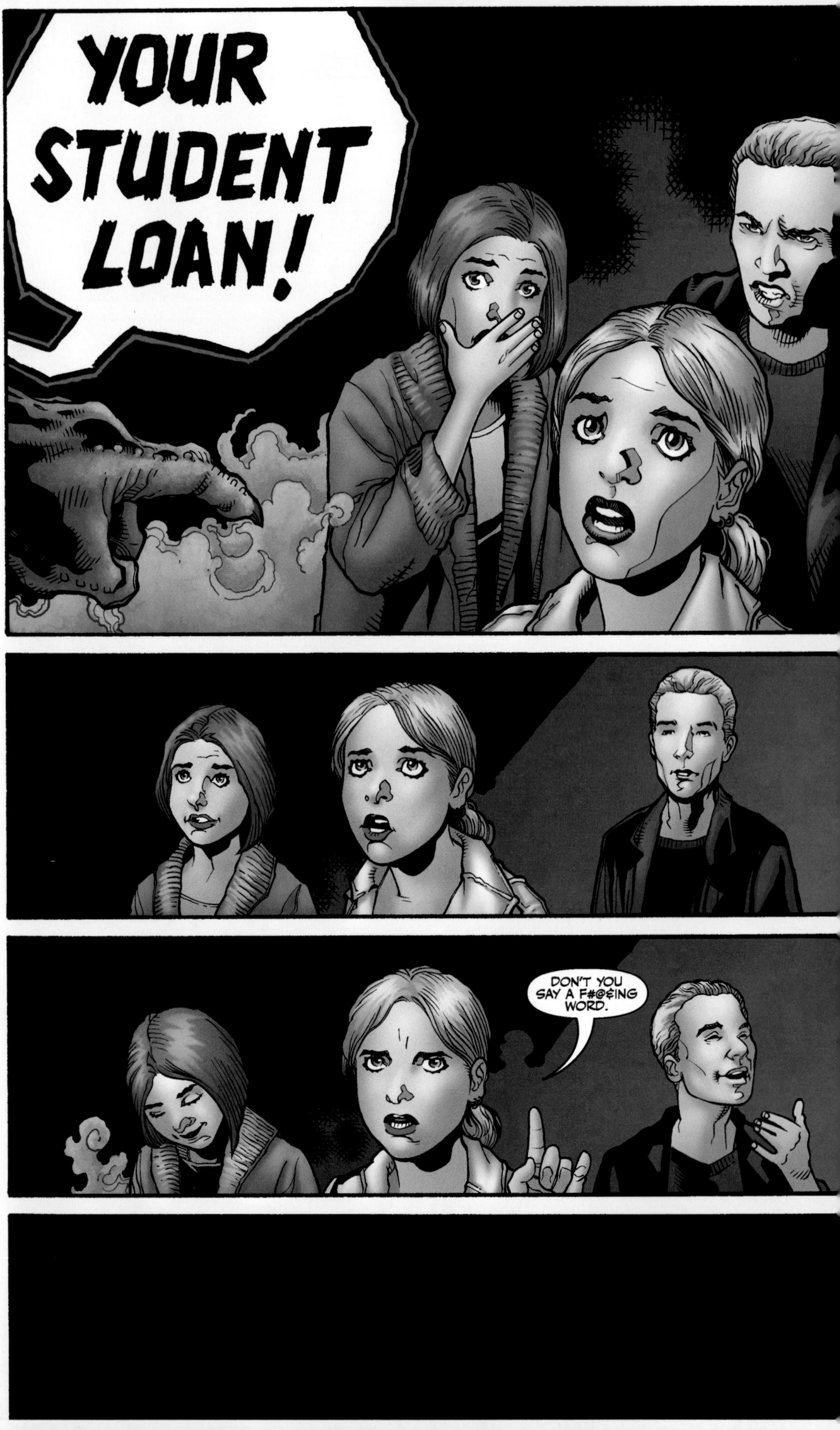
YOUR STUDENT LOAN!
DON'T YOU SAY A F#@&ING WORD.

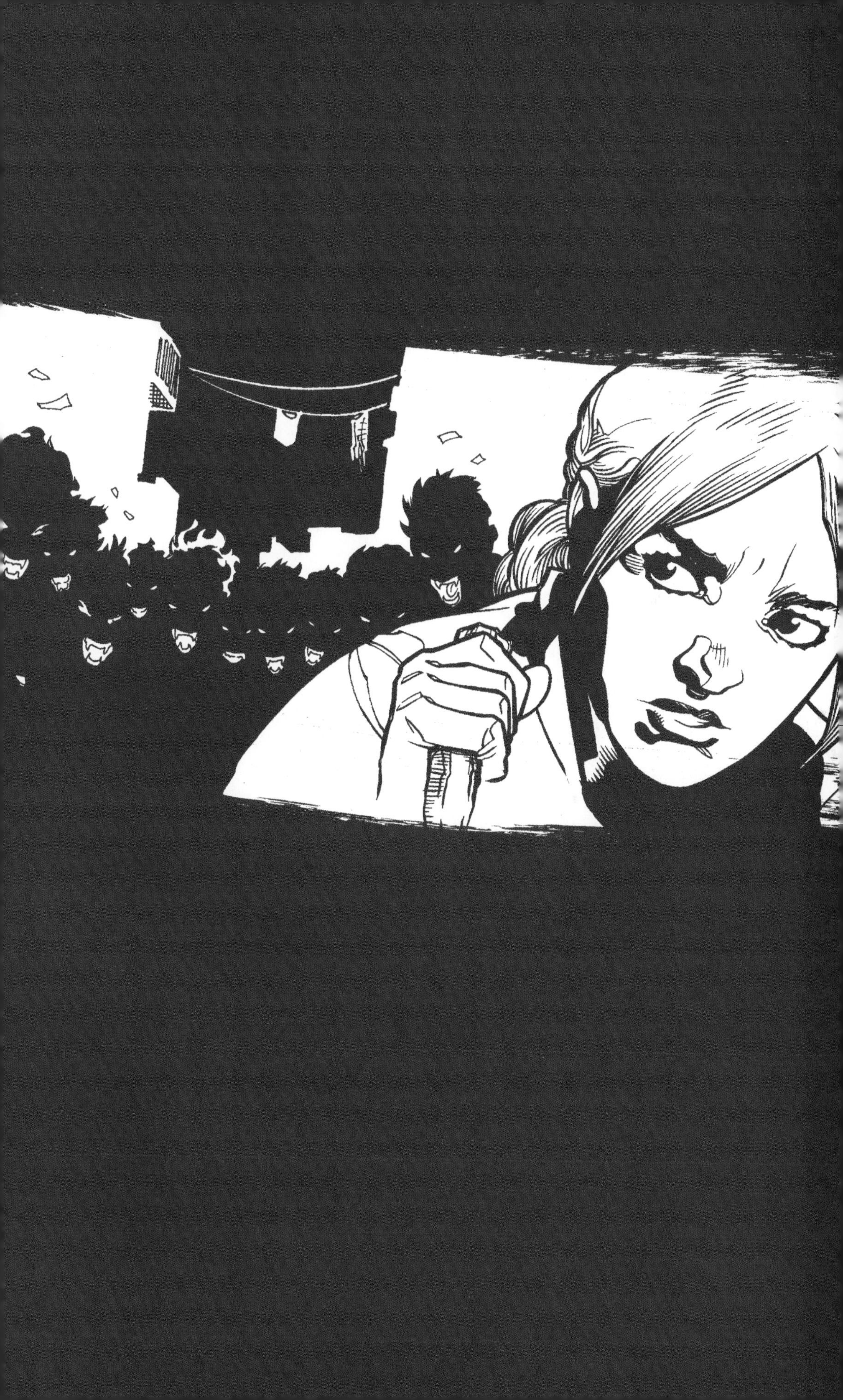

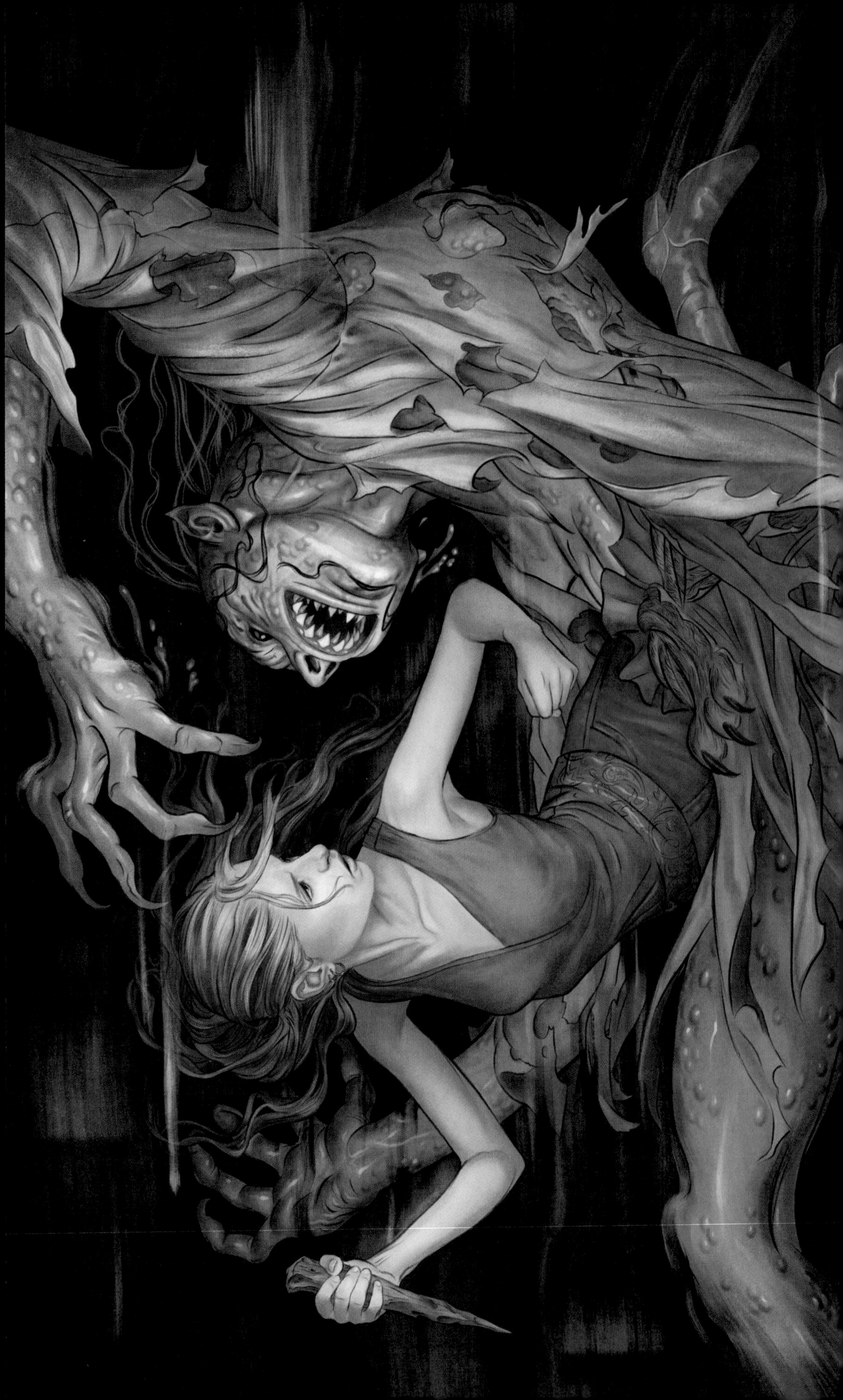

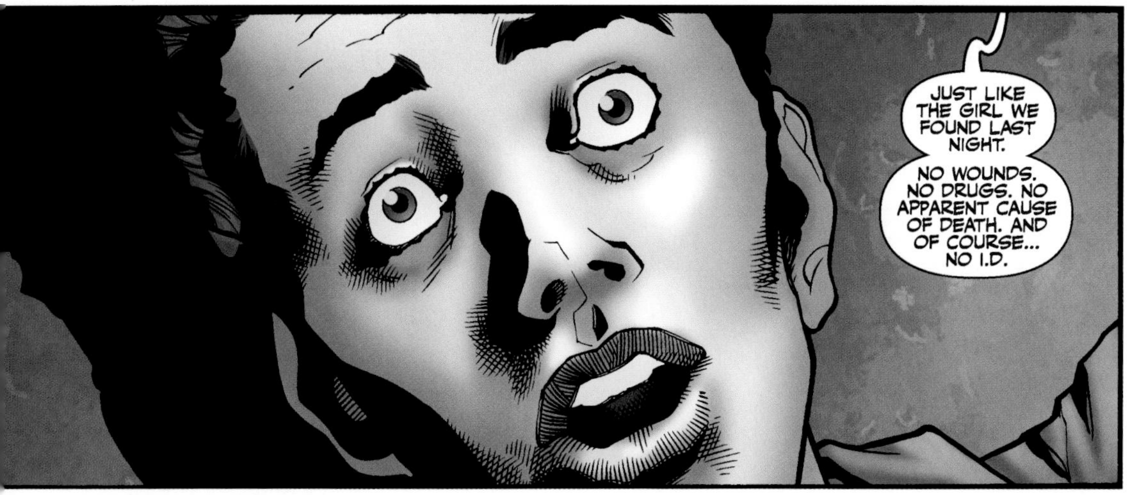
JUST LIKE THE GIRL WE FOUND LAST NIGHT.
NO WOUNDS. NO DRUGS. NO APPARENT CAUSE OF DEATH. AND OF COURSE... NO I.D.

FREEFALL

Part Two

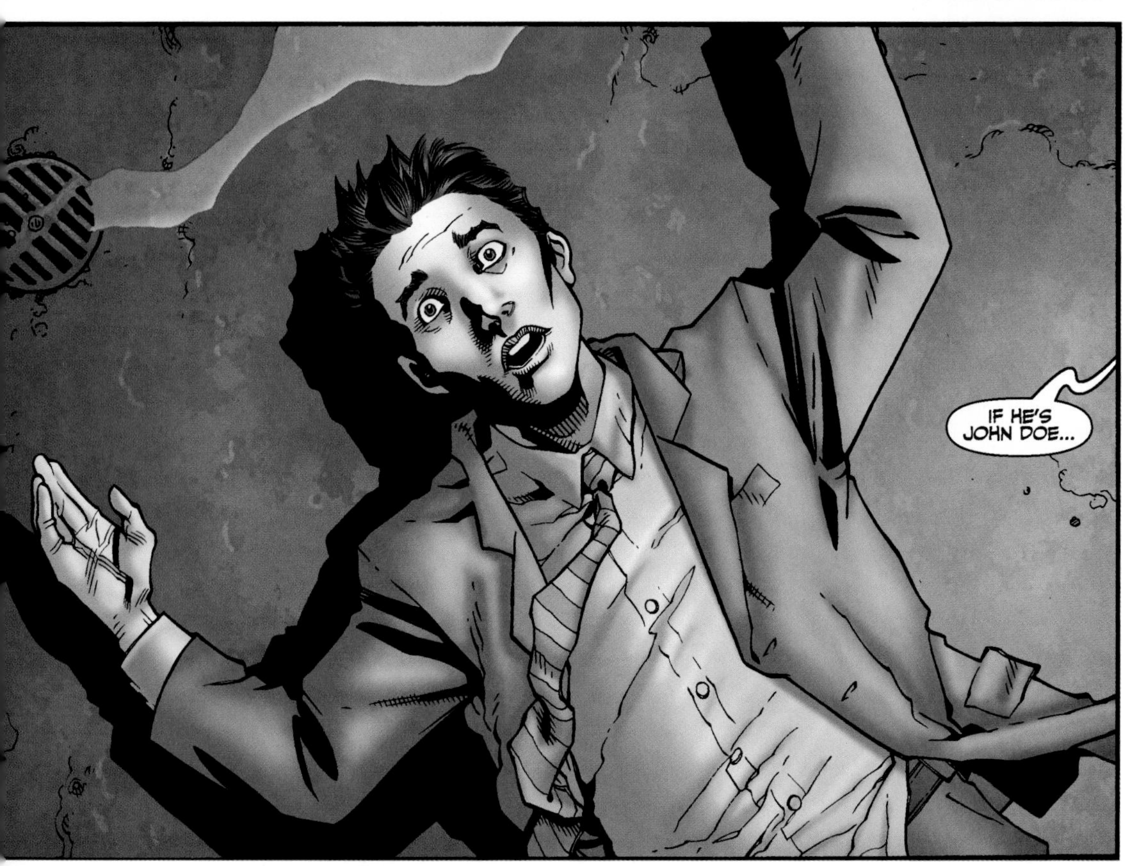
IF HE'S JOHN DOE...

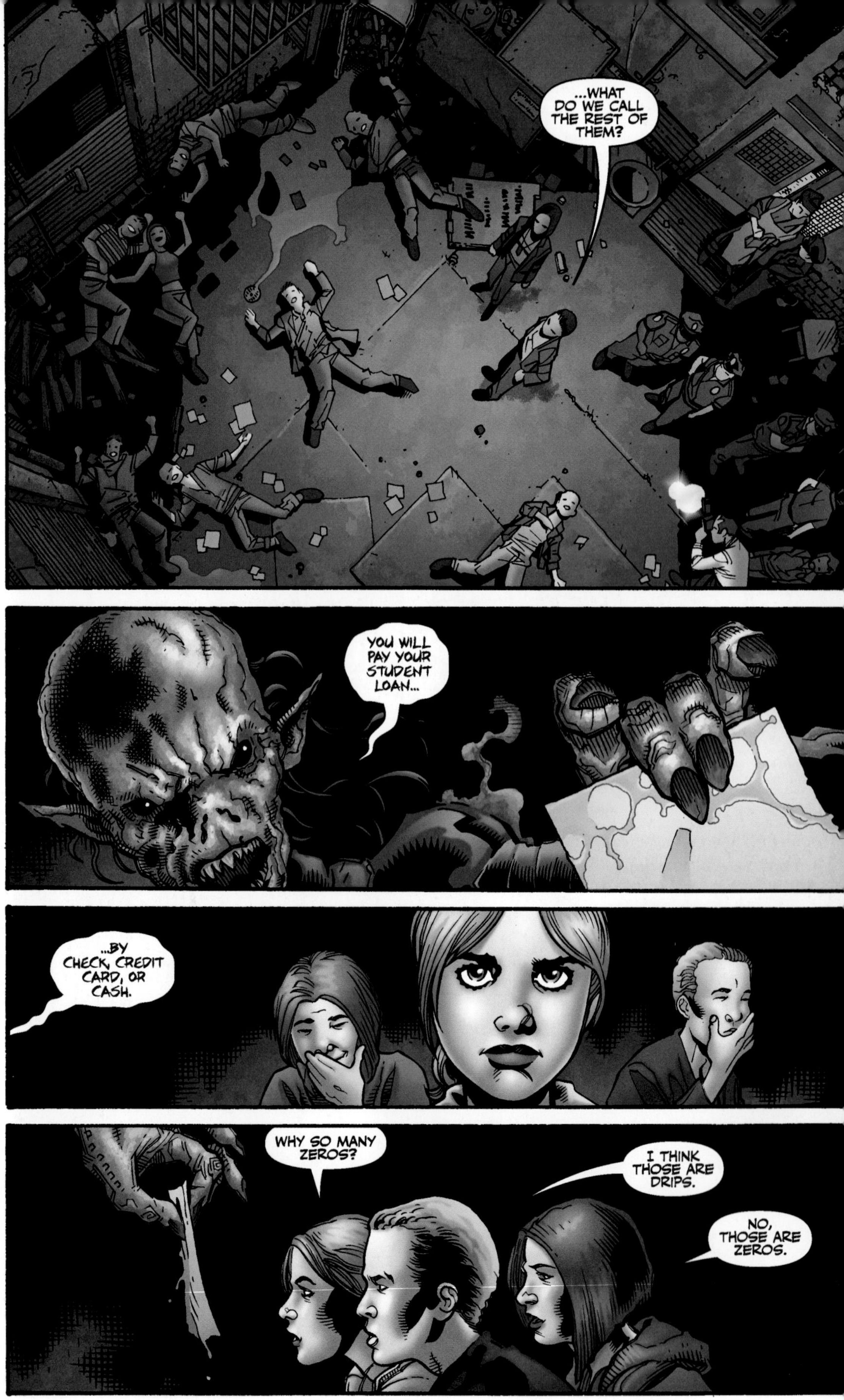

...WHAT DO WE CALL THE REST OF THEM?
YOU WILL PAY YOUR STUDENT LOAN...
...BY CHECK, CREDIT CARD, OR CASH.
WHY SO MANY ZEROS?
I THINK THOSE ARE DRIPS.
NO, THOSE ARE ZEROS.

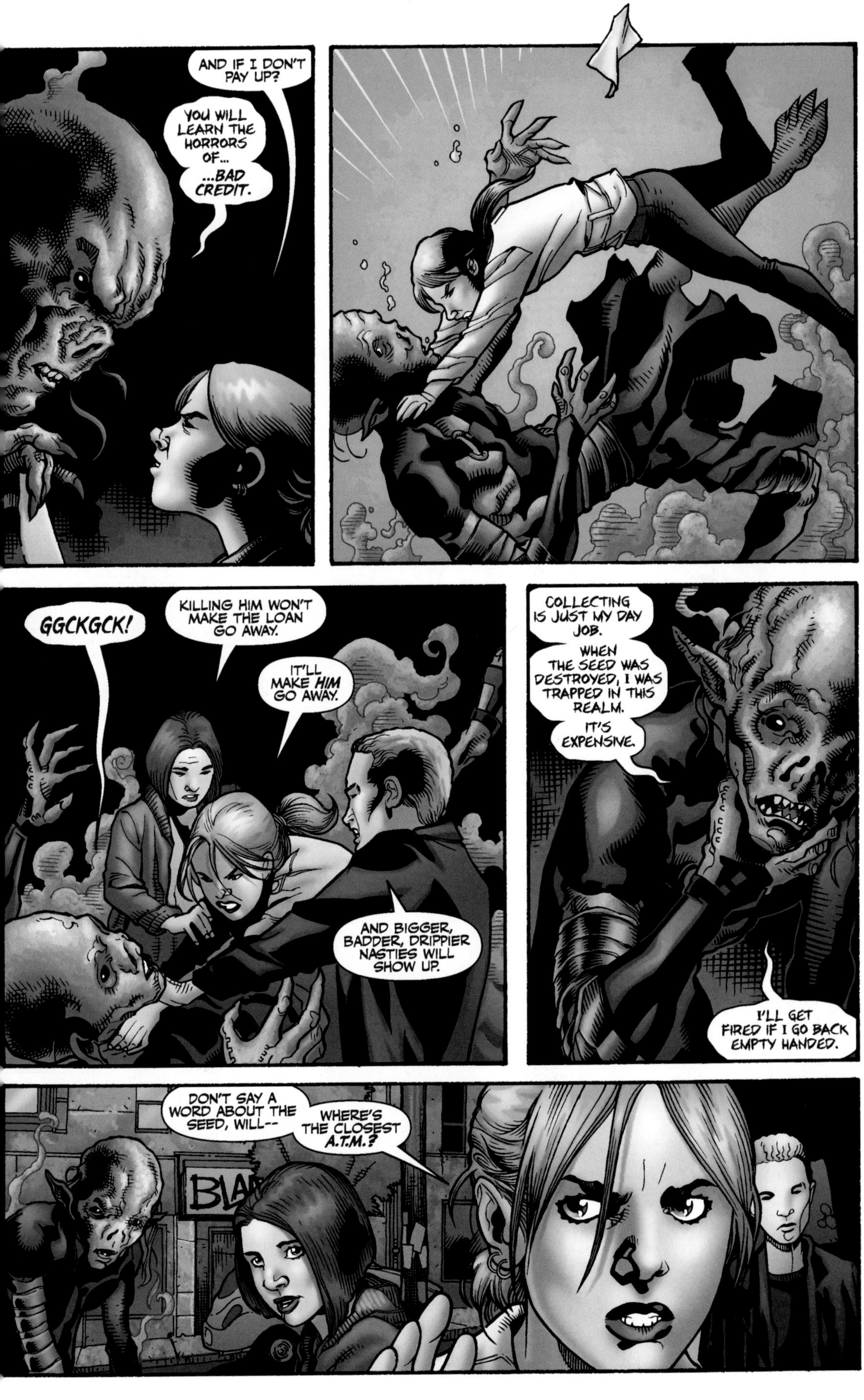
AND IF I DON'T PAY UP?
YOU WILL LEARN THE HORRORS OF...
...BAD CREDIT.
GGCKGCK!
KILLING HIM WON'T MAKE THE LOAN GO AWAY.
IT'LL MAKE HIM GO AWAY.
AND BIGGER, BADDER, DRIPPIER NASTIES WILL SHOW UP.
COLLECTING IS JUST MY DAY JOB.
WHEN THE SEED WAS DESTROYED, I WAS TRAPPED IN THIS REALM.
IT'S EXPENSIVE.
I'LL GET FIRED IF I GO BACK EMPTY HANDED.
DON'T SAY A WORD ABOUT THE SEED, WILL--
WHERE'S THE CLOSEST A.T.M.?
BLA

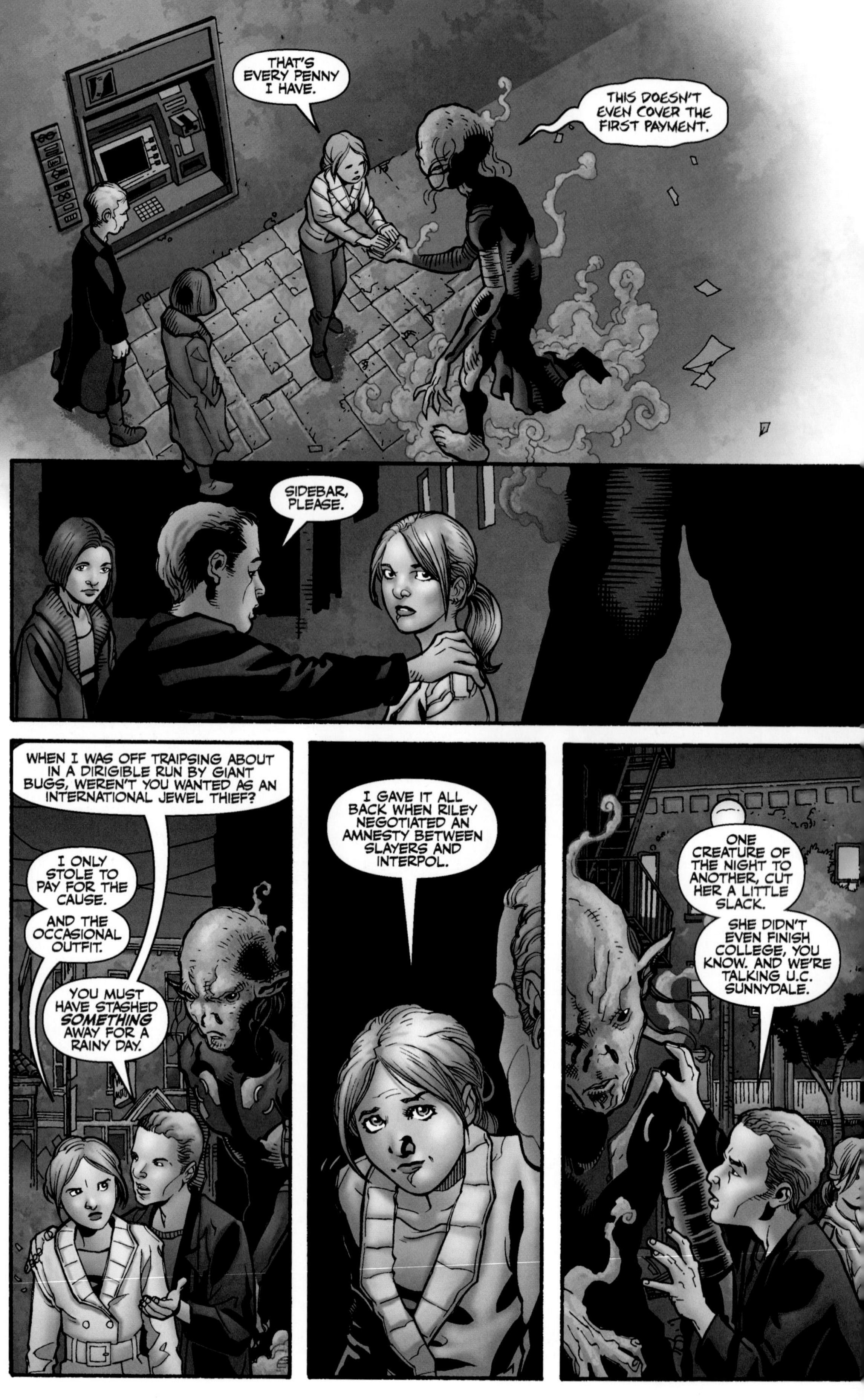
THAT'S EVERY PENNY I HAVE.
THIS DOESN'T EVEN COVER THE FIRST PAYMENT.
SIDEBAR, PLEASE.
WHEN I WAS OFF TRAIPSING ABOUT IN A DIRIGIBLE RUN BY GIANT BUGS, WEREN'T YOU WANTED AS AN INTERNATIONAL JEWEL THIEF?
I ONLY STOLE TO PAY FOR THE CAUSE.
AND THE OCCASIONAL OUTFIT.
YOU MUST HAVE STASHED *SOMETHING* AWAY FOR A RAINY DAY.
I GAVE IT ALL BACK WHEN RILEY NEGOTIATED AN AMNESTY BETWEEN SLAYERS AND INTERPOL.
ONE CREATURE OF THE NIGHT TO ANOTHER, CUT HER A LITTLE SLACK.
SHE DIDN'T EVEN FINISH COLLEGE, YOU KNOW. AND WE'RE TALKING U.C. SUNNYDALE.

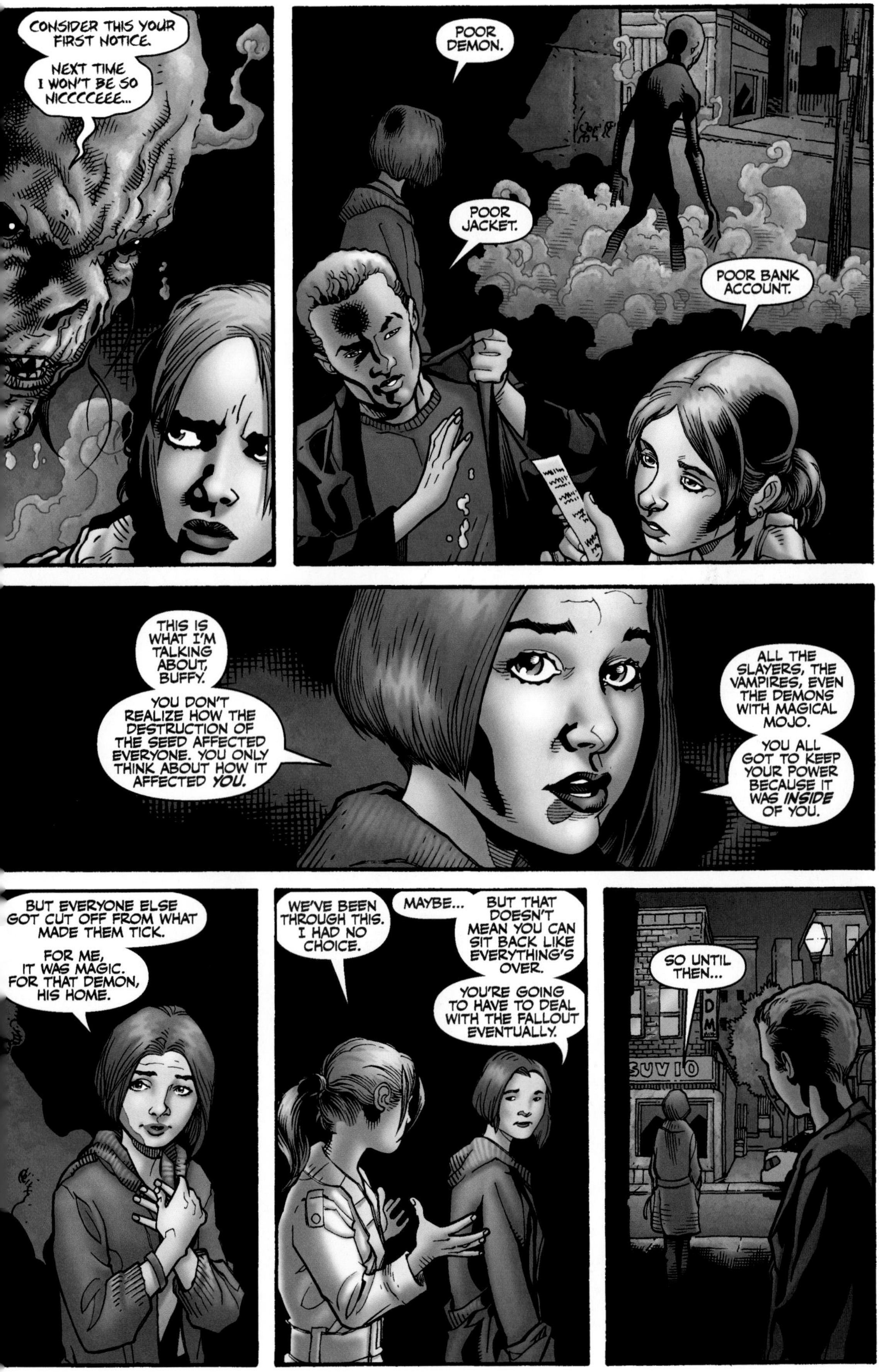
CONSIDER THIS YOUR FIRST NOTICE.
NEXT TIME I WON'T BE SO NICCCCEEE...
POOR DEMON.
POOR JACKET.
POOR BANK ACCOUNT.
THIS IS WHAT I'M TALKING ABOUT, BUFFY.
YOU DON'T REALIZE HOW THE DESTRUCTION OF THE SEED AFFECTED EVERYONE. YOU ONLY THINK ABOUT HOW IT AFFECTED *YOU.*
ALL THE SLAYERS, THE VAMPIRES, EVEN THE DEMONS WITH MAGICAL MOJO.
YOU ALL GOT TO KEEP YOUR POWER BECAUSE IT WAS *INSIDE* OF YOU.
BUT EVERYONE ELSE GOT CUT OFF FROM WHAT MADE THEM TICK.
FOR ME, IT WAS MAGIC. FOR THAT DEMON, HIS HOME.
WE'VE BEEN THROUGH THIS. I HAD NO CHOICE.
MAYBE...
BUT THAT DOESN'T MEAN YOU CAN SIT BACK LIKE EVERYTHING'S OVER.
YOU'RE GOING TO HAVE TO DEAL WITH THE FALLOUT EVENTUALLY.
SO UNTIL THEN...
SUVIO

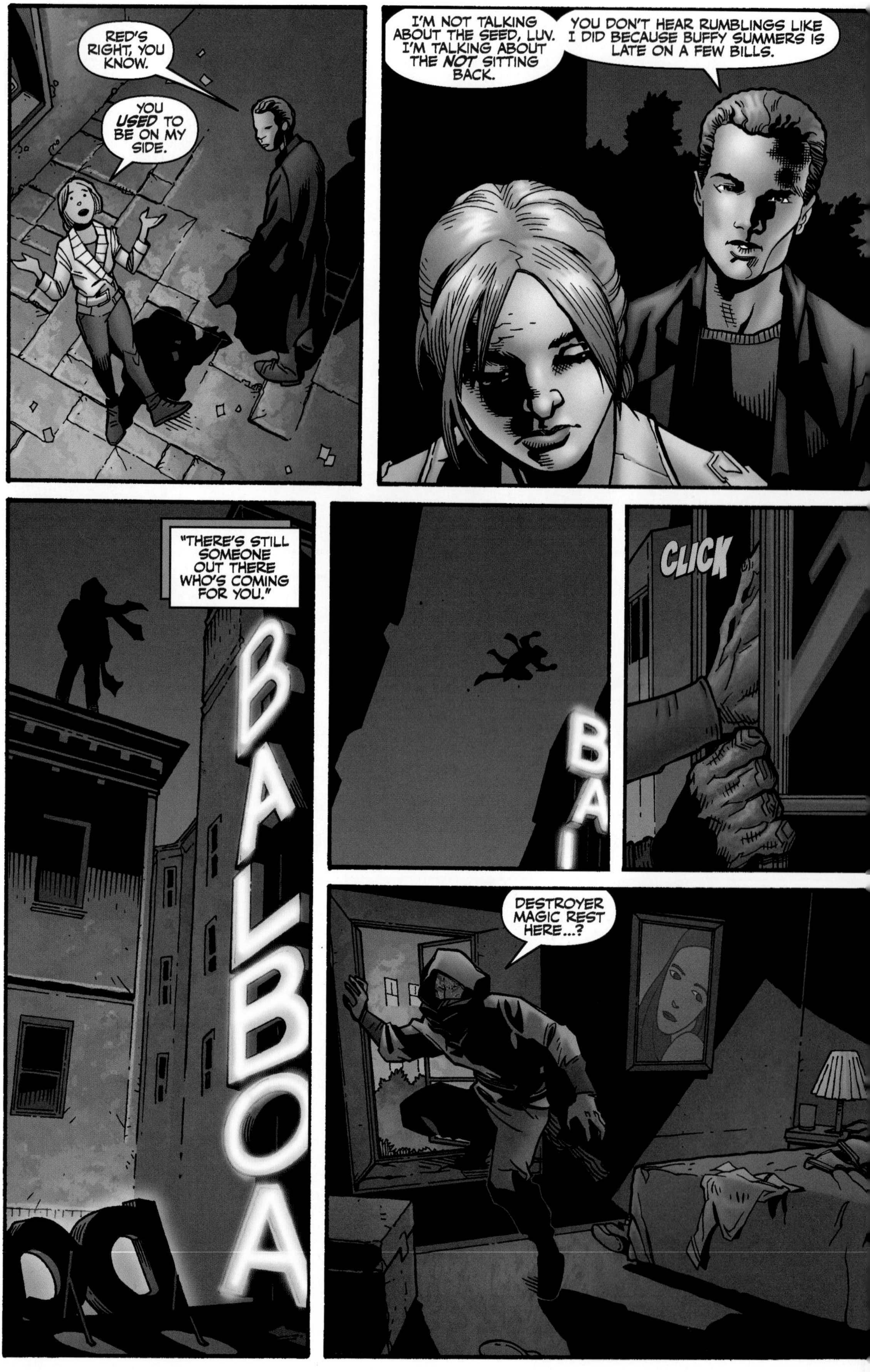
RED'S RIGHT, YOU KNOW.
YOU USED TO BE ON MY SIDE.
I'M NOT TALKING ABOUT THE SEED, LUV. I'M TALKING ABOUT THE NOT SITTING BACK.
YOU DON'T HEAR RUMBLINGS LIKE I DID BECAUSE BUFFY SUMMERS IS LATE ON A FEW BILLS.
"THERE'S STILL SOMEONE OUT THERE WHO'S COMING FOR YOU."
BALBOA
BAI
CLICK
DESTROYER MAGIC REST HERE...?

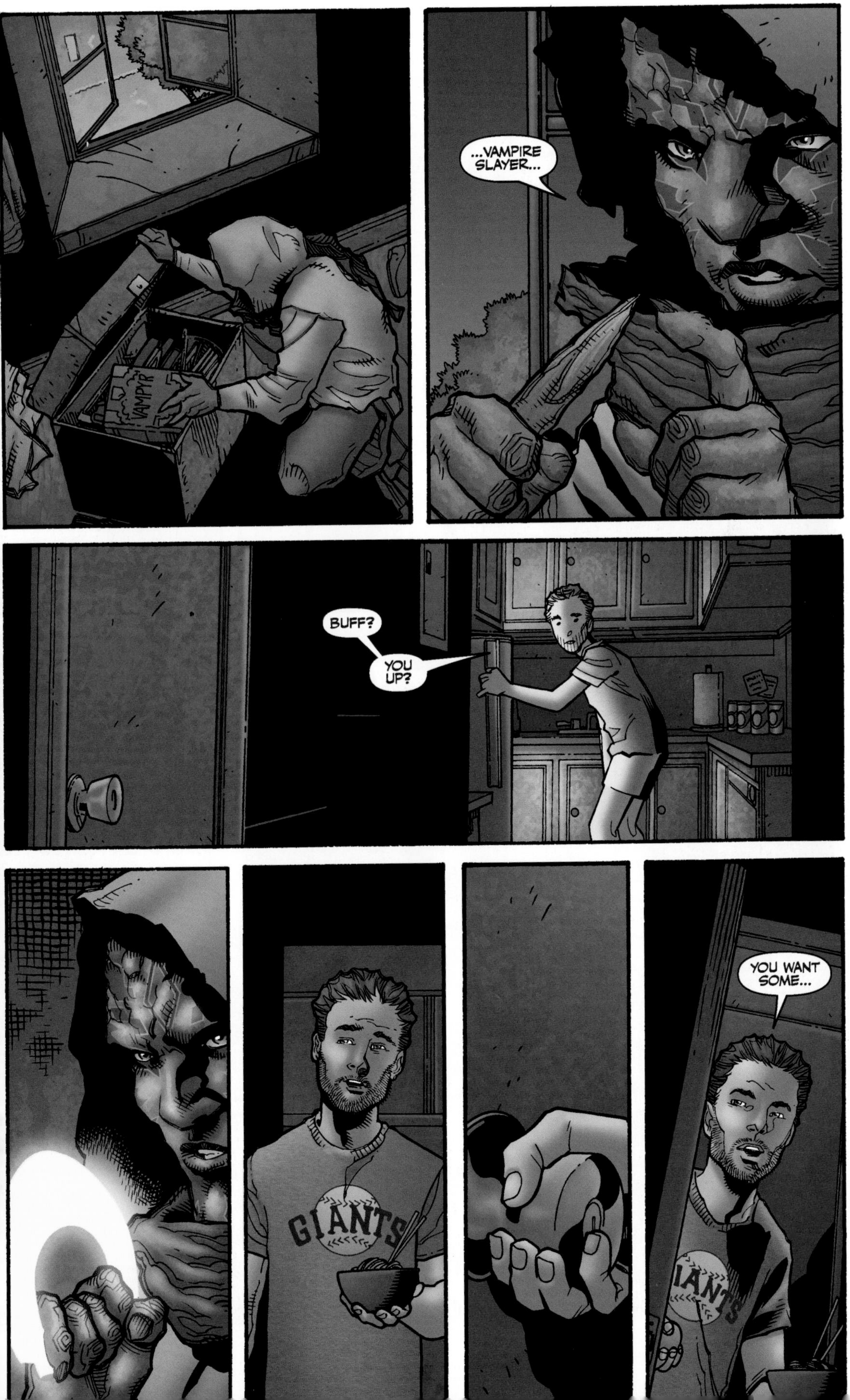
VAMPYR
...VAMPIRE SLAYER...
BUFF?
YOU UP?
GIANTS
YOU WANT SOME...

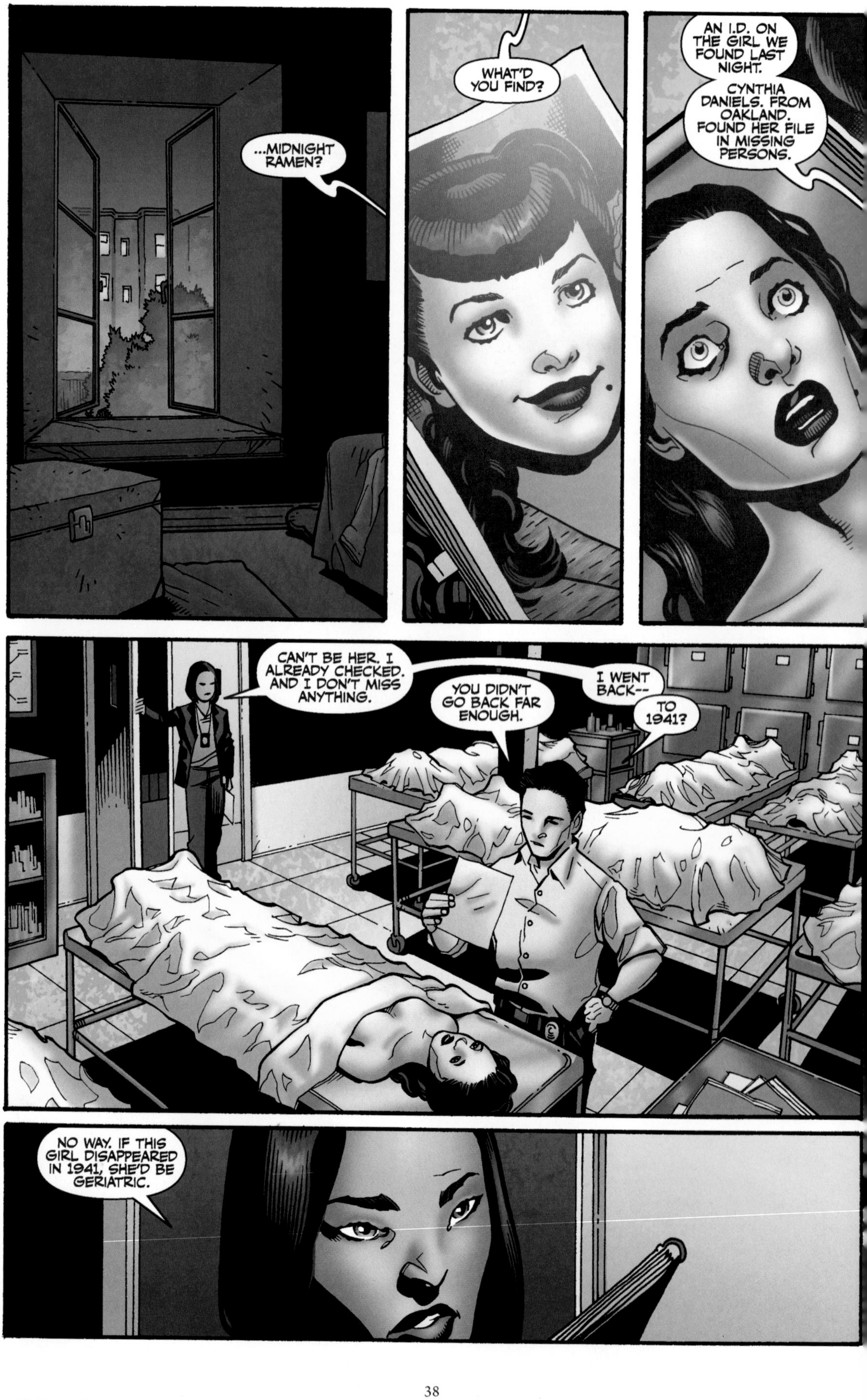
...MIDNIGHT RAMEN?
WHAT'D YOU FIND?
AN I.D. ON THE GIRL WE FOUND LAST NIGHT.
CYNTHIA DANIELS. FROM OAKLAND. FOUND HER FILE IN MISSING PERSONS.
CAN'T BE HER. I ALREADY CHECKED. AND I DON'T MISS ANYTHING.
YOU DIDN'T GO BACK FAR ENOUGH.
I WENT BACK--
TO 1941?
NO WAY. IF THIS GIRL DISAPPEARED IN 1941, SHE'D BE GERIATRIC.

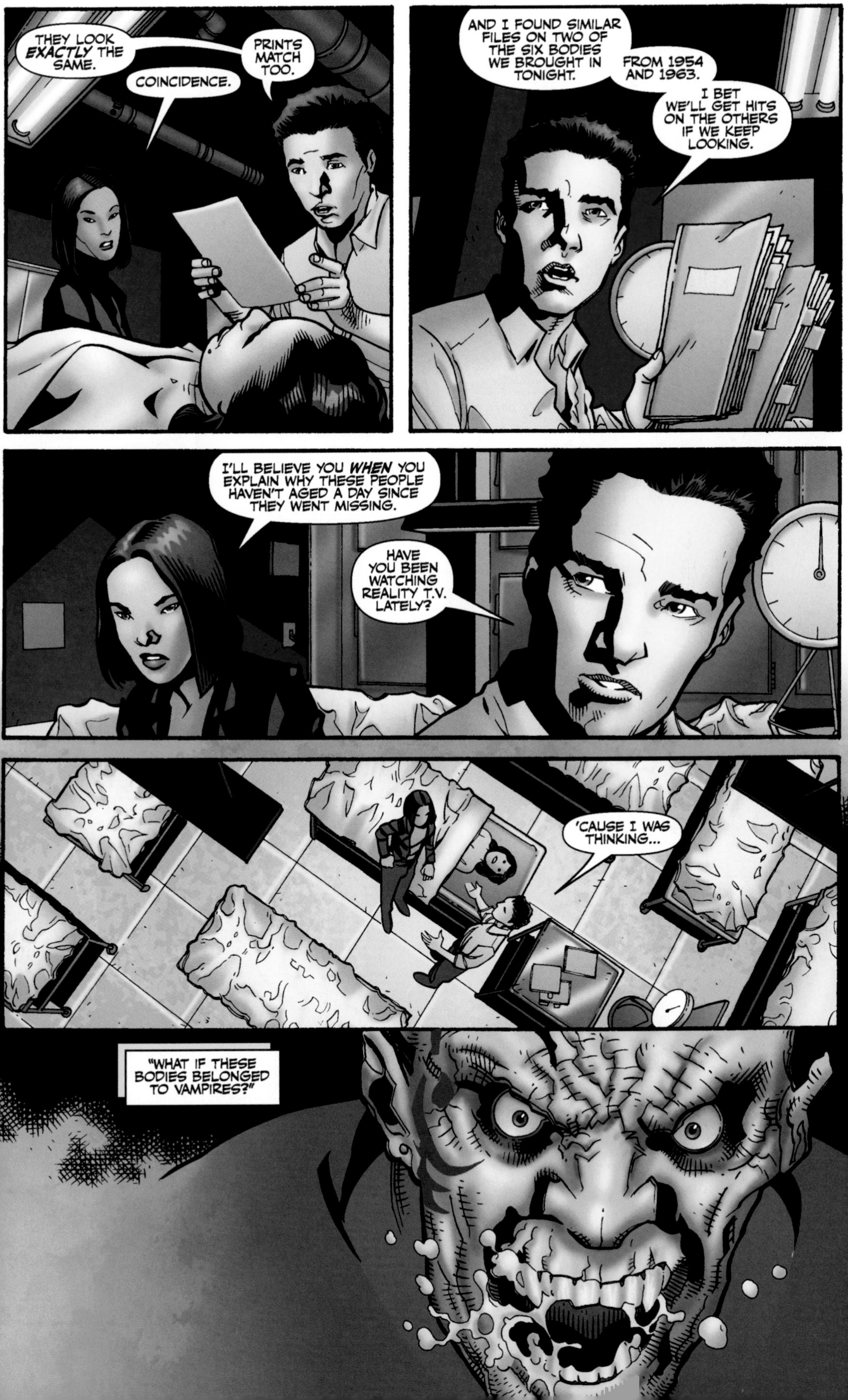
THEY LOOK EXACTLY THE SAME.
PRINTS MATCH TOO.
COINCIDENCE.
AND I FOUND SIMILAR FILES ON TWO OF THE SIX BODIES WE BROUGHT IN TONIGHT.
FROM 1954 AND 1963.
I BET WE'LL GET HITS ON THE OTHERS IF WE KEEP LOOKING.
I'LL BELIEVE YOU WHEN YOU EXPLAIN WHY THESE PEOPLE HAVEN'T AGED A DAY SINCE THEY WENT MISSING.
HAVE YOU BEEN WATCHING REALITY T.V. LATELY?
'CAUSE I WAS THINKING...
"WHAT IF THESE BODIES BELONGED TO VAMPIRES?"

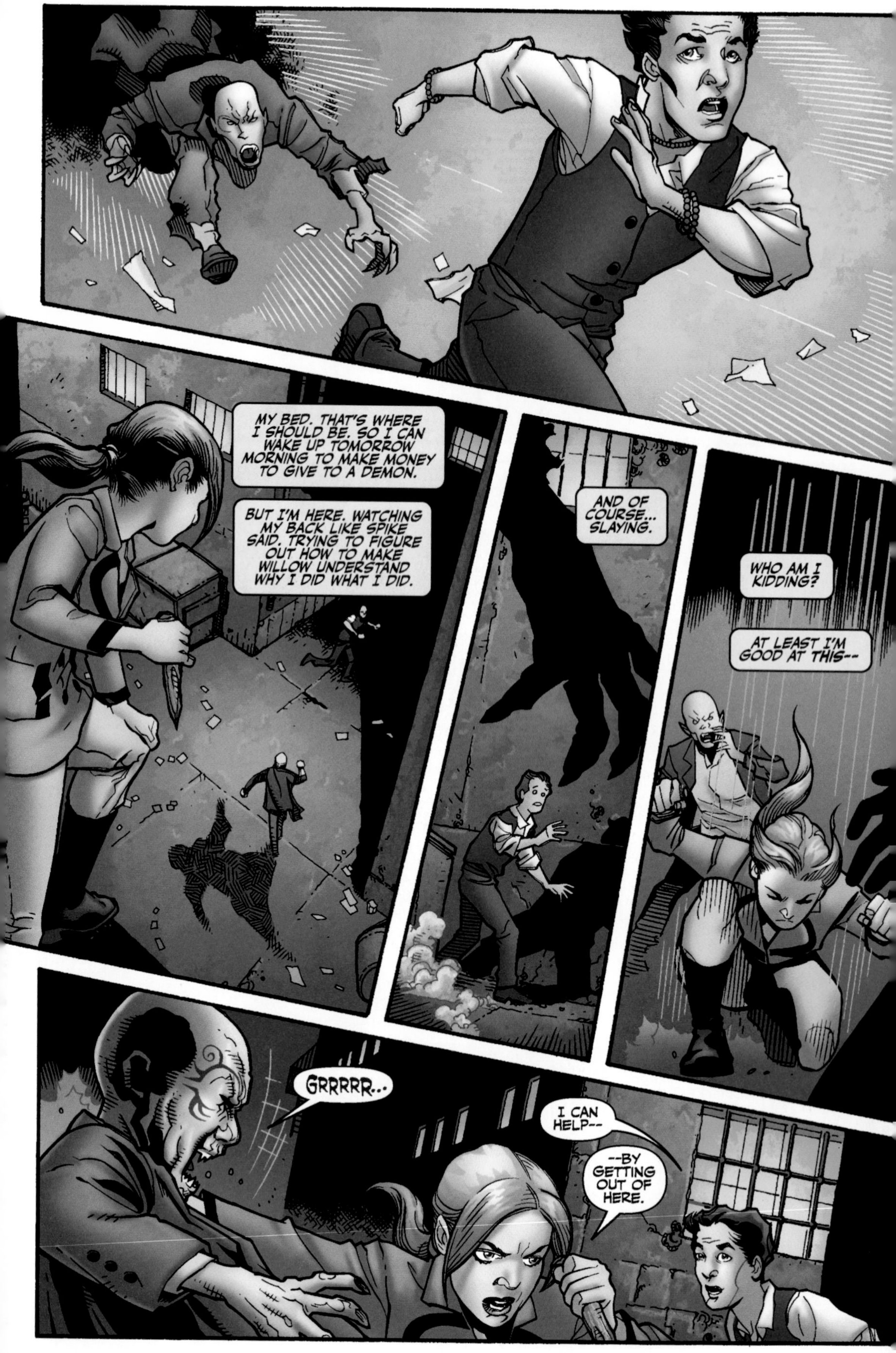
MY BED. THAT'S WHERE I SHOULD BE. SO I CAN WAKE UP TOMORROW MORNING TO MAKE MONEY TO GIVE TO A DEMON.
BUT I'M HERE. WATCHING MY BACK LIKE SPIKE SAID. TRYING TO FIGURE OUT HOW TO MAKE WILLOW UNDERSTAND WHY I DID WHAT I DID.
AND OF COURSE... SLAYING.
WHO AM I KIDDING?
AT LEAST I'M GOOD AT THIS--
GRRRRR...
I CAN HELP--
--BY GETTING OUT OF HERE.

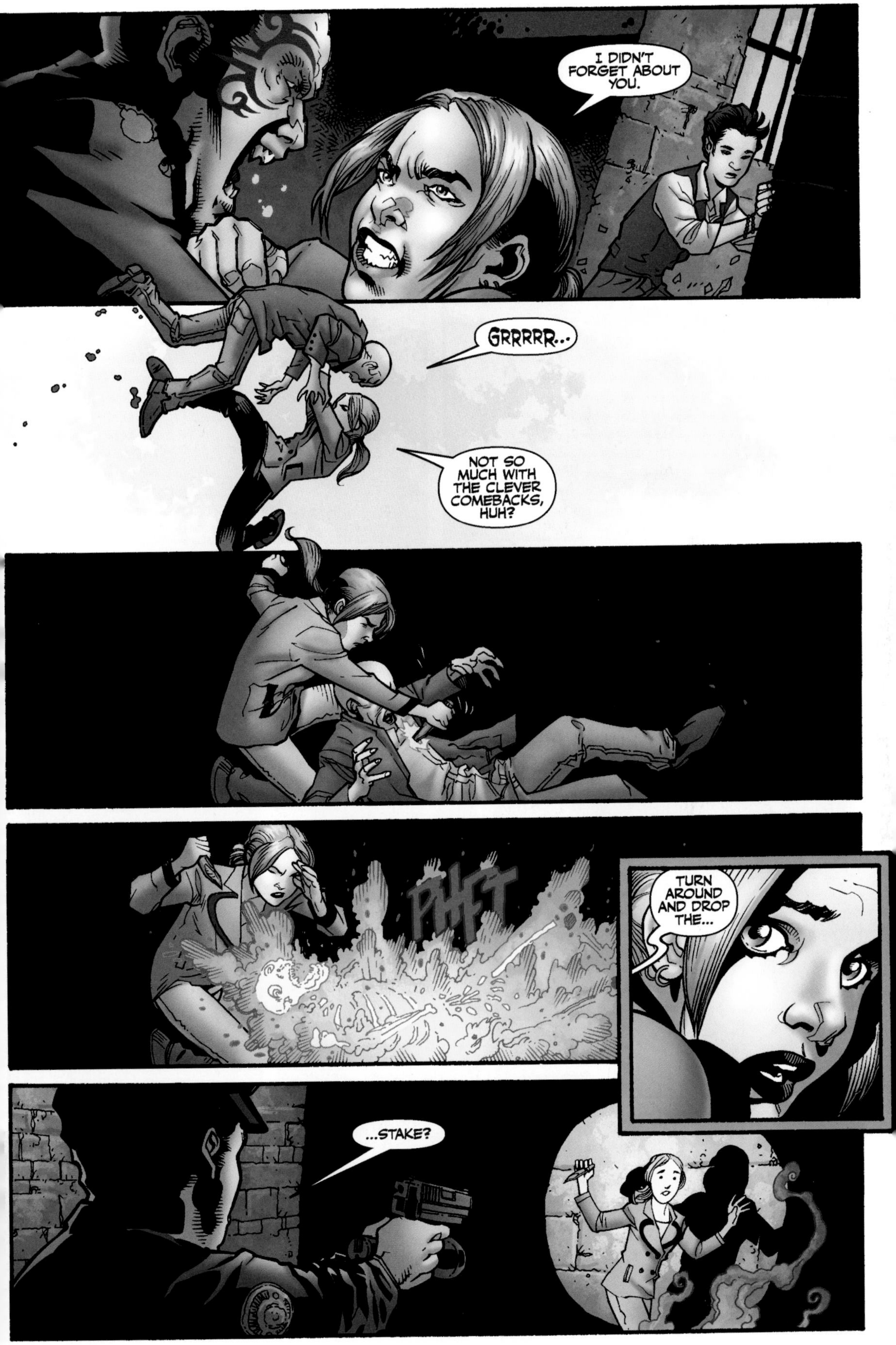
I DIDN'T FORGET ABOUT YOU.
GRRRRR...
NOT SO MUCH WITH THE CLEVER COMEBACKS, HUH?
PHFT
TURN AROUND AND DROP THE...
...STAKE?

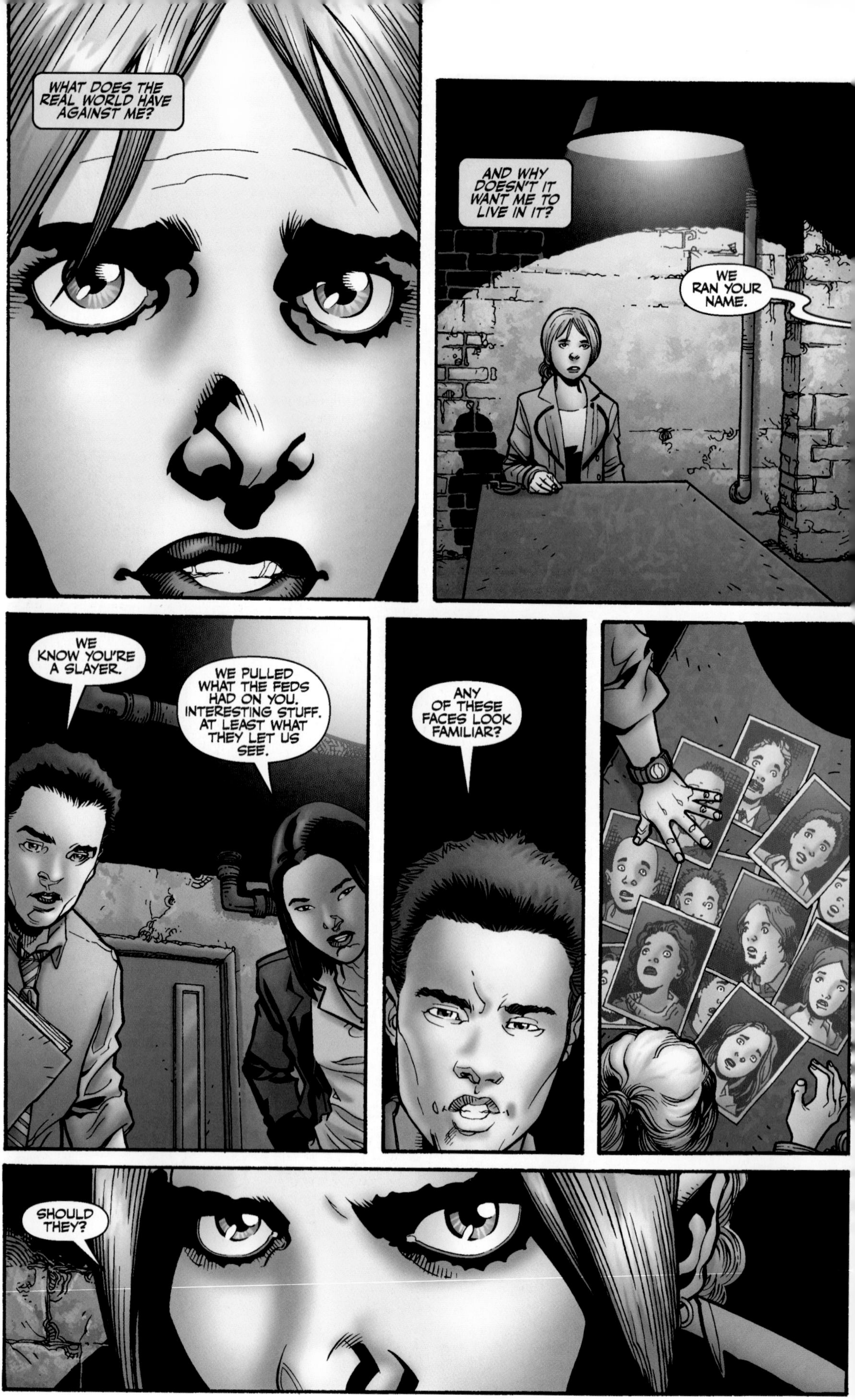
WHAT DOES THE REAL WORLD HAVE AGAINST ME?
AND WHY DOESN'T IT WANT ME TO LIVE IN IT?
WE RAN YOUR NAME.
WE KNOW YOU'RE A SLAYER.
WE PULLED WHAT THE FEDS HAD ON YOU. INTERESTING STUFF. AT LEAST WHAT THEY LET US SEE.
ANY OF THESE FACES LOOK FAMILIAR?
SHOULD THEY?

DETECTIVE DOWLING HAS THE NOVEL THEORY THAT THESE BODIES BELONG TO VAMPIRES.

AND SINCE YOU'RE A SLAYER...

YOU THINK I KILLED THEM?

THEY'RE NOT EVEN VAMPIRES.

WHAT MAKES YOU SO SURE?

UNDEAD 101. NO MATTER HOW A VAMP DIES--STAKE TO THE CHEST, DECAPITATION, SUNLIGHT--

IT ALWAYS ENDS IN ONE BIG POOF.

LIKE THE VAMPIRE YOU KILLED TONIGHT?

THE TERM IS SLAYED. AND IS NOW WHEN I ASK FOR A LAWYER?

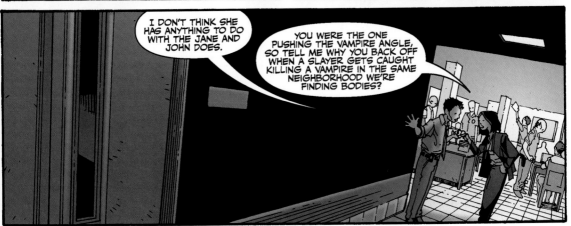

I DON'T THINK SHE HAS ANYTHING TO DO WITH THE JANE AND JOHN DOES.

YOU WERE THE ONE PUSHING THE VAMPIRE ANGLE, SO TELL ME WHY YOU BACK OFF WHEN A SLAYER GETS CAUGHT KILLING A VAMPIRE IN THE SAME NEIGHBORHOOD WE'RE FINDING BODIES?

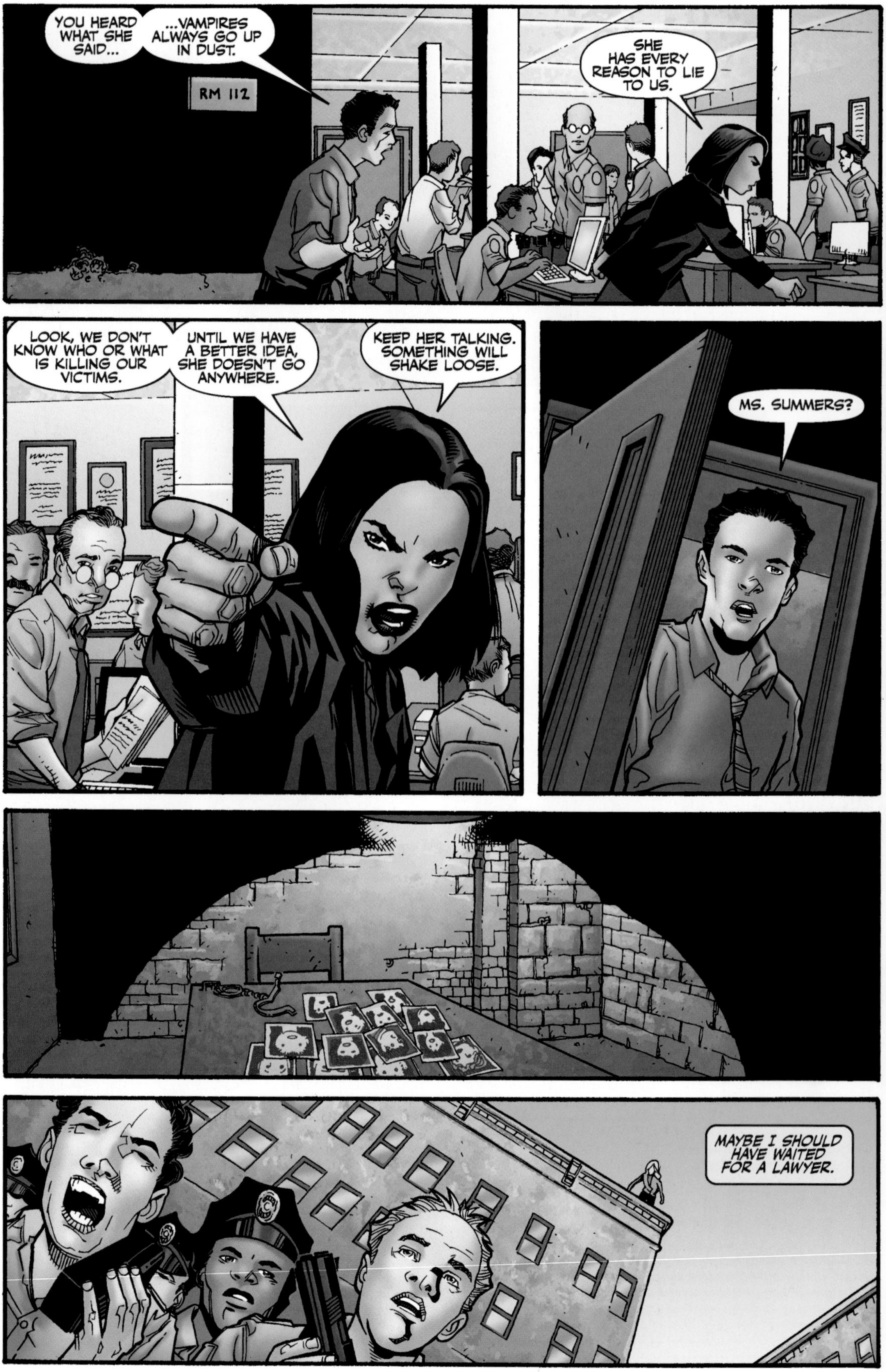
YOU HEARD WHAT SHE SAID...
...VAMPIRES ALWAYS GO UP IN DUST.
RM 112
SHE HAS EVERY REASON TO LIE TO US.
LOOK, WE DON'T KNOW WHO OR WHAT IS KILLING OUR VICTIMS.
UNTIL WE HAVE A BETTER IDEA, SHE DOESN'T GO ANYWHERE.
KEEP HER TALKING. SOMETHING WILL SHAKE LOOSE.
MS. SUMMERS?
MAYBE I SHOULD HAVE WAITED FOR A LAWYER.

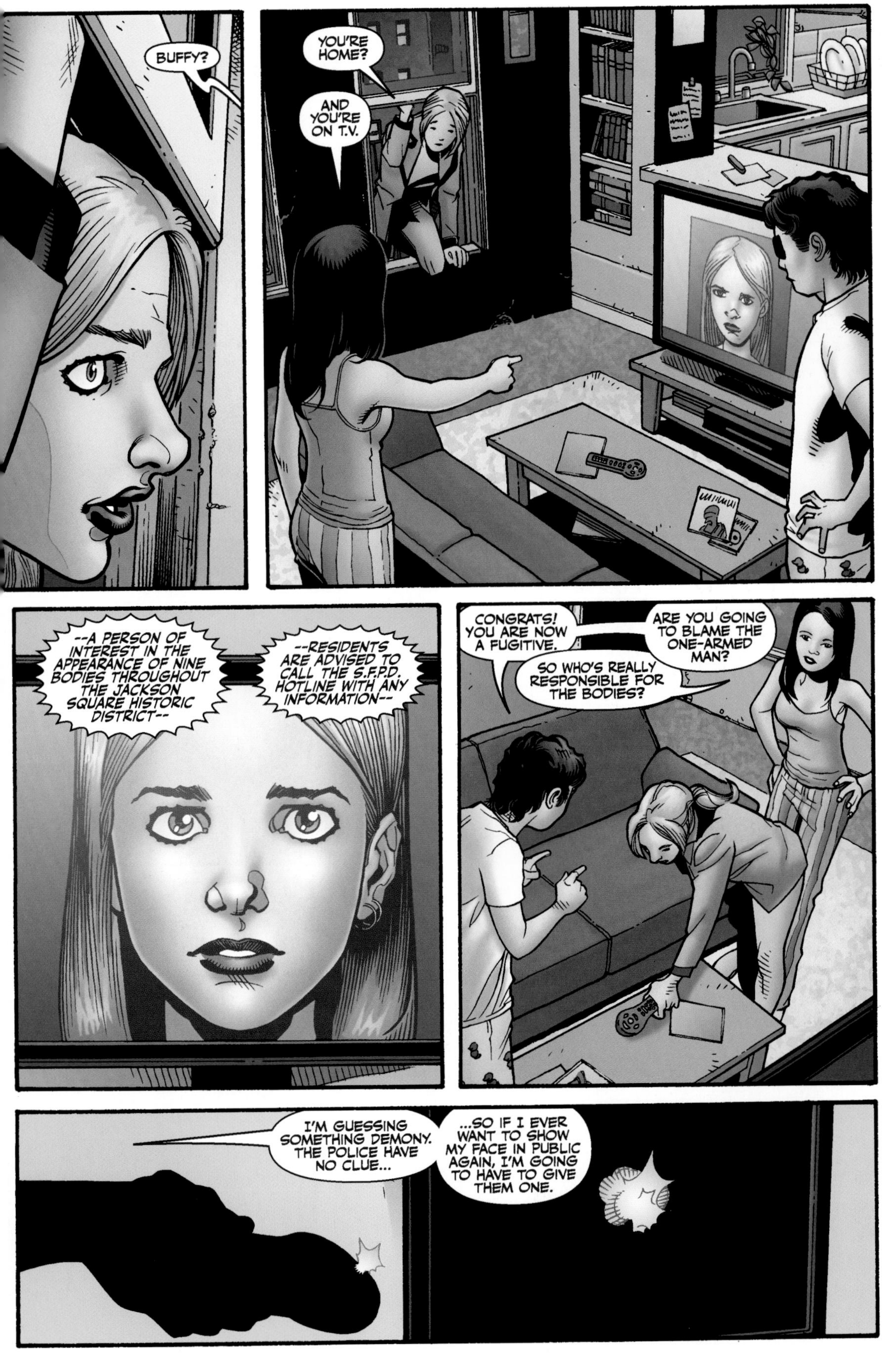
BUFFY?
YOU'RE HOME?
AND YOU'RE ON T.V.
--A PERSON OF INTEREST IN THE APPEARANCE OF NINE BODIES THROUGHOUT THE JACKSON SQUARE HISTORIC DISTRICT--
--RESIDENTS ARE ADVISED TO CALL THE S.F.P.D. HOTLINE WITH ANY INFORMATION--
CONGRATS! YOU ARE NOW A FUGITIVE.
ARE YOU GOING TO BLAME THE ONE-ARMED MAN?
SO WHO'S REALLY RESPONSIBLE FOR THE BODIES?
I'M GUESSING SOMETHING DEMONY. THE POLICE HAVE NO CLUE...
...SO IF I EVER WANT TO SHOW MY FACE IN PUBLIC AGAIN, I'M GOING TO HAVE TO GIVE THEM ONE.

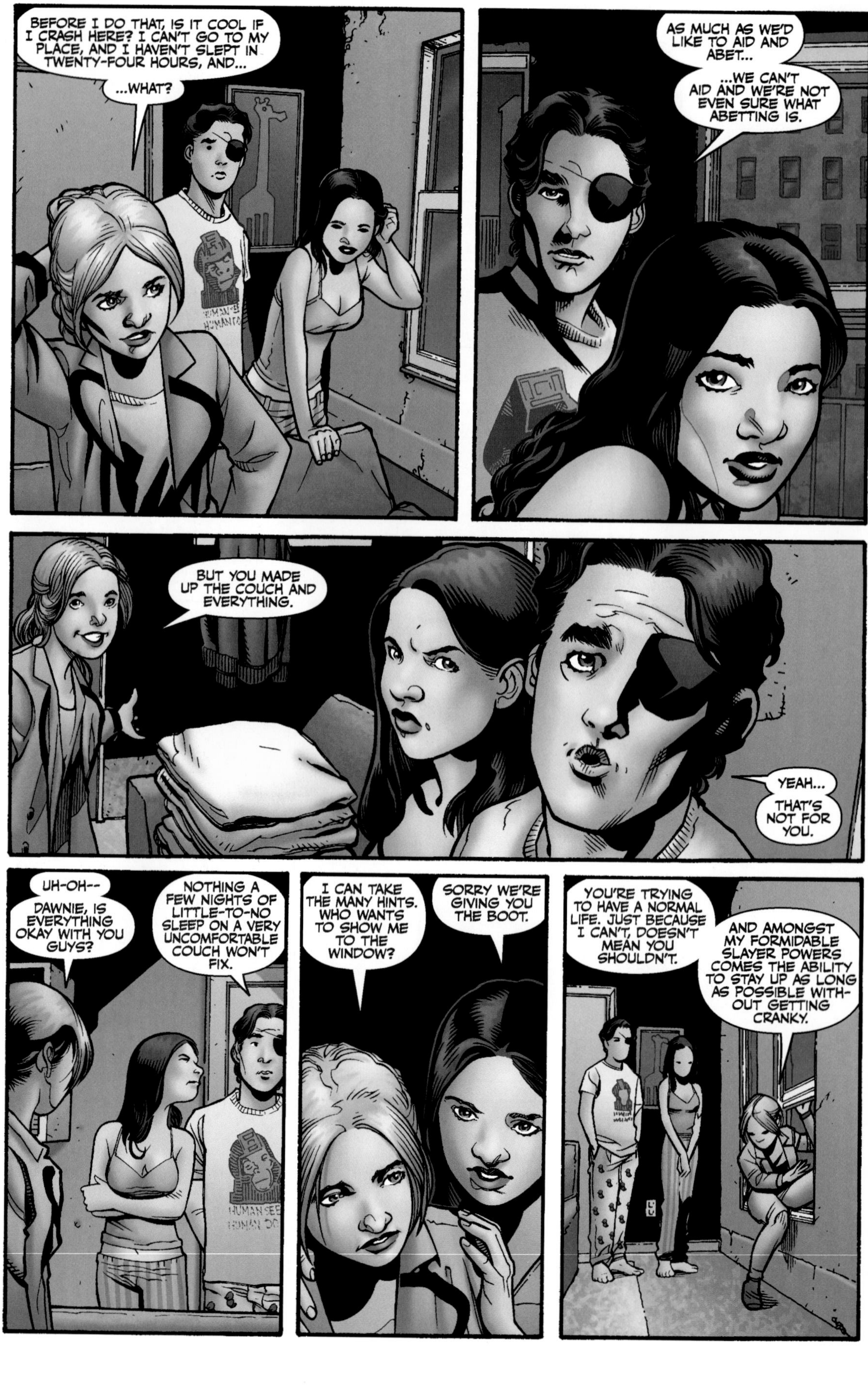
BEFORE I DO THAT, IS IT COOL IF I CRASH HERE? I CAN'T GO TO MY PLACE, AND I HAVEN'T SLEPT IN TWENTY-FOUR HOURS, AND...
...WHAT?
AS MUCH AS WE'D LIKE TO AID AND ABET...
...WE CAN'T AID AND WE'RE NOT EVEN SURE WHAT ABETTING IS.
BUT YOU MADE UP THE COUCH AND EVERYTHING.
YEAH...
THAT'S NOT FOR YOU.
UH-OH--
DAWNIE, IS EVERYTHING OKAY WITH YOU GUYS?
NOTHING A FEW NIGHTS OF LITTLE-TO-NO SLEEP ON A VERY UNCOMFORTABLE COUCH WON'T FIX.
I CAN TAKE THE MANY HINTS. WHO WANTS TO SHOW ME TO THE WINDOW?
SORRY WE'RE GIVING YOU THE BOOT.
YOU'RE TRYING TO HAVE A NORMAL LIFE. JUST BECAUSE I CAN'T, DOESN'T MEAN YOU SHOULDN'T.
AND AMONGST MY FORMIDABLE SLAYER POWERS COMES THE ABILITY TO STAY UP AS LONG AS POSSIBLE WITHOUT GETTING CRANKY.

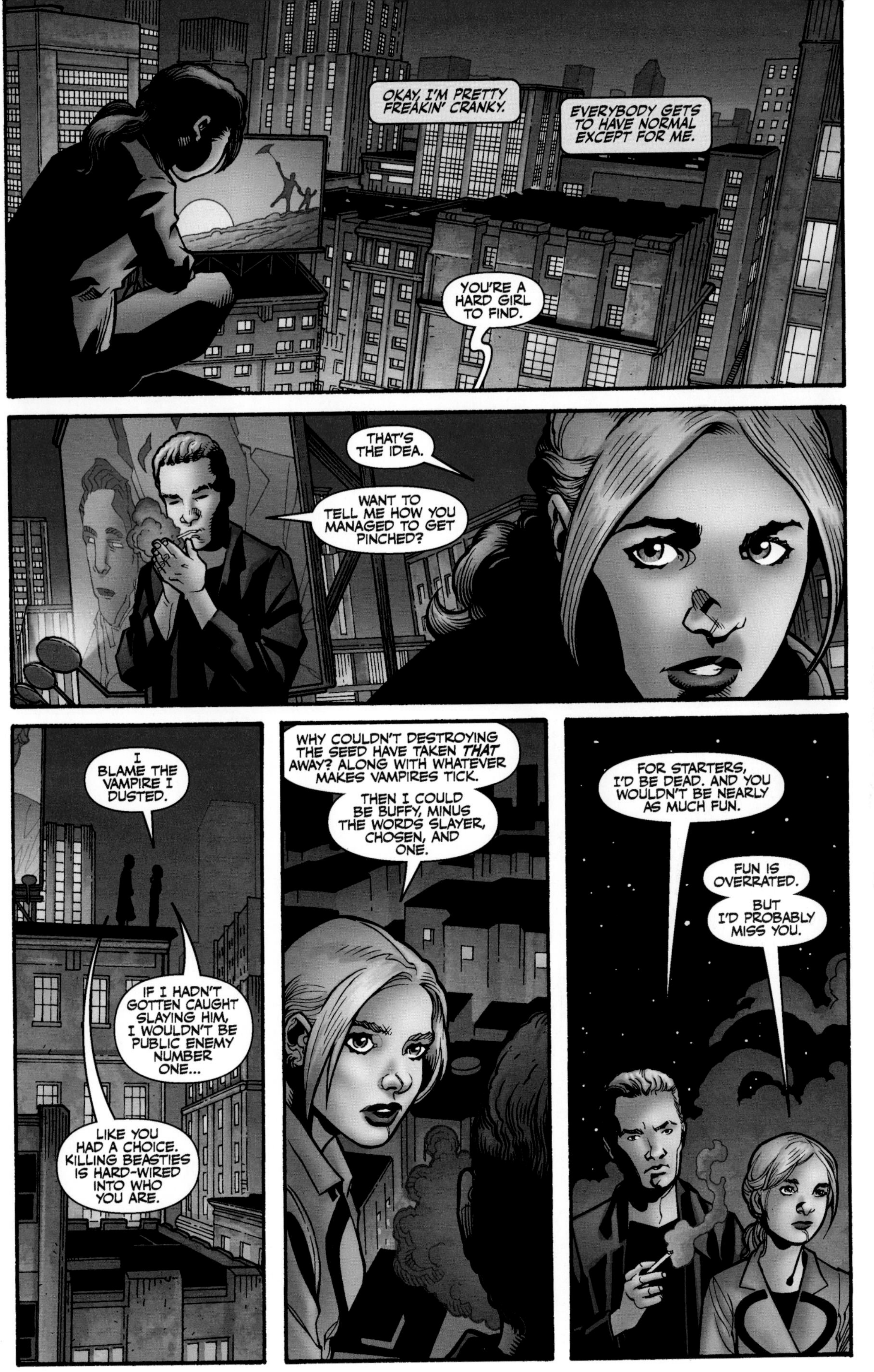

OKAY, I'M PRETTY FREAKIN' CRANKY.
EVERYBODY GETS TO HAVE NORMAL EXCEPT FOR ME.
YOU'RE A HARD GIRL TO FIND.
THAT'S THE IDEA.
WANT TO TELL ME HOW YOU MANAGED TO GET PINCHED?
I BLAME THE VAMPIRE I DUSTED.
IF I HADN'T GOTTEN CAUGHT SLAYING HIM, I WOULDN'T BE PUBLIC ENEMY NUMBER ONE...
LIKE YOU HAD A CHOICE. KILLING BEASTIES IS HARD-WIRED INTO WHO YOU ARE.
WHY COULDN'T DESTROYING THE SEED HAVE TAKEN *THAT* AWAY? ALONG WITH WHATEVER MAKES VAMPIRES TICK.
THEN I COULD BE BUFFY, MINUS THE WORDS SLAYER, CHOSEN, AND ONE.
FOR STARTERS, I'D BE DEAD. AND YOU WOULDN'T BE NEARLY AS MUCH FUN.
FUN IS OVERRATED.
BUT I'D PROBABLY MISS YOU.

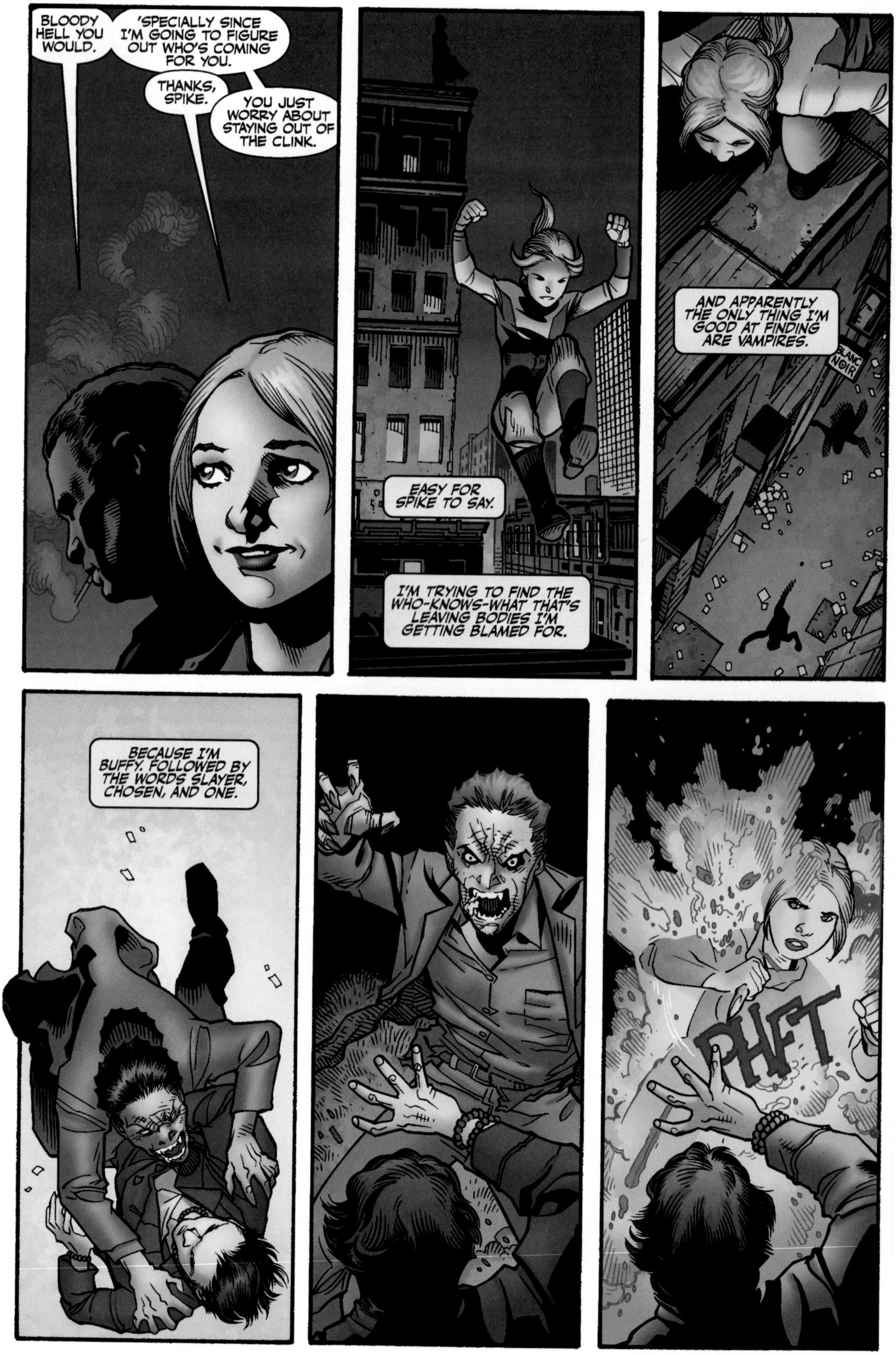

BLOODY HELL YOU WOULD.
'SPECIALLY SINCE I'M GOING TO FIGURE OUT WHO'S COMING FOR YOU.
THANKS, SPIKE.
YOU JUST WORRY ABOUT STAYING OUT OF THE CLINK.
EASY FOR SPIKE TO SAY.
I'M TRYING TO FIND THE WHO-KNOWS-WHAT THAT'S LEAVING BODIES I'M GETTING BLAMED FOR.
AND APPARENTLY THE ONLY THING I'M GOOD AT FINDING ARE VAMPIRES.
BLANC NOIR
BECAUSE I'M BUFFY. FOLLOWED BY THE WORDS SLAYER, CHOSEN, AND ONE.
PHFT

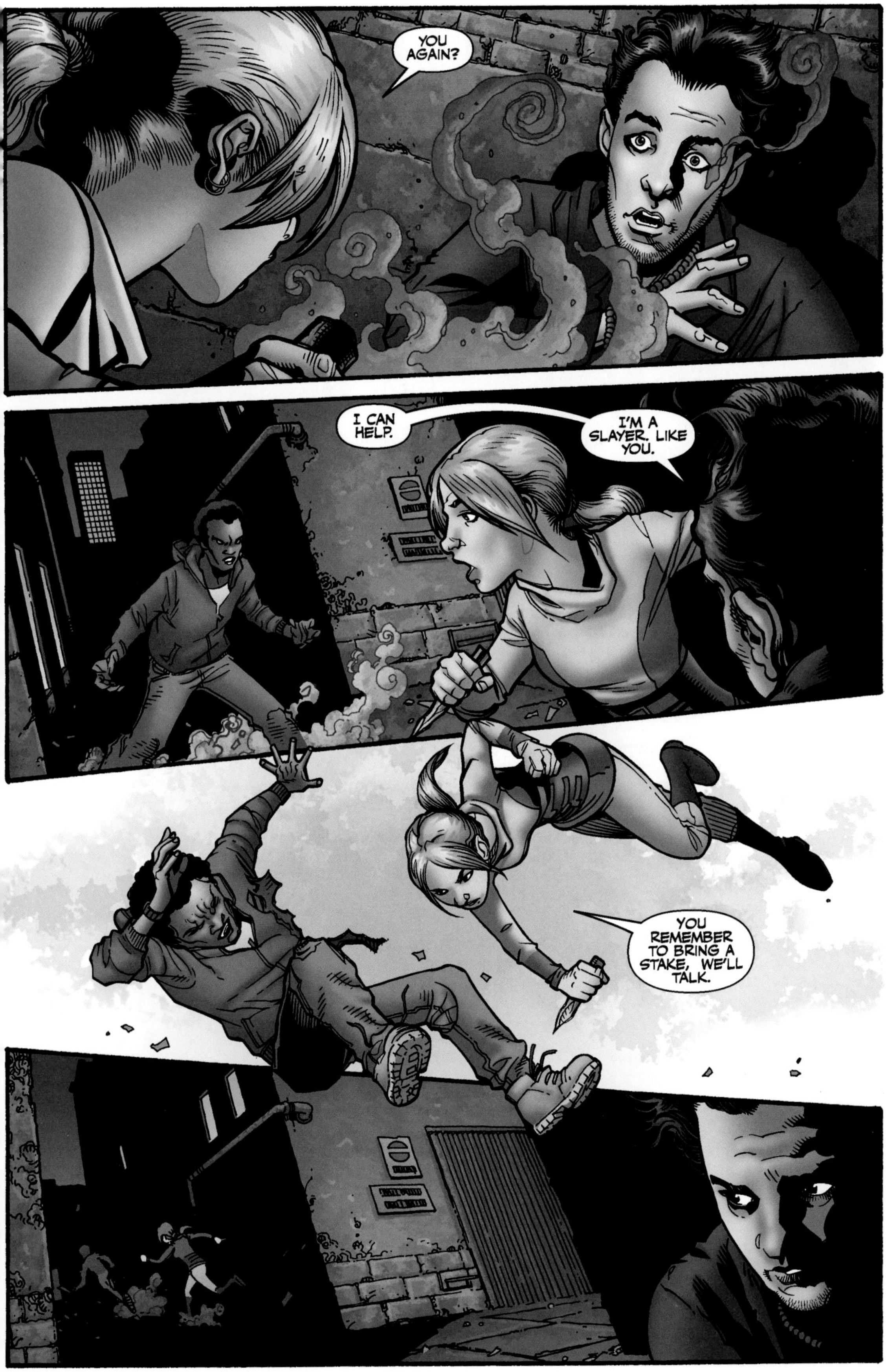
YOU AGAIN?
I CAN HELP.
I'M A SLAYER. LIKE YOU.
YOU REMEMBER TO BRING A STAKE, WE'LL TALK.

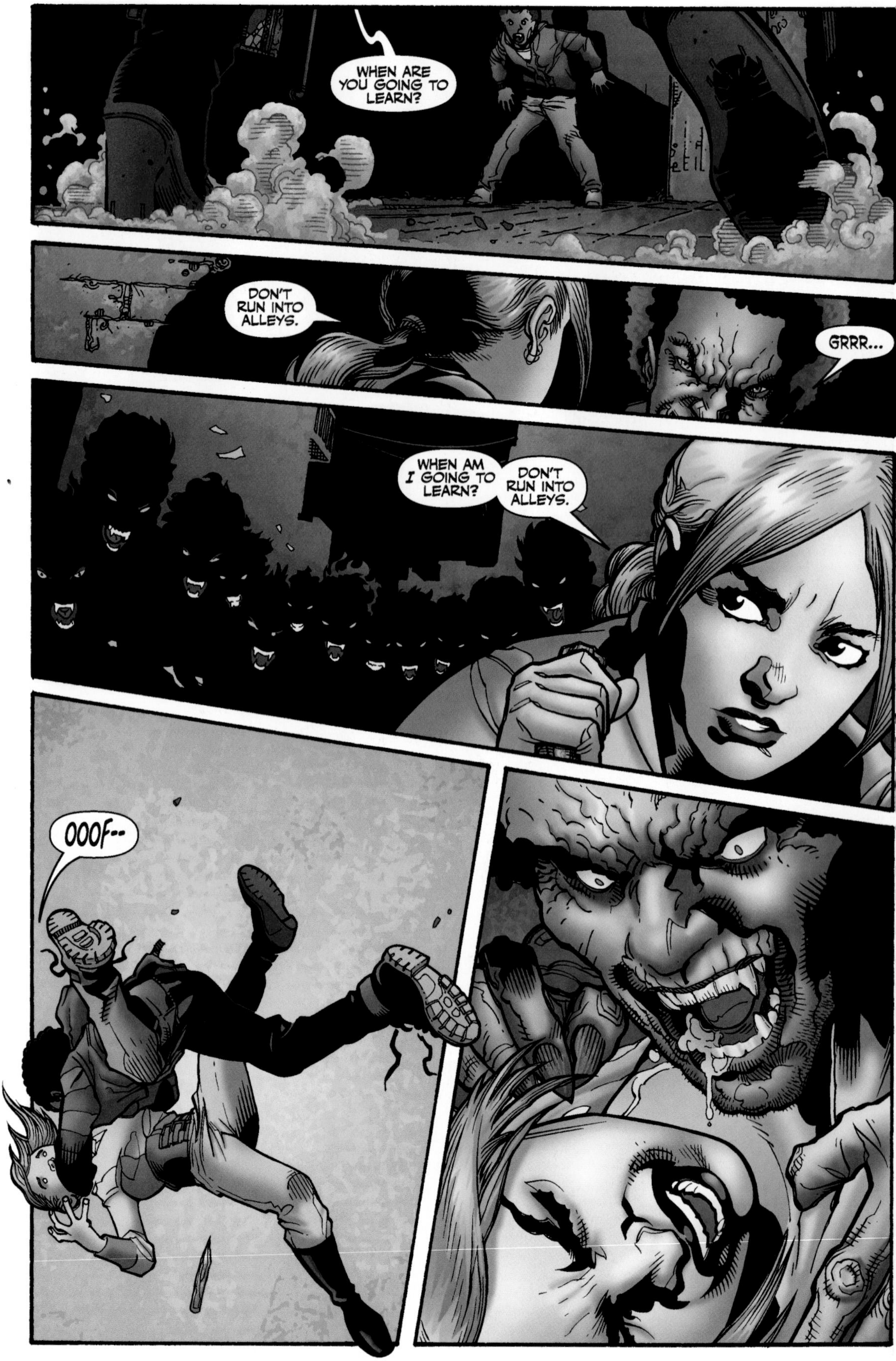
WHEN ARE YOU GOING TO LEARN?
DON'T RUN INTO ALLEYS.
GRRR...
WHEN AM I GOING TO LEARN?
DON'T RUN INTO ALLEYS.
OOOF--

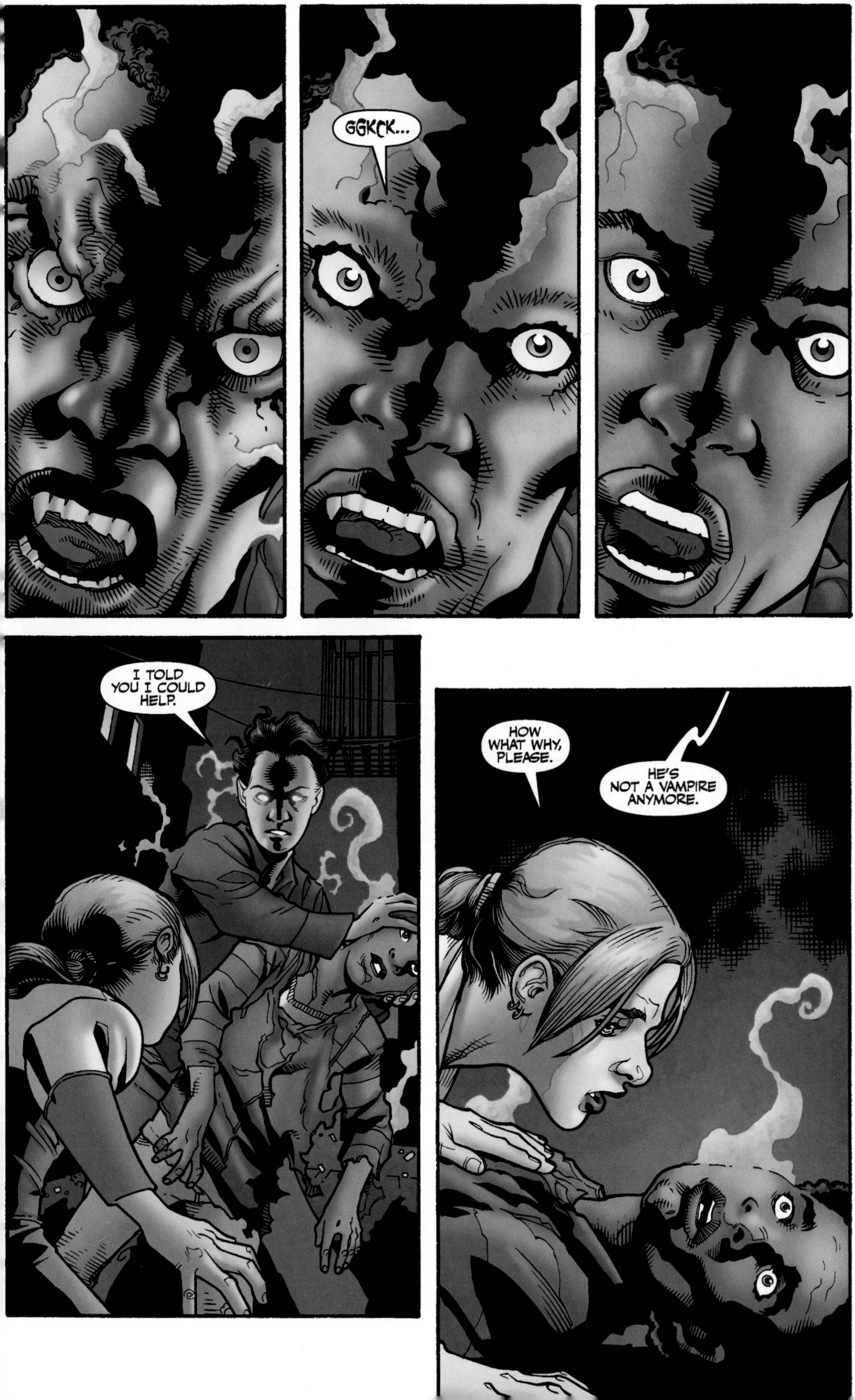
GGKCK...
I TOLD YOU I COULD HELP.
HOW WHAT WHY, PLEASE.
HE'S NOT A VAMPIRE ANYMORE.

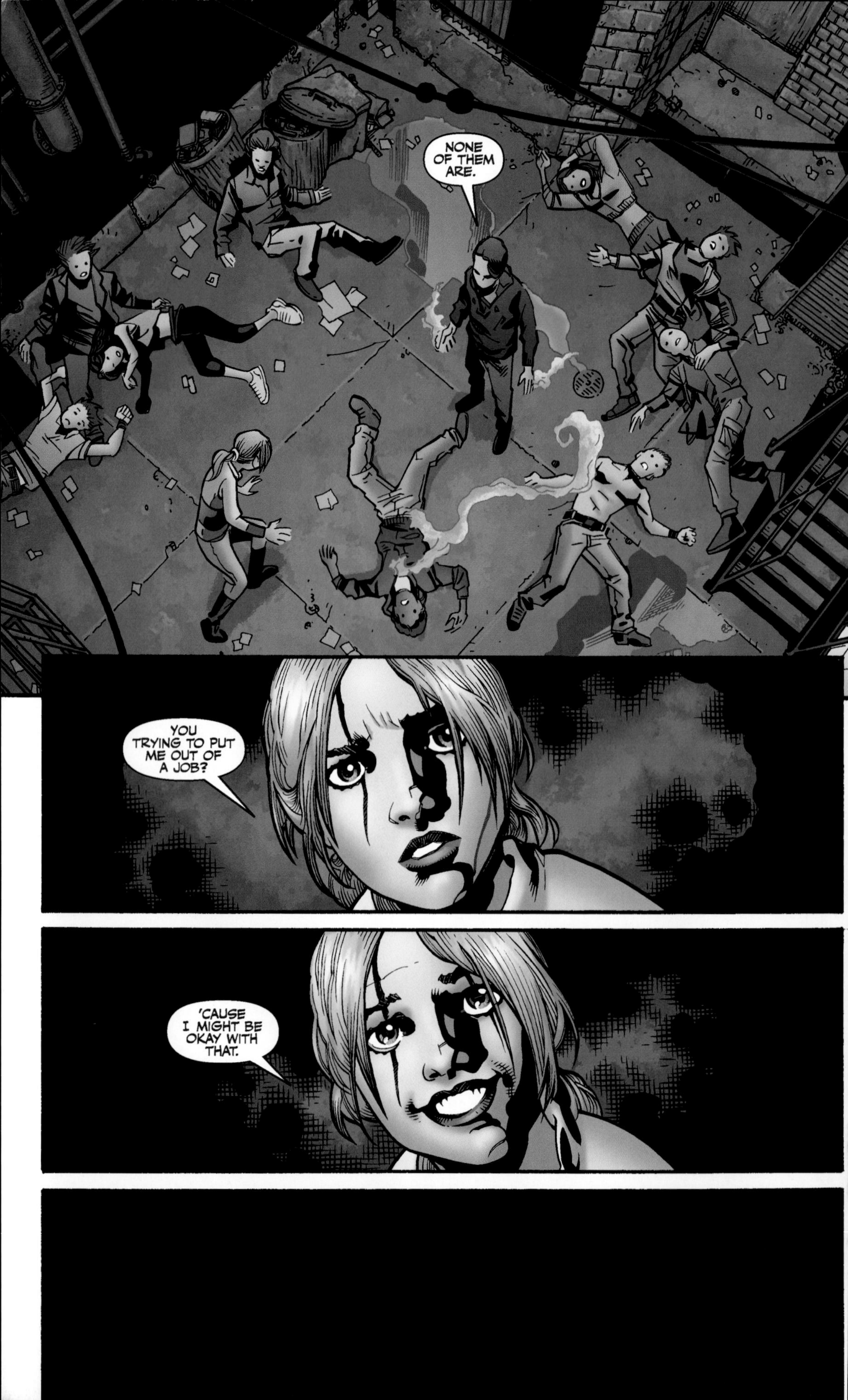
NONE OF THEM ARE.
YOU TRYING TO PUT ME OUT OF A JOB?
'CAUSE I MIGHT BE OKAY WITH THAT.

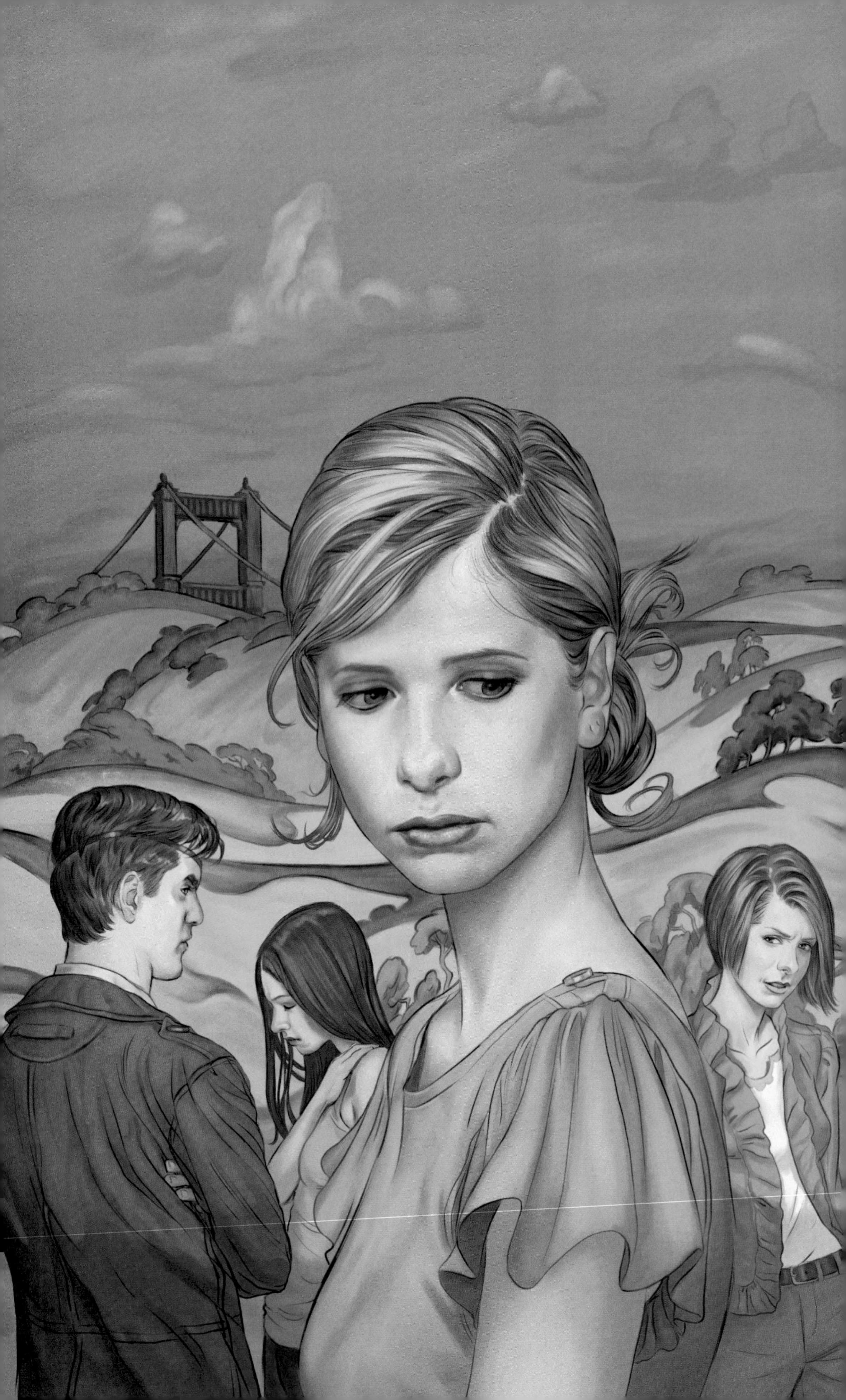

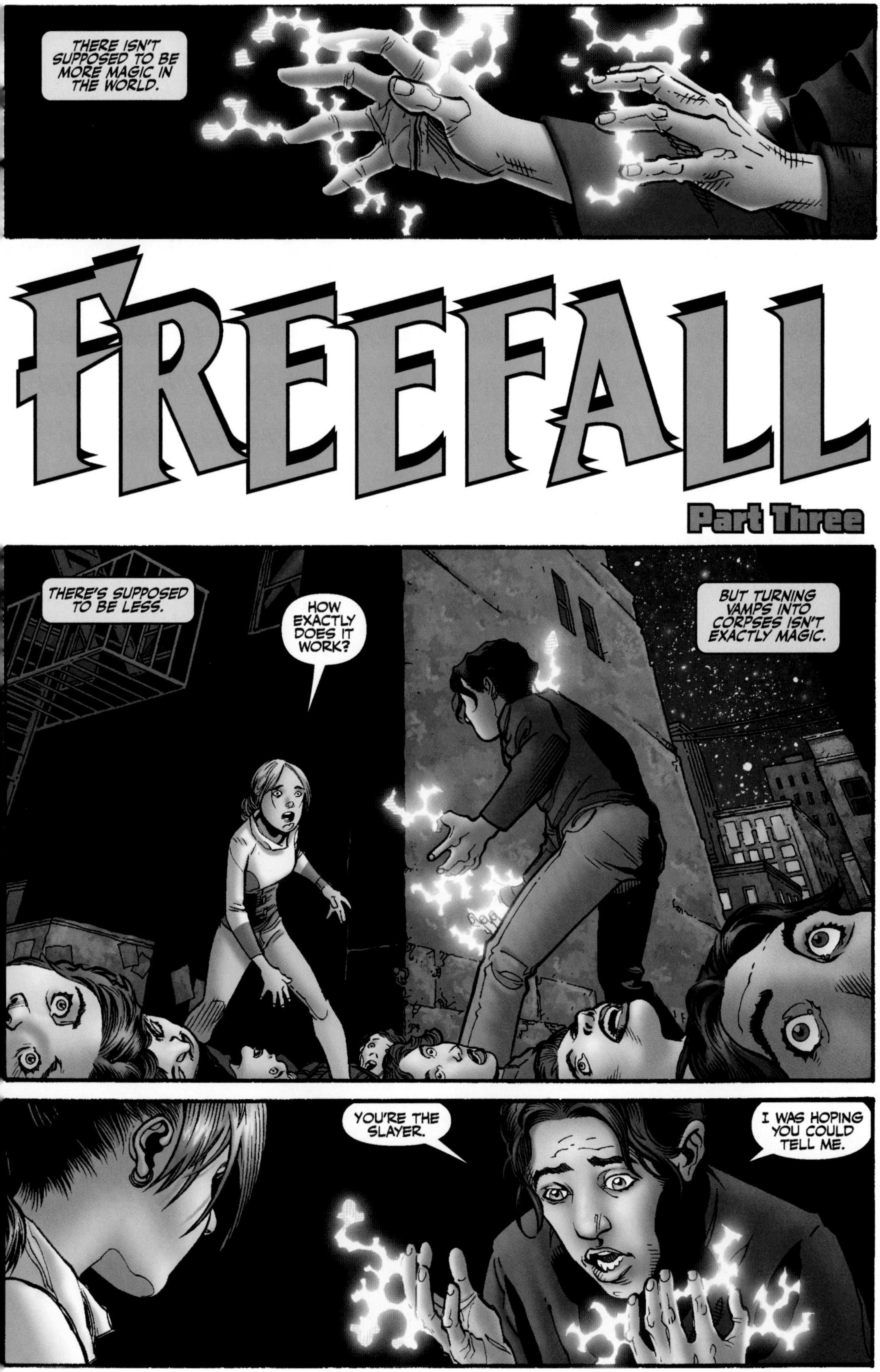
THERE ISN'T SUPPOSED TO BE MORE MAGIC IN THE WORLD.
FREEFALL
Part Three
THERE'S SUPPOSED TO BE LESS.
HOW EXACTLY DOES IT WORK?
BUT TURNING VAMPS INTO CORPSES ISN'T EXACTLY MAGIC.
YOU'RE THE SLAYER.
I WAS HOPING YOU COULD TELL ME.

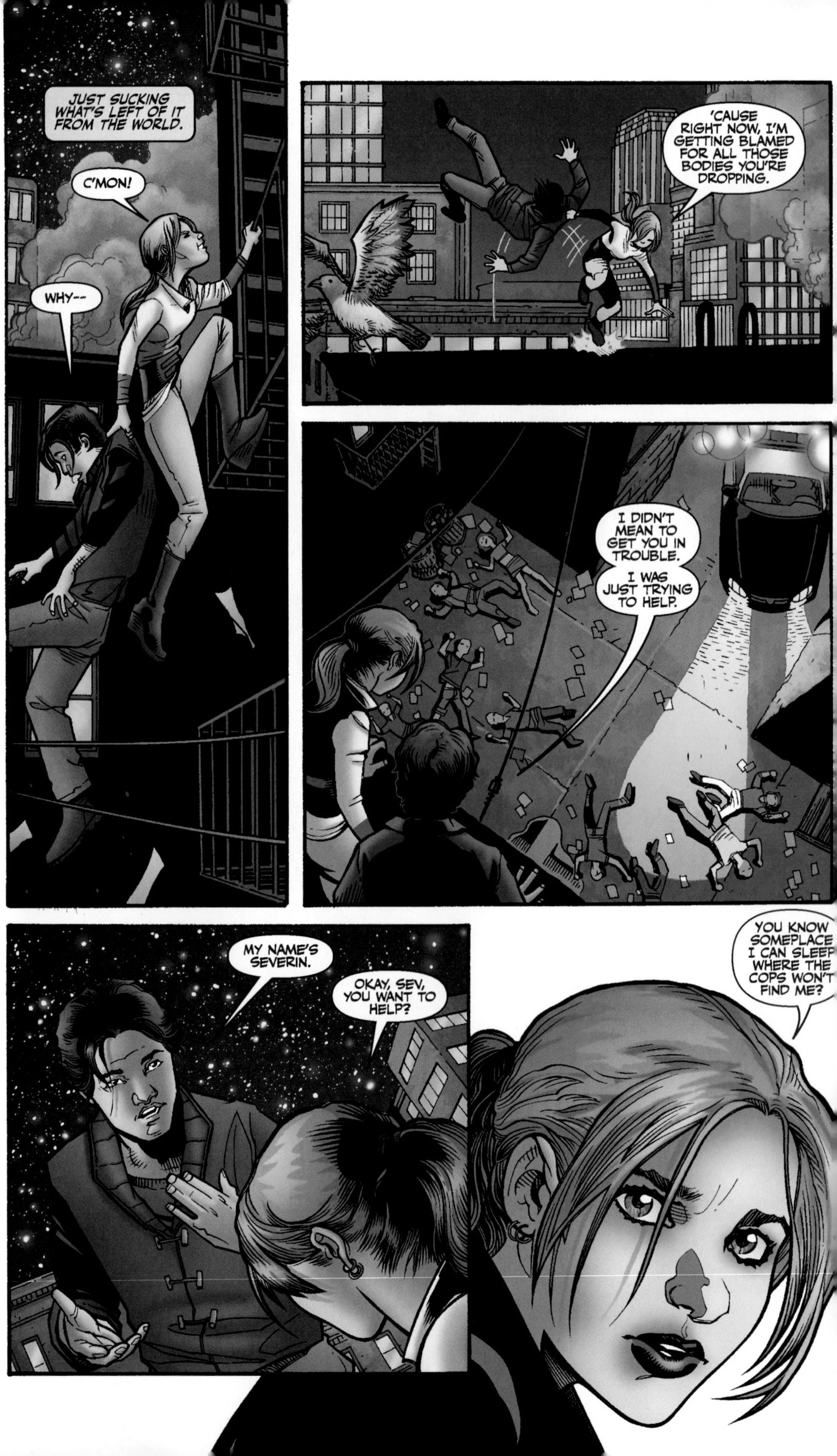

JUST SUCKING WHAT'S LEFT OF IT FROM THE WORLD.
C'MON!
WHY--
'CAUSE RIGHT NOW, I'M GETTING BLAMED FOR ALL THOSE BODIES YOU'RE DROPPING.
I DIDN'T MEAN TO GET YOU IN TROUBLE.
I WAS JUST TRYING TO HELP.
MY NAME'S SEVERIN.
OKAY, SEV, YOU WANT TO HELP?
YOU KNOW SOMEPLACE I CAN SLEEP WHERE THE COPS WON'T FIND ME?

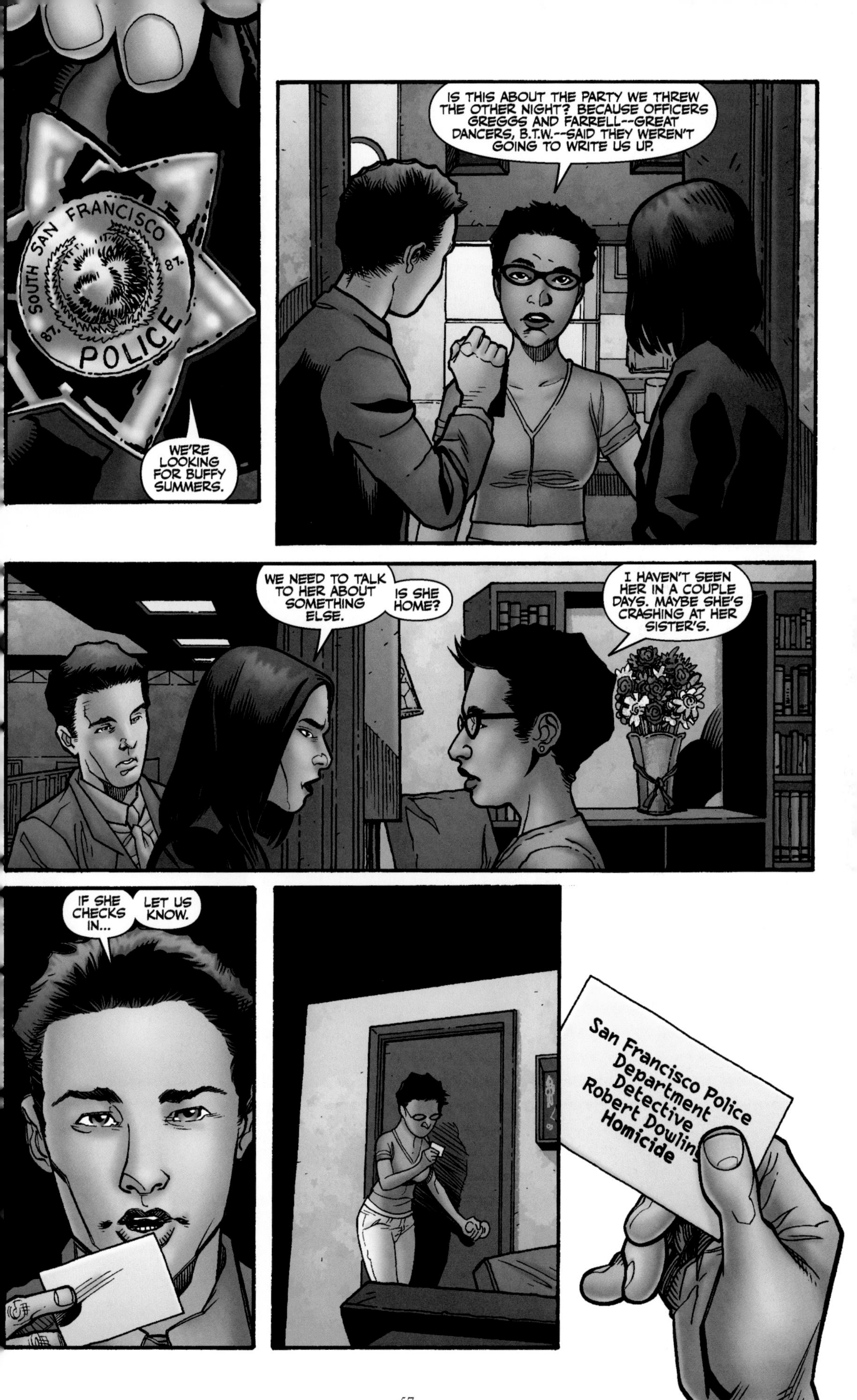
SOUTH SAN FRANCISCO 87. 87. POLICE
WE'RE LOOKING FOR BUFFY SUMMERS.
IS THIS ABOUT THE PARTY WE THREW THE OTHER NIGHT? BECAUSE OFFICERS GREGGS AND FARRELL--GREAT DANCERS, B.T.W.--SAID THEY WEREN'T GOING TO WRITE US UP.
WE NEED TO TALK TO HER ABOUT SOMETHING ELSE.
IS SHE HOME?
I HAVEN'T SEEN HER IN A COUPLE DAYS. MAYBE SHE'S CRASHING AT HER SISTER'S.
IF SHE CHECKS IN...
LET US KNOW.
San Francisco Police
Department
Detective
Robert Dowling
Homicide

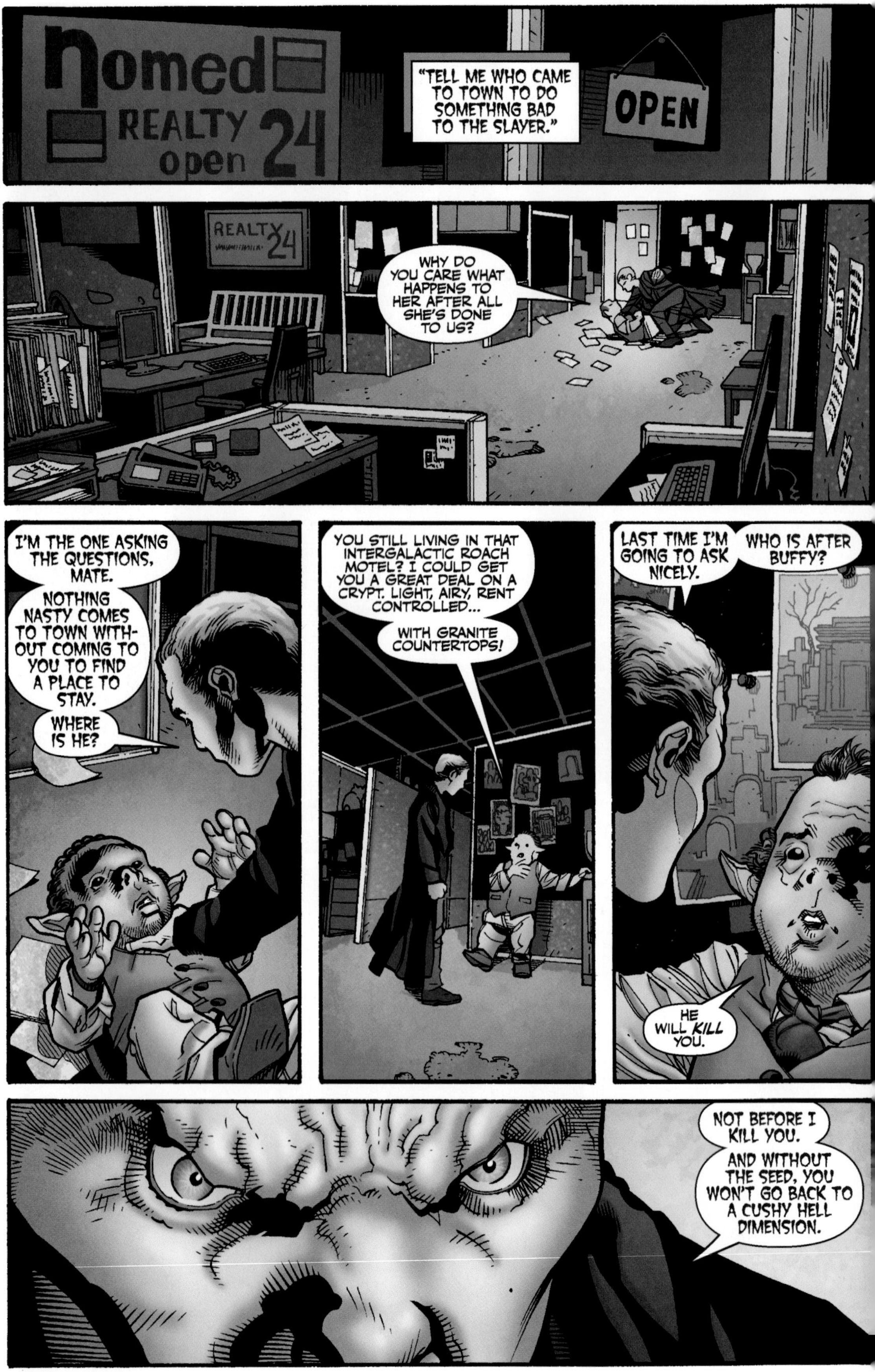
nomed
REALTY open 24
"TELL ME WHO CAME TO TOWN TO DO SOMETHING BAD TO THE SLAYER."
OPEN
REALTY 24
WHY DO YOU CARE WHAT HAPPENS TO HER AFTER ALL SHE'S DONE TO US?
I'M THE ONE ASKING THE QUESTIONS, MATE.
NOTHING NASTY COMES TO TOWN WITHOUT COMING TO YOU TO FIND A PLACE TO STAY.
WHERE IS HE?
YOU STILL LIVING IN THAT INTERGALACTIC ROACH MOTEL? I COULD GET YOU A GREAT DEAL ON A CRYPT. LIGHT, AIRY, RENT CONTROLLED...
WITH GRANITE COUNTERTOPS!
LAST TIME I'M GOING TO ASK NICELY.
WHO IS AFTER BUFFY?
HE WILL *KILL* YOU.
NOT BEFORE I KILL YOU.
AND WITHOUT THE SEED, YOU WON'T GO BACK TO A CUSHY HELL DIMENSION.

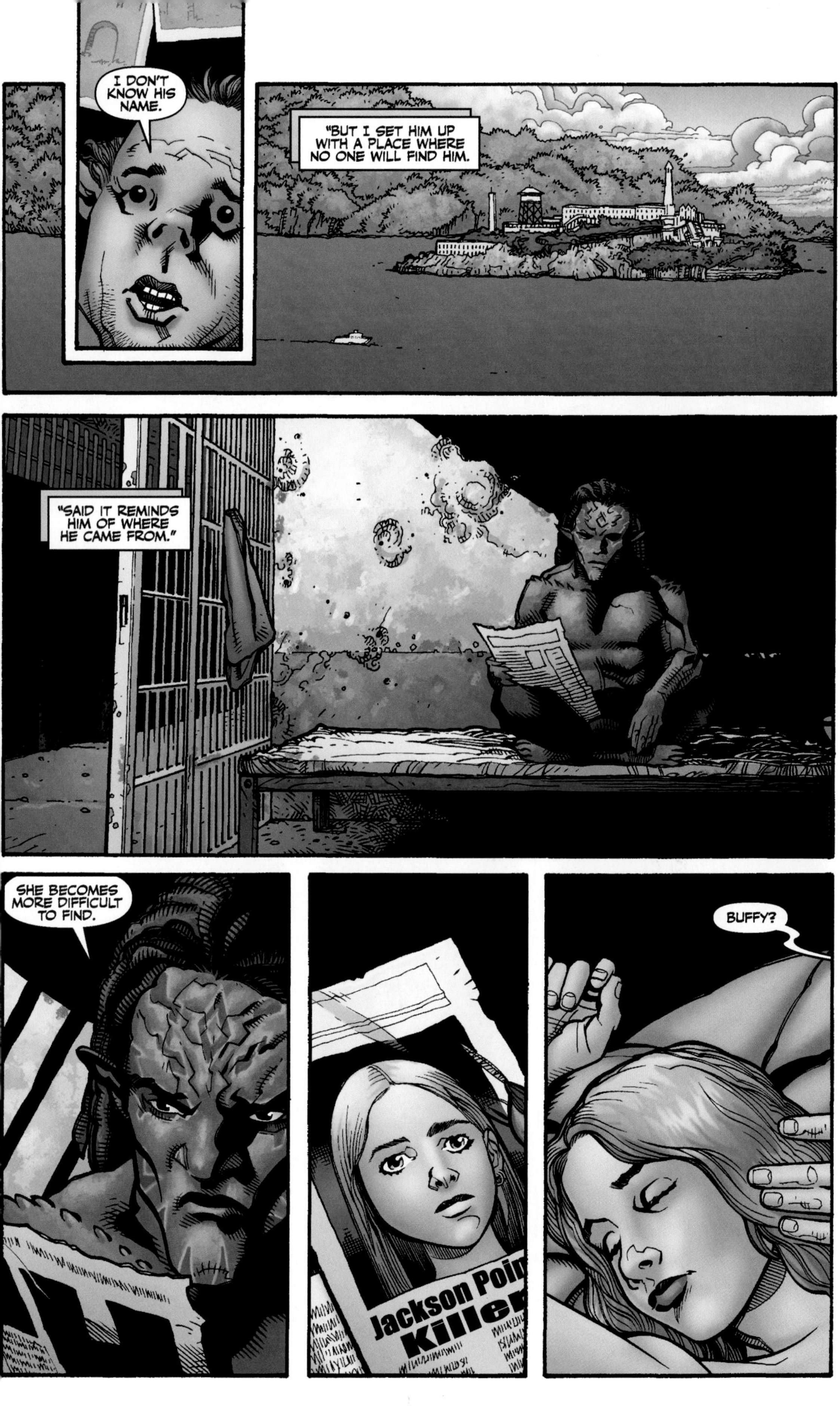
I DON'T KNOW HIS NAME.
"BUT I SET HIM UP WITH A PLACE WHERE NO ONE WILL FIND HIM.
"SAID IT REMINDS HIM OF WHERE HE CAME FROM."
SHE BECOMES MORE DIFFICULT TO FIND.
Jackson Poi
Killer
BUFFY?

OW. OW. OW.

JUST BRINGING YOU COFFEE.

OH, RIGHT. WANNABE SLAYER WITH THE MYSTERY TOUCH WHO LET ME CRASH HERE FOR THE NIGHT.

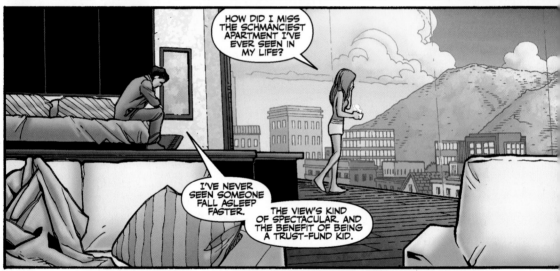

HOW DID I MISS THE SCHMANCIEST APARTMENT I'VE EVER SEEN IN MY LIFE?

I'VE NEVER SEEN SOMEONE FALL ASLEEP FASTER.

THE VIEW'S KIND OF SPECTACULAR. AND THE BENEFIT OF BEING A TRUST-FUND KID.

WHY WOULD YOU RISK THIS AWESOMENESS TO PLAY EXORCIST TO A BUNCH OF VAMPIRES?

THAT'S THE THING, BUFFY. I NEVER WANTED TO KILL VAMPIRES.

I WANTED TO BE ONE.

YOU TOO?

60

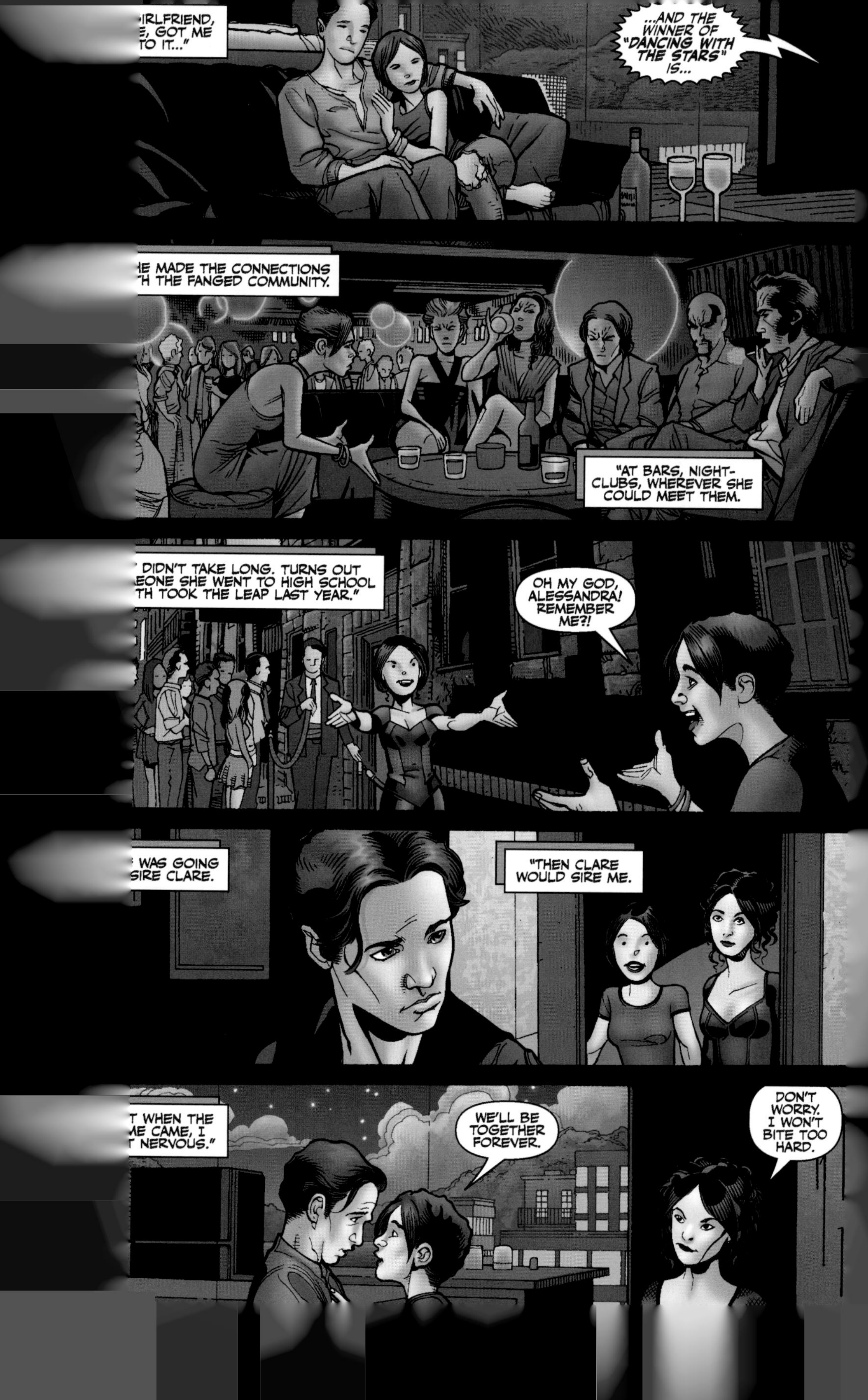

IRLFRIEND,
E, GOT ME
TO IT..."
...AND THE WINNER OF "DANCING WITH THE STARS" IS...
HE MADE THE CONNECTIONS
TH THE FANGED COMMUNITY.
"AT BARS, NIGHT-CLUBS, WHEREVER SHE COULD MEET THEM.
DIDN'T TAKE LONG. TURNS OUT
EONE SHE WENT TO HIGH SCHOOL
TH TOOK THE LEAP LAST YEAR."
OH MY GOD, ALESSANDRA! REMEMBER ME?!
WAS GOING
SIRE CLARE.
"THEN CLARE WOULD SIRE ME.
T WHEN THE
ME CAME, I
T NERVOUS."
WE'LL BE TOGETHER FOREVER.
DON'T WORRY. I WON'T BITE TOO HARD.

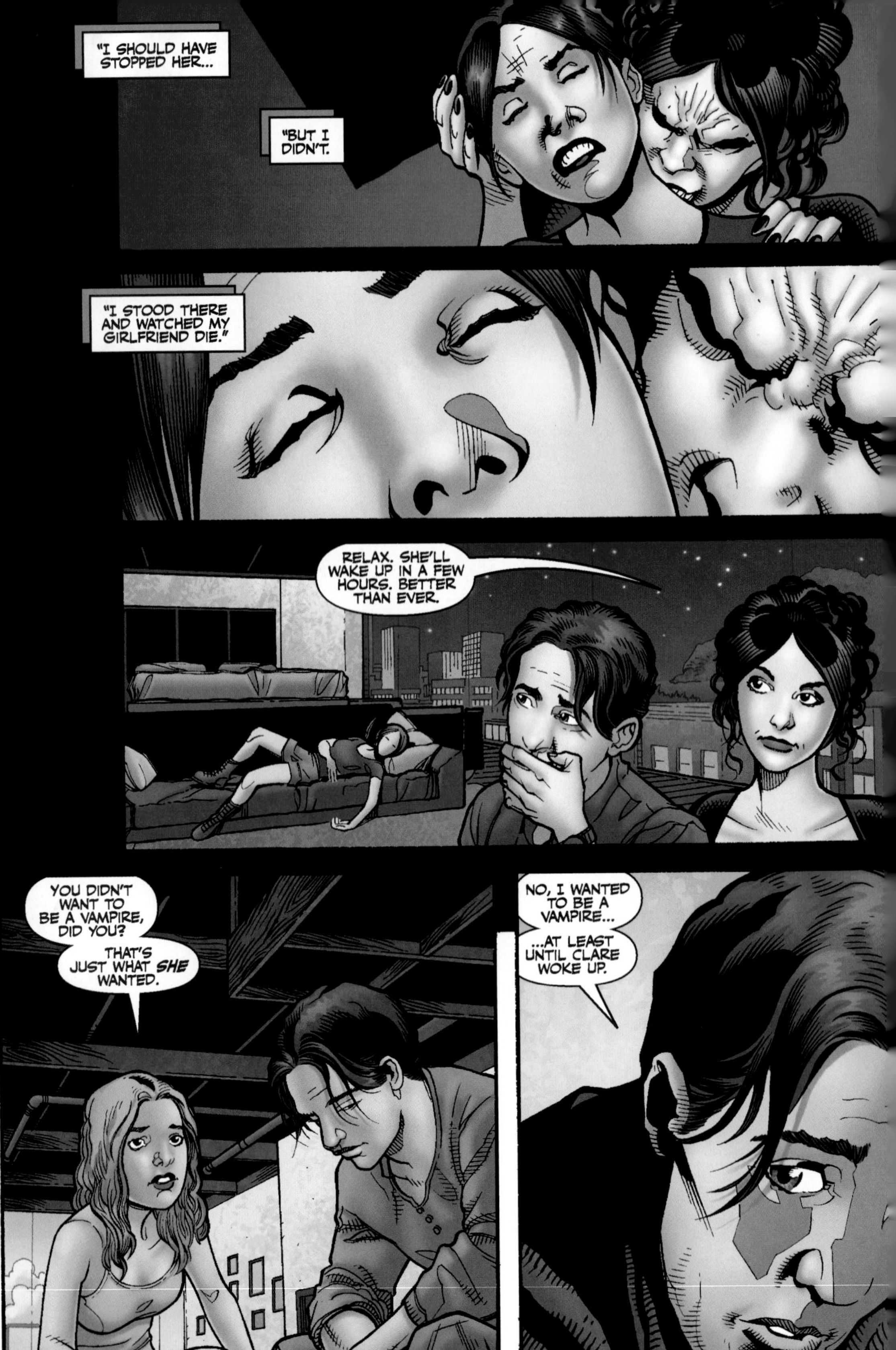
"I SHOULD HAVE STOPPED HER...
"BUT I DIDN'T.
"I STOOD THERE AND WATCHED MY GIRLFRIEND DIE."
RELAX. SHE'LL WAKE UP IN A FEW HOURS. BETTER THAN EVER.
YOU DIDN'T WANT TO BE A VAMPIRE, DID YOU?
THAT'S JUST WHAT SHE WANTED.
NO, I WANTED TO BE A VAMPIRE...
...AT LEAST UNTIL CLARE WOKE UP.

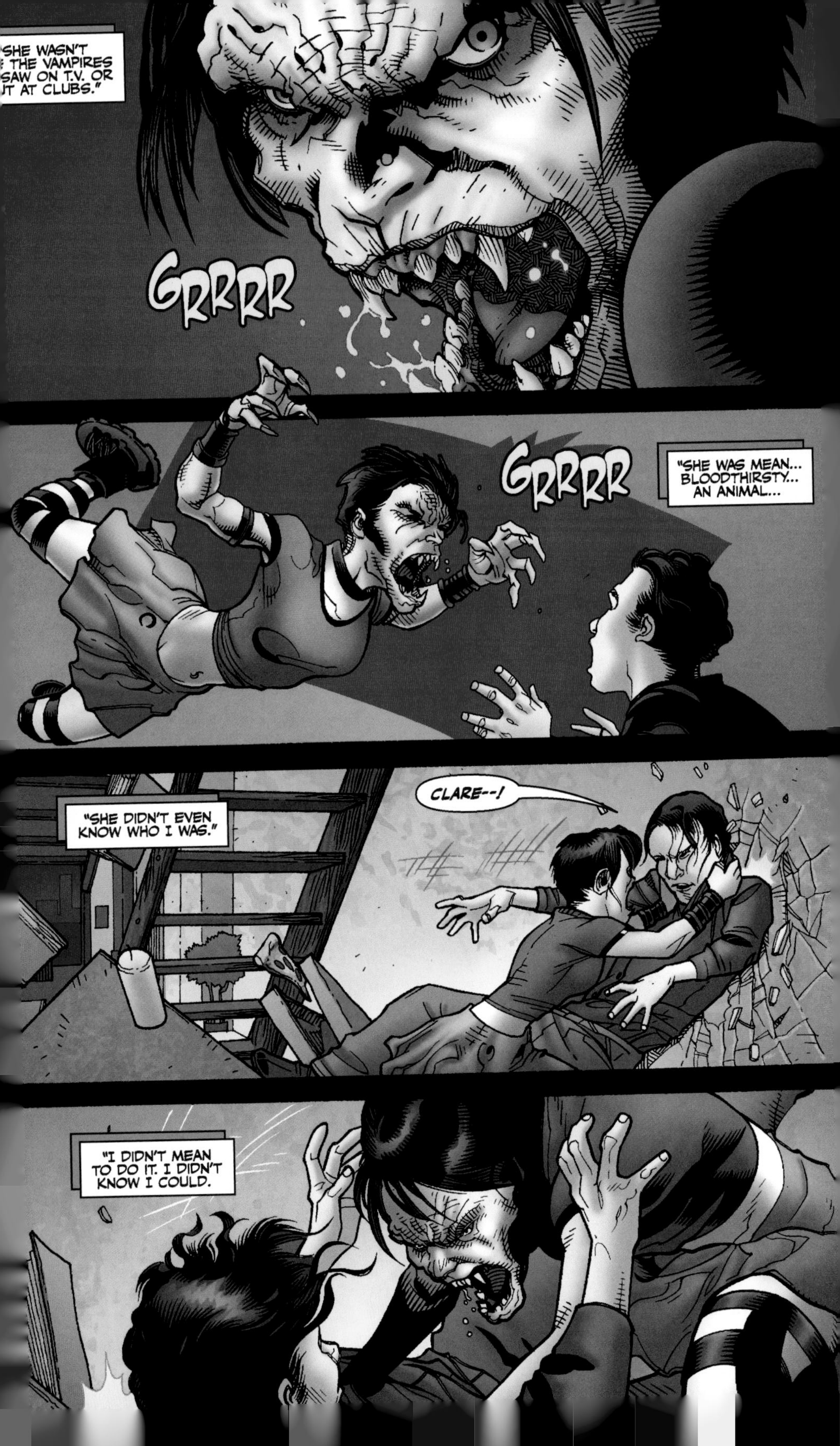
"SHE WASN'T
E THE VAMPIRES
SAW ON T.V. OR
T AT CLUBS."
GRRRR
GRRRR
"SHE WAS MEAN... BLOODTHIRSTY... AN ANIMAL...
"SHE DIDN'T EVEN KNOW WHO I WAS."
CLARE--!
"I DIDN'T MEAN TO DO IT. I DIDN'T KNOW I COULD.

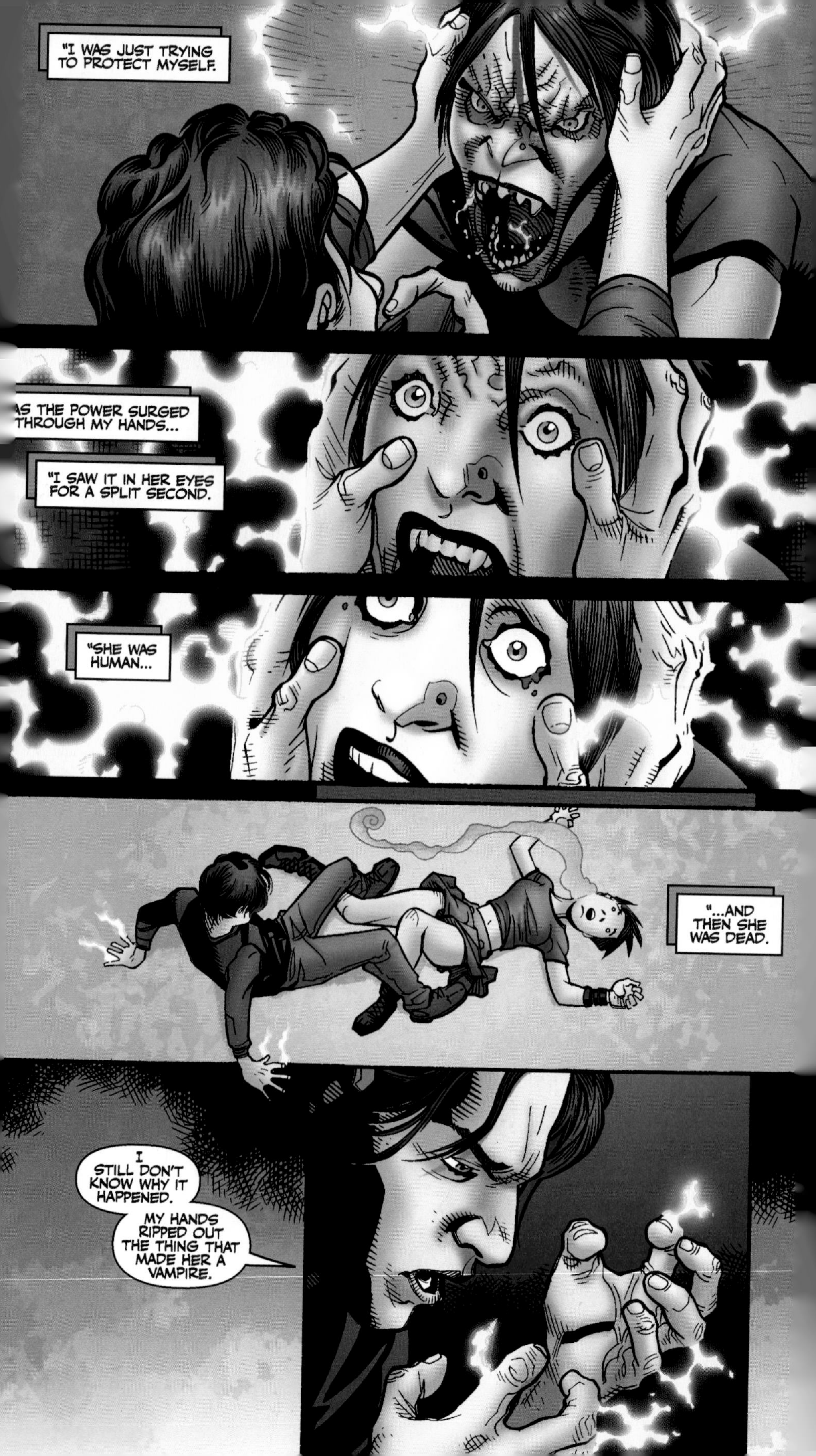
"I WAS JUST TRYING TO PROTECT MYSELF.
AS THE POWER SURGED THROUGH MY HANDS...
"I SAW IT IN HER EYES FOR A SPLIT SECOND.
"SHE WAS HUMAN...
"...AND THEN SHE WAS DEAD.
I STILL DON'T KNOW WHY IT HAPPENED.
MY HANDS RIPPED OUT THE THING THAT MADE HER A VAMPIRE.

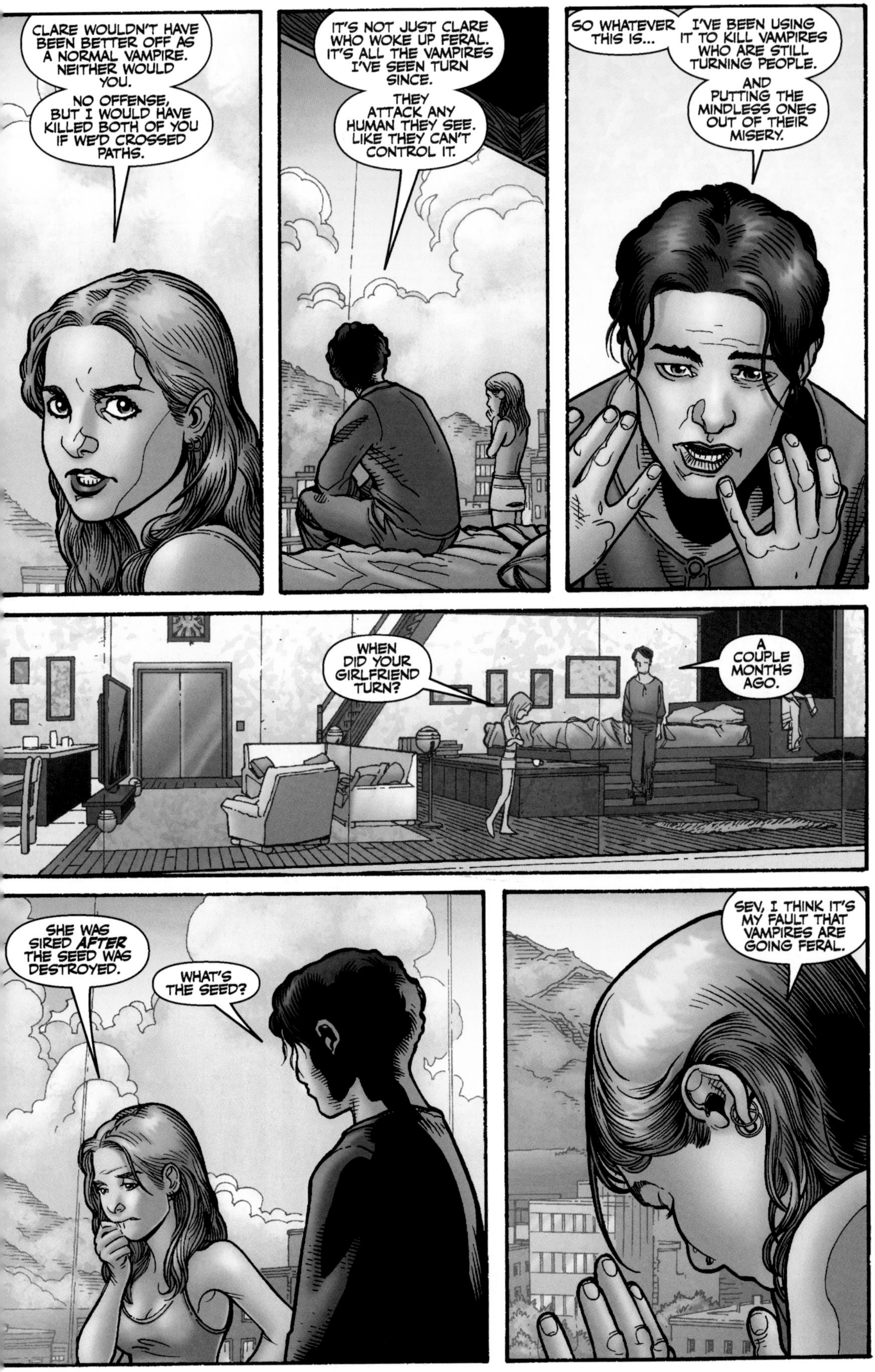
CLARE WOULDN'T HAVE BEEN BETTER OFF AS A NORMAL VAMPIRE. NEITHER WOULD YOU.
NO OFFENSE, BUT I WOULD HAVE KILLED BOTH OF YOU IF WE'D CROSSED PATHS.
IT'S NOT JUST CLARE WHO WOKE UP FERAL. IT'S ALL THE VAMPIRES I'VE SEEN TURN SINCE.
THEY ATTACK ANY HUMAN THEY SEE. LIKE THEY CAN'T CONTROL IT.
SO WHATEVER THIS IS...
I'VE BEEN USING IT TO KILL VAMPIRES WHO ARE STILL TURNING PEOPLE.
AND PUTTING THE MINDLESS ONES OUT OF THEIR MISERY.
WHEN DID YOUR GIRLFRIEND TURN?
A COUPLE MONTHS AGO.
SHE WAS SIRED *AFTER* THE SEED WAS DESTROYED.
WHAT'S THE SEED?
SEV, I THINK IT'S MY FAULT THAT VAMPIRES ARE GOING FERAL.

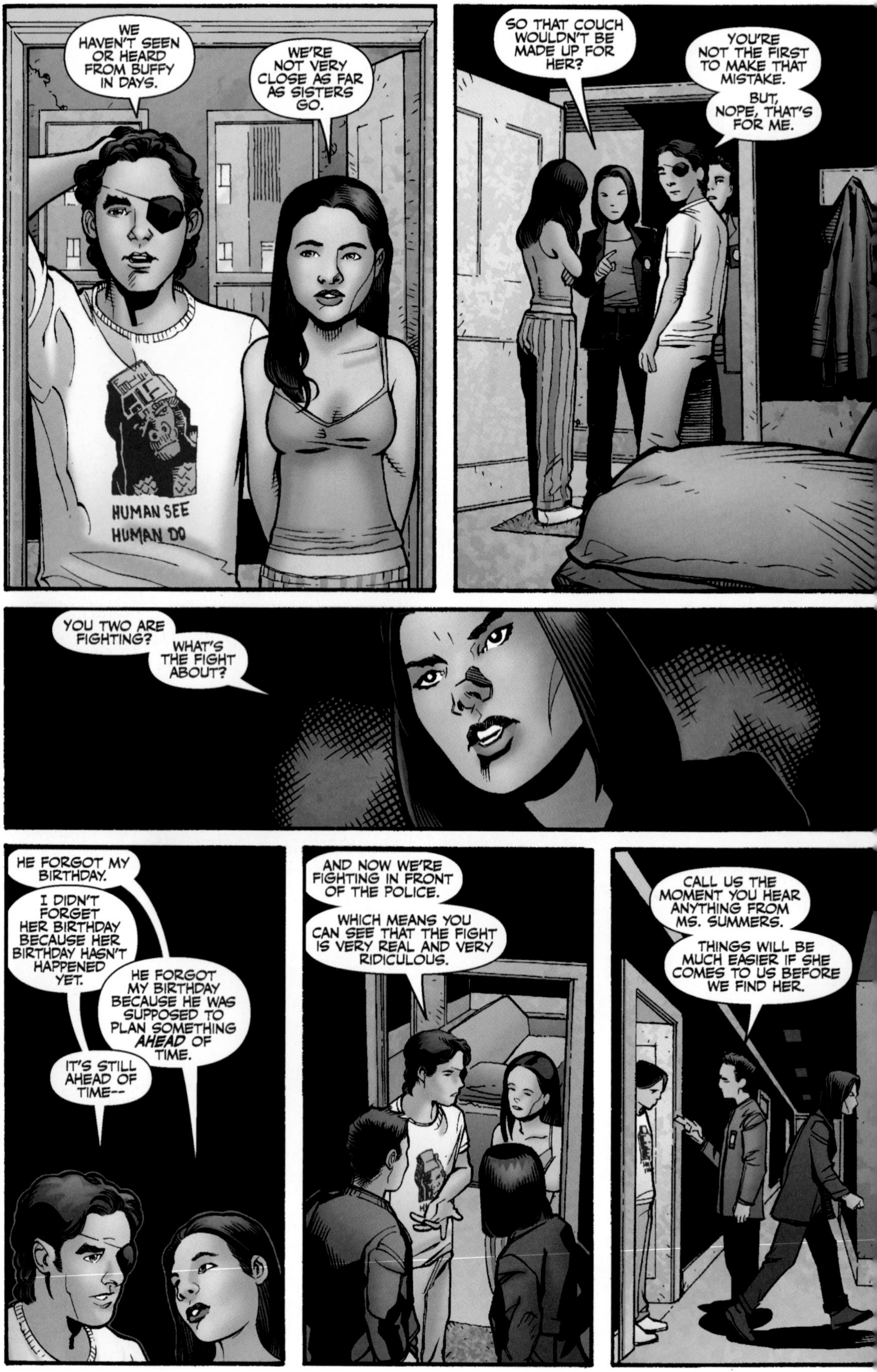
WE HAVEN'T SEEN OR HEARD FROM BUFFY IN DAYS.
WE'RE NOT VERY CLOSE AS FAR AS SISTERS GO.
HUMAN SEE HUMAN DO
SO THAT COUCH WOULDN'T BE MADE UP FOR HER?
YOU'RE NOT THE FIRST TO MAKE THAT MISTAKE.
BUT, NOPE, THAT'S FOR ME.
YOU TWO ARE FIGHTING?
WHAT'S THE FIGHT ABOUT?
HE FORGOT MY BIRTHDAY.
I DIDN'T FORGET HER BIRTHDAY BECAUSE HER BIRTHDAY HASN'T HAPPENED YET.
HE FORGOT MY BIRTHDAY BECAUSE HE WAS SUPPOSED TO PLAN SOMETHING *AHEAD* OF TIME.
IT'S STILL AHEAD OF TIME--
AND NOW WE'RE FIGHTING IN FRONT OF THE POLICE.
WHICH MEANS YOU CAN SEE THAT THE FIGHT IS VERY REAL AND VERY RIDICULOUS.
CALL US THE MOMENT YOU HEAR ANYTHING FROM MS. SUMMERS.
THINGS WILL BE MUCH EASIER IF SHE COMES TO US BEFORE WE FIND HER.

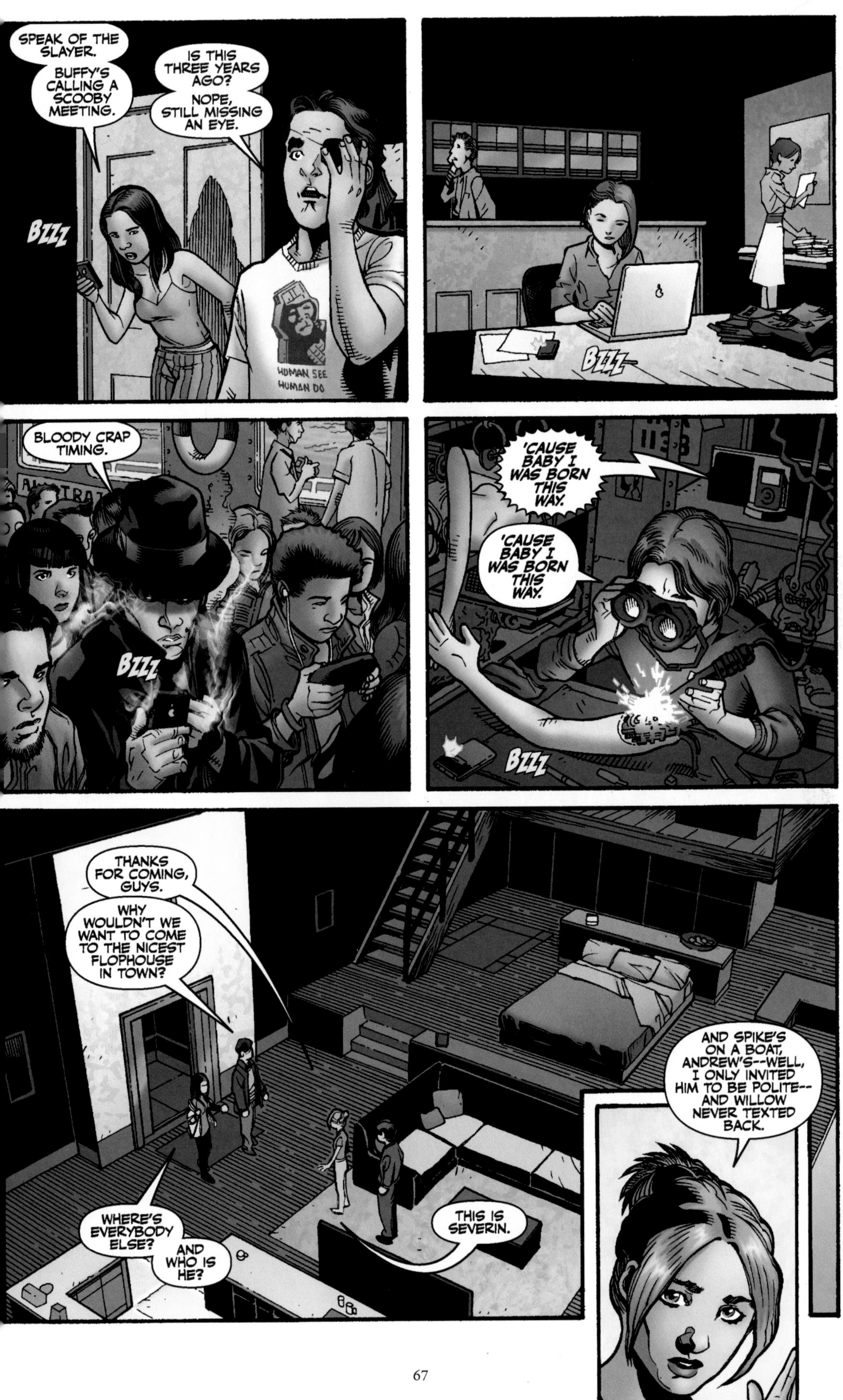
SPEAK OF THE SLAYER.
BUFFY'S CALLING A SCOOBY MEETING.
IS THIS THREE YEARS AGO?
NOPE, STILL MISSING AN EYE.
BZZZ
HUMAN SEE HUMAN DO
BZZZ
BLOODY CRAP TIMING.
BZZZ
'CAUSE BABY I WAS BORN THIS WAY.
'CAUSE BABY I WAS BORN THIS WAY.
BZZZ
THANKS FOR COMING, GUYS.
WHY WOULDN'T WE WANT TO COME TO THE NICEST FLOPHOUSE IN TOWN?
WHERE'S EVERYBODY ELSE?
AND WHO IS HE?
THIS IS SEVERIN.
AND SPIKE'S ON A BOAT, ANDREW'S--WELL, I ONLY INVITED HIM TO BE POLITE-- AND WILLOW NEVER TEXTED BACK.

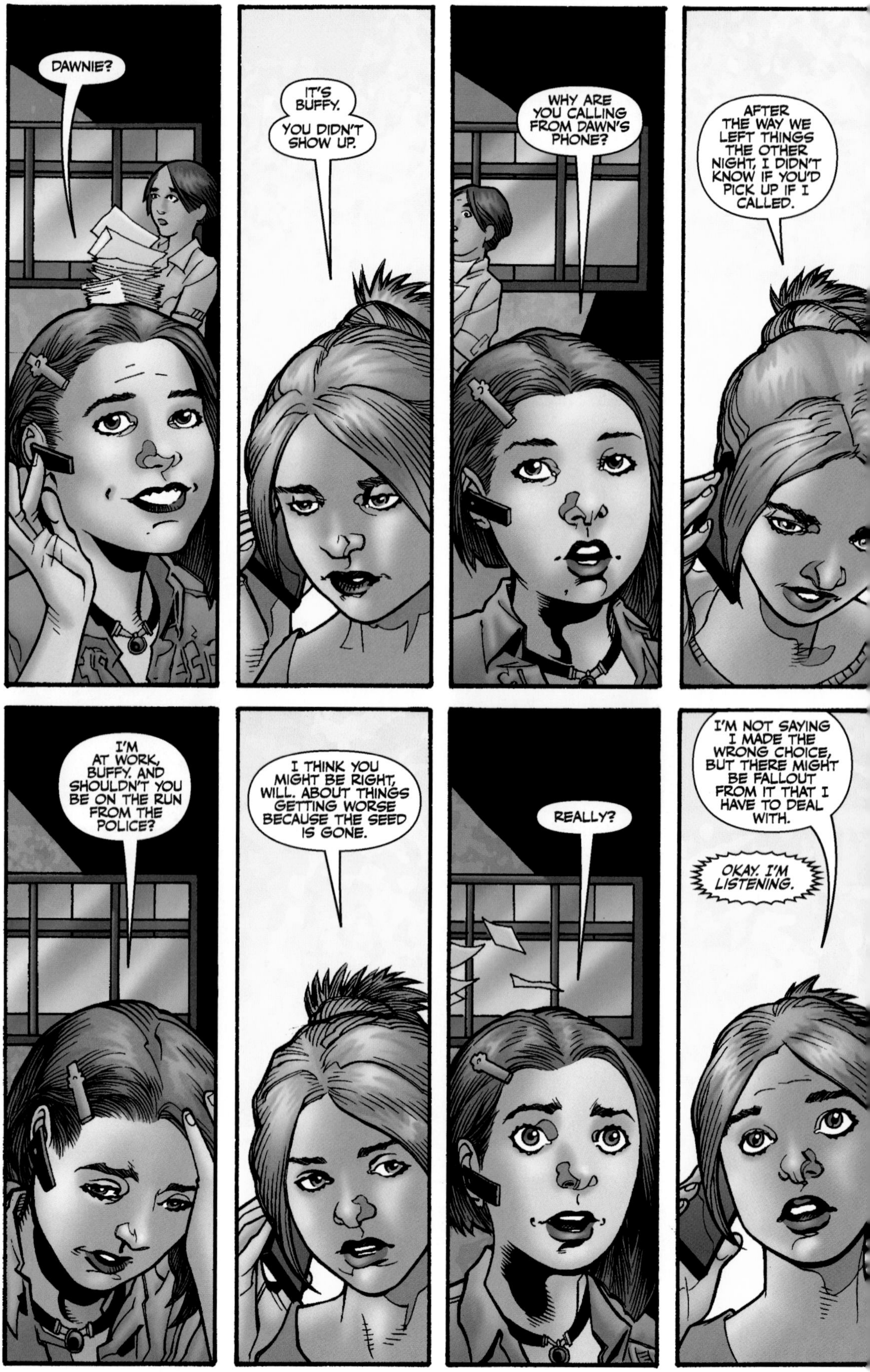
DAWNIE?
IT'S BUFFY.
YOU DIDN'T SHOW UP.
WHY ARE YOU CALLING FROM DAWN'S PHONE?
AFTER THE WAY WE LEFT THINGS THE OTHER NIGHT, I DIDN'T KNOW IF YOU'D PICK UP IF I CALLED.
I'M AT WORK, BUFFY. AND SHOULDN'T YOU BE ON THE RUN FROM THE POLICE?
I THINK YOU MIGHT BE RIGHT, WILL. ABOUT THINGS GETTING WORSE BECAUSE THE SEED IS GONE.
REALLY?
I'M NOT SAYING I MADE THE WRONG CHOICE, BUT THERE MIGHT BE FALLOUT FROM IT THAT I HAVE TO DEAL WITH.
OKAY. I'M LISTENING.

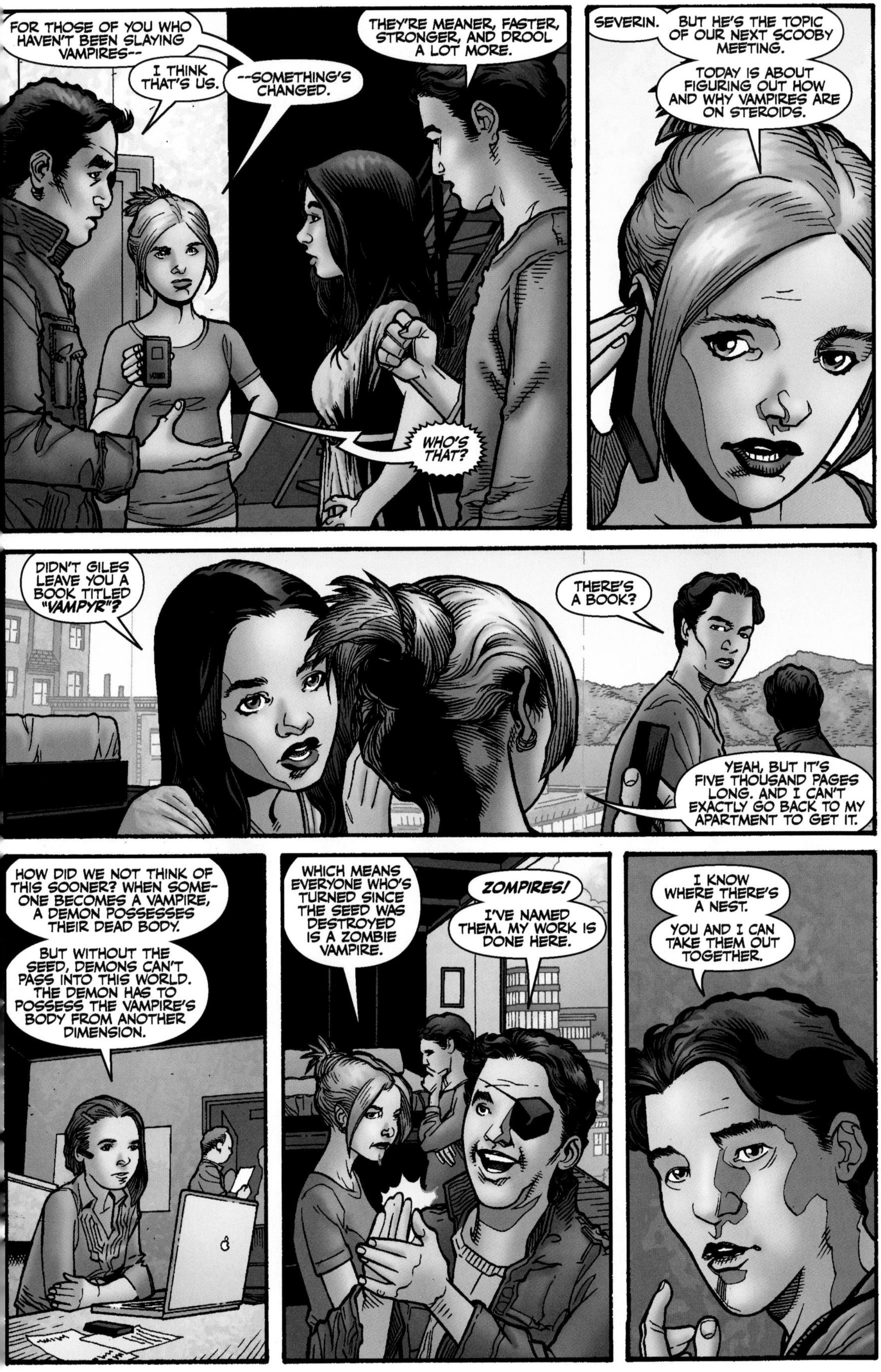
FOR THOSE OF YOU WHO HAVEN'T BEEN SLAYING VAMPIRES--
I THINK THAT'S US.
--SOMETHING'S CHANGED.
THEY'RE MEANER, FASTER, STRONGER, AND DROOL A LOT MORE.
WHO'S THAT?
SEVERIN.
BUT HE'S THE TOPIC OF OUR NEXT SCOOBY MEETING.
TODAY IS ABOUT FIGURING OUT HOW AND WHY VAMPIRES ARE ON STEROIDS.
DIDN'T GILES LEAVE YOU A BOOK TITLED "VAMPYR"?
THERE'S A BOOK?
YEAH, BUT IT'S FIVE THOUSAND PAGES LONG. AND I CAN'T EXACTLY GO BACK TO MY APARTMENT TO GET IT.
HOW DID WE NOT THINK OF THIS SOONER? WHEN SOME-ONE BECOMES A VAMPIRE, A DEMON POSSESSES THEIR DEAD BODY.
BUT WITHOUT THE SEED, DEMONS CAN'T PASS INTO THIS WORLD. THE DEMON HAS TO POSSESS THE VAMPIRE'S BODY FROM ANOTHER DIMENSION.
WHICH MEANS EVERYONE WHO'S TURNED SINCE THE SEED WAS DESTROYED IS A ZOMBIE VAMPIRE.
ZOMPIRES!
I'VE NAMED THEM. MY WORK IS DONE HERE.
I KNOW WHERE THERE'S A NEST.
YOU AND I CAN TAKE THEM OUT TOGETHER.

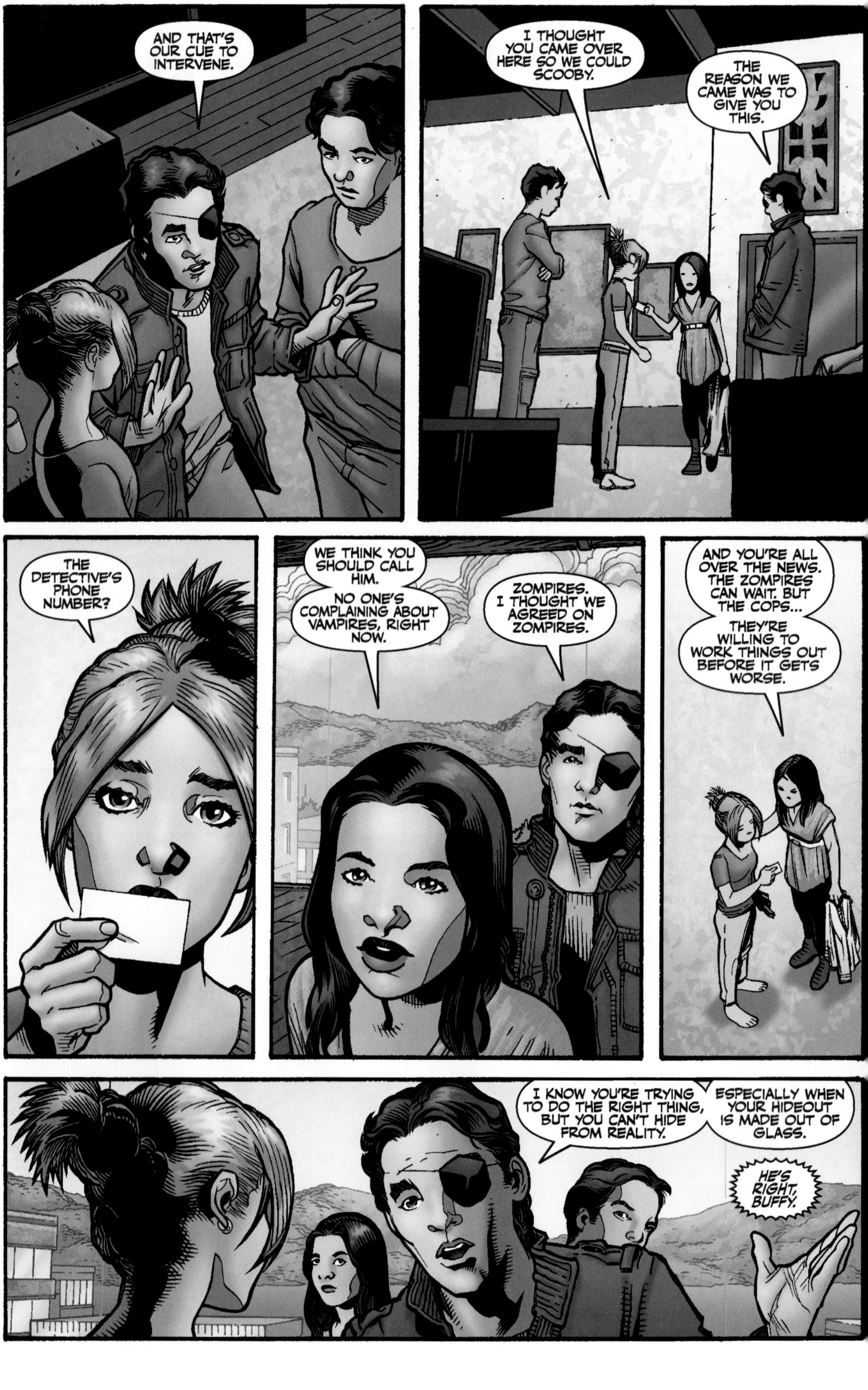
AND THAT'S OUR CUE TO INTERVENE.
I THOUGHT YOU CAME OVER HERE SO WE COULD SCOOBY.
THE REASON WE CAME WAS TO GIVE YOU THIS.
THE DETECTIVE'S PHONE NUMBER?
WE THINK YOU SHOULD CALL HIM.
NO ONE'S COMPLAINING ABOUT VAMPIRES, RIGHT NOW.
ZOMPIRES. I THOUGHT WE AGREED ON ZOMPIRES.
AND YOU'RE ALL OVER THE NEWS. THE ZOMPIRES CAN WAIT. BUT THE COPS...
THEY'RE WILLING TO WORK THINGS OUT BEFORE IT GETS WORSE.
I KNOW YOU'RE TRYING TO DO THE RIGHT THING, BUT YOU CAN'T HIDE FROM REALITY.
ESPECIALLY WHEN YOUR HIDEOUT IS MADE OUT OF GLASS.
HE'S RIGHT, BUFFY.

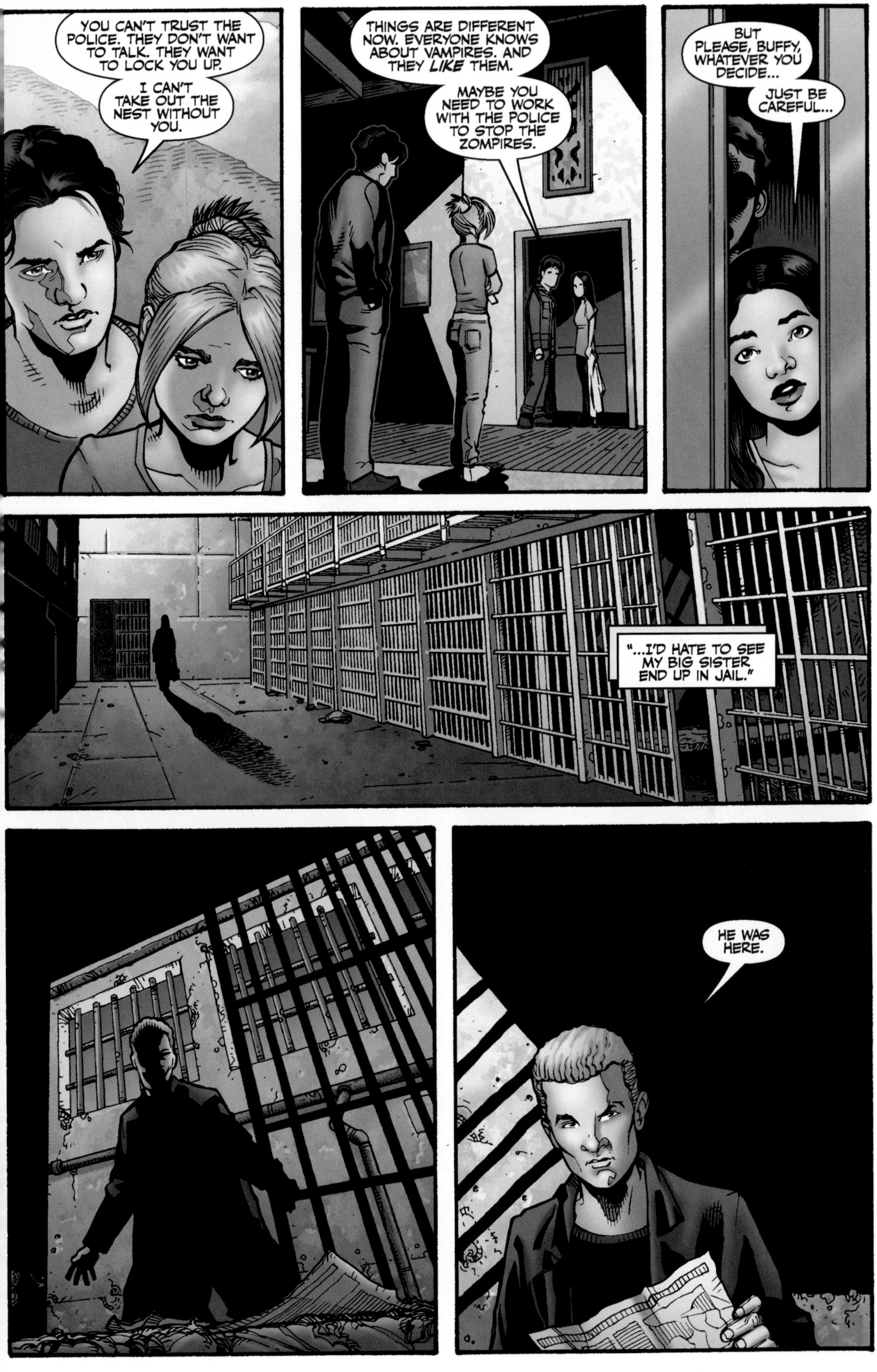
YOU CAN'T TRUST THE POLICE. THEY DON'T WANT TO TALK. THEY WANT TO LOCK YOU UP.
I CAN'T TAKE OUT THE NEST WITHOUT YOU.
THINGS ARE DIFFERENT NOW. EVERYONE KNOWS ABOUT VAMPIRES. AND THEY LIKE THEM.
MAYBE YOU NEED TO WORK WITH THE POLICE TO STOP THE ZOMPIRES.
BUT PLEASE, BUFFY, WHATEVER YOU DECIDE...
JUST BE CAREFUL...
"...I'D HATE TO SEE MY BIG SISTER END UP IN JAIL."
HE WAS HERE.

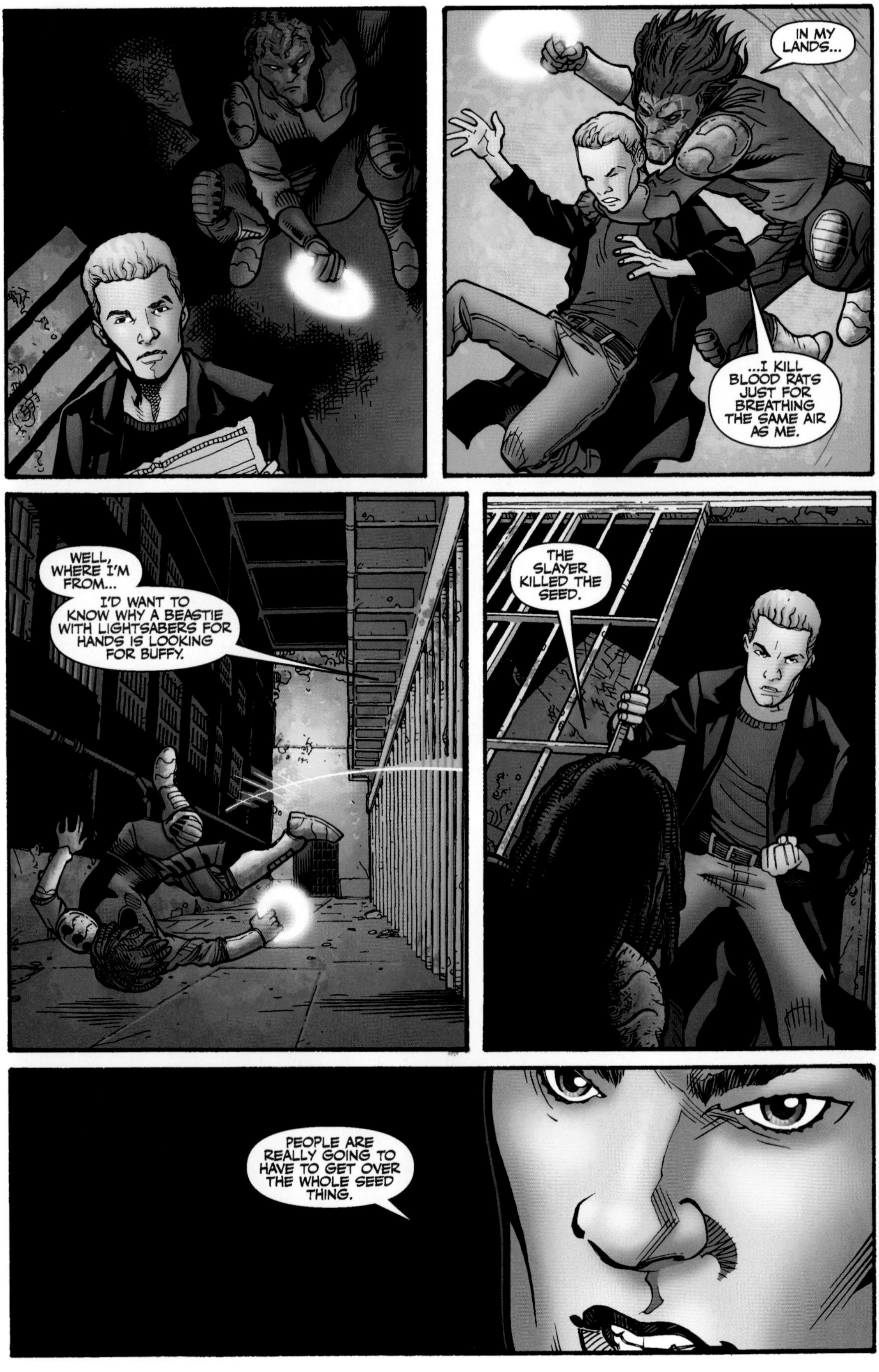
IN MY LANDS...
...I KILL BLOOD RATS JUST FOR BREATHING THE SAME AIR AS ME.
WELL, WHERE I'M FROM...
I'D WANT TO KNOW WHY A BEASTIE WITH LIGHTSABERS FOR HANDS IS LOOKING FOR BUFFY.
THE SLAYER KILLED THE SEED.
PEOPLE ARE REALLY GOING TO HAVE TO GET OVER THE WHOLE SEED THING.

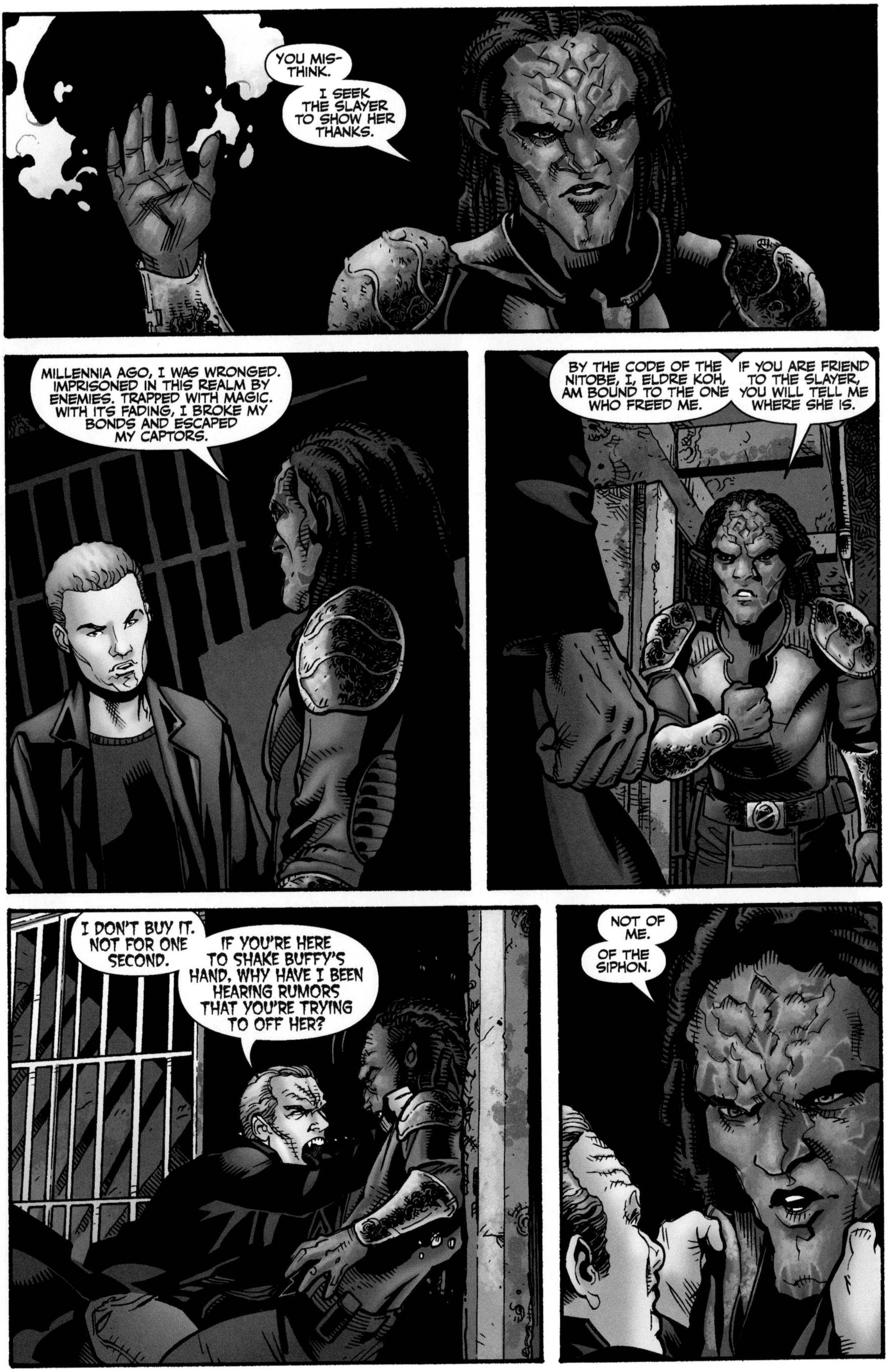
YOU MIS-THINK.
I SEEK THE SLAYER TO SHOW HER THANKS.
MILLENNIA AGO, I WAS WRONGED. IMPRISONED IN THIS REALM BY ENEMIES. TRAPPED WITH MAGIC. WITH ITS FADING, I BROKE MY BONDS AND ESCAPED MY CAPTORS.
BY THE CODE OF THE NITOBE, I, ELDRE KOH, AM BOUND TO THE ONE WHO FREED ME.
IF YOU ARE FRIEND TO THE SLAYER, YOU WILL TELL ME WHERE SHE IS.
I DON'T BUY IT. NOT FOR ONE SECOND.
IF YOU'RE HERE TO SHAKE BUFFY'S HAND, WHY HAVE I BEEN HEARING RUMORS THAT YOU'RE TRYING TO OFF HER?
NOT OF ME.
OF THE SIPHON.

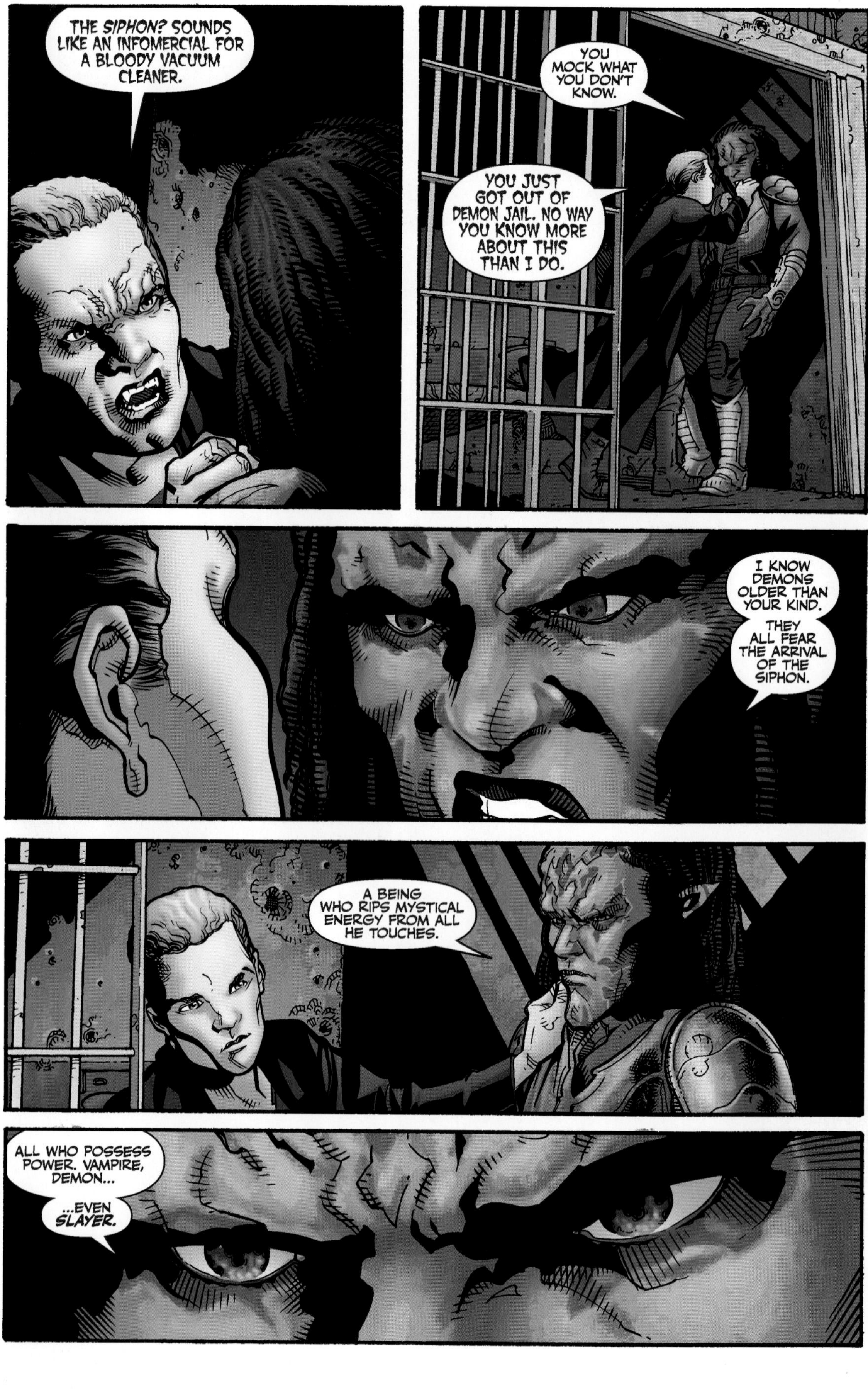
THE SIPHON? SOUNDS LIKE AN INFOMERCIAL FOR A BLOODY VACUUM CLEANER.
YOU MOCK WHAT YOU DON'T KNOW.
YOU JUST GOT OUT OF DEMON JAIL. NO WAY YOU KNOW MORE ABOUT THIS THAN I DO.
I KNOW DEMONS OLDER THAN YOUR KIND.
THEY ALL FEAR THE ARRIVAL OF THE SIPHON.
A BEING WHO RIPS MYSTICAL ENERGY FROM ALL HE TOUCHES.
ALL WHO POSSESS POWER. VAMPIRE, DEMON...
...EVEN SLAYER.

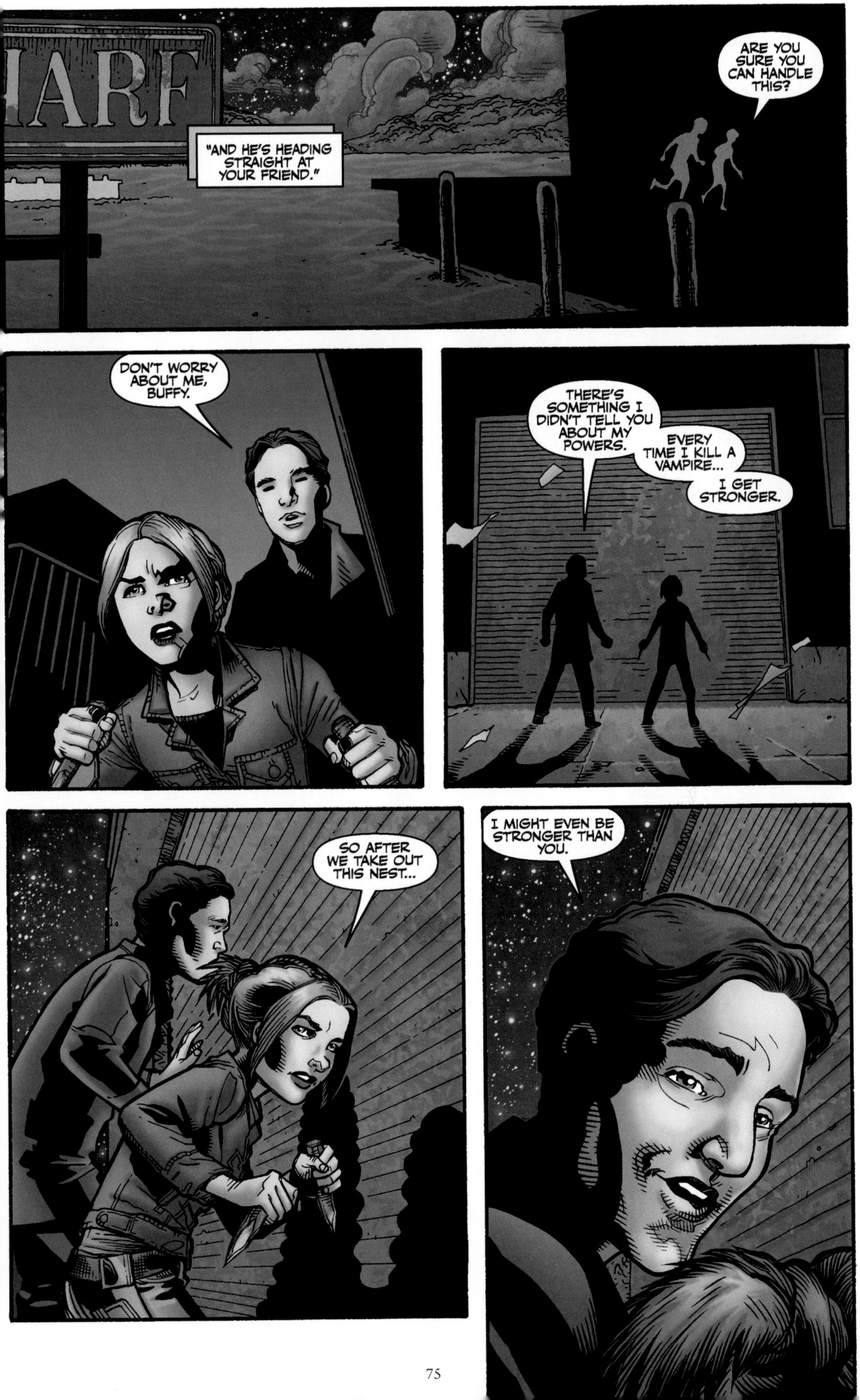
"AND HE'S HEADING STRAIGHT AT YOUR FRIEND."
ARE YOU SURE YOU CAN HANDLE THIS?
DON'T WORRY ABOUT ME, BUFFY.
THERE'S SOMETHING I DIDN'T TELL YOU ABOUT MY POWERS.
EVERY TIME I KILL A VAMPIRE...
I GET STRONGER.
SO AFTER WE TAKE OUT THIS NEST...
I MIGHT EVEN BE STRONGER THAN YOU.

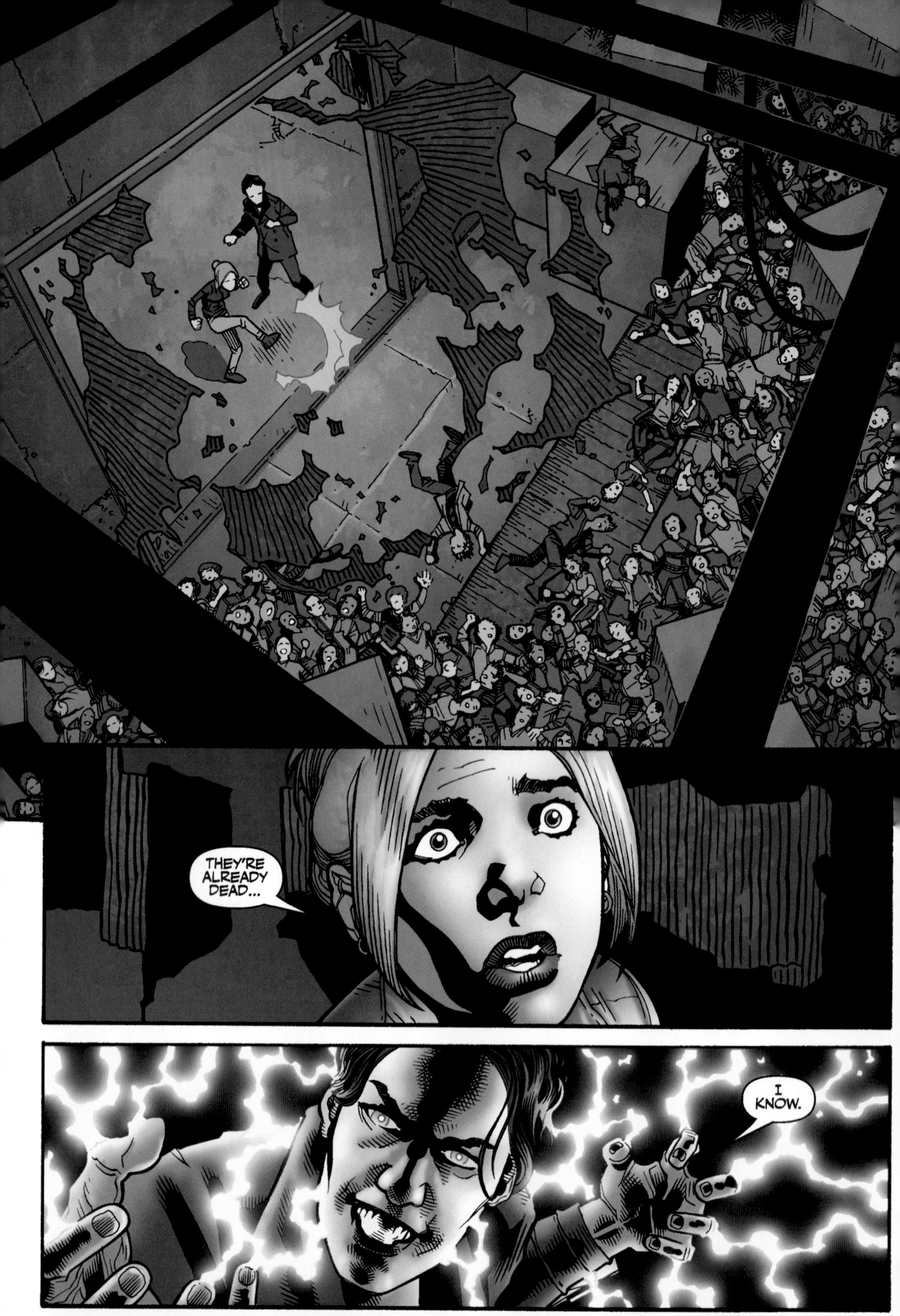
THEY'RE ALREADY DEAD...
I KNOW.

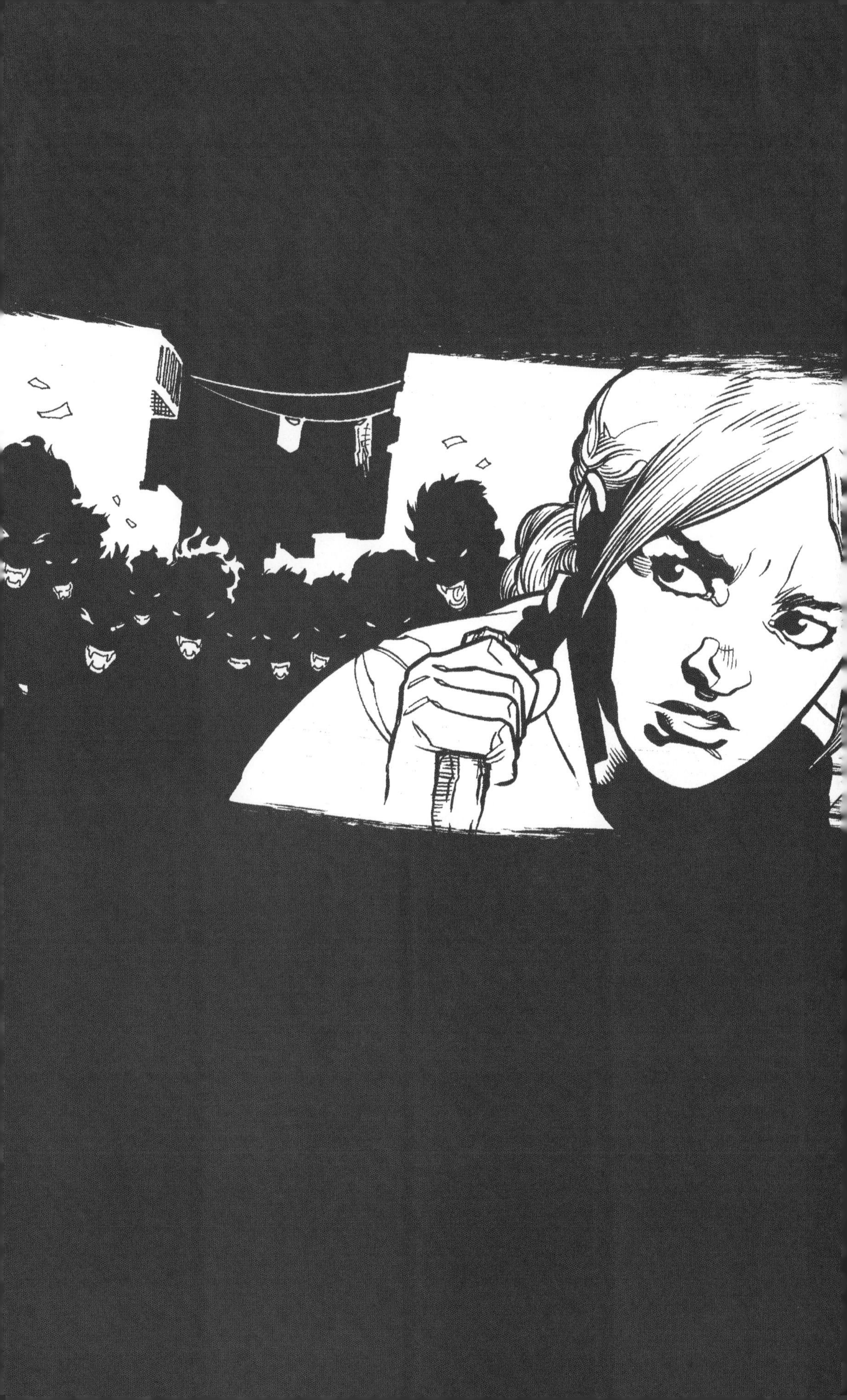

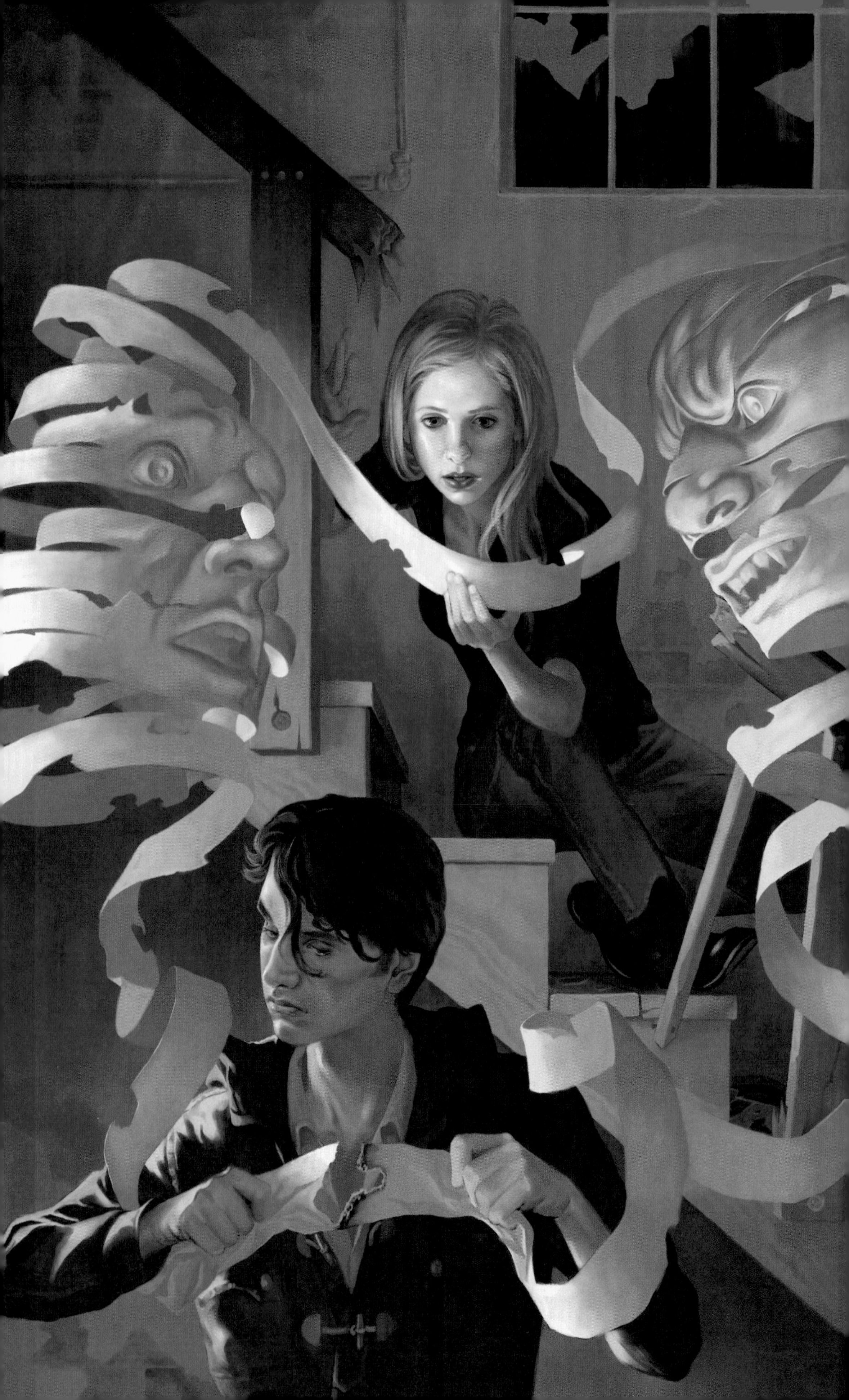

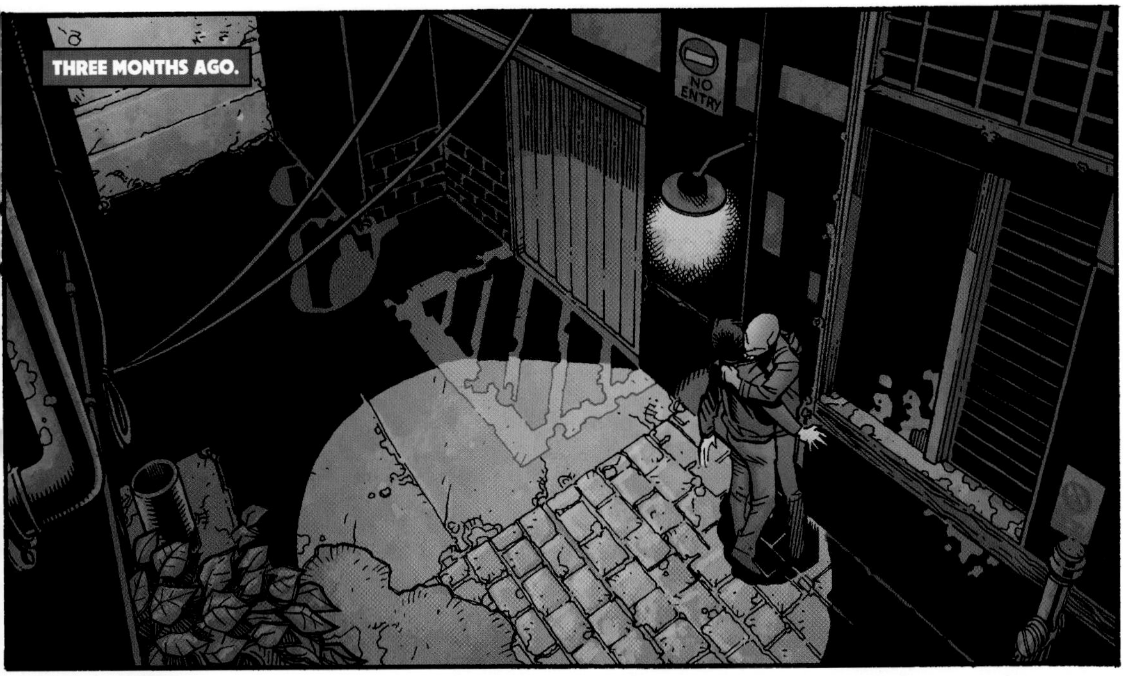
THREE MONTHS AGO.
NO ENTRY

FREEFALL

Part Four

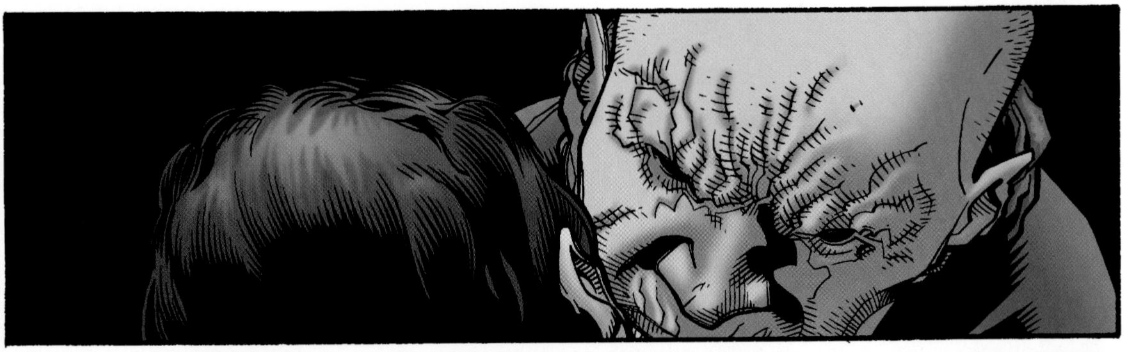

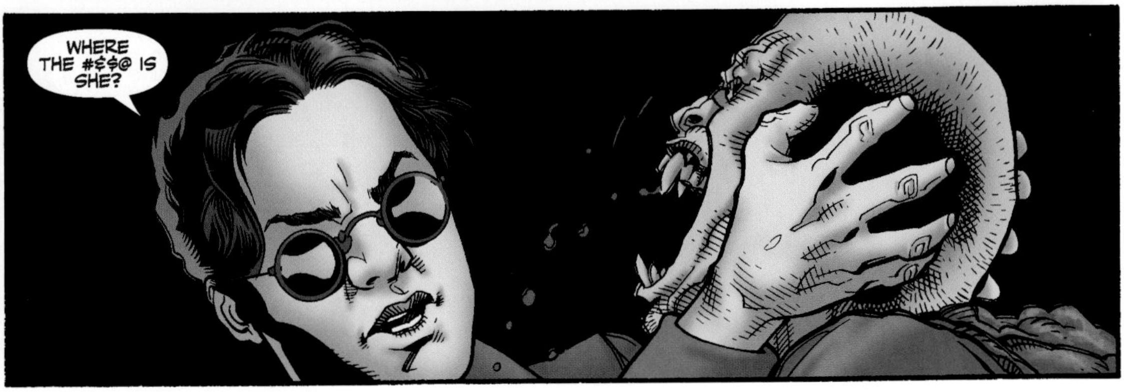
WHERE THE #$$@ IS SHE?

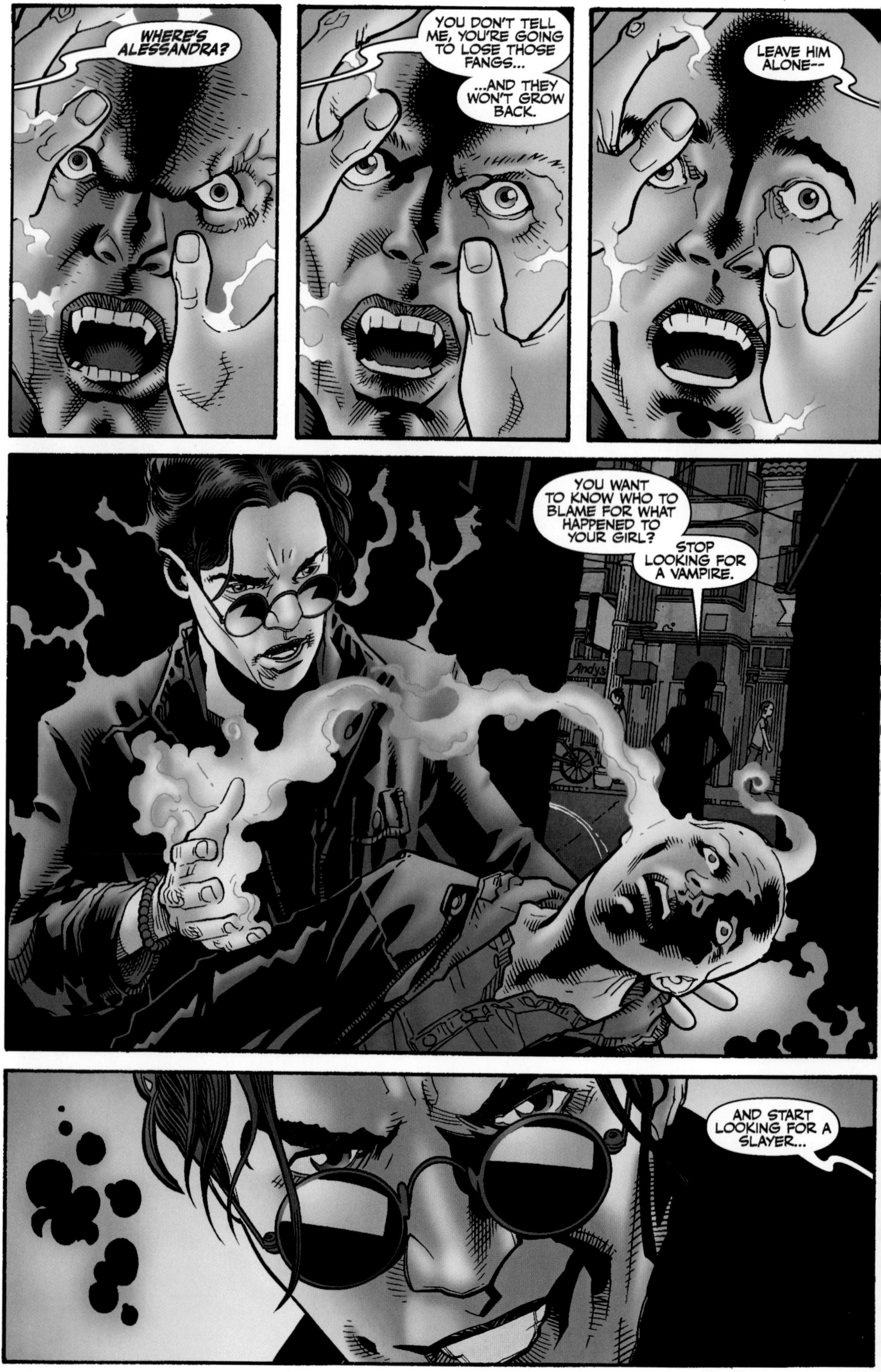
WHERE'S ALESSANDRA?
YOU DON'T TELL ME, YOU'RE GOING TO LOSE THOSE FANGS...
...AND THEY WON'T GROW BACK.
LEAVE HIM ALONE--
YOU WANT TO KNOW WHO TO BLAME FOR WHAT HAPPENED TO YOUR GIRL?
STOP LOOKING FOR A VAMPIRE.
Andys
AND START LOOKING FOR A SLAYER...

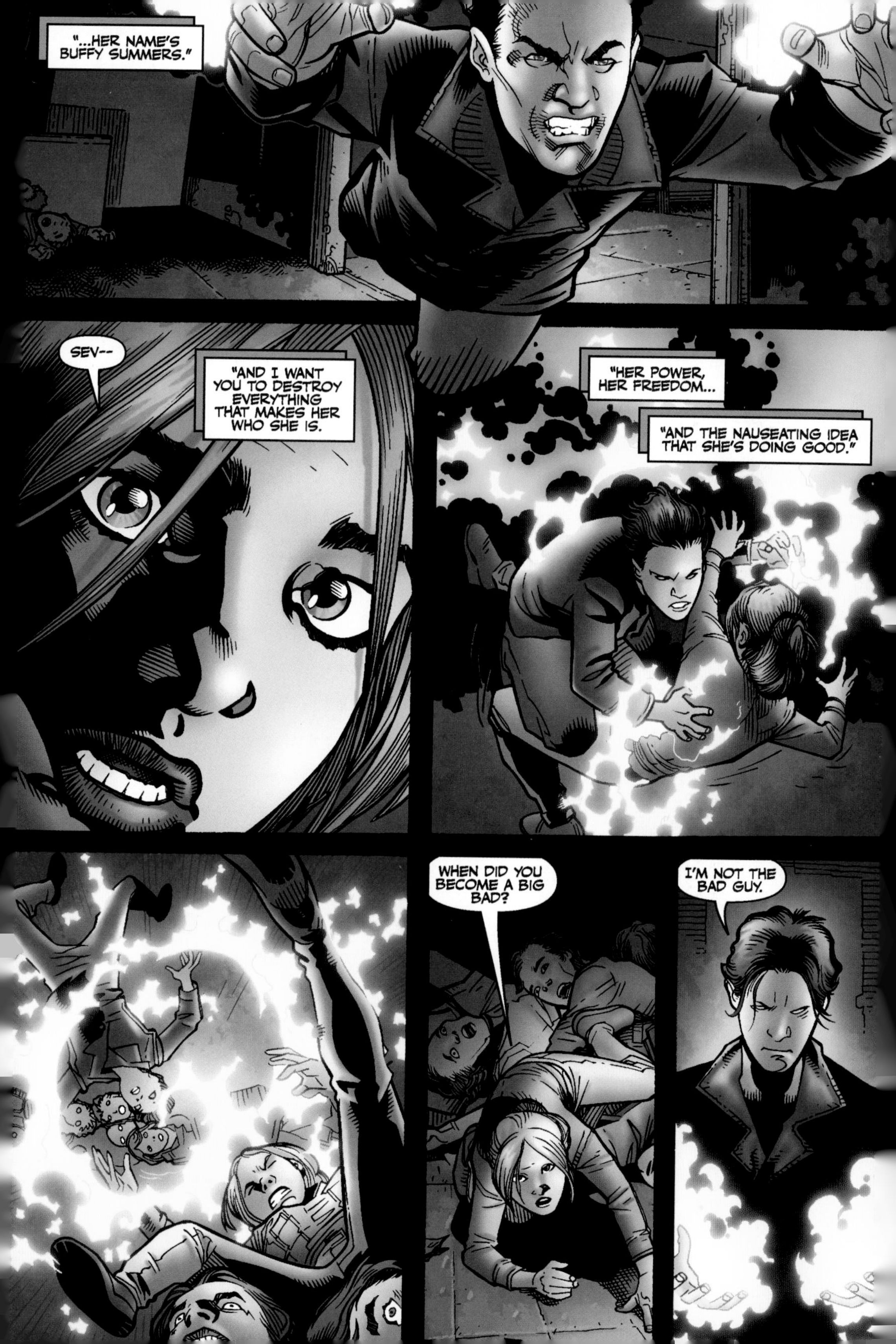
"...HER NAME'S BUFFY SUMMERS."
SEV--
"AND I WANT YOU TO DESTROY EVERYTHING THAT MAKES HER WHO SHE IS.
"HER POWER, HER FREEDOM...
"AND THE NAUSEATING IDEA THAT SHE'S DOING GOOD."
WHEN DID YOU BECOME A BIG BAD?
I'M NOT THE BAD GUY.

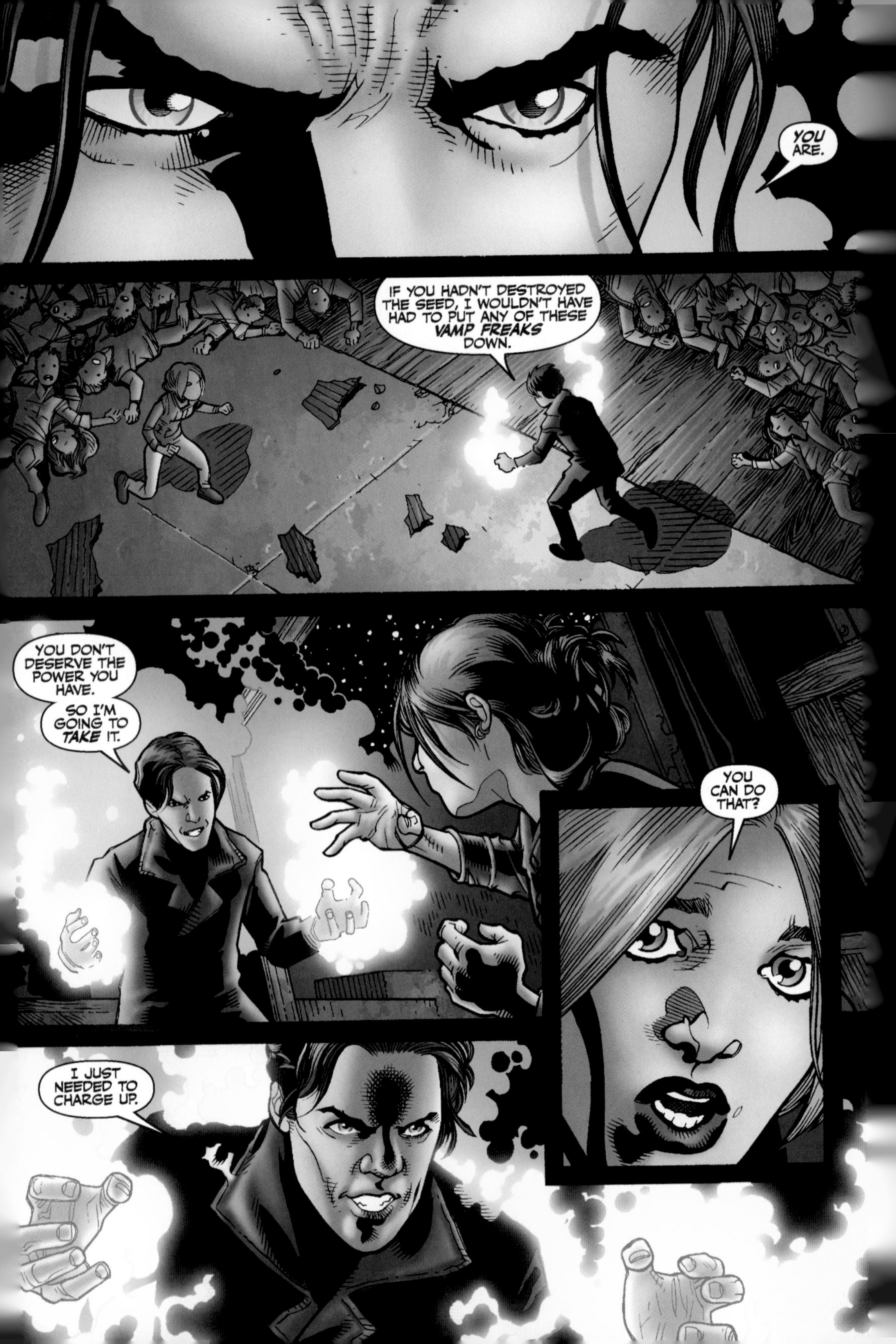
YOU ARE.
IF YOU HADN'T DESTROYED THE SEED, I WOULDN'T HAVE HAD TO PUT ANY OF THESE VAMP FREAKS DOWN.
YOU DON'T DESERVE THE POWER YOU HAVE.
SO I'M GOING TO TAKE IT.
YOU CAN DO THAT?
I JUST NEEDED TO CHARGE UP.

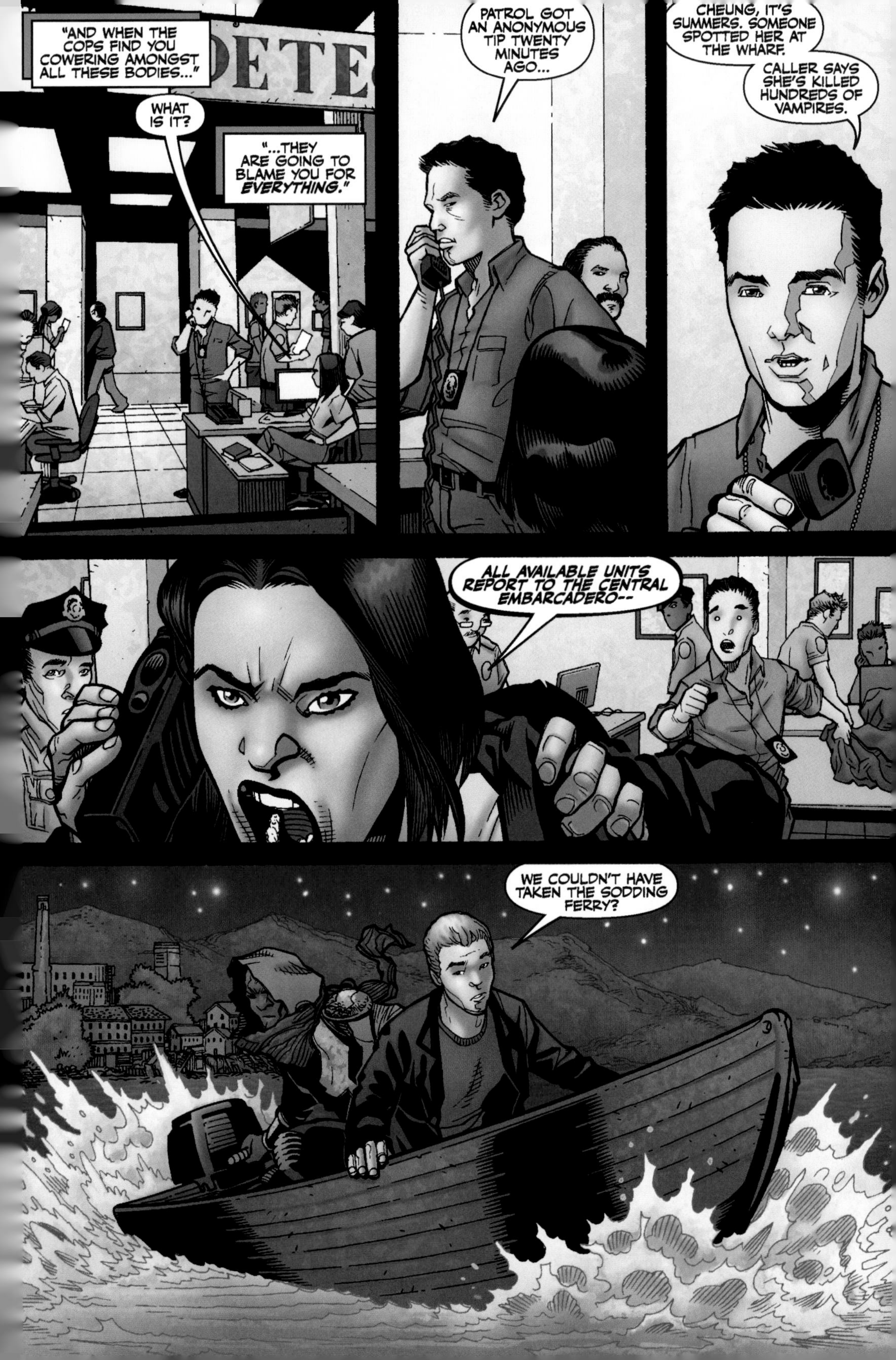

"AND WHEN THE COPS FIND YOU COWERING AMONGST ALL THESE BODIES..."
WHAT IS IT?
"...THEY ARE GOING TO BLAME YOU FOR *EVERYTHING*."
PATROL GOT AN ANONYMOUS TIP TWENTY MINUTES AGO...
CHEUNG, IT'S SUMMERS. SOMEONE SPOTTED HER AT THE WHARF.
CALLER SAYS SHE'S KILLED HUNDREDS OF VAMPIRES.
ALL AVAILABLE UNITS REPORT TO THE CENTRAL EMBARCADERO--
WE COULDN'T HAVE TAKEN THE SODDING FERRY?

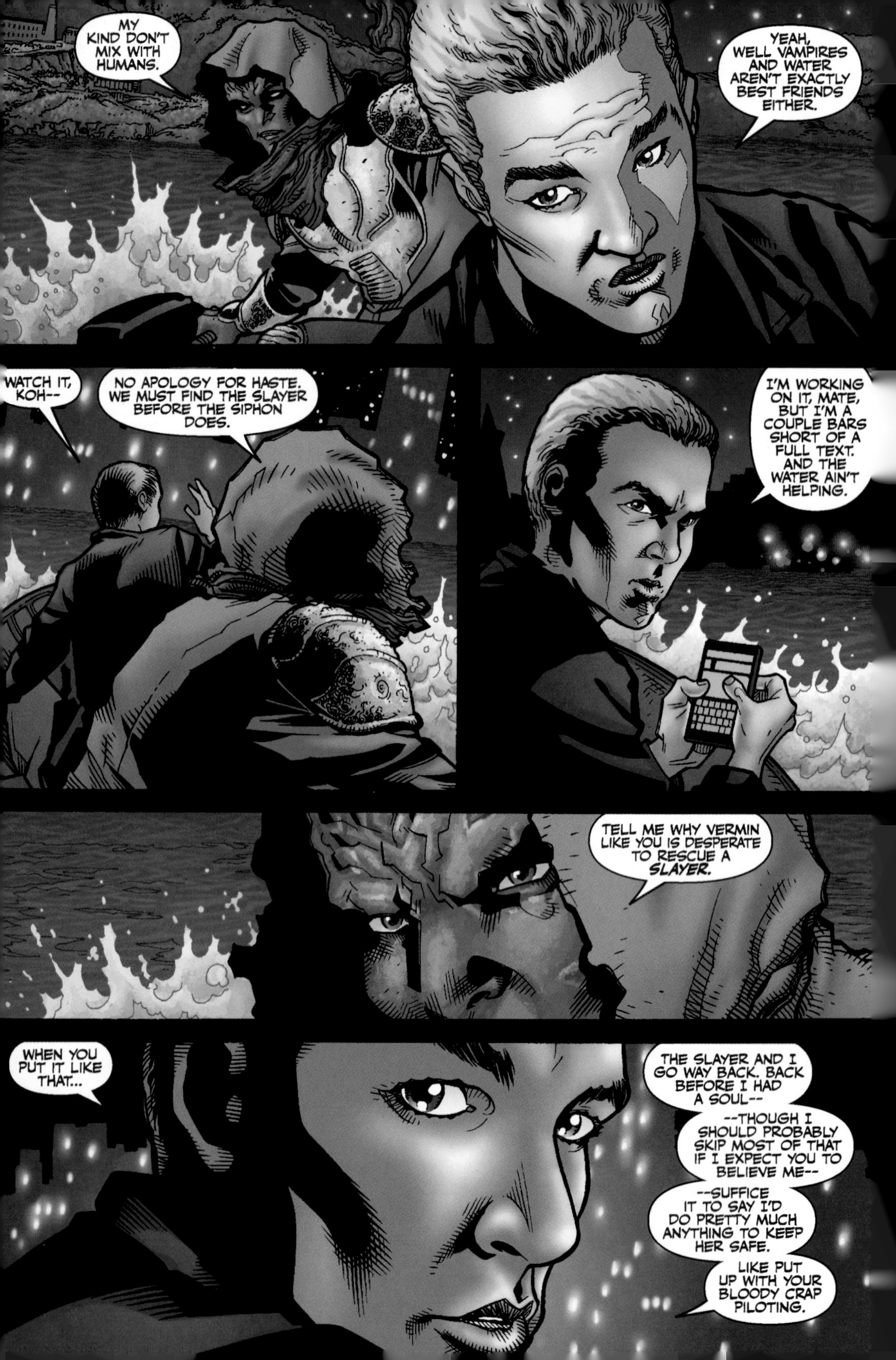
MY KIND DON'T MIX WITH HUMANS.
YEAH, WELL VAMPIRES AND WATER AREN'T EXACTLY BEST FRIENDS EITHER.
WATCH IT, KOH--
NO APOLOGY FOR HASTE. WE MUST FIND THE SLAYER BEFORE THE SIPHON DOES.
I'M WORKING ON IT, MATE, BUT I'M A COUPLE BARS SHORT OF A FULL TEXT. AND THE WATER AIN'T HELPING.
TELL ME WHY VERMIN LIKE YOU IS DESPERATE TO RESCUE A SLAYER.
WHEN YOU PUT IT LIKE THAT...
THE SLAYER AND I GO WAY BACK. BACK BEFORE I HAD A SOUL--
--THOUGH I SHOULD PROBABLY SKIP MOST OF THAT IF I EXPECT YOU TO BELIEVE ME--
--SUFFICE IT TO SAY I'D DO PRETTY MUCH ANYTHING TO KEEP HER SAFE.
LIKE PUT UP WITH YOUR BLOODY CRAP PILOTING.

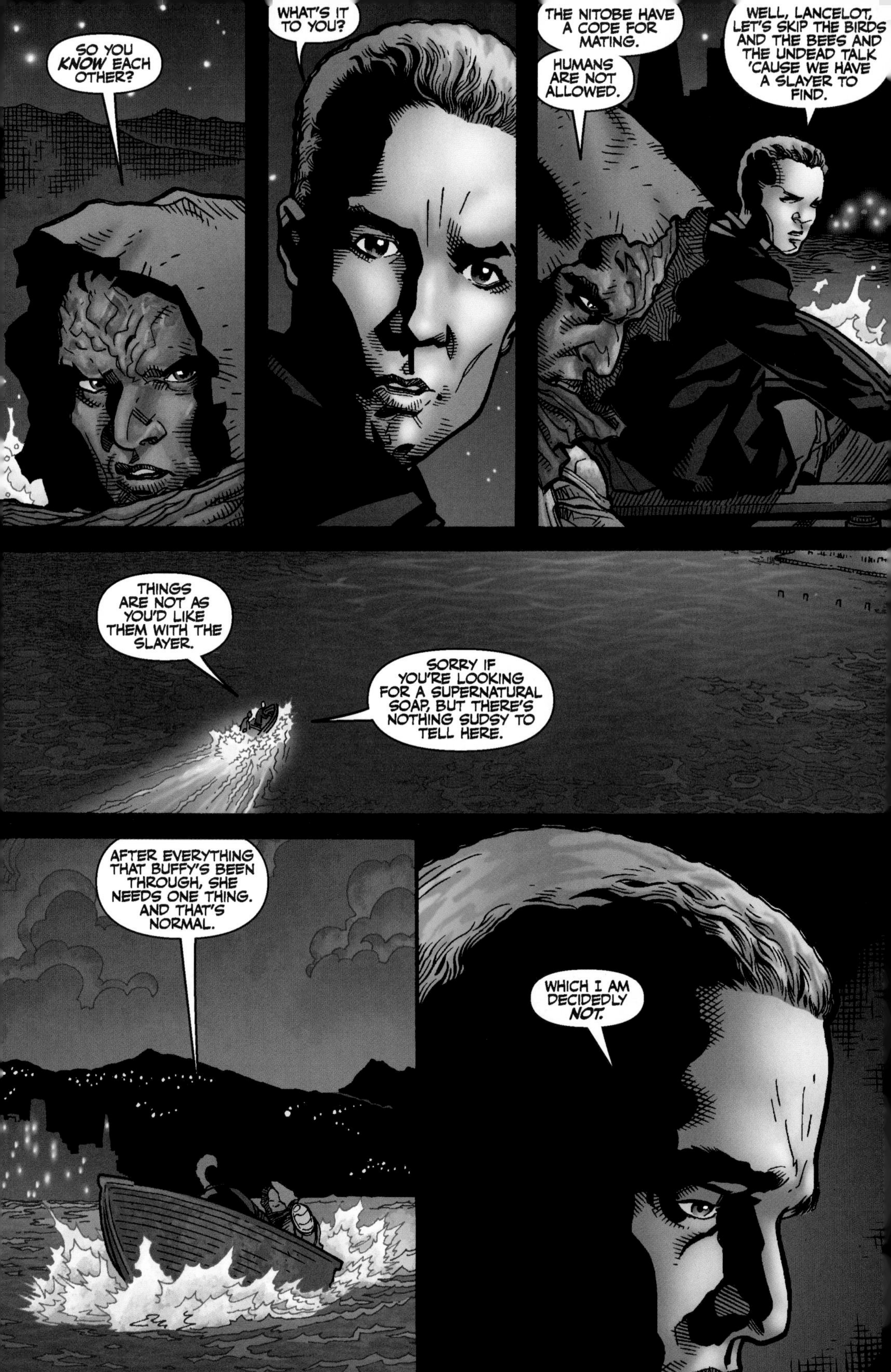

SO YOU KNOW EACH OTHER?
WHAT'S IT TO YOU?
THE NITOBE HAVE A CODE FOR MATING.
HUMANS ARE NOT ALLOWED.
WELL, LANCELOT, LET'S SKIP THE BIRDS AND THE BEES AND THE UNDEAD TALK 'CAUSE WE HAVE A SLAYER TO FIND.
THINGS ARE NOT AS YOU'D LIKE THEM WITH THE SLAYER.
SORRY IF YOU'RE LOOKING FOR A SUPERNATURAL SOAP, BUT THERE'S NOTHING SUDSY TO TELL HERE.
AFTER EVERYTHING THAT BUFFY'S BEEN THROUGH, SHE NEEDS ONE THING. AND THAT'S NORMAL.
WHICH I AM DECIDEDLY NOT.

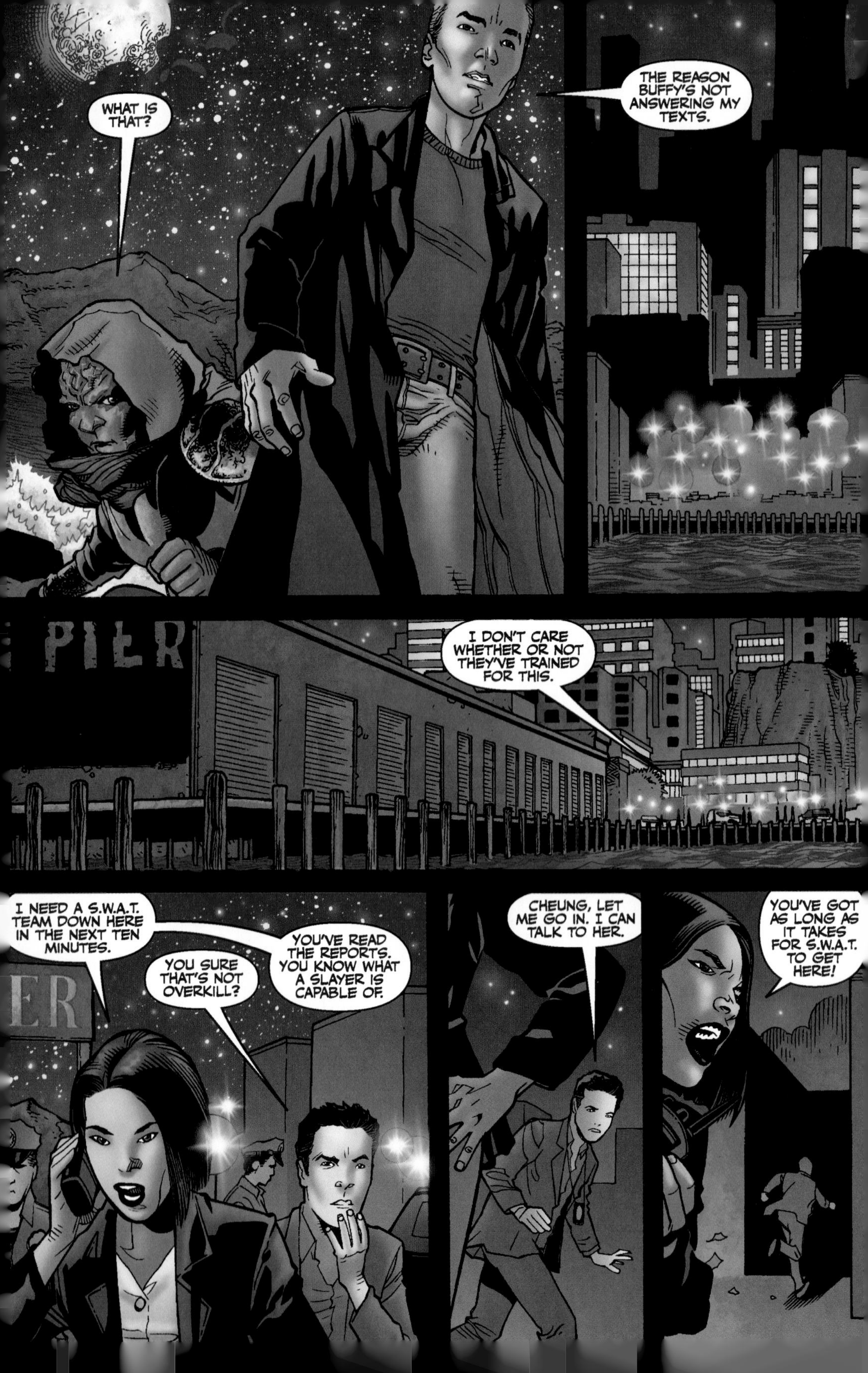

WHAT IS THAT?
THE REASON BUFFY'S NOT ANSWERING MY TEXTS.
PIER
I DON'T CARE WHETHER OR NOT THEY'VE TRAINED FOR THIS.
I NEED A S.W.A.T. TEAM DOWN HERE IN THE NEXT TEN MINUTES.
YOU SURE THAT'S NOT OVERKILL?
YOU'VE READ THE REPORTS. YOU KNOW WHAT A SLAYER IS CAPABLE OF.
CHEUNG, LET ME GO IN. I CAN TALK TO HER.
YOU'VE GOT AS LONG AS IT TAKES FOR S.W.A.T. TO GET HERE!

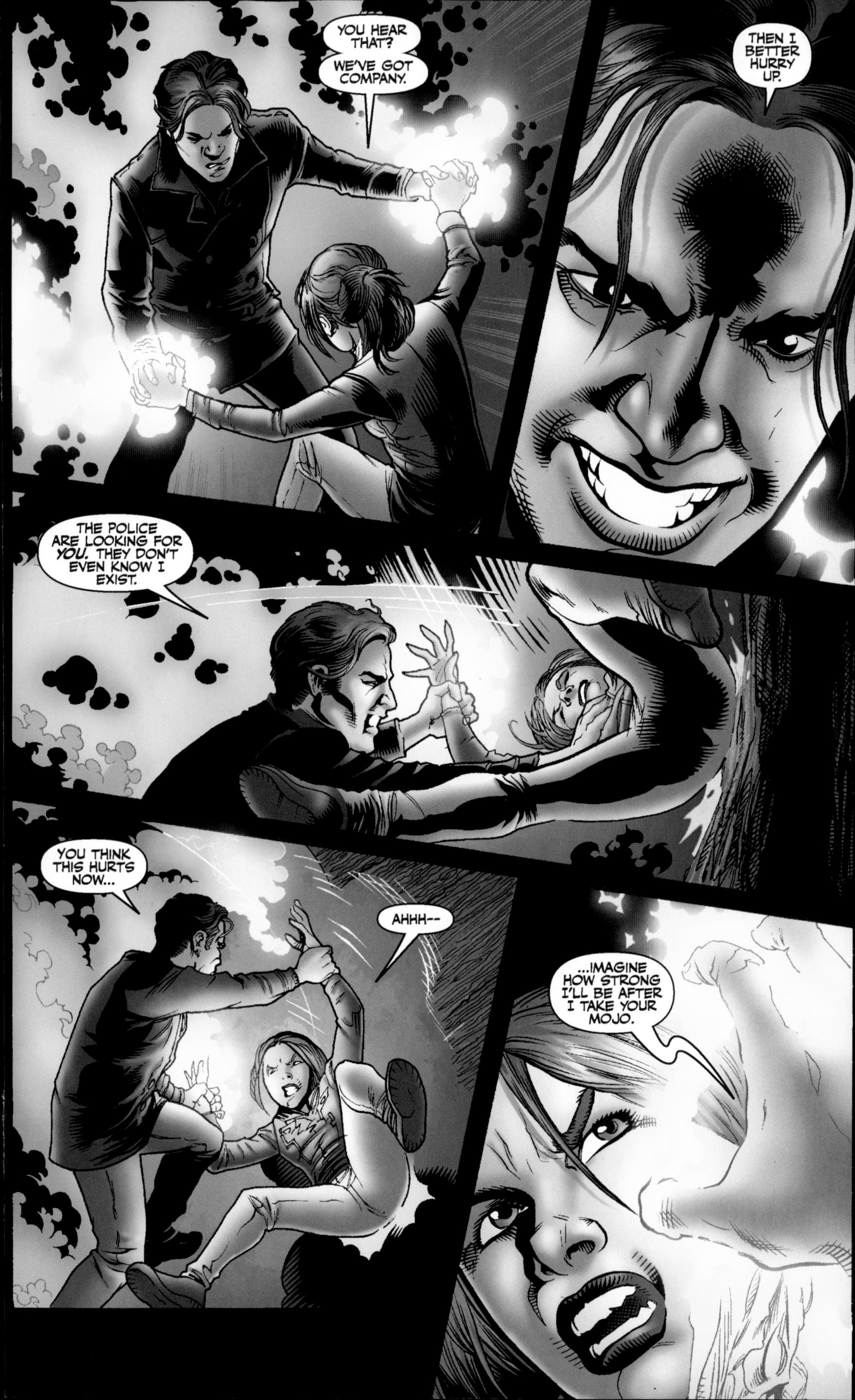
YOU HEAR THAT?
WE'VE GOT COMPANY.
THEN I BETTER HURRY UP.
THE POLICE ARE LOOKING FOR *YOU*. THEY DON'T EVEN KNOW I EXIST.
YOU THINK THIS HURTS NOW...
AHHH--
...IMAGINE HOW STRONG I'LL BE AFTER I TAKE YOUR MOJO.

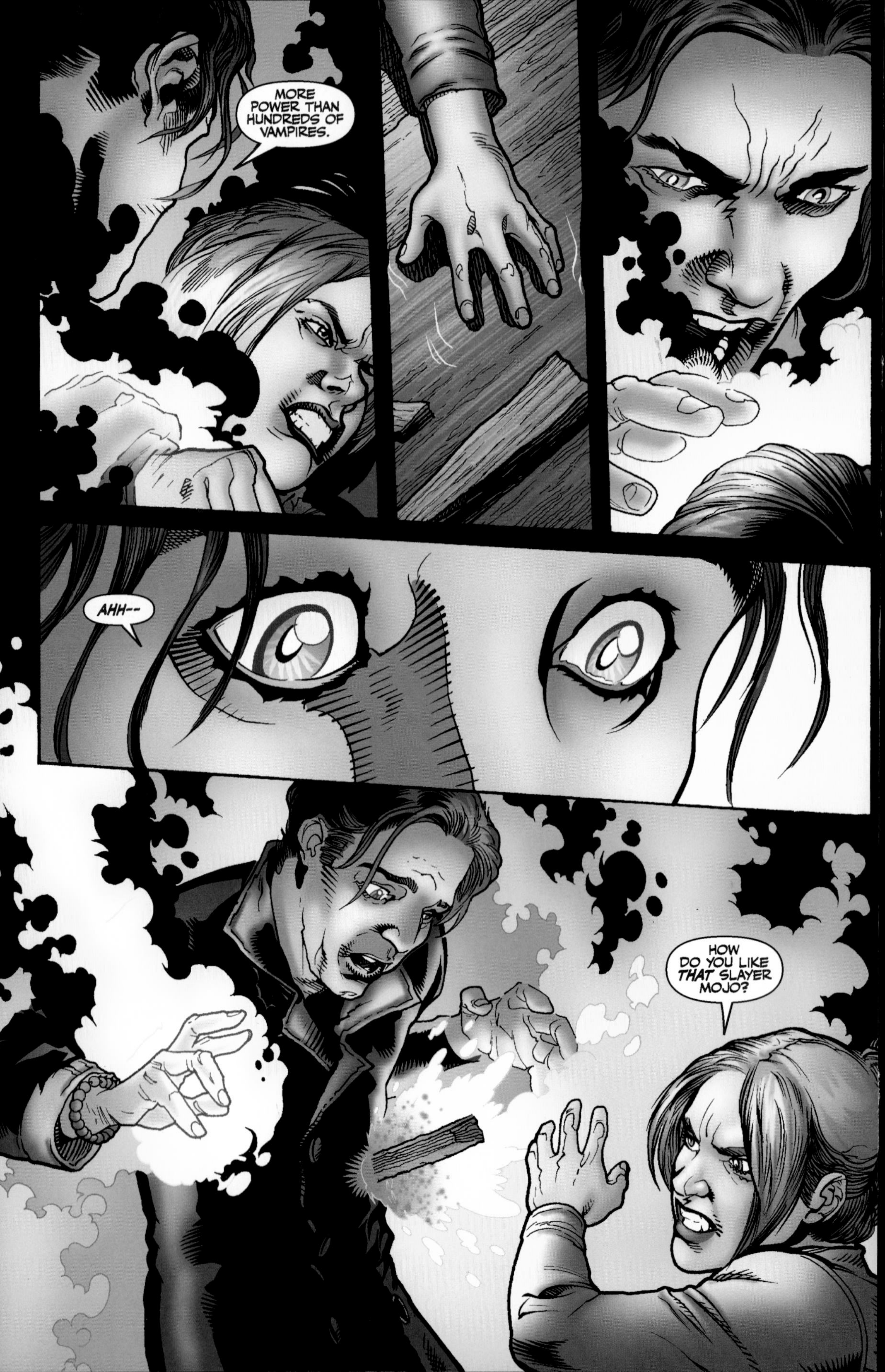
MORE POWER THAN HUNDREDS OF VAMPIRES.
AHH--
HOW DO YOU LIKE *THAT* SLAYER MOJO?

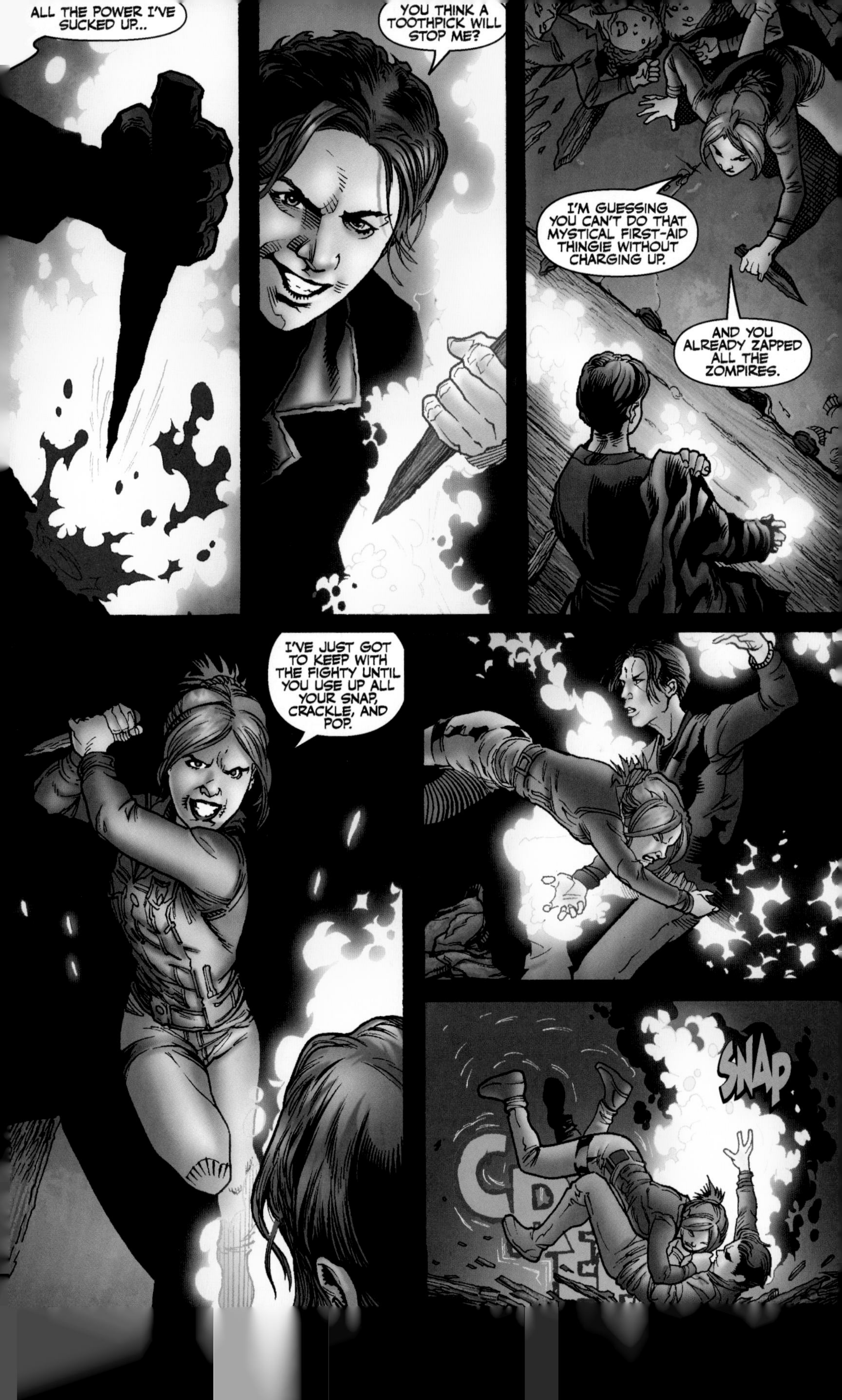
ALL THE POWER I'VE SUCKED UP...
YOU THINK A TOOTHPICK WILL STOP ME?
I'M GUESSING YOU CAN'T DO THAT MYSTICAL FIRST-AID THINGIE WITHOUT CHARGING UP.
AND YOU ALREADY ZAPPED ALL THE ZOMPIRES.
I'VE JUST GOT TO KEEP WITH THE FIGHTY UNTIL YOU USE UP ALL YOUR SNAP, CRACKLE, AND POP.
SNAP

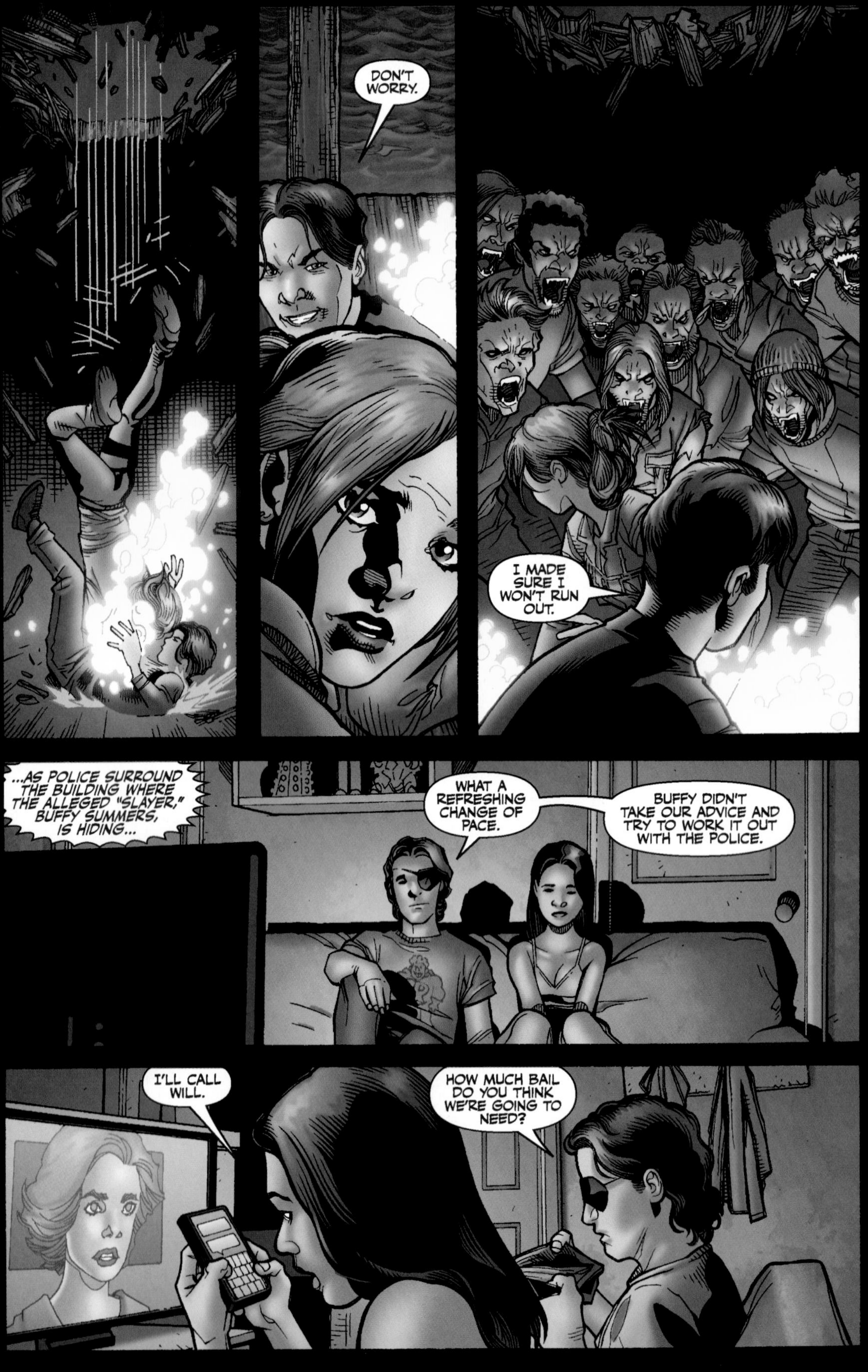

DON'T WORRY.
I MADE SURE I WON'T RUN OUT.
...AS POLICE SURROUND THE BUILDING WHERE THE ALLEGED "SLAYER," BUFFY SUMMERS, IS HIDING...
WHAT A REFRESHING CHANGE OF PACE.
BUFFY DIDN'T TAKE OUR ADVICE AND TRY TO WORK IT OUT WITH THE POLICE.
I'LL CALL WILL.
HOW MUCH BAIL DO YOU THINK WE'RE GOING TO NEED?

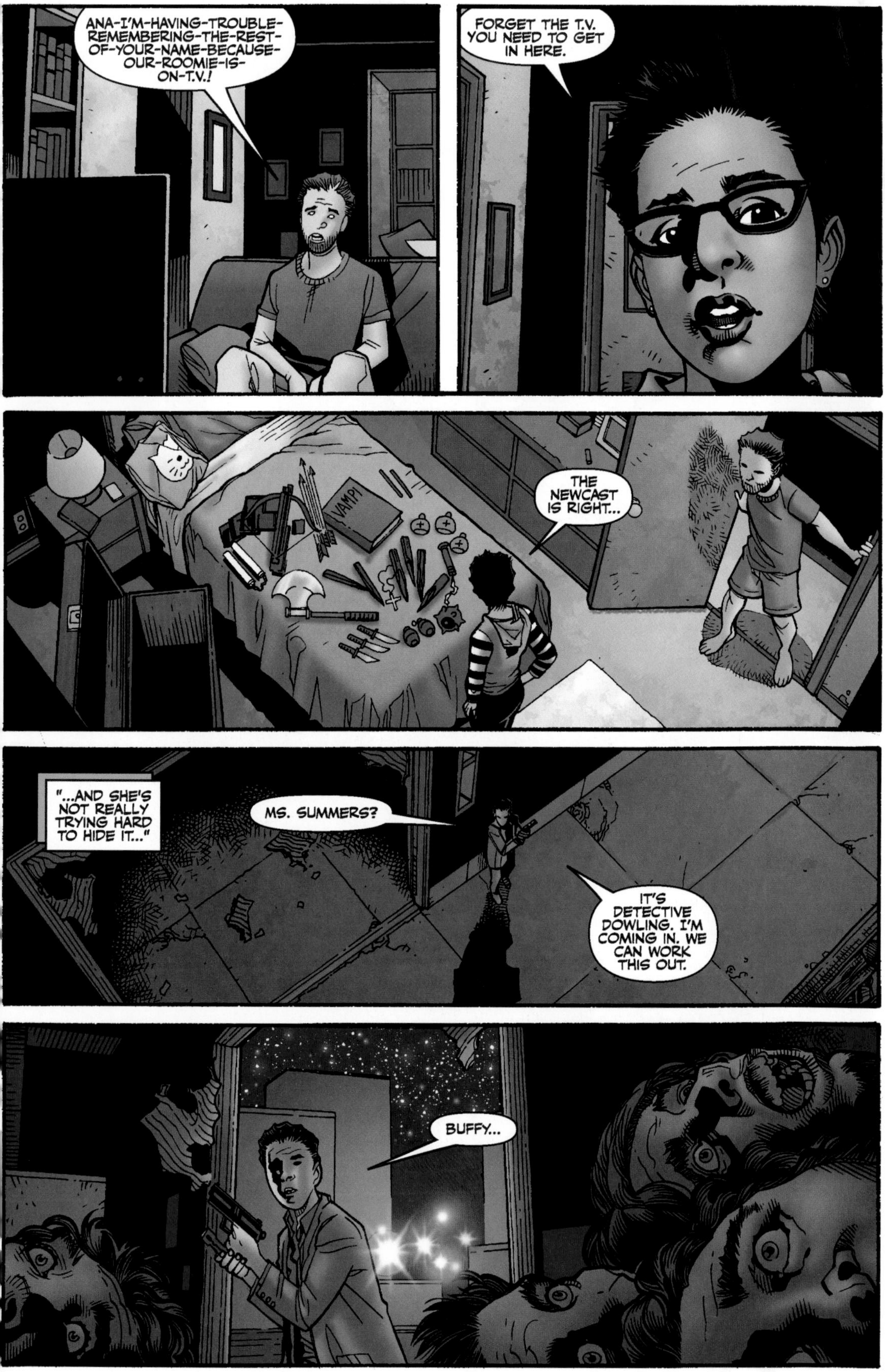
ANA-I'M-HAVING-TROUBLE-REMEMBERING-THE-REST-OF-YOUR-NAME-BECAUSE-OUR-ROOMIE-IS-ON-T.V.!
FORGET THE T.V. YOU NEED TO GET IN HERE.
VAMPI
THE NEWCAST IS RIGHT...
"...AND SHE'S NOT REALLY TRYING HARD TO HIDE IT..."
MS. SUMMERS?
IT'S DETECTIVE DOWLING. I'M COMING IN. WE CAN WORK THIS OUT.
BUFFY...

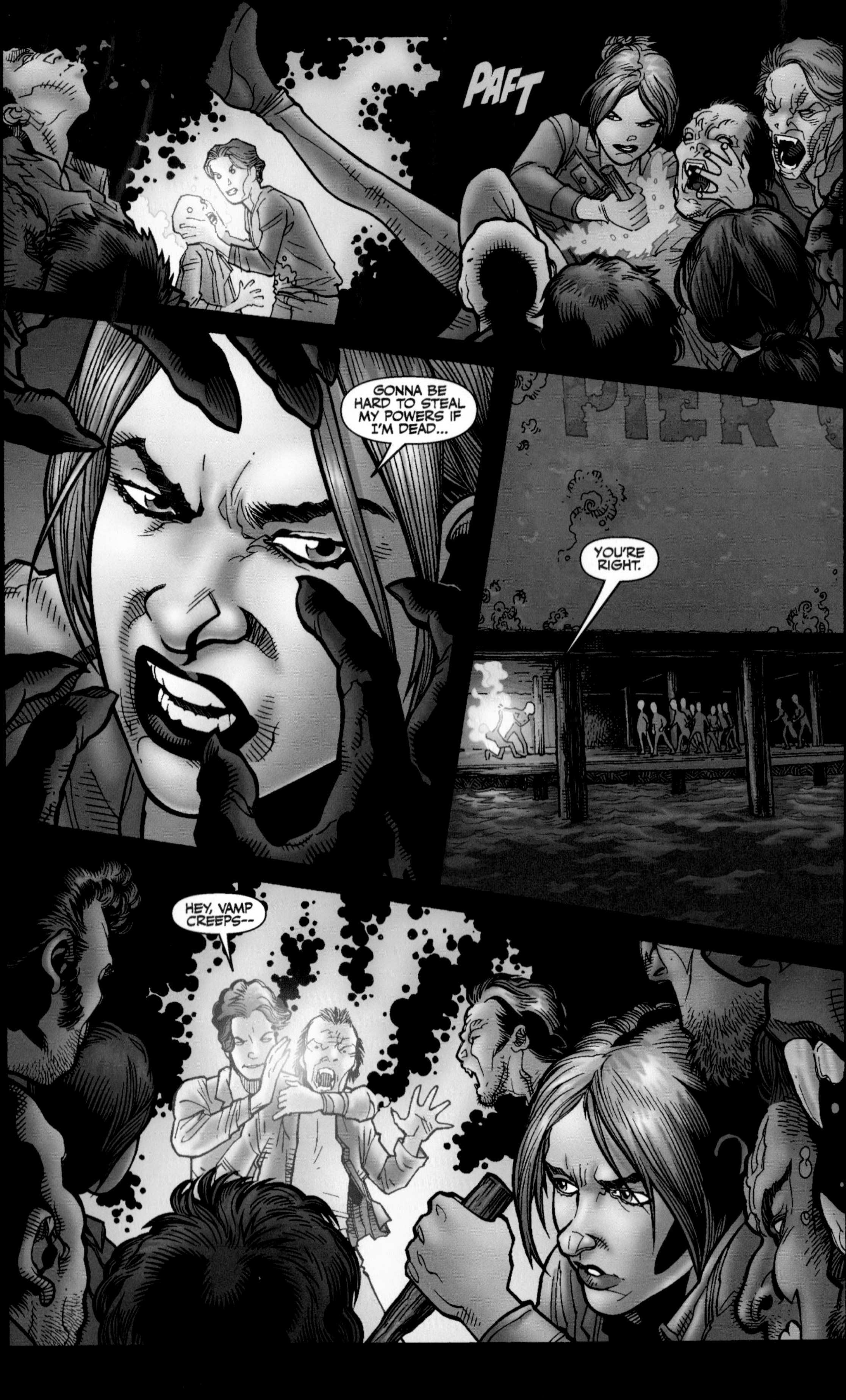
PAFT
GONNA BE HARD TO STEAL MY POWERS IF I'M DEAD...
PIER
YOU'RE RIGHT.
HEY, VAMP CREEPS--

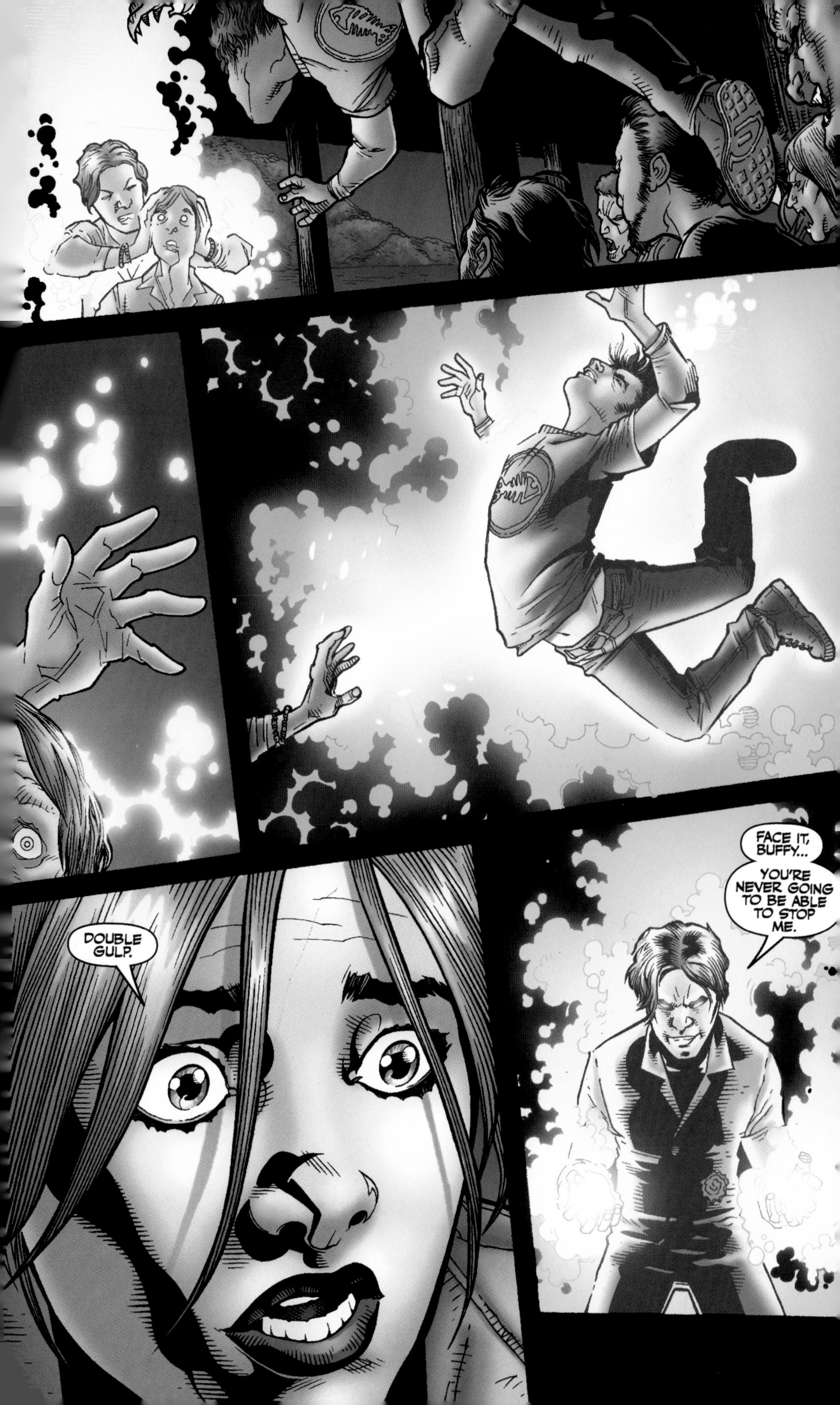
DOUBLE GULP.
FACE IT, BUFFY...
YOU'RE NEVER GOING TO BE ABLE TO STOP ME.

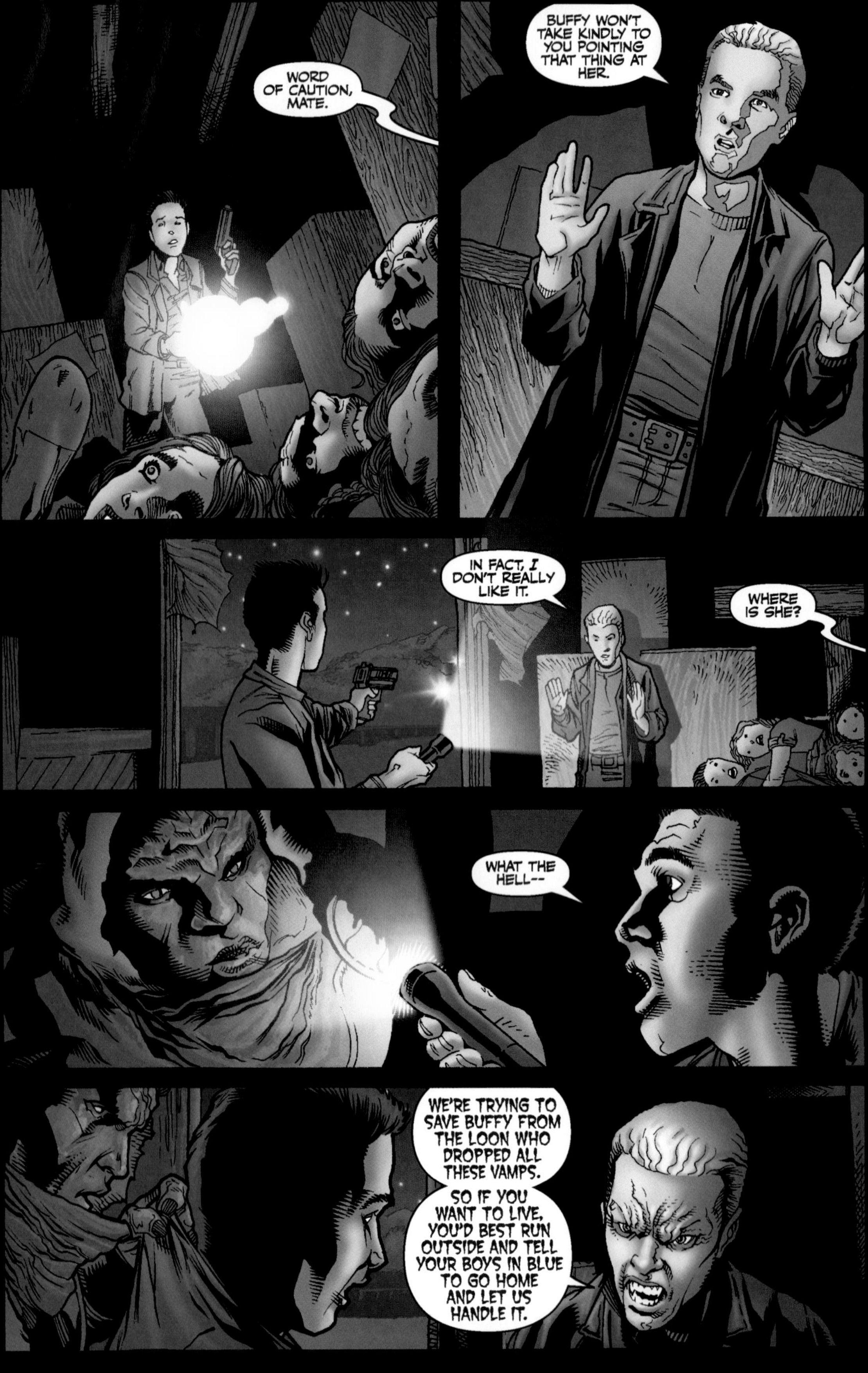
WORD OF CAUTION, MATE.
BUFFY WON'T TAKE KINDLY TO YOU POINTING THAT THING AT HER.
IN FACT, I DON'T REALLY LIKE IT.
WHERE IS SHE?
WHAT THE HELL--
WE'RE TRYING TO SAVE BUFFY FROM THE LOON WHO DROPPED ALL THESE VAMPS.
SO IF YOU WANT TO LIVE, YOU'D BEST RUN OUTSIDE AND TELL YOUR BOYS IN BLUE TO GO HOME AND LET US HANDLE IT.

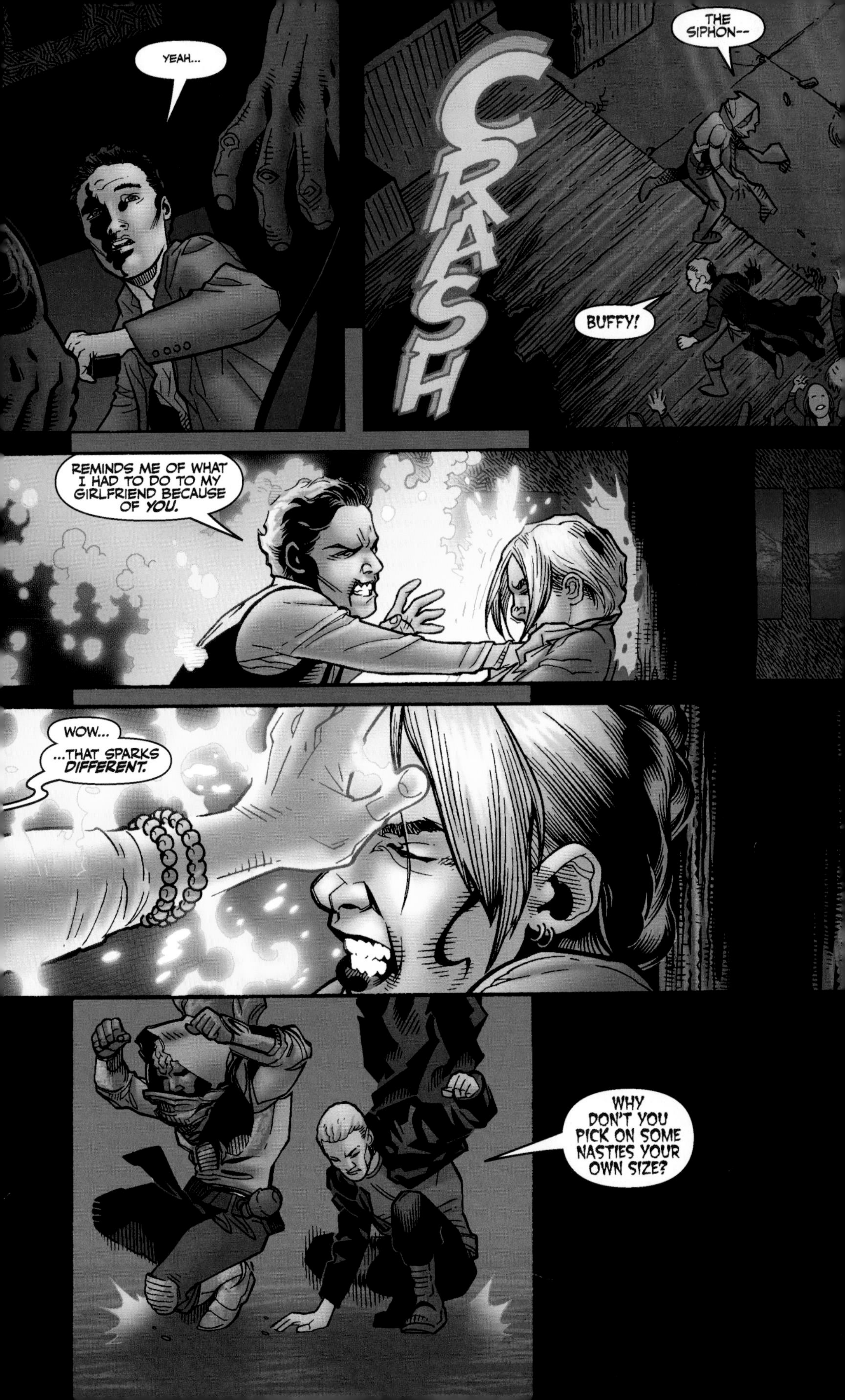
YEAH...
CRASH
THE SIPHON--
BUFFY!
REMINDS ME OF WHAT I HAD TO DO TO MY GIRLFRIEND BECAUSE OF YOU.
WOW...
...THAT SPARKS DIFFERENT.
WHY DON'T YOU PICK ON SOME NASTIES YOUR OWN SIZE?

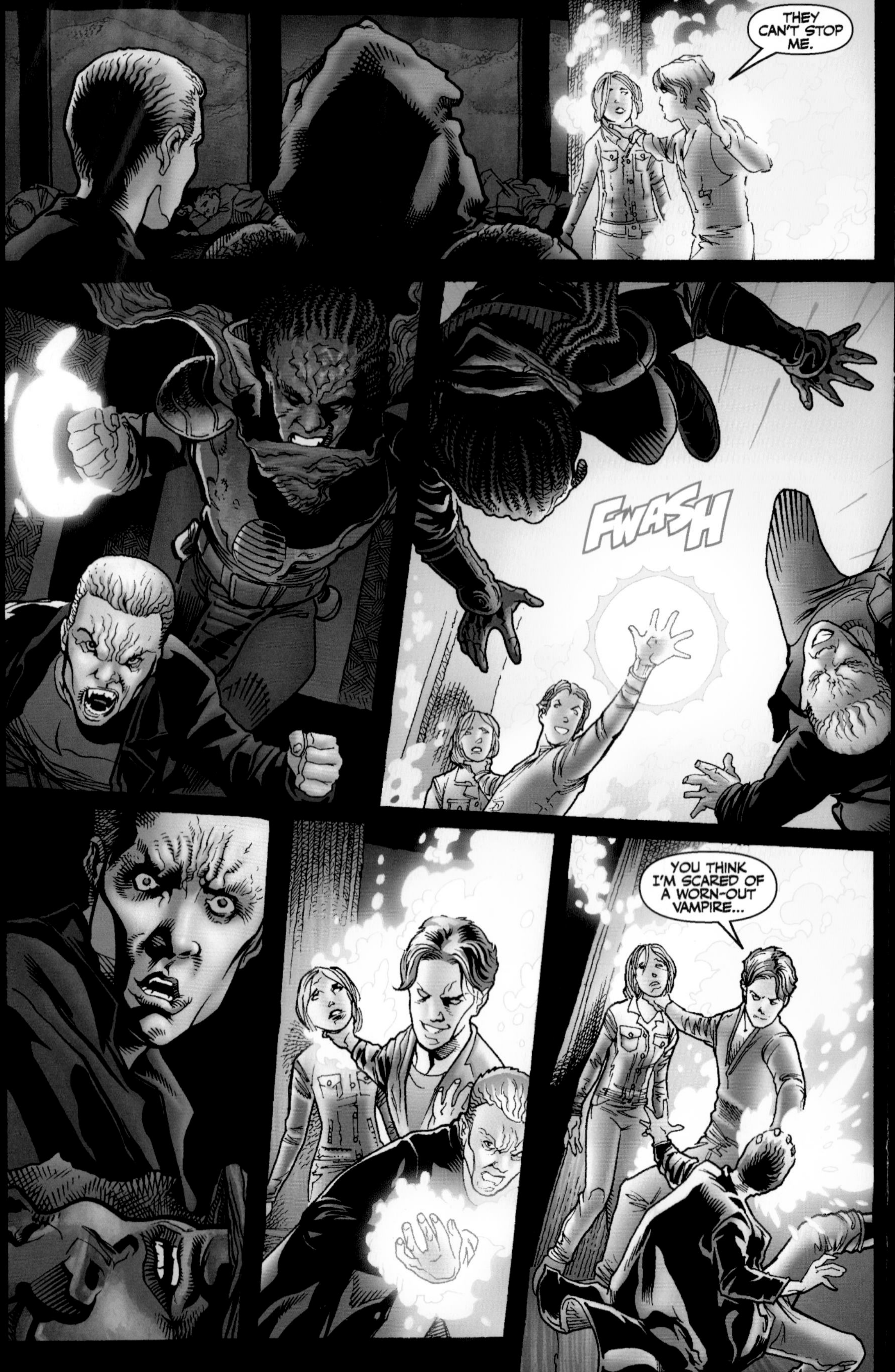

THEY CAN'T STOP ME.
FWASH
YOU THINK I'M SCARED OF A WORN-OUT VAMPIRE...

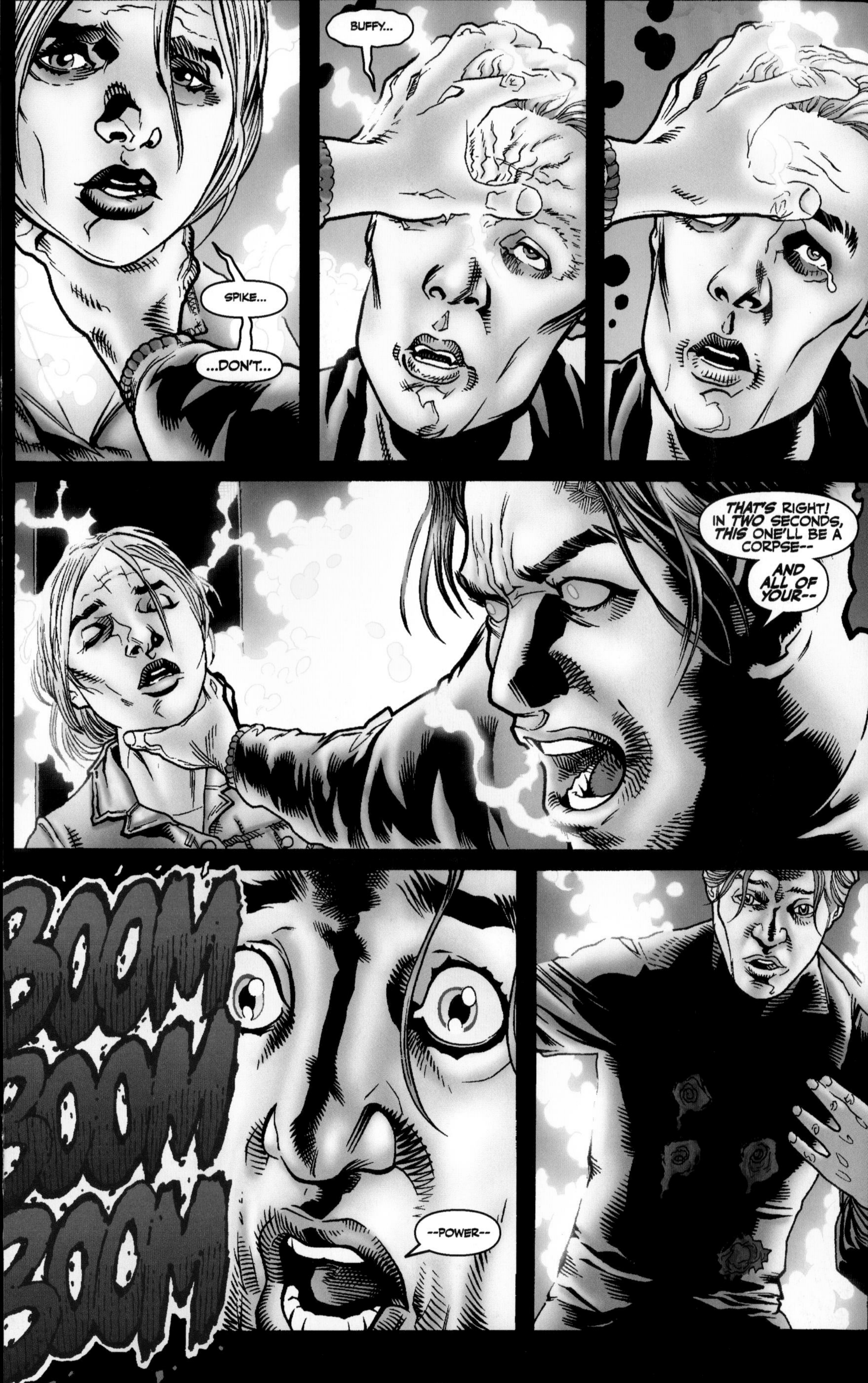
SPIKE...
...DON'T...
BUFFY...
THAT'S RIGHT! IN TWO SECONDS, THIS ONE'LL BE A CORPSE--
AND ALL OF YOUR--
BOOM
BOOM
BOOM
--POWER--

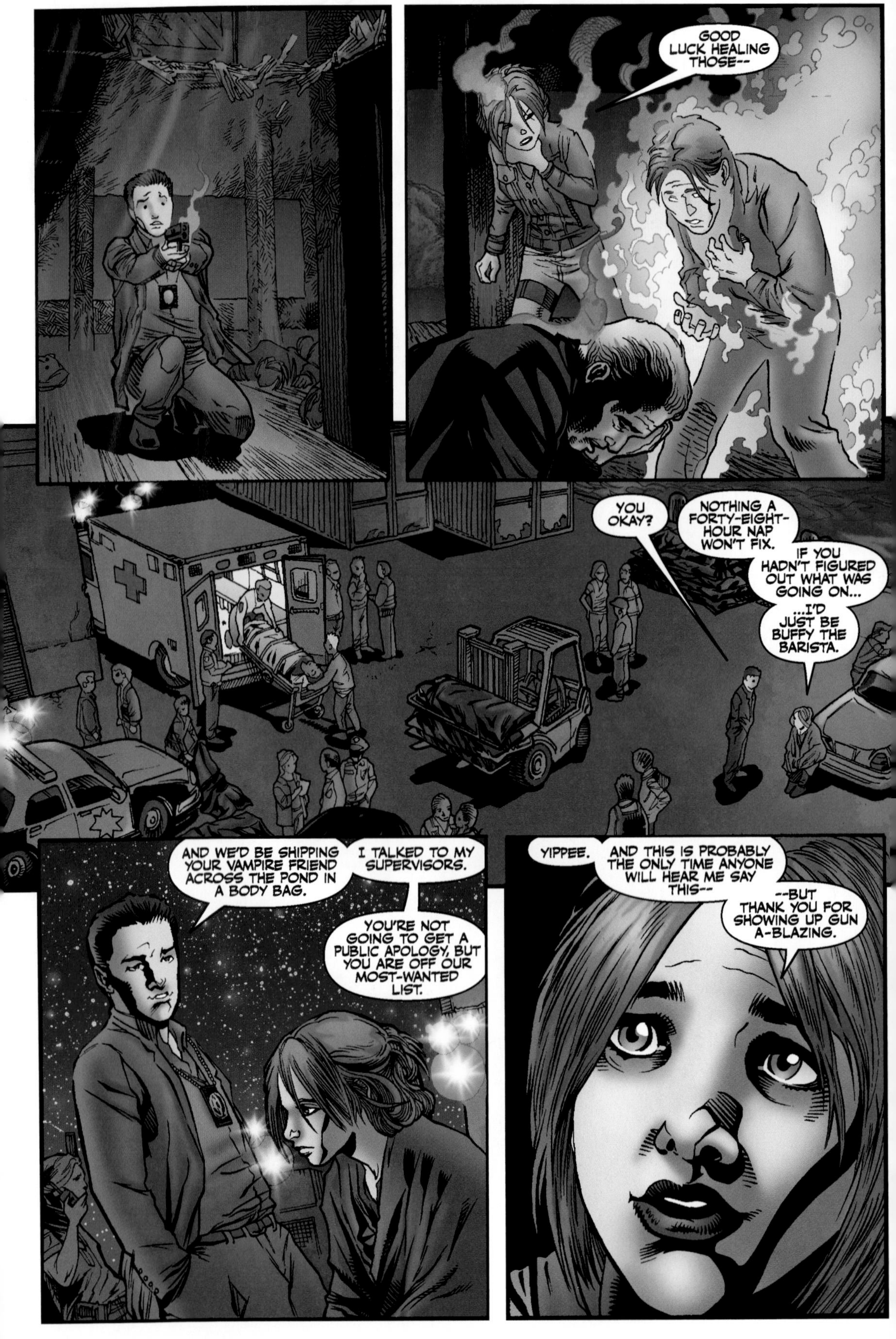

GOOD LUCK HEALING THOSE--
YOU OKAY?
NOTHING A FORTY-EIGHT-HOUR NAP WON'T FIX.
IF YOU HADN'T FIGURED OUT WHAT WAS GOING ON...
...I'D JUST BE BUFFY THE BARISTA.
AND WE'D BE SHIPPING YOUR VAMPIRE FRIEND ACROSS THE POND IN A BODY BAG.
I TALKED TO MY SUPERVISORS.
YOU'RE NOT GOING TO GET A PUBLIC APOLOGY, BUT YOU ARE OFF OUR MOST-WANTED LIST.
YIPPEE.
AND THIS IS PROBABLY THE ONLY TIME ANYONE WILL HEAR ME SAY THIS--
--BUT THANK YOU FOR SHOWING UP GUN A-BLAZING.

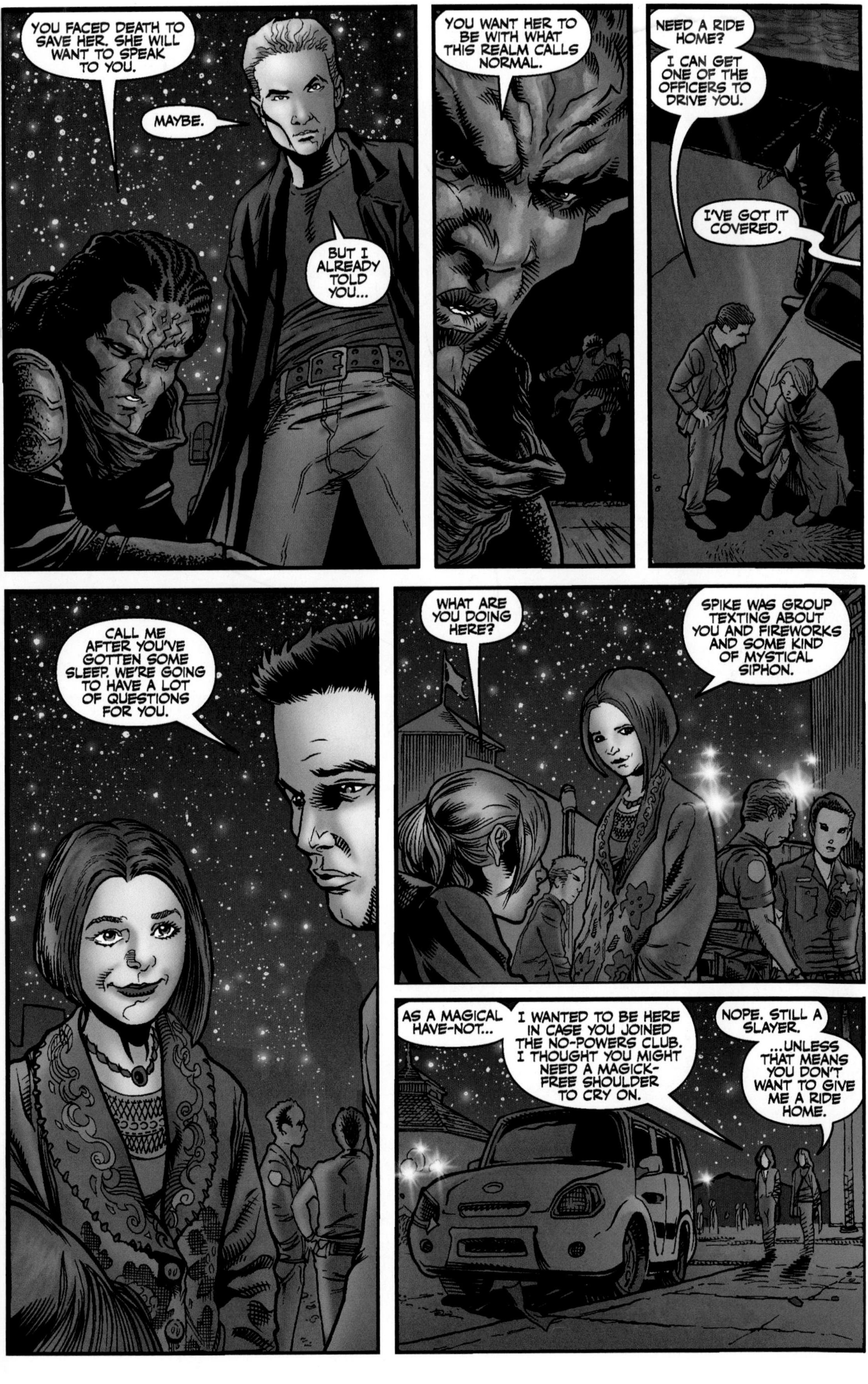
YOU FACED DEATH TO SAVE HER. SHE WILL WANT TO SPEAK TO YOU.
MAYBE.
BUT I ALREADY TOLD YOU...
YOU WANT HER TO BE WITH WHAT THIS REALM CALLS NORMAL.
NEED A RIDE HOME?
I CAN GET ONE OF THE OFFICERS TO DRIVE YOU.
I'VE GOT IT COVERED.
CALL ME AFTER YOU'VE GOTTEN SOME SLEEP. WE'RE GOING TO HAVE A LOT OF QUESTIONS FOR YOU.
WHAT ARE YOU DOING HERE?
SPIKE WAS GROUP TEXTING ABOUT YOU AND FIREWORKS AND SOME KIND OF MYSTICAL SIPHON.
AS A MAGICAL HAVE-NOT...
I WANTED TO BE HERE IN CASE YOU JOINED THE NO-POWERS CLUB. I THOUGHT YOU MIGHT NEED A MAGICK-FREE SHOULDER TO CRY ON.
NOPE. STILL A SLAYER.
...UNLESS THAT MEANS YOU DON'T WANT TO GIVE ME A RIDE HOME.

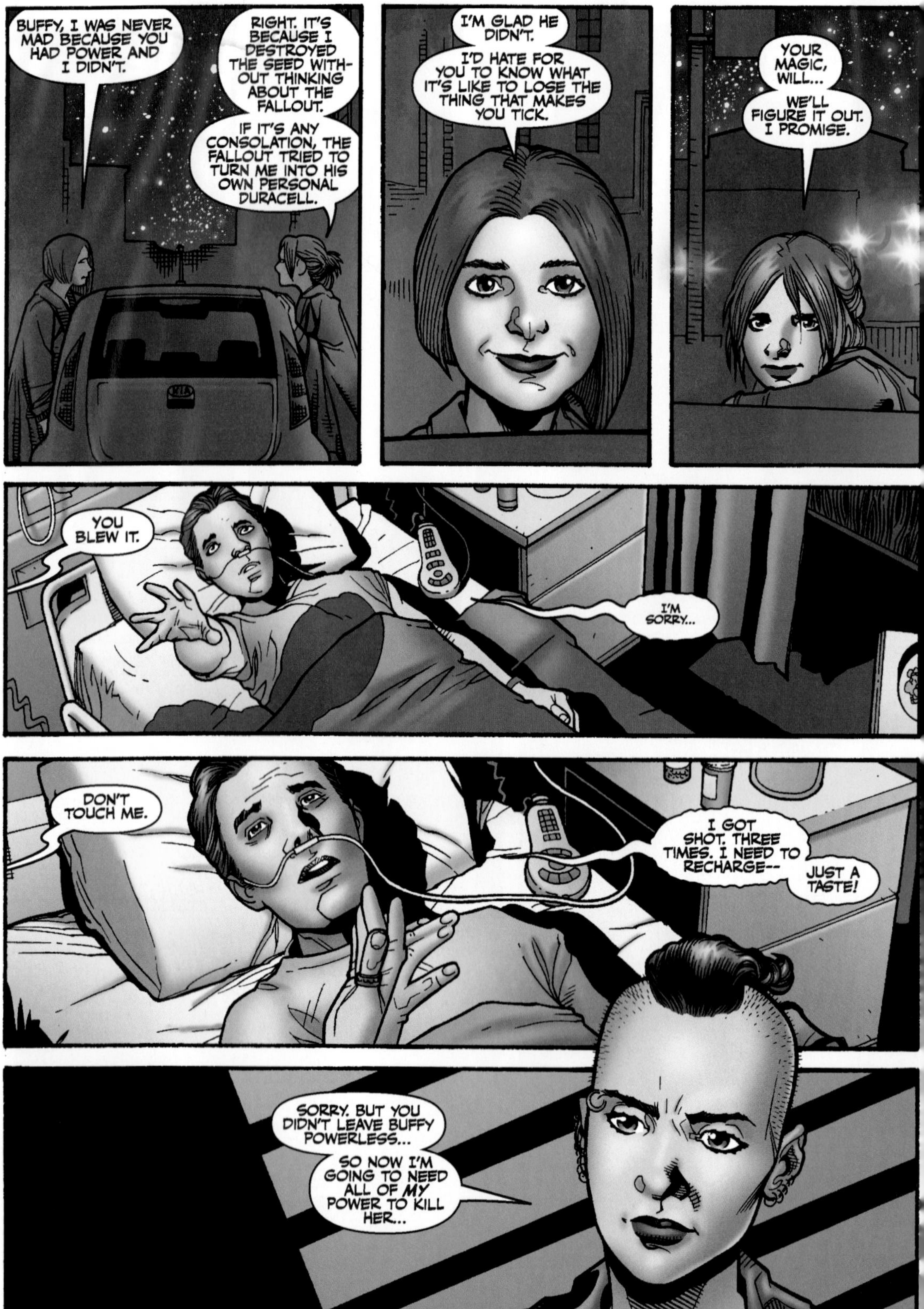
BUFFY, I WAS NEVER MAD BECAUSE YOU HAD POWER AND I DIDN'T.
RIGHT. IT'S BECAUSE I DESTROYED THE SEED WITHOUT THINKING ABOUT THE FALLOUT.
IF IT'S ANY CONSOLATION, THE FALLOUT TRIED TO TURN ME INTO HIS OWN PERSONAL DURACELL.
I'M GLAD HE DIDN'T.
I'D HATE FOR YOU TO KNOW WHAT IT'S LIKE TO LOSE THE THING THAT MAKES YOU TICK.
YOUR MAGIC, WILL...
WE'LL FIGURE IT OUT. I PROMISE.
YOU BLEW IT.
I'M SORRY...
DON'T TOUCH ME.
I GOT SHOT. THREE TIMES. I NEED TO RECHARGE--
JUST A TASTE!
SORRY. BUT YOU DIDN'T LEAVE BUFFY POWERLESS...
SO NOW I'M GOING TO NEED ALL OF *MY* POWER TO KILL HER...

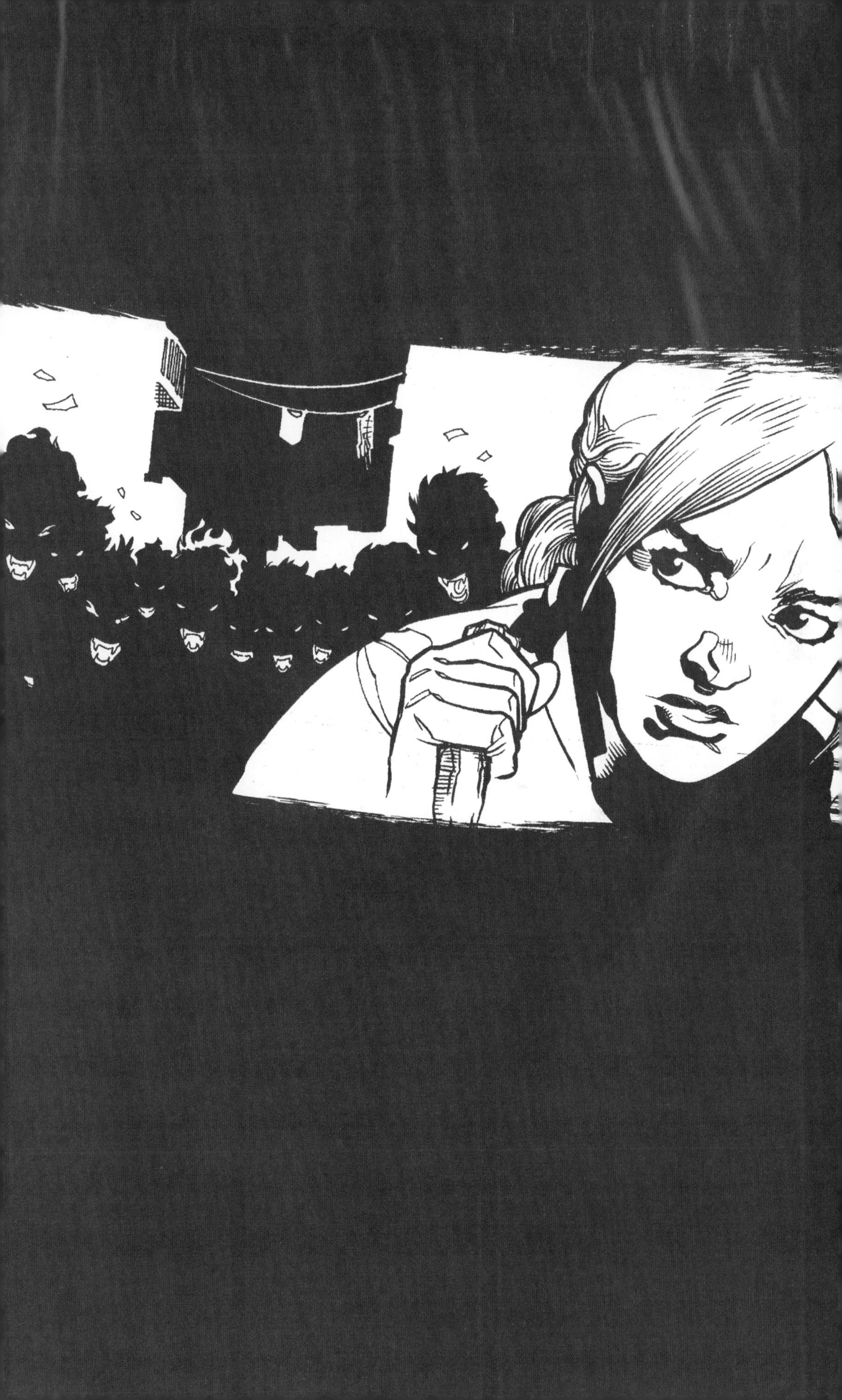

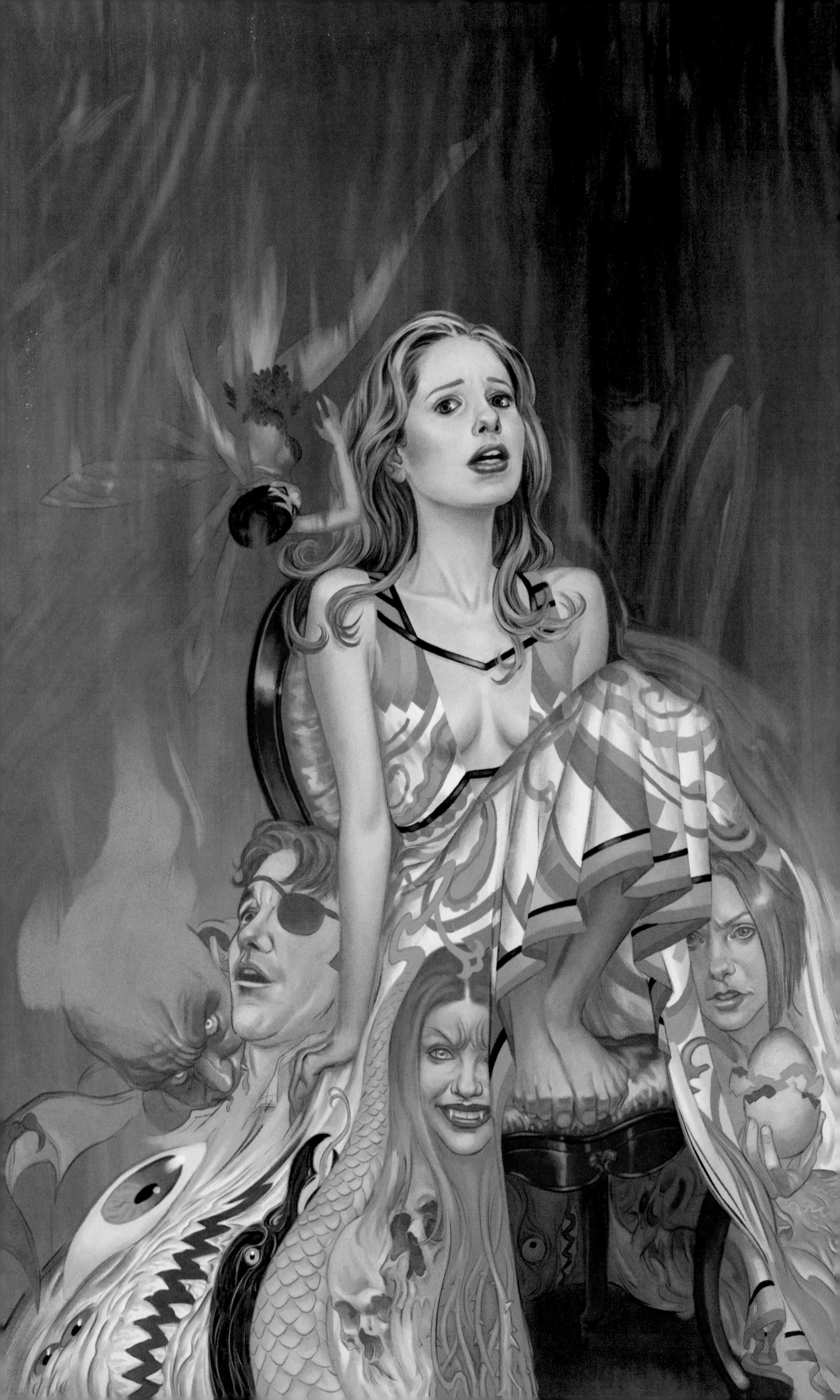

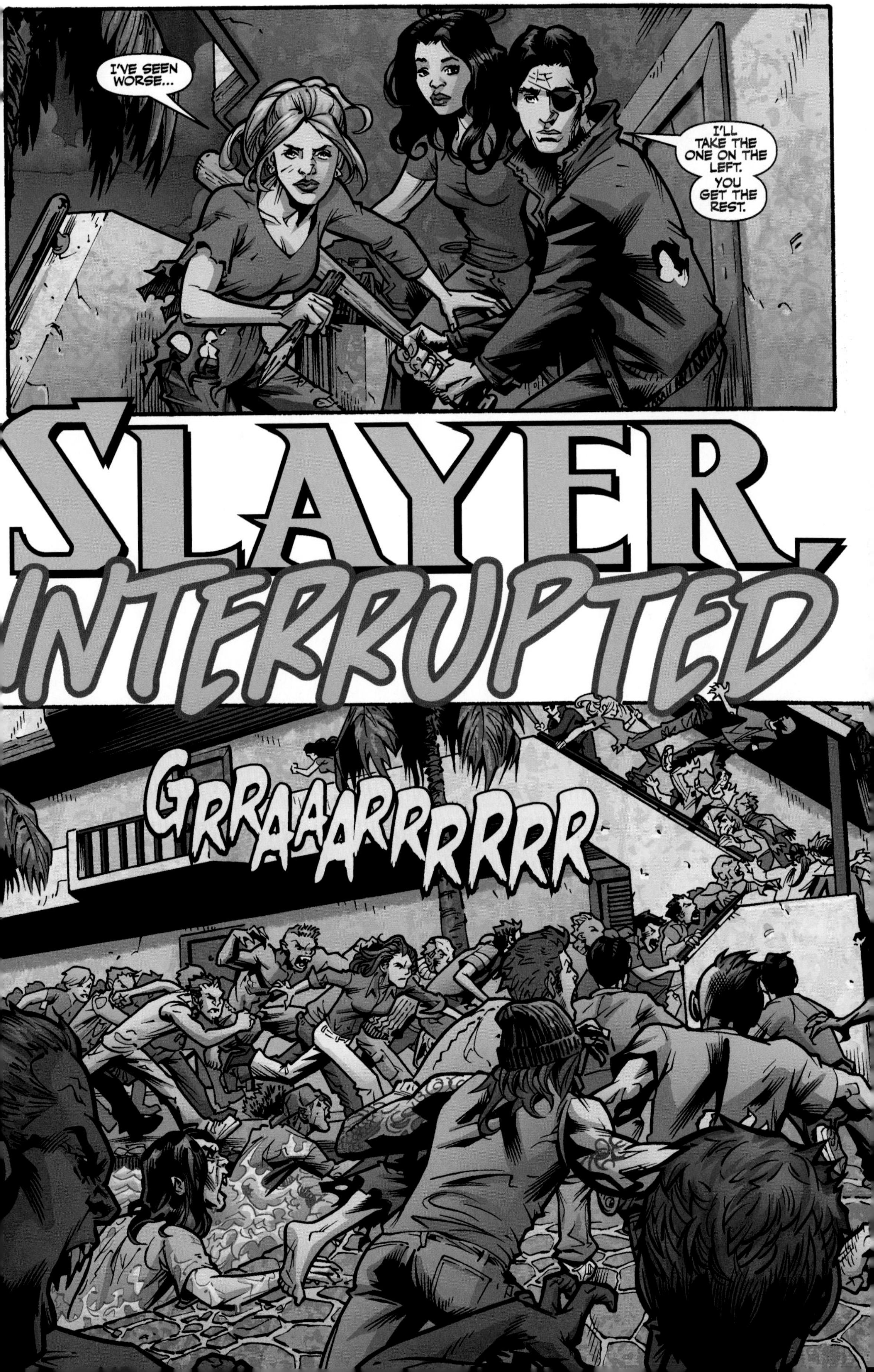
I'VE SEEN WORSE...
I'LL TAKE THE ONE ON THE LEFT. YOU GET THE REST.
SLAYER, INTERRUPTED
GRRAAARRRRRR

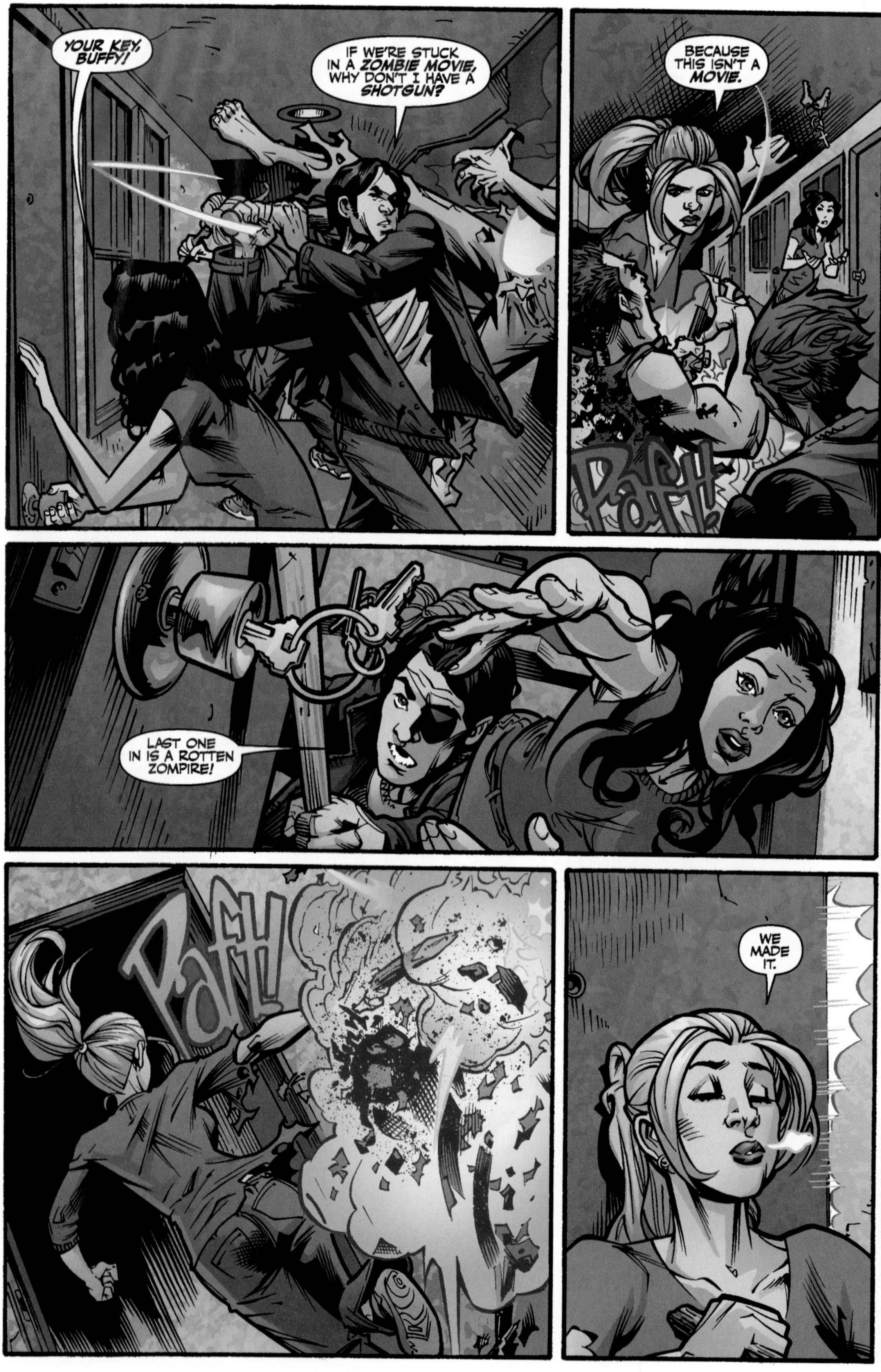
YOUR KEY, BUFFY!
IF WE'RE STUCK IN A ZOMBIE MOVIE, WHY DON'T I HAVE A SHOTGUN?
BECAUSE THIS ISN'T A MOVIE.
LAST ONE IN IS A ROTTEN ZOMPIRE!
WE MADE IT.

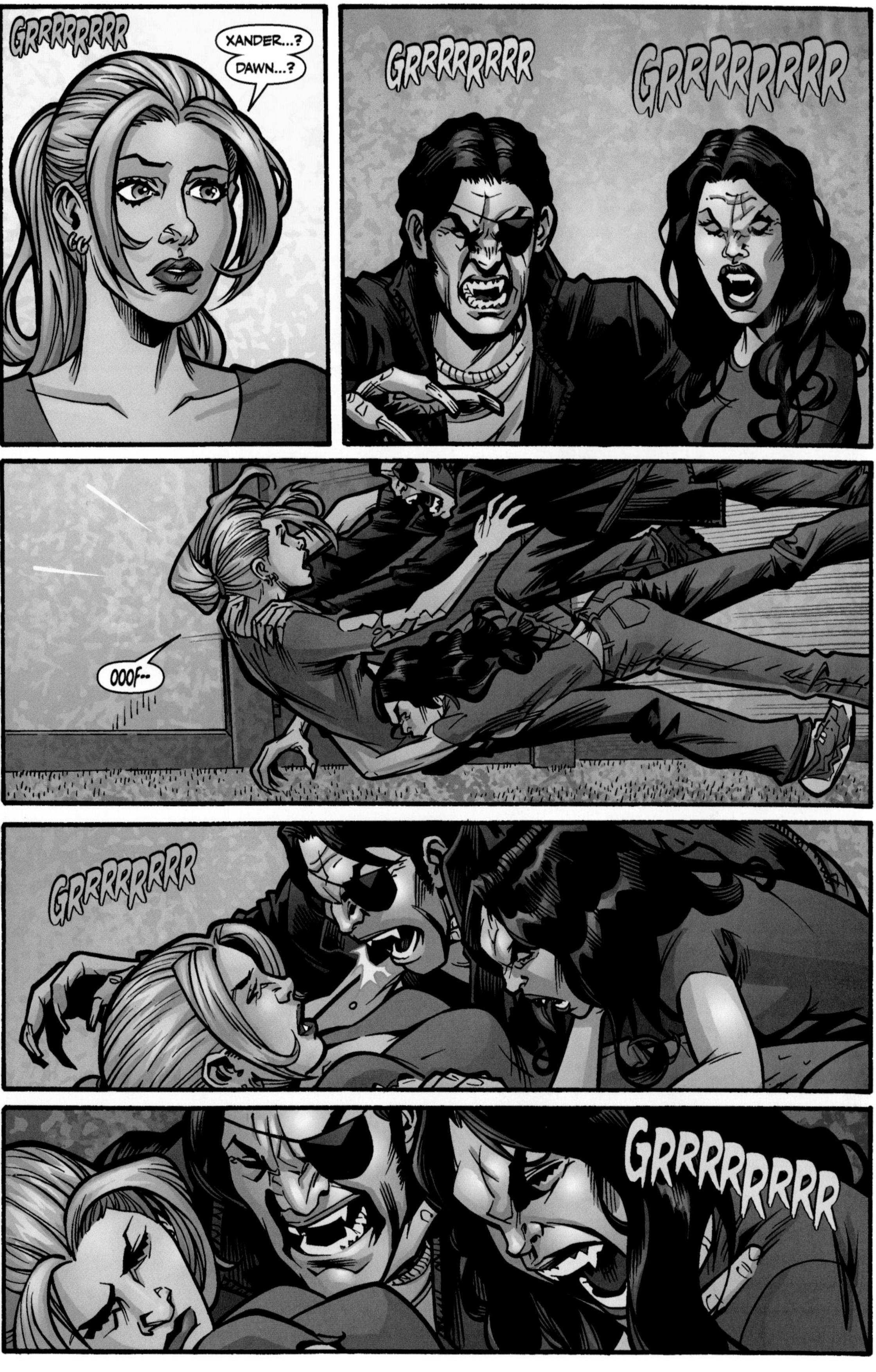
GRRRRRRRR
XANDER...?
DAWN...?
GRRRRRRRR
GRRRRRRRR
OOOF--
GRRRRRRRR
GRRRRRRRR

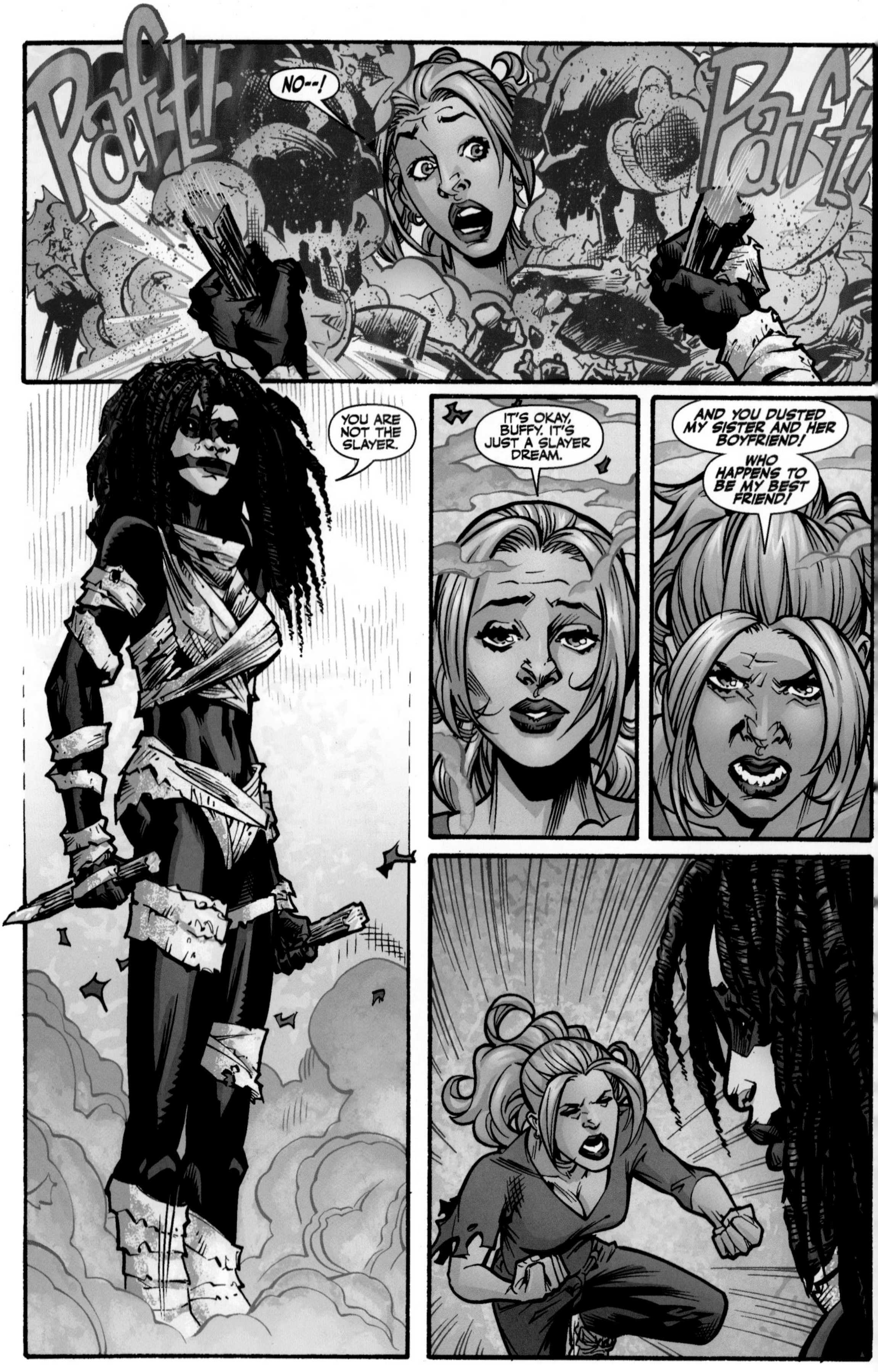
Paft!
NO--!
Paft!
YOU ARE NOT THE SLAYER.
IT'S OKAY, BUFFY. IT'S JUST A SLAYER DREAM.
AND YOU DUSTED MY SISTER AND HER BOYFRIEND!
WHO HAPPENS TO BE MY BEST FRIEND!

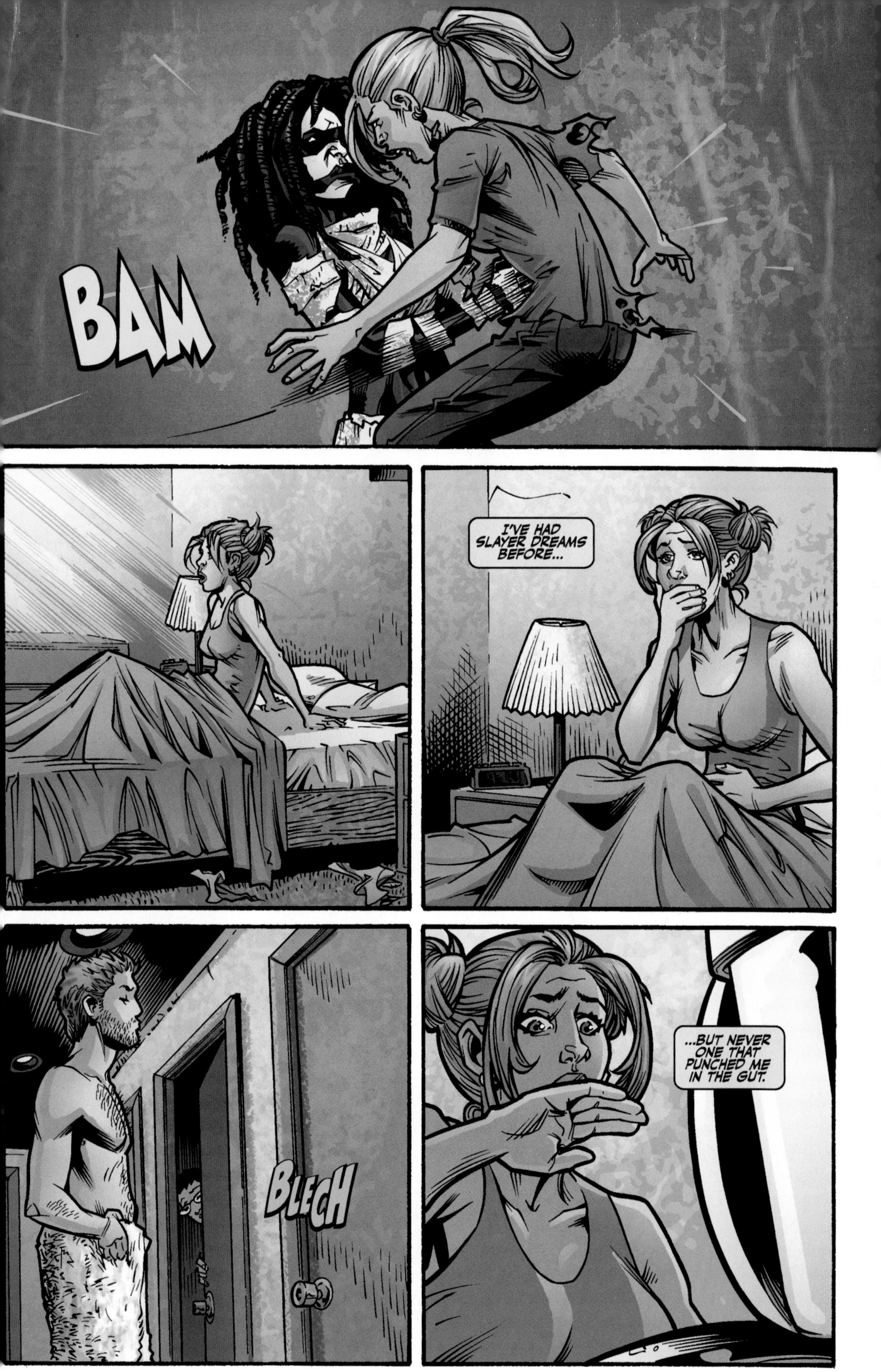
BAM
I'VE HAD SLAYER DREAMS BEFORE...
BLECH
...BUT NEVER ONE THAT PUNCHED ME IN THE GUT.

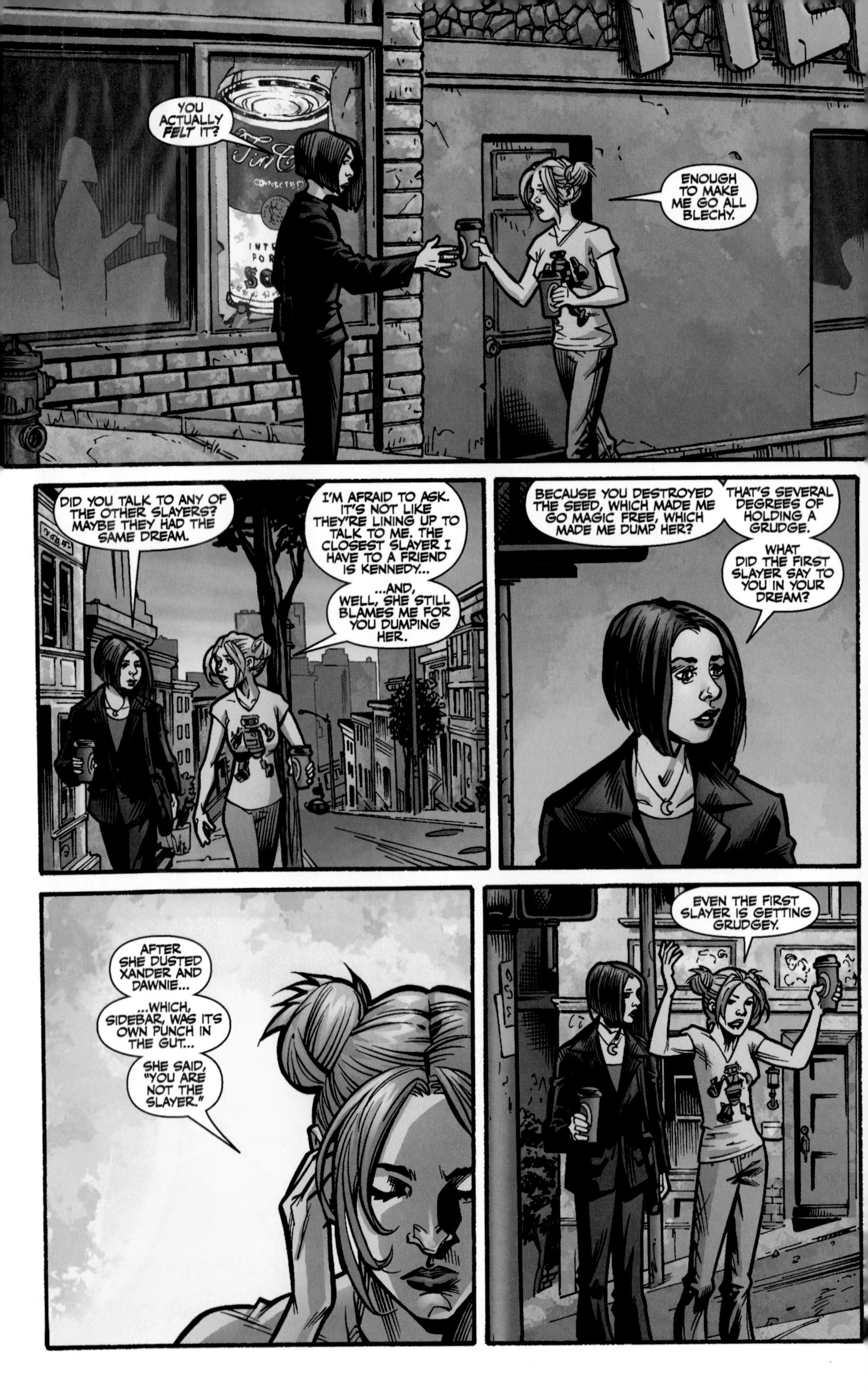
YOU ACTUALLY *FELT* IT?
ENOUGH TO MAKE ME GO ALL BLECHY.
DID YOU TALK TO ANY OF THE OTHER SLAYERS? MAYBE THEY HAD THE SAME DREAM.
I'M AFRAID TO ASK. IT'S NOT LIKE THEY'RE LINING UP TO TALK TO ME. THE CLOSEST SLAYER I HAVE TO A FRIEND IS KENNEDY...
...AND, WELL, SHE STILL BLAMES ME FOR YOU DUMPING HER.
BECAUSE YOU DESTROYED THE SEED, WHICH MADE ME GO MAGIC FREE, WHICH MADE ME DUMP HER?
THAT'S SEVERAL DEGREES OF HOLDING A GRUDGE.
WHAT DID THE FIRST SLAYER SAY TO YOU IN YOUR DREAM?
AFTER SHE DUSTED XANDER AND DAWNIE...
...WHICH, SIDEBAR, WAS ITS OWN PUNCH IN THE GUT...
SHE SAID, "YOU ARE NOT THE SLAYER."
EVEN THE FIRST SLAYER IS GETTING GRUDGEY.

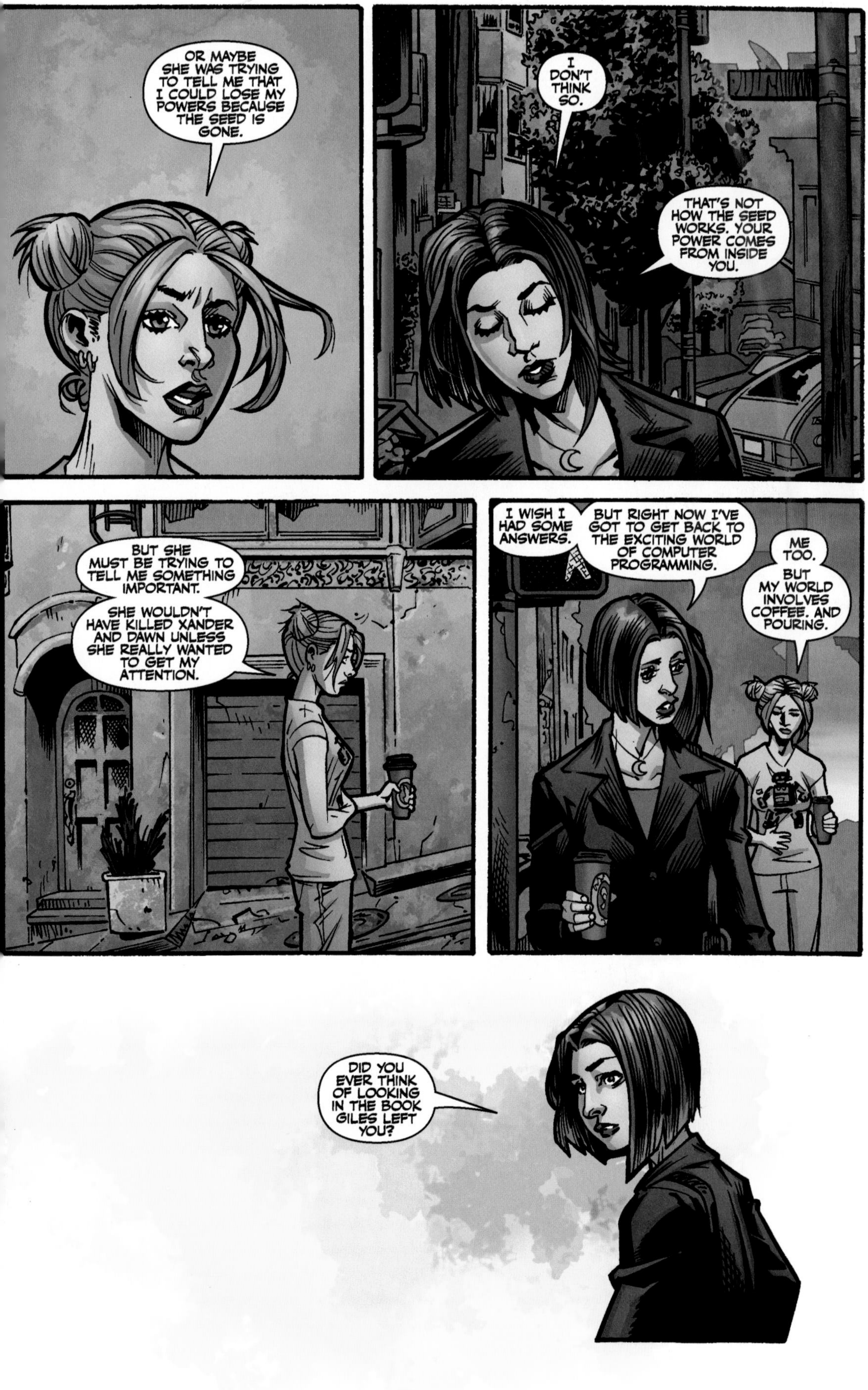
OR MAYBE SHE WAS TRYING TO TELL ME THAT I COULD LOSE MY POWERS BECAUSE THE SEED IS GONE.
I DON'T THINK SO.
THAT'S NOT HOW THE SEED WORKS. YOUR POWER COMES FROM INSIDE YOU.
BUT SHE MUST BE TRYING TO TELL ME SOMETHING IMPORTANT.
SHE WOULDN'T HAVE KILLED XANDER AND DAWN UNLESS SHE REALLY WANTED TO GET MY ATTENTION.
I WISH I HAD SOME ANSWERS.
BUT RIGHT NOW I'VE GOT TO GET BACK TO THE EXCITING WORLD OF COMPUTER PROGRAMMING.
ME TOO.
BUT MY WORLD INVOLVES COFFEE. AND POURING.
DID YOU EVER THINK OF LOOKING IN THE BOOK GILES LEFT YOU?

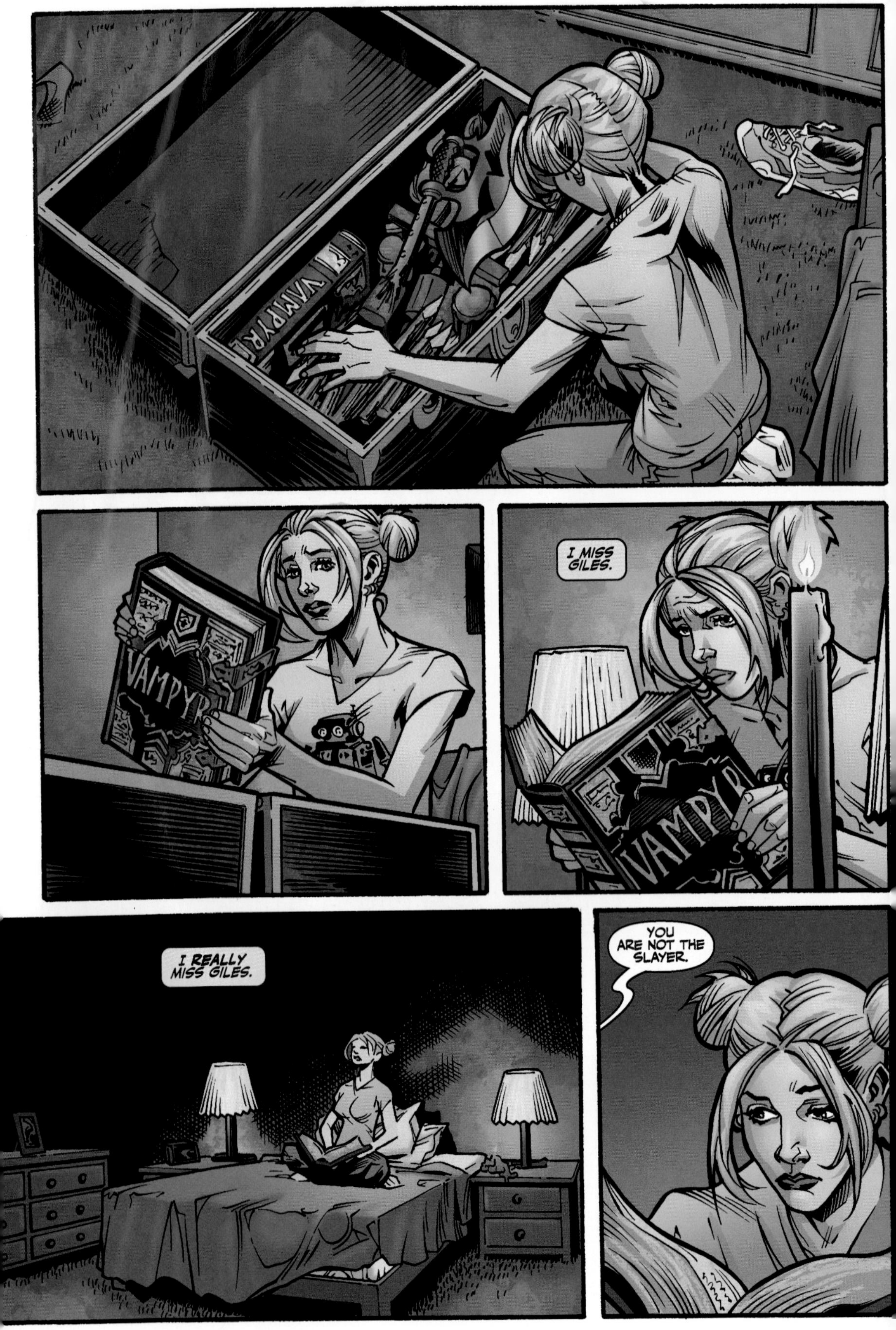
VAMPYR
I MISS GILES.
I REALLY MISS GILES.
YOU ARE NOT THE SLAYER.

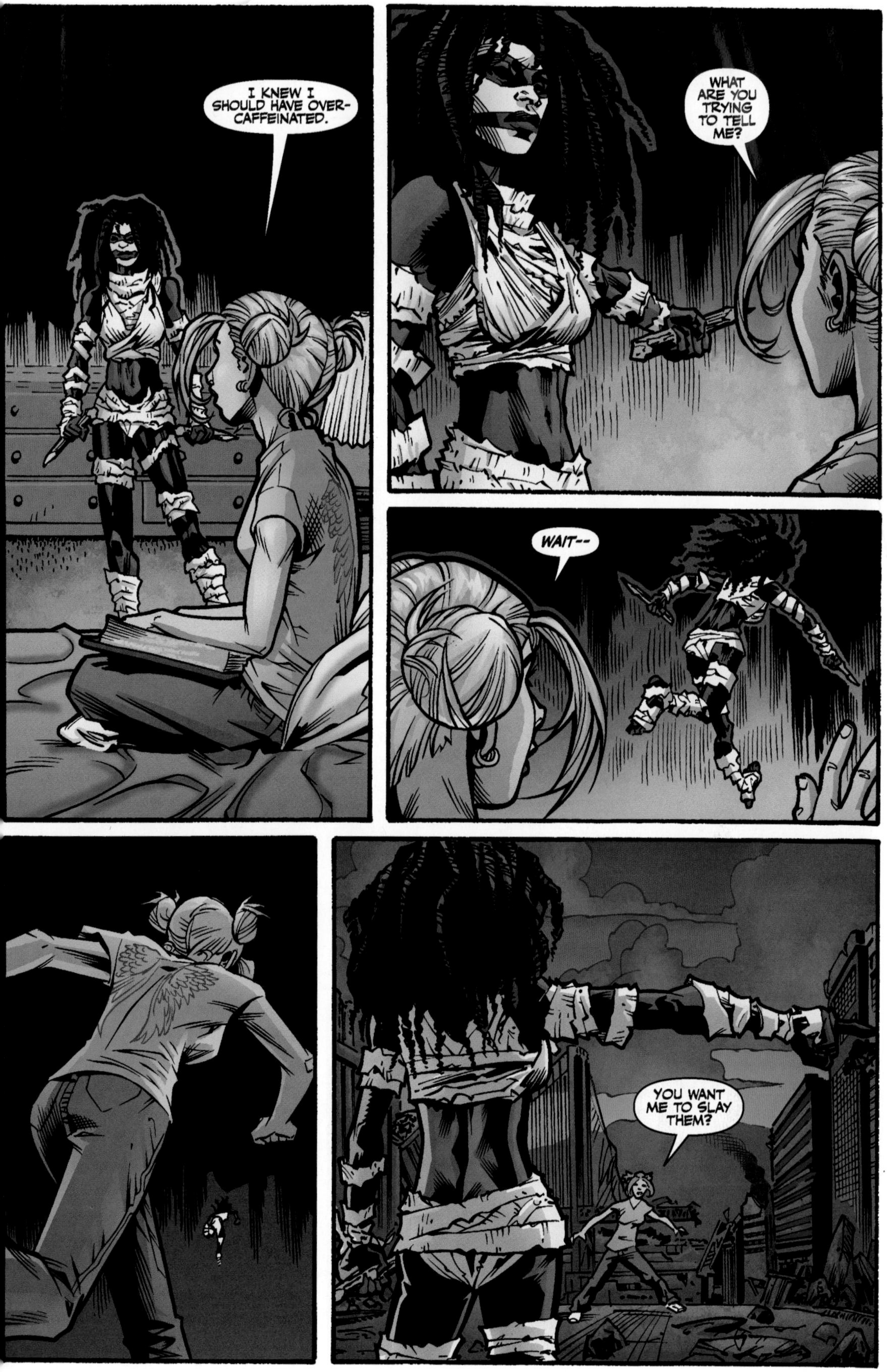
I KNEW I SHOULD HAVE OVER-CAFFEINATED.
WHAT ARE YOU TRYING TO TELL ME?
WAIT--
YOU WANT ME TO SLAY THEM?

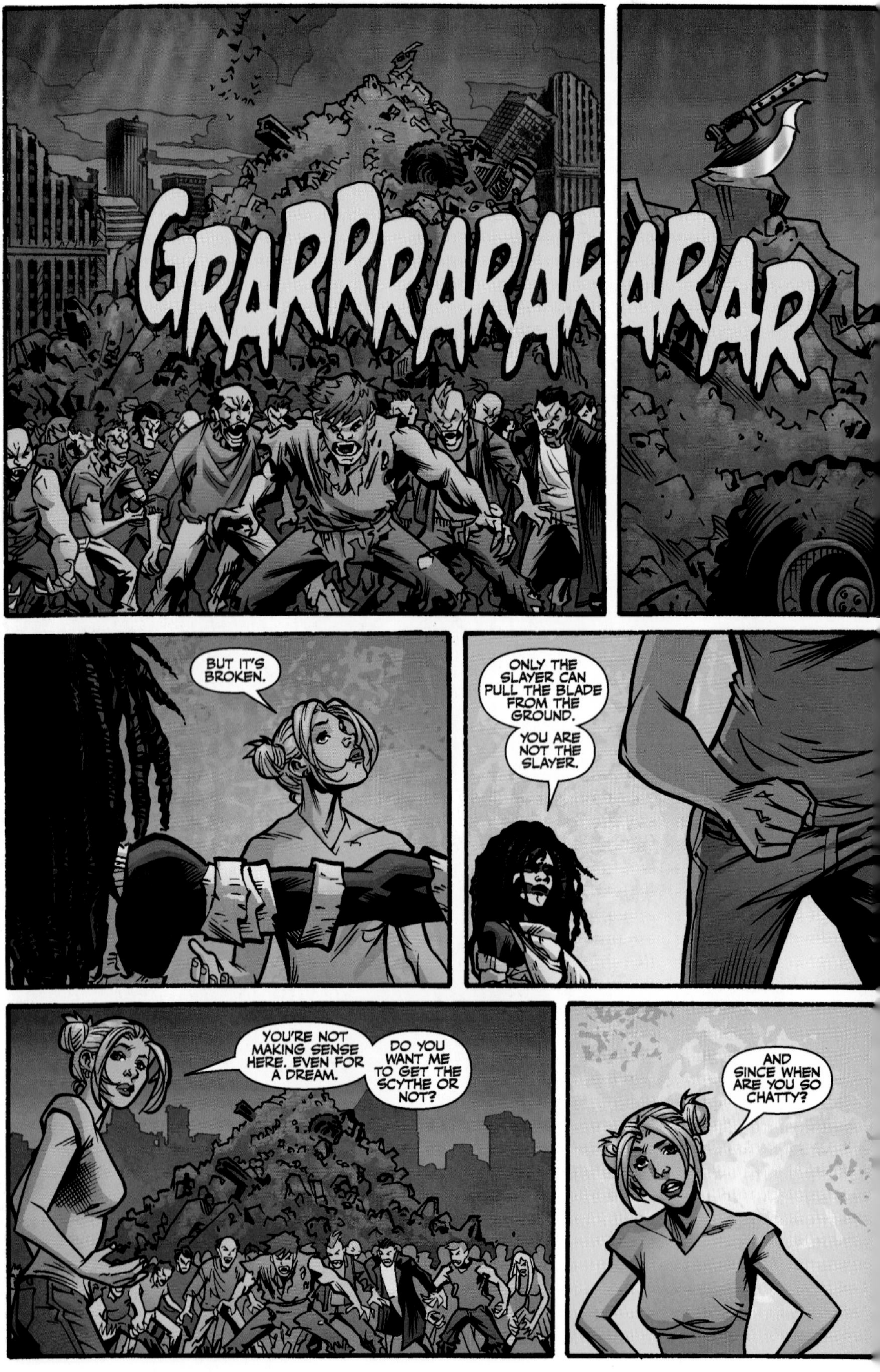
GRARRRARARARAR
BUT IT'S BROKEN.
ONLY THE SLAYER CAN PULL THE BLADE FROM THE GROUND.
YOU ARE NOT THE SLAYER.
YOU'RE NOT MAKING SENSE HERE. EVEN FOR A DREAM.
DO YOU WANT ME TO GET THE SCYTHE OR NOT?
AND SINCE WHEN ARE YOU SO CHATTY?

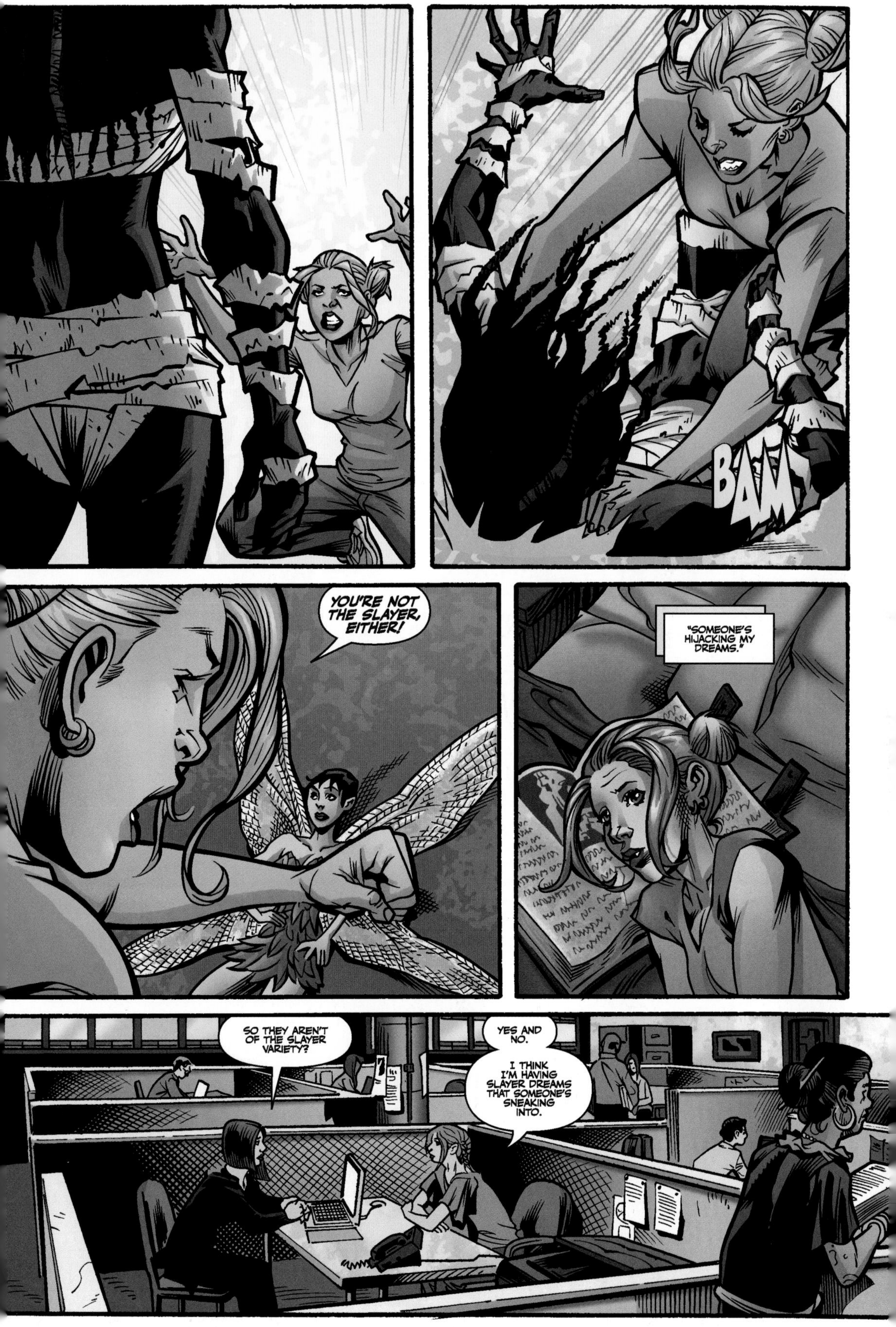
BAM
YOU'RE NOT THE SLAYER, EITHER!
"SOMEONE'S HIJACKING MY DREAMS."
SO THEY AREN'T OF THE SLAYER VARIETY?
YES AND NO.
I THINK I'M HAVING SLAYER DREAMS THAT SOMEONE'S SNEAKING INTO.

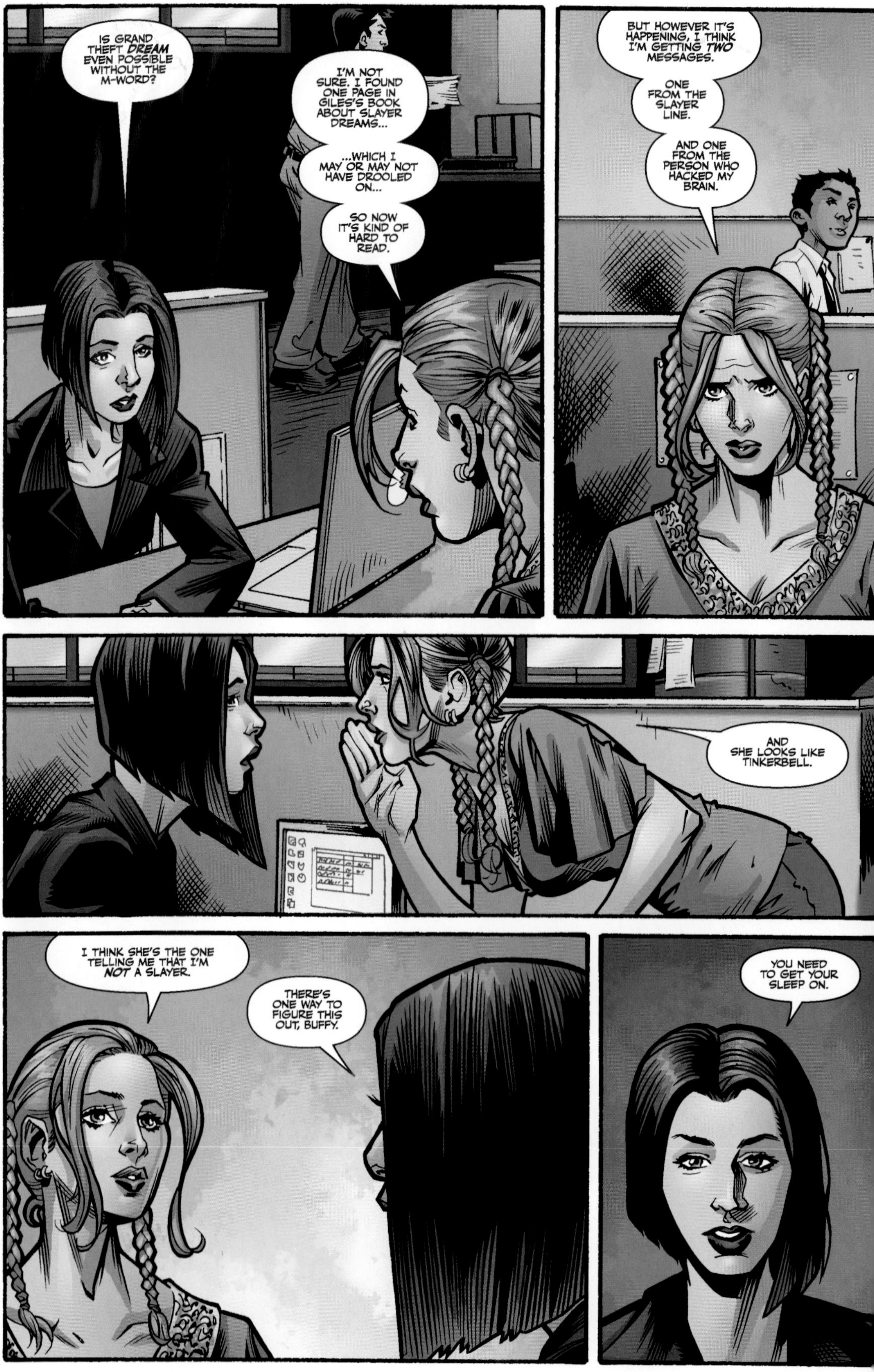
IS GRAND THEFT DREAM EVEN POSSIBLE WITHOUT THE M-WORD?
I'M NOT SURE. I FOUND ONE PAGE IN GILES'S BOOK ABOUT SLAYER DREAMS...
...WHICH I MAY OR MAY NOT HAVE DROOLED ON...
SO NOW IT'S KIND OF HARD TO READ.
BUT HOWEVER IT'S HAPPENING, I THINK I'M GETTING TWO MESSAGES.
ONE FROM THE SLAYER LINE.
AND ONE FROM THE PERSON WHO HACKED MY BRAIN.
AND SHE LOOKS LIKE TINKERBELL.
I THINK SHE'S THE ONE TELLING ME THAT I'M NOT A SLAYER.
THERE'S ONE WAY TO FIGURE THIS OUT, BUFFY.
YOU NEED TO GET YOUR SLEEP ON.

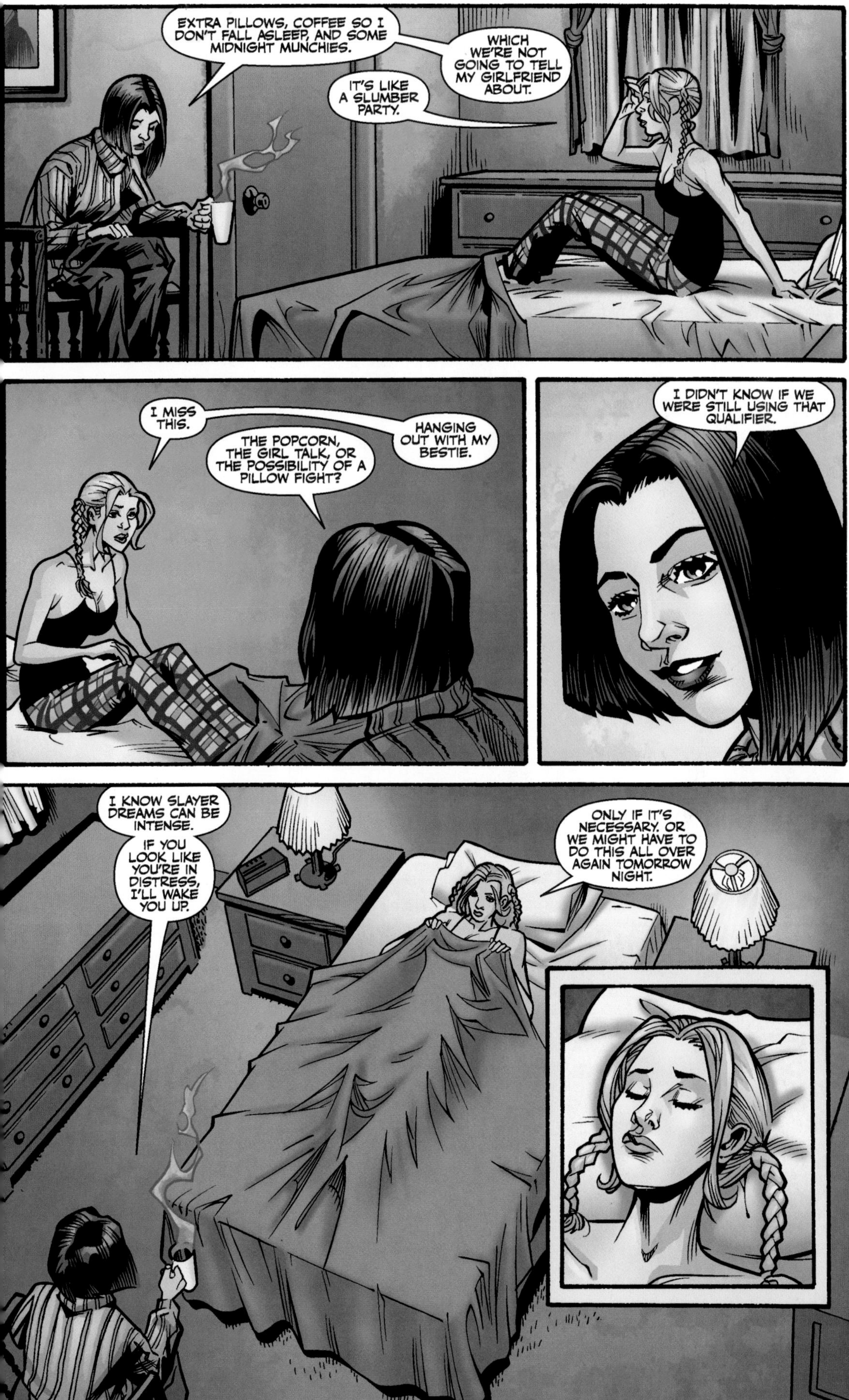
EXTRA PILLOWS, COFFEE SO I DON'T FALL ASLEEP, AND SOME MIDNIGHT MUNCHIES.
IT'S LIKE A SLUMBER PARTY.
WHICH WE'RE NOT GOING TO TELL MY GIRLFRIEND ABOUT.
I MISS THIS.
THE POPCORN, THE GIRL TALK, OR THE POSSIBILITY OF A PILLOW FIGHT?
HANGING OUT WITH MY BESTIE.
I DIDN'T KNOW IF WE WERE STILL USING THAT QUALIFIER.
I KNOW SLAYER DREAMS CAN BE INTENSE.
IF YOU LOOK LIKE YOU'RE IN DISTRESS, I'LL WAKE YOU UP.
ONLY IF IT'S NECESSARY. OR WE MIGHT HAVE TO DO THIS ALL OVER AGAIN TOMORROW NIGHT.

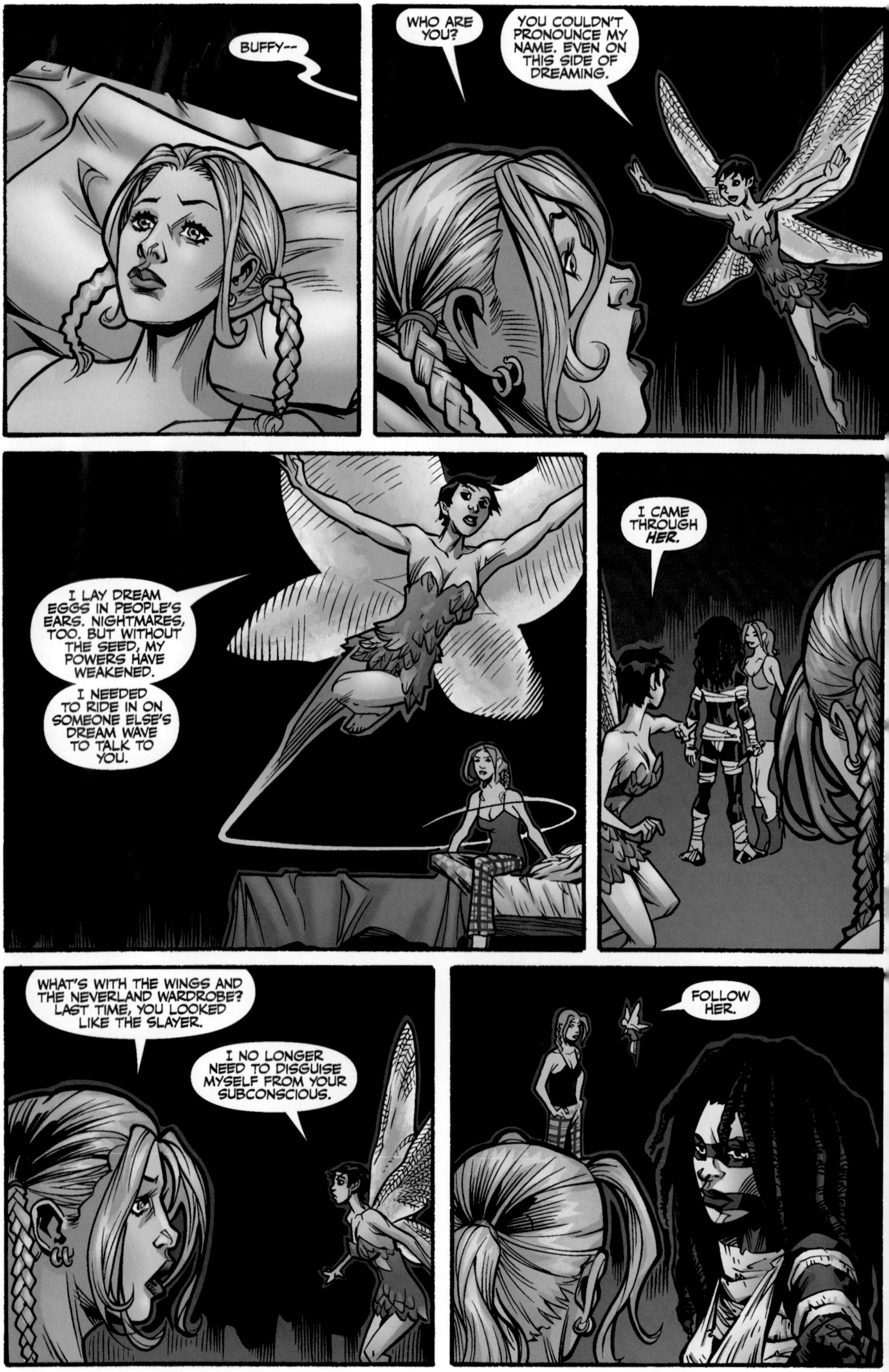
BUFFY--
WHO ARE YOU?
YOU COULDN'T PRONOUNCE MY NAME. EVEN ON THIS SIDE OF DREAMING.
I LAY DREAM EGGS IN PEOPLE'S EARS. NIGHTMARES, TOO. BUT WITHOUT THE SEED, MY POWERS HAVE WEAKENED.
I NEEDED TO RIDE IN ON SOMEONE ELSE'S DREAM WAVE TO TALK TO YOU.
I CAME THROUGH *HER*.
WHAT'S WITH THE WINGS AND THE NEVERLAND WARDROBE? LAST TIME, YOU LOOKED LIKE THE SLAYER.
I NO LONGER NEED TO DISGUISE MYSELF FROM YOUR SUBCONSCIOUS.
FOLLOW HER.

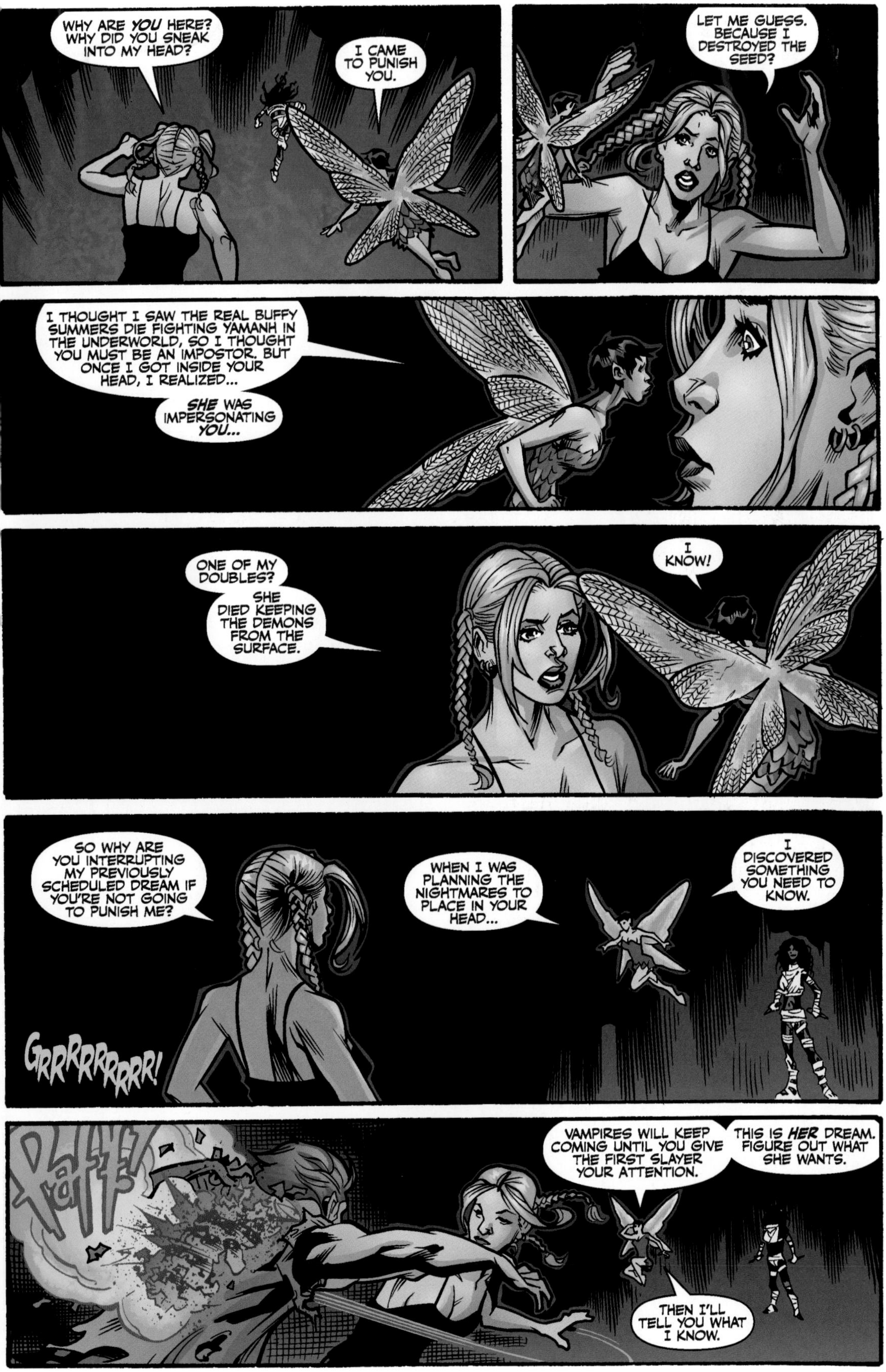

WHY ARE YOU HERE? WHY DID YOU SNEAK INTO MY HEAD?
I CAME TO PUNISH YOU.
LET ME GUESS. BECAUSE I DESTROYED THE SEED?
I THOUGHT I SAW THE REAL BUFFY SUMMERS DIE FIGHTING YAMANH IN THE UNDERWORLD, SO I THOUGHT YOU MUST BE AN IMPOSTOR. BUT ONCE I GOT INSIDE YOUR HEAD, I REALIZED...
SHE WAS IMPERSONATING YOU...
ONE OF MY DOUBLES?
SHE DIED KEEPING THE DEMONS FROM THE SURFACE.
I KNOW!
SO WHY ARE YOU INTERRUPTING MY PREVIOUSLY SCHEDULED DREAM IF YOU'RE NOT GOING TO PUNISH ME?
WHEN I WAS PLANNING THE NIGHTMARES TO PLACE IN YOUR HEAD...
I DISCOVERED SOMETHING YOU NEED TO KNOW.
GRRRRRRRRR!
VAMPIRES WILL KEEP COMING UNTIL YOU GIVE THE FIRST SLAYER YOUR ATTENTION.
THIS IS HER DREAM. FIGURE OUT WHAT SHE WANTS.
THEN I'LL TELL YOU WHAT I KNOW.

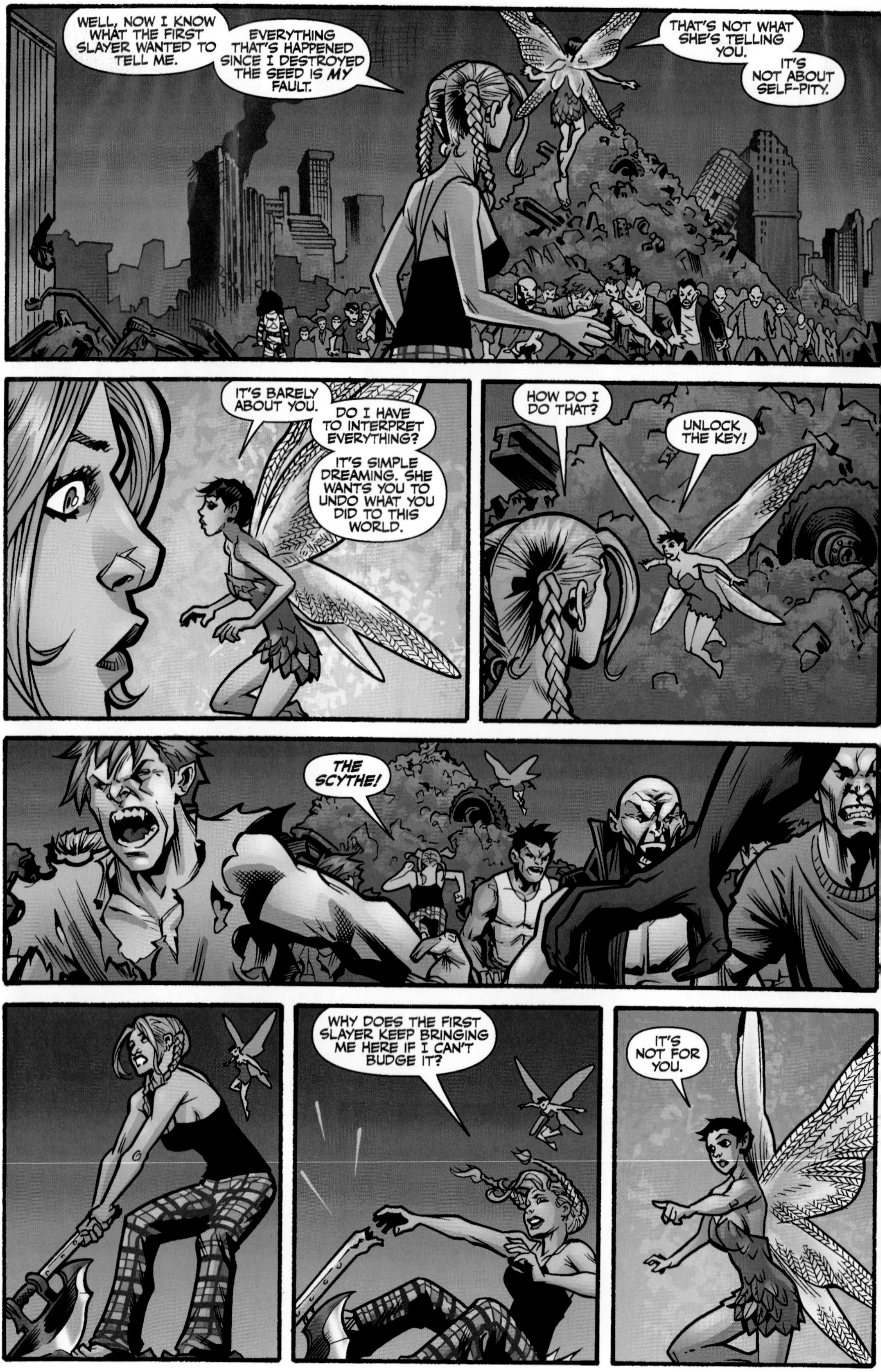
WELL, NOW I KNOW WHAT THE FIRST SLAYER WANTED TO TELL ME.
EVERYTHING THAT'S HAPPENED SINCE I DESTROYED THE SEED IS *MY* FAULT.
THAT'S NOT WHAT SHE'S TELLING YOU.
IT'S NOT ABOUT SELF-PITY.
IT'S BARELY ABOUT YOU.
DO I HAVE TO INTERPRET EVERYTHING?
IT'S SIMPLE DREAMING. SHE WANTS YOU TO UNDO WHAT YOU DID TO THIS WORLD.
HOW DO I DO THAT?
UNLOCK THE KEY!
THE SCYTHE!
WHY DOES THE FIRST SLAYER KEEP BRINGING ME HERE IF I CAN'T BUDGE IT?
IT'S NOT FOR YOU.

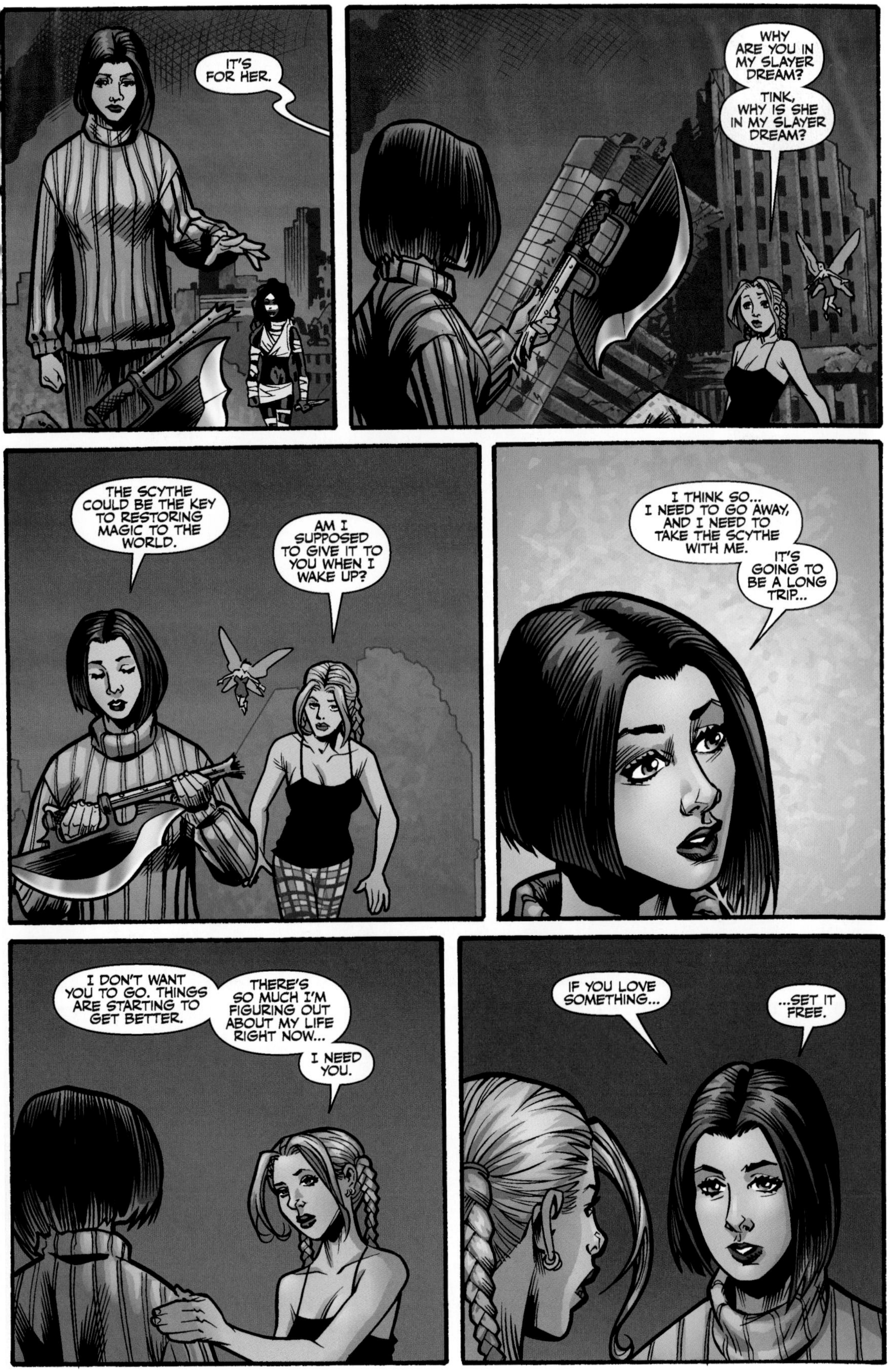
IT'S FOR HER.
WHY ARE YOU IN MY SLAYER DREAM?
TINK, WHY IS SHE IN MY SLAYER DREAM?
THE SCYTHE COULD BE THE KEY TO RESTORING MAGIC TO THE WORLD.
AM I SUPPOSED TO GIVE IT TO YOU WHEN I WAKE UP?
I THINK SO... I NEED TO GO AWAY, AND I NEED TO TAKE THE SCYTHE WITH ME.
IT'S GOING TO BE A LONG TRIP...
I DON'T WANT YOU TO GO. THINGS ARE STARTING TO GET BETTER.
THERE'S SO MUCH I'M FIGURING OUT ABOUT MY LIFE RIGHT NOW...
I NEED YOU.
IF YOU LOVE SOMETHING...
...SET IT FREE.

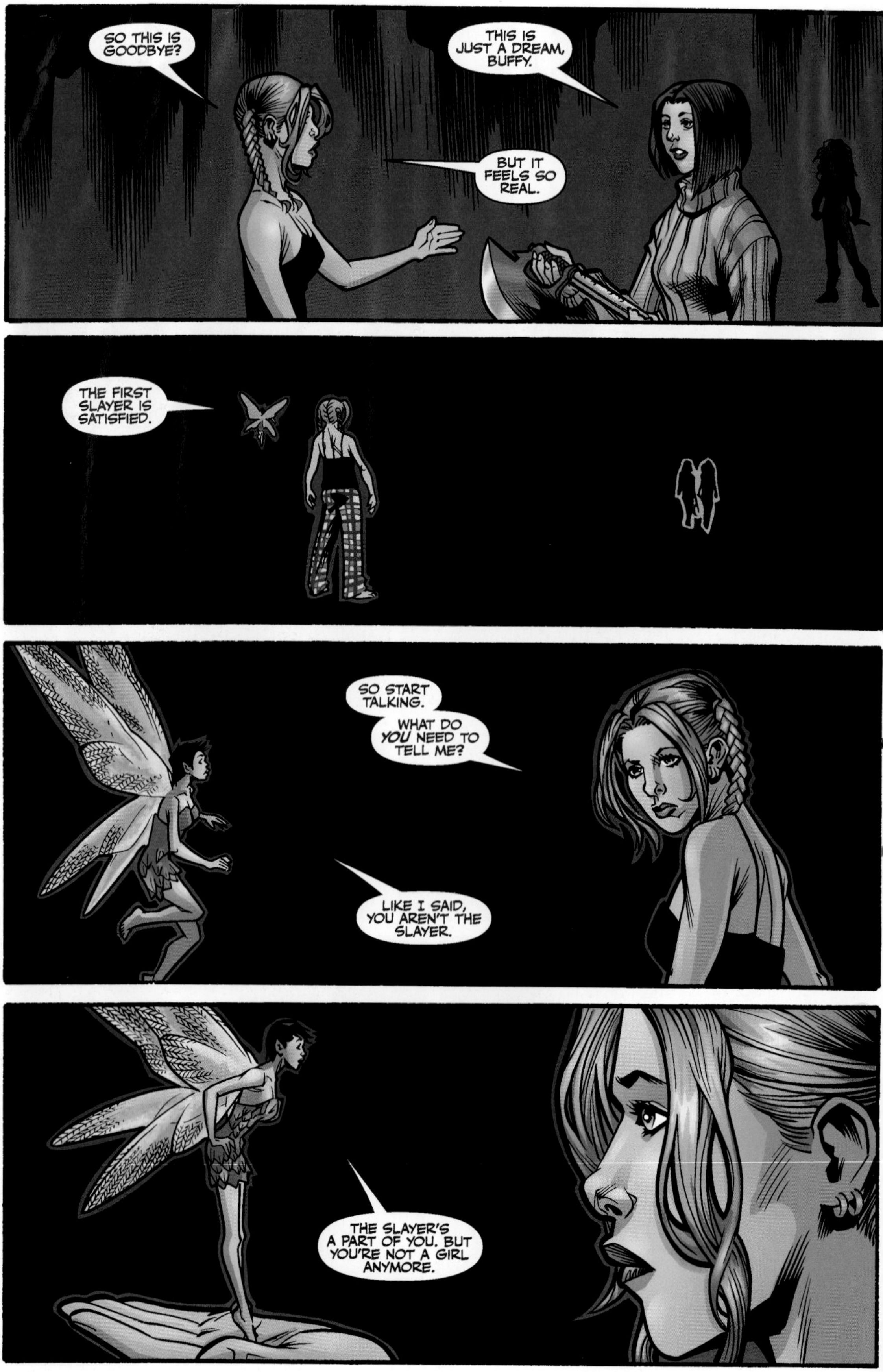
SO THIS IS GOODBYE?
THIS IS JUST A DREAM, BUFFY.
BUT IT FEELS SO REAL.
THE FIRST SLAYER IS SATISFIED.
SO START TALKING.
WHAT DO *YOU* NEED TO TELL ME?
LIKE I SAID, YOU AREN'T THE SLAYER.
THE SLAYER'S A PART OF YOU. BUT YOU'RE NOT A GIRL ANYMORE.

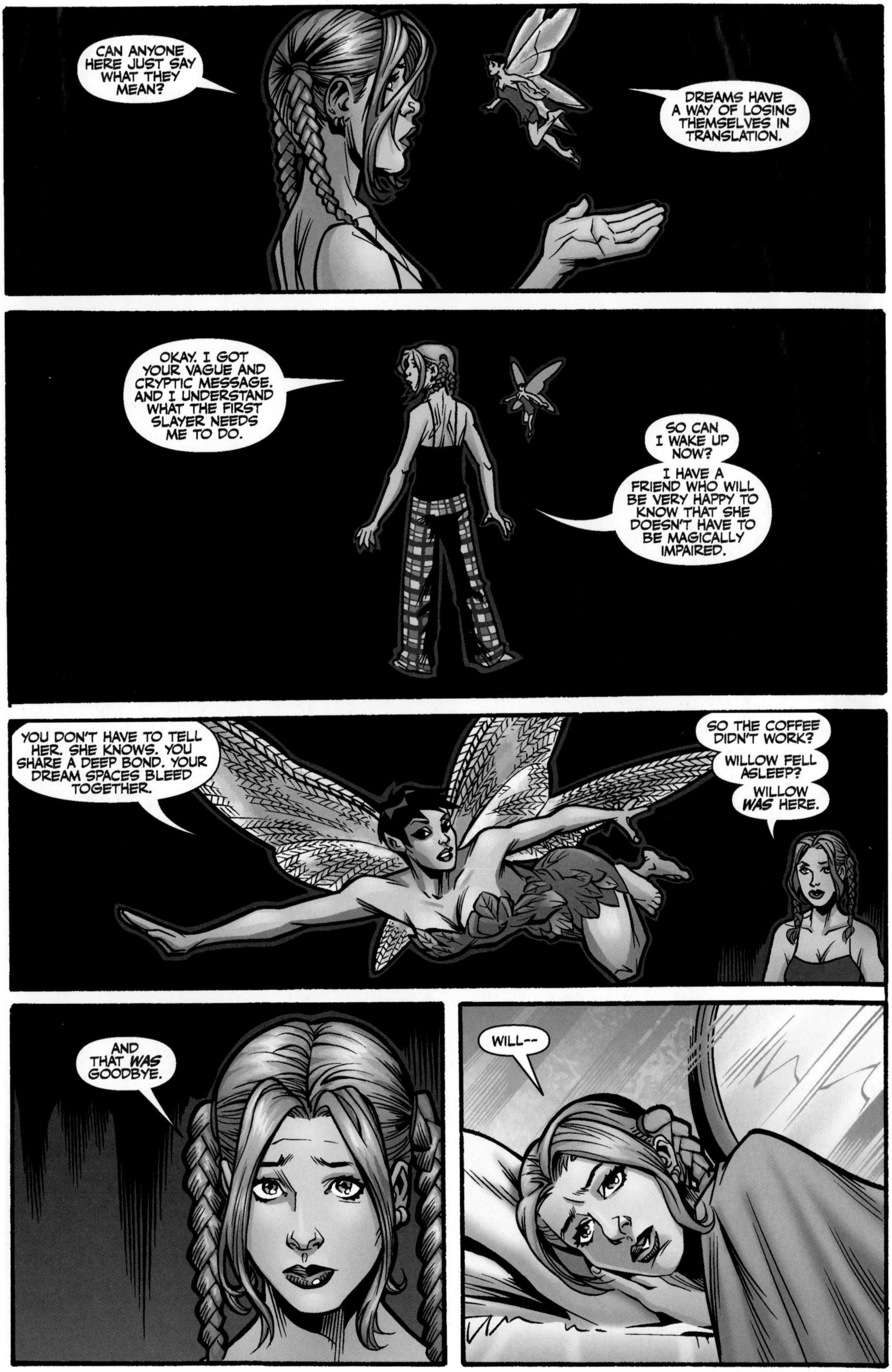
CAN ANYONE HERE JUST SAY WHAT THEY MEAN?
DREAMS HAVE A WAY OF LOSING THEMSELVES IN TRANSLATION.
OKAY. I GOT YOUR VAGUE AND CRYPTIC MESSAGE. AND I UNDERSTAND WHAT THE FIRST SLAYER NEEDS ME TO DO.
SO CAN I WAKE UP NOW?
I HAVE A FRIEND WHO WILL BE VERY HAPPY TO KNOW THAT SHE DOESN'T HAVE TO BE MAGICALLY IMPAIRED.
YOU DON'T HAVE TO TELL HER. SHE KNOWS. YOU SHARE A DEEP BOND. YOUR DREAM SPACES BLEED TOGETHER.
SO THE COFFEE DIDN'T WORK?
WILLOW FELL ASLEEP?
WILLOW *WAS* HERE.
AND THAT *WAS* GOODBYE.
WILL--

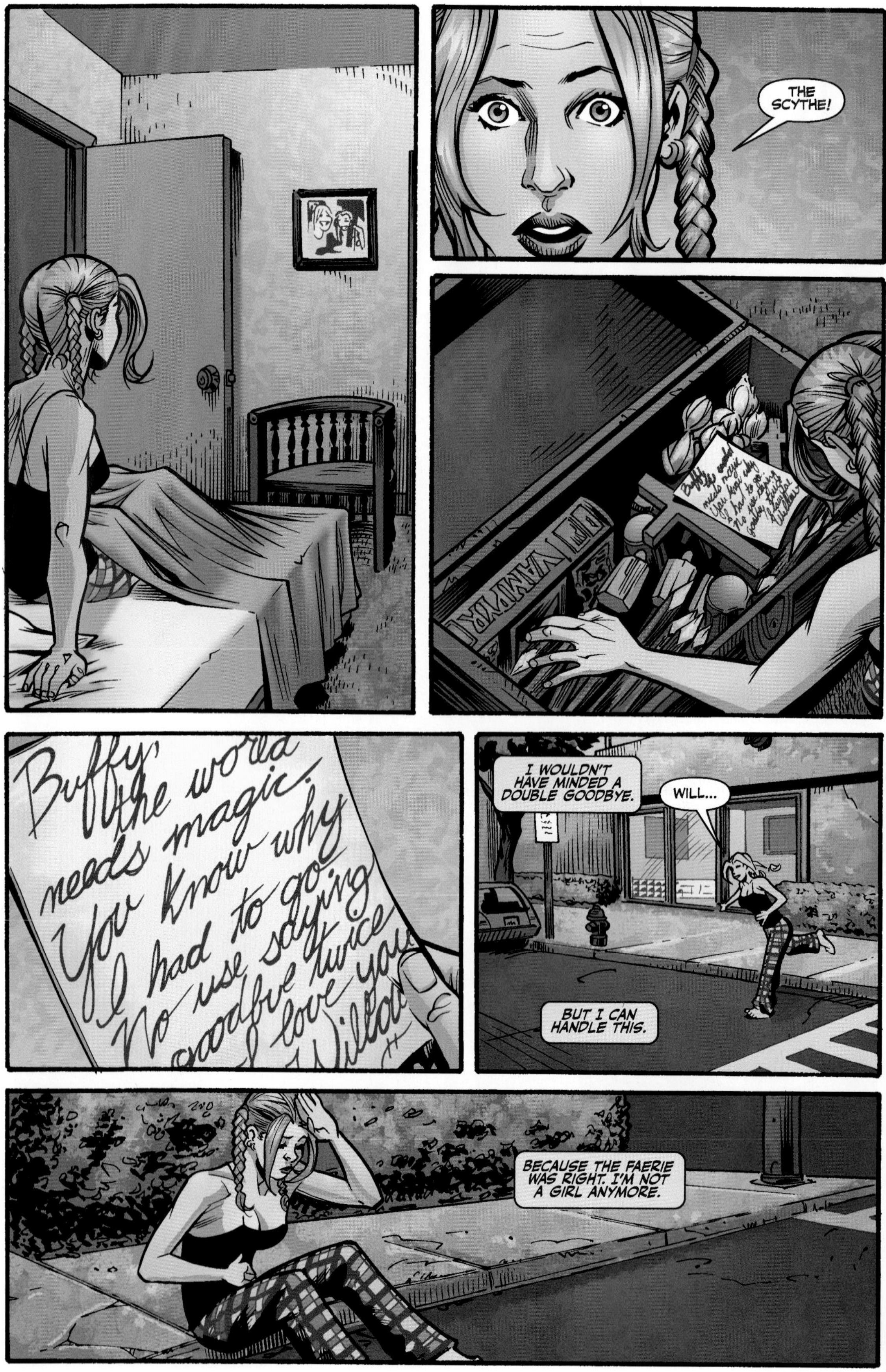
THE SCYTHE!
Buffy,
the world
needs magic.
You know why
I had to go.
No use saying
goodbye twice
I love you
I WOULDN'T HAVE MINDED A DOUBLE GOODBYE.
WILL...
BUT I CAN HANDLE THIS.
BECAUSE THE FAERIE WAS RIGHT. I'M NOT A GIRL ANYMORE.

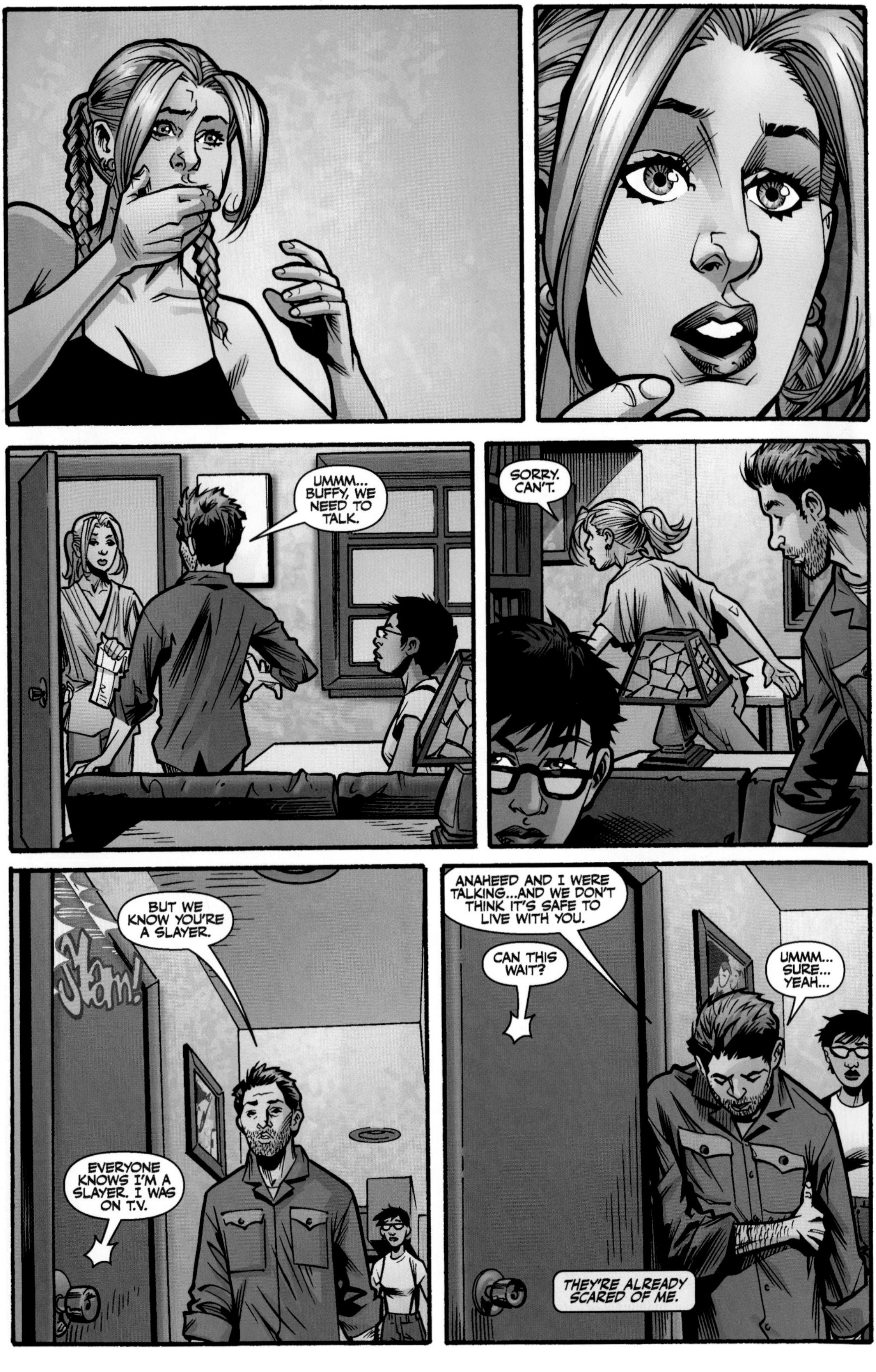
UMMM... BUFFY, WE NEED TO TALK.
SORRY. CAN'T.
BUT WE KNOW YOU'RE A SLAYER.
EVERYONE KNOWS I'M A SLAYER. I WAS ON T.V.
ANAHEED AND I WERE TALKING...AND WE DON'T THINK IT'S SAFE TO LIVE WITH YOU.
CAN THIS WAIT?
UMMM... SURE... YEAH...
THEY'RE ALREADY SCARED OF ME.

BECAUSE I'M A SLAYER.

BUT THAT'S OKAY...

BECAUSE I'M SCARED TOO.

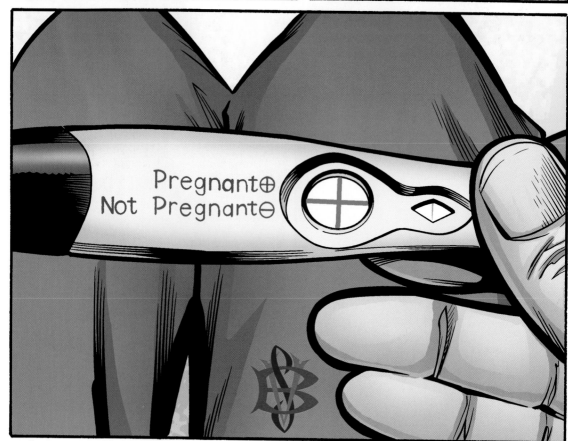

Pregnant ⊕
Not Pregnant ⊖

BUFFY *the* VAMPIRE SLAYER COVER GALLERY *and* SKETCHBOOK

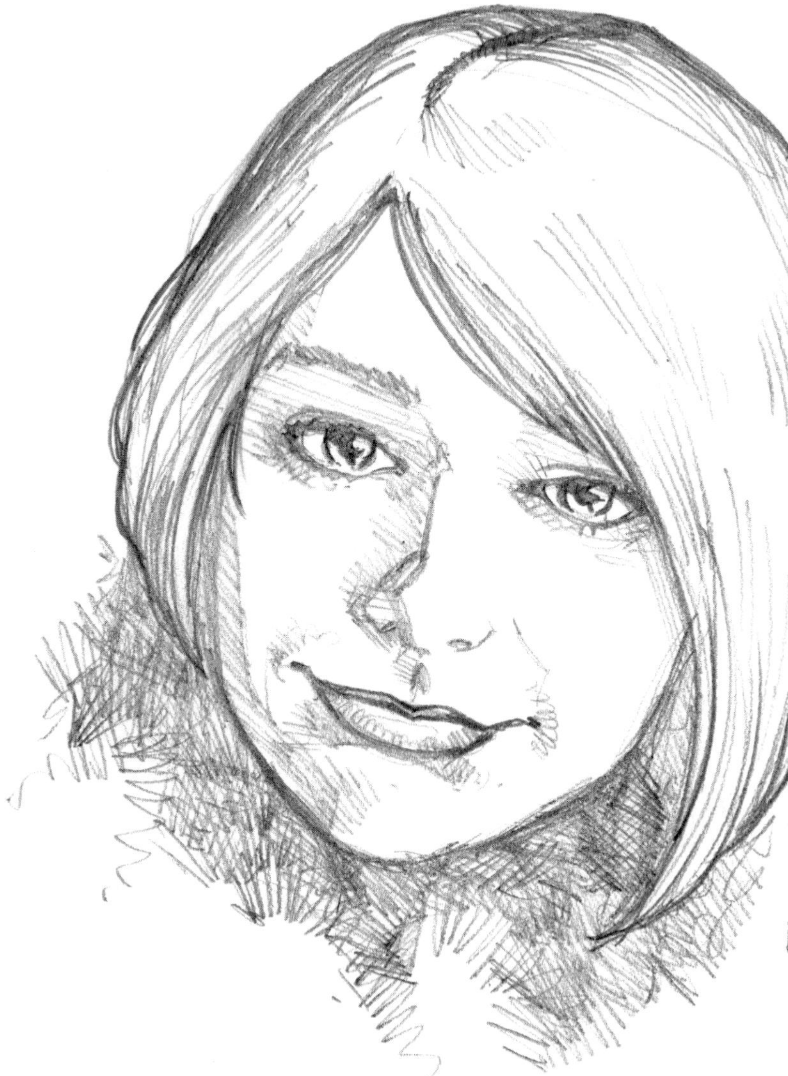

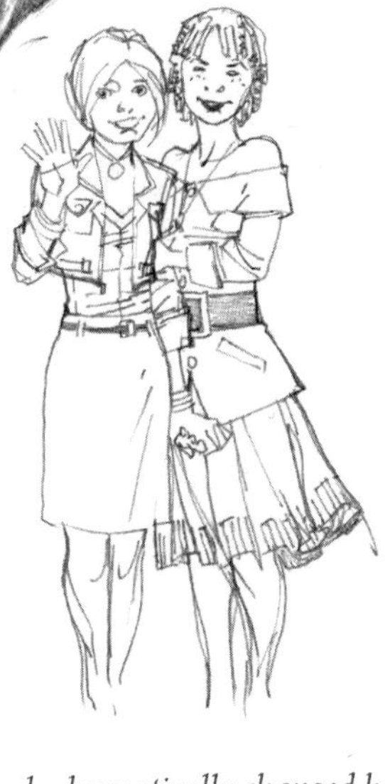

As we started work on Season 9, Joss requested that Willow get a new look. Because she was now living in San Francisco with a fancy new job under her belt, we wanted to see the more cosmopolitan side of Willow.

ABOVE: *Georges gave us several haircut options, and Joss chose the short, uneven style.*

RIGHT: *Willow not only dramatically changed her hair; she also broke up with Kennedy and attached herself to a very tall, very aloof, very bored model.*

FOLLOWING PAGES: *Dark Horse twenty-fifth anniversary special edition cover to Buffy S9 #1 and variant cover to Buffy S9 #2 , both by Georges Jeanty, Dexter Vines, and JD Mettler.*

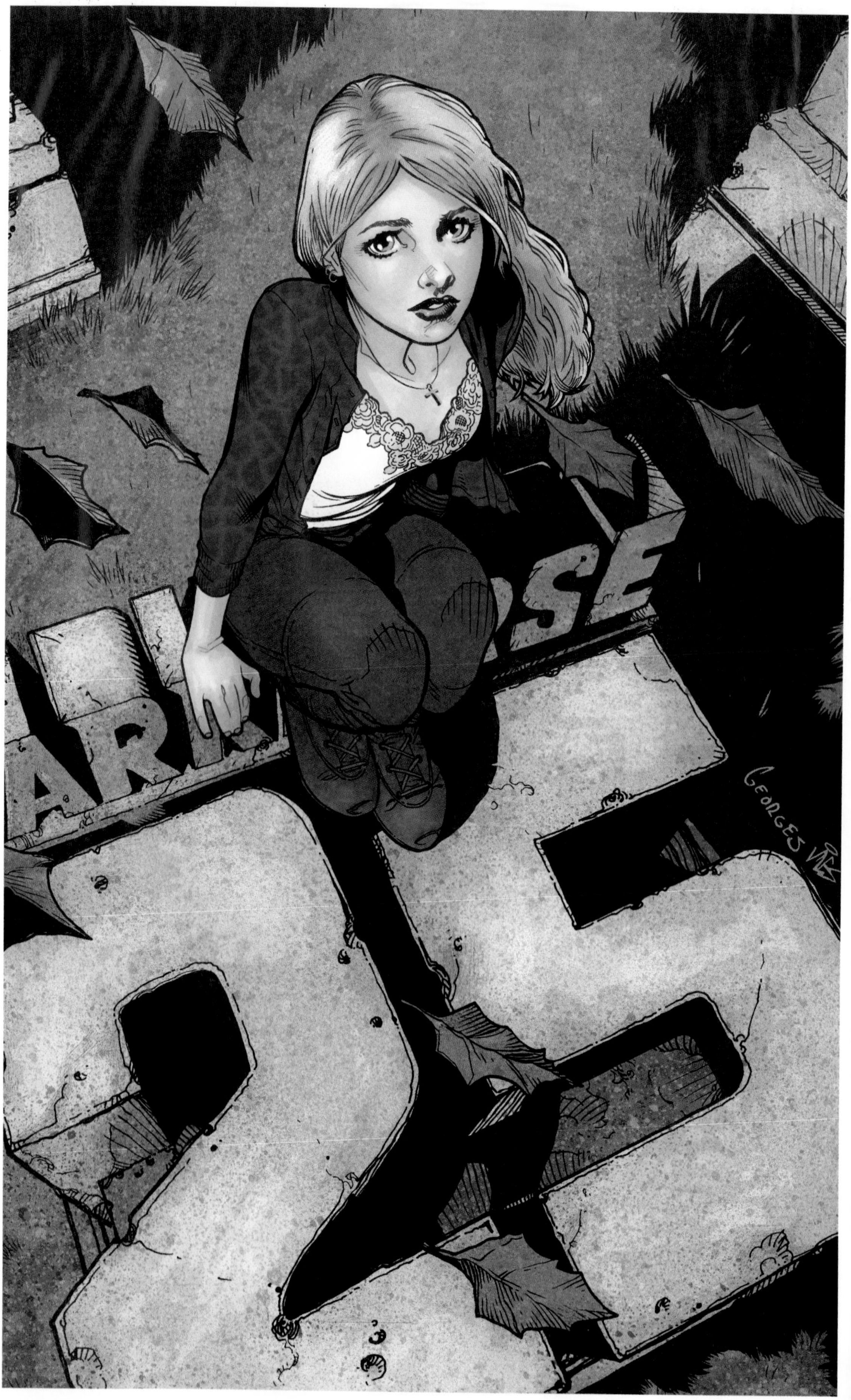
GEORGES

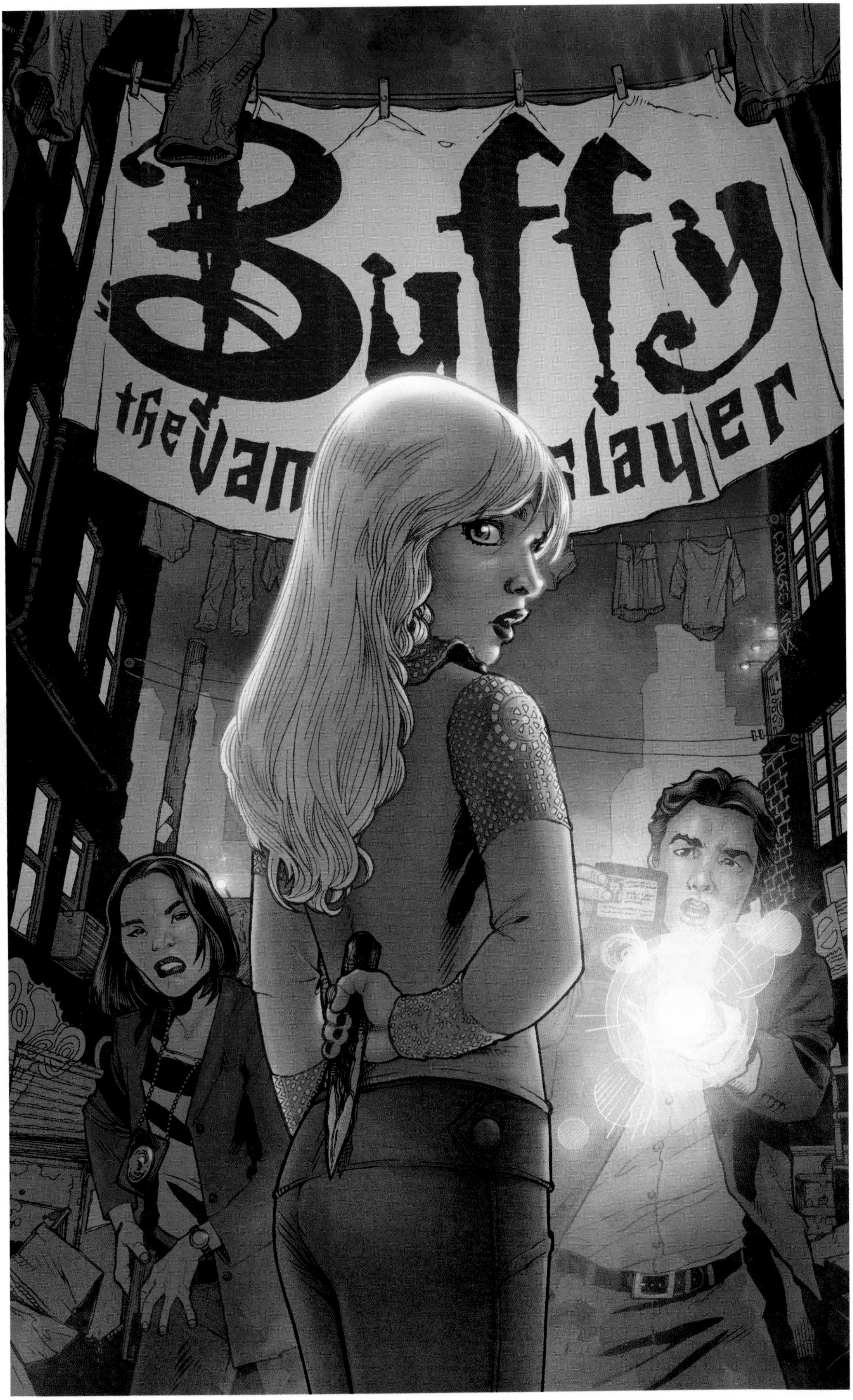
Buffy
the vam
slayer

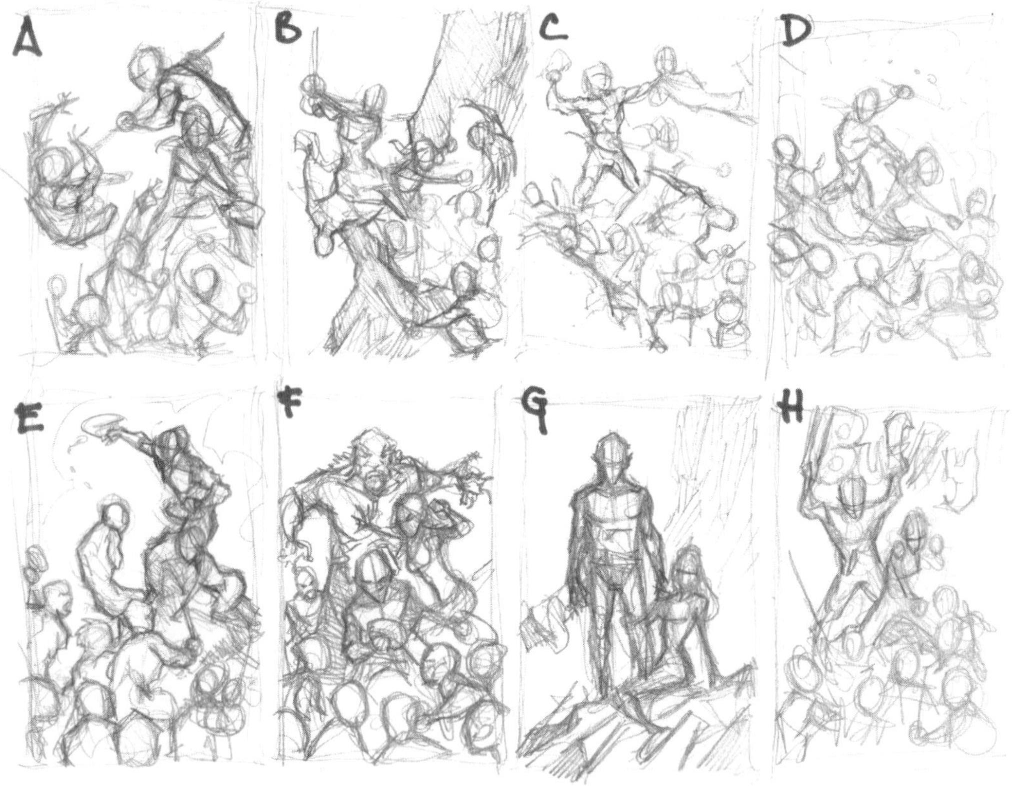
A
B
C
D
E
F
G
H

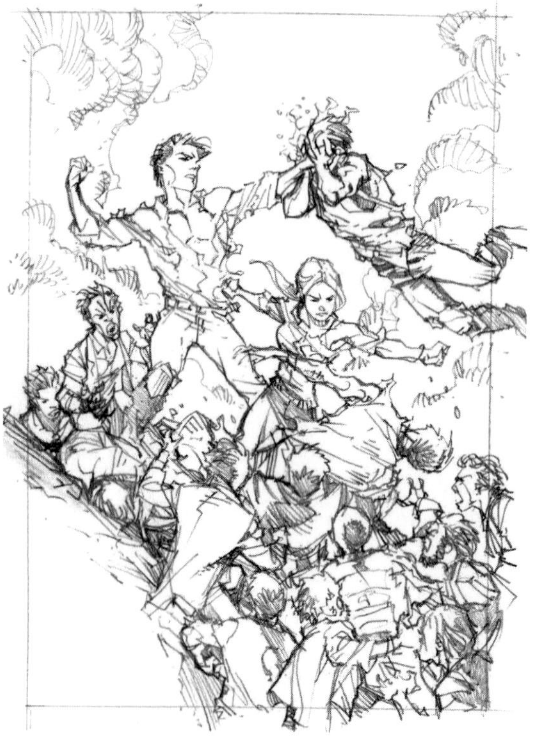

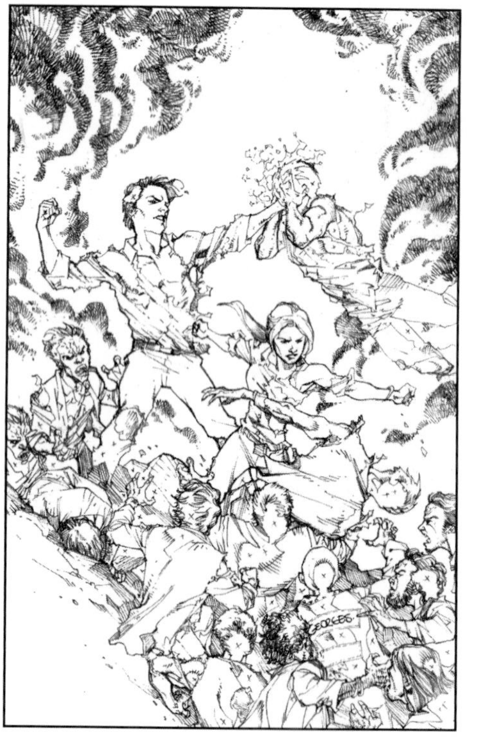

For the cover of issue #3 we wanted to pay homage to artist Frank Frazetta and feature Buffy and newcomer Detective Dowling taking on the new threat—zompires (aptly described by the wonderful Xander Harris). Georges gave us many options (the rough layouts are at the top).

We chose option C, and he then gave us loose pencils, followed by tighter pencils that were eventually inked and colored.

OPPOSITE: *Cover to Buffy S9 #3 by Georges Jeanty, Dexter Vines, and JD Mettler.*

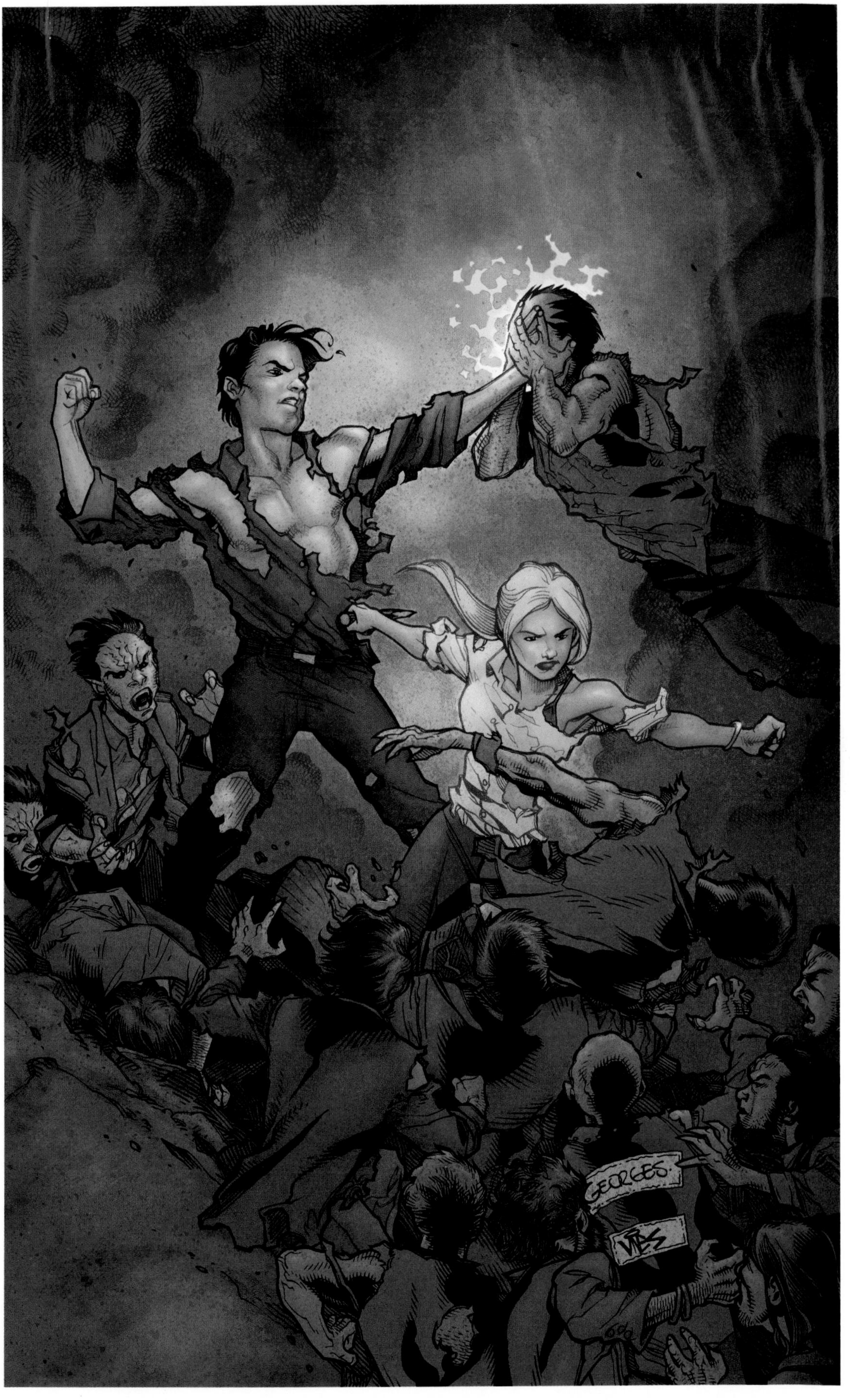
GEORGES

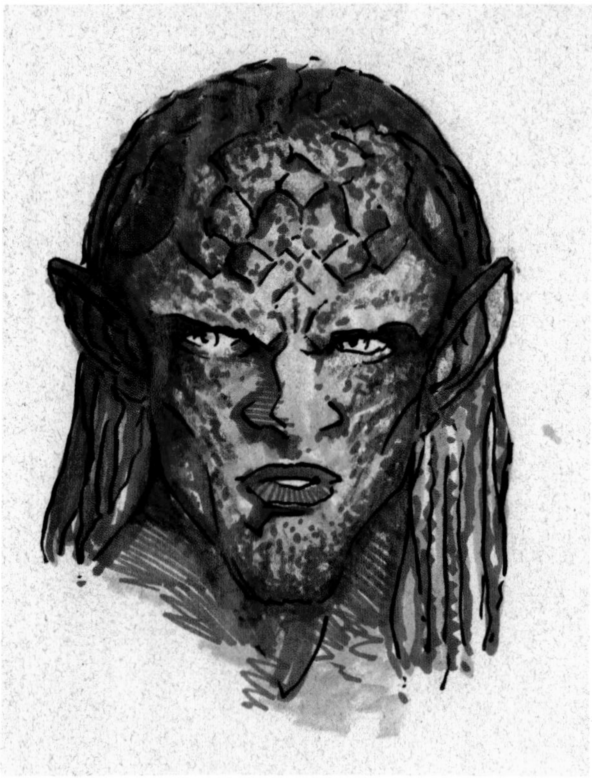

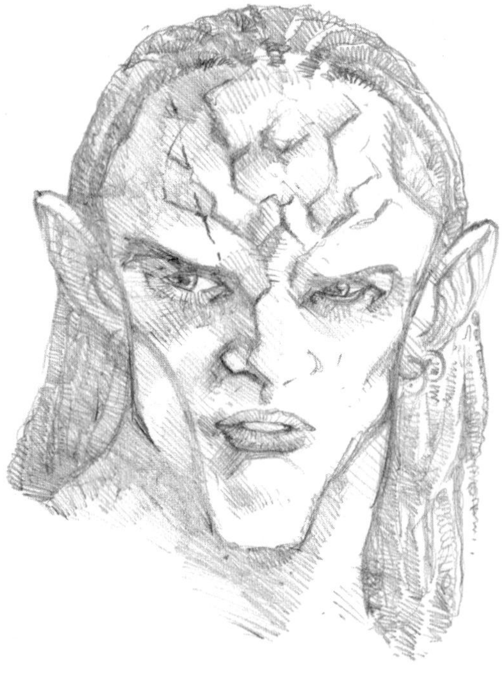

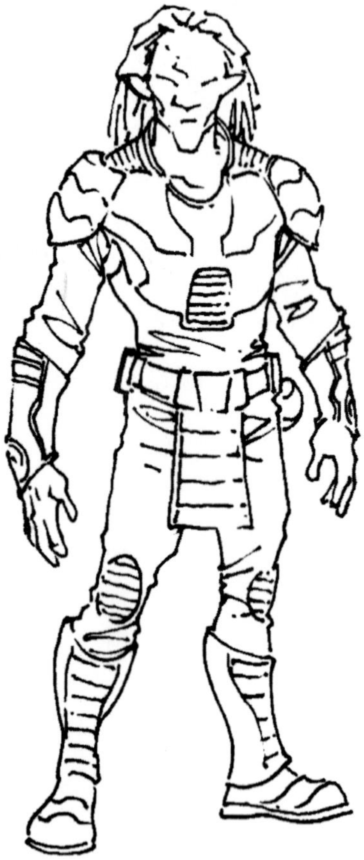

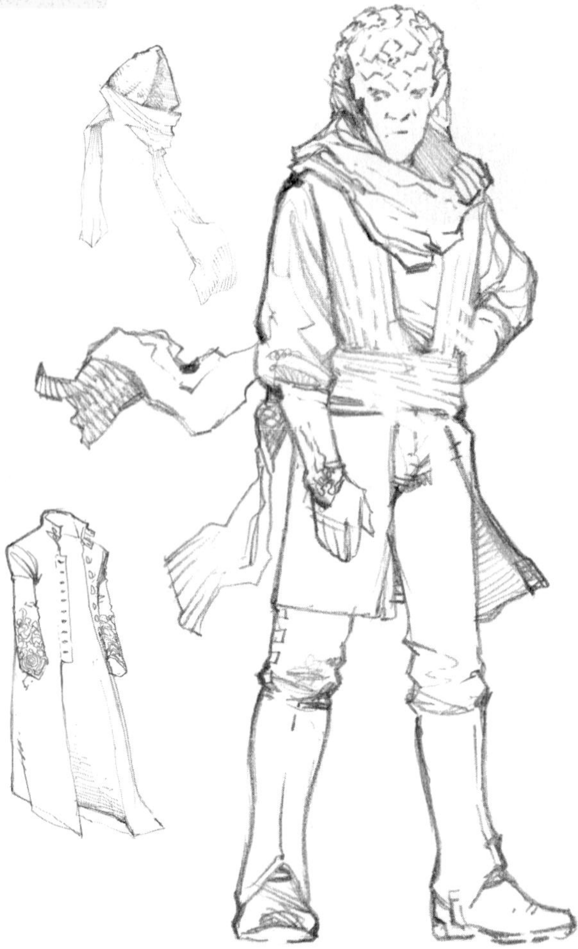

Here are the designs for our newest antihero and demon—Eldre Koh. Joss wanted someone who resembled a "steampunk Civil War Jedi" and would be sexy . . . like Beauty and the Beast *sexy.*

OPPOSITE: *Cover to* Buffy S9 #4 *by Georges Jeanty, Dexter Vines, and Dave Stewart.*

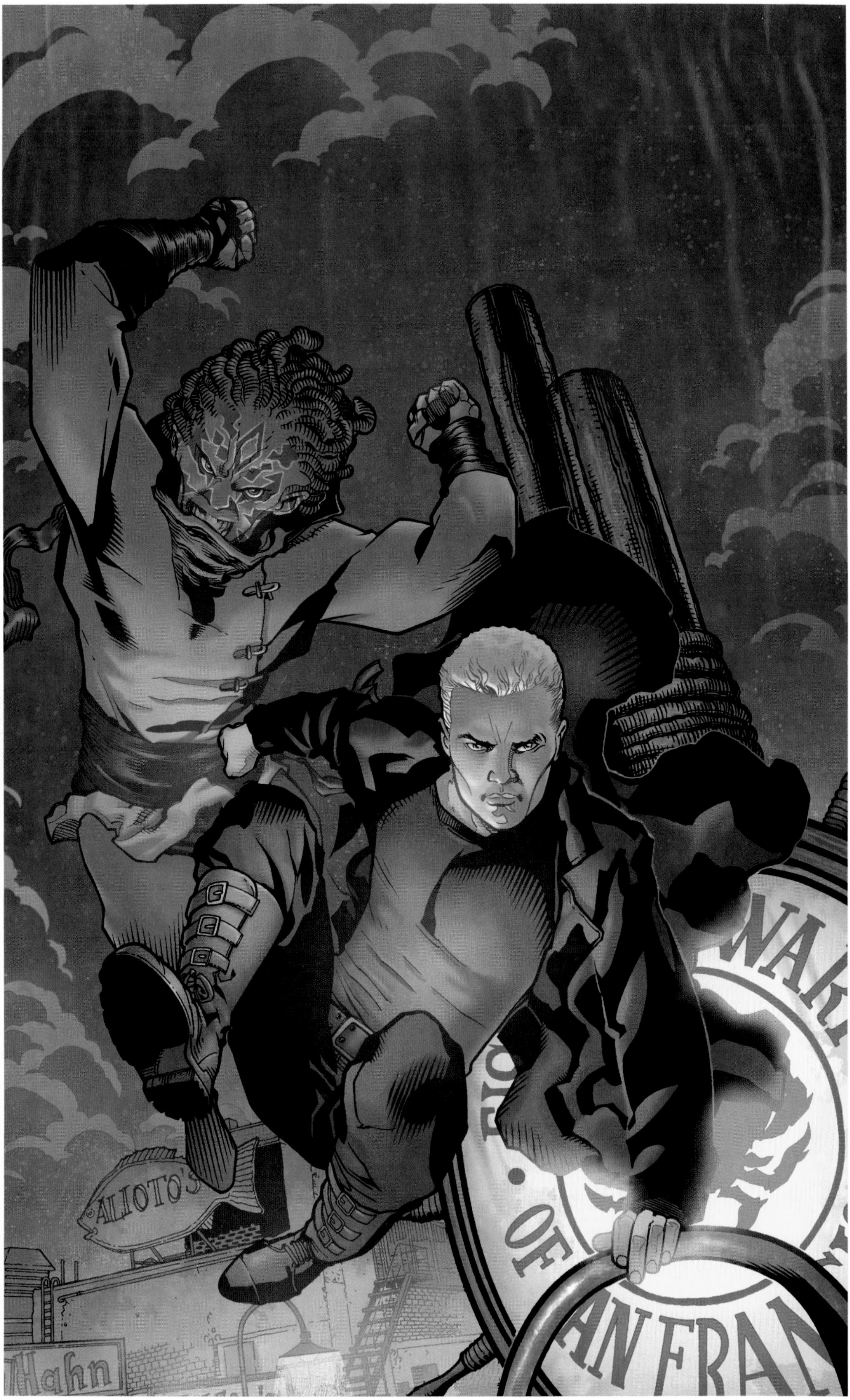
ALIOTO'S
Hahn
OF

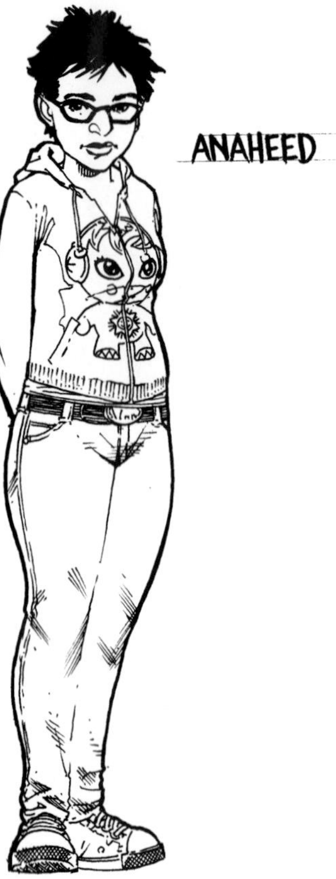
ANAHEED

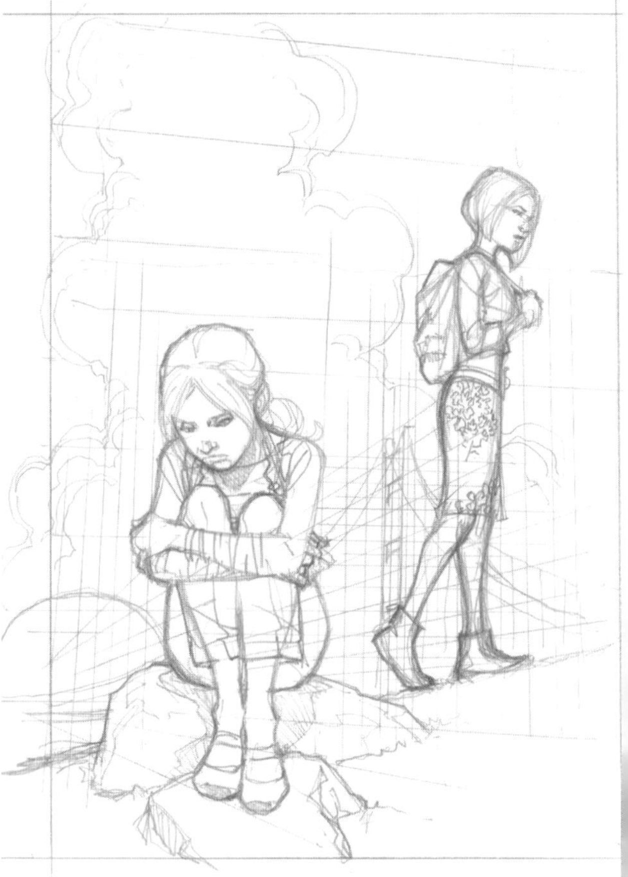

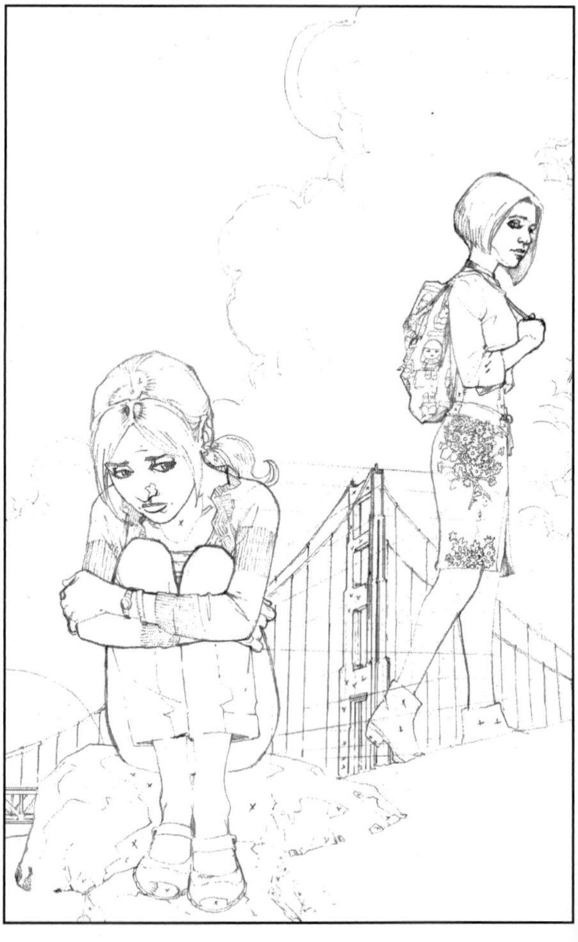

ABOVE: *Here is the character design for Anaheed, one of Buffy's adorable new roomies.*

RIGHT: *Layouts and pencils for* Buffy *S9 #5, marking Willow's departure.*

OPPOSITE: *Cover to* Buffy *S9 #5 by Georges Jeanty, Dexter Vines, and Michelle Madsen.*

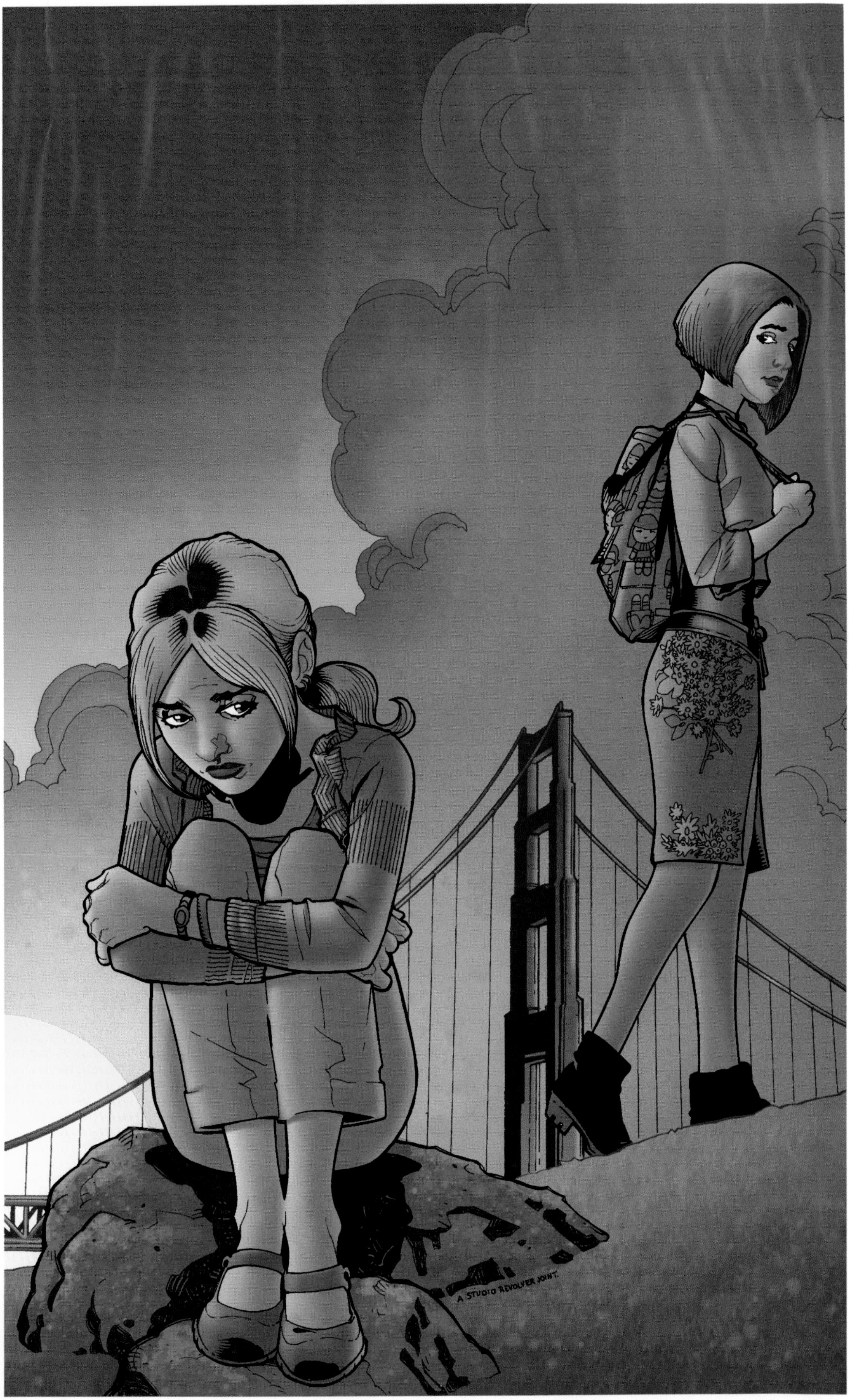
A STUDIO REVOLVER JOINT.

MAGICAL MYSTERY TOUR
FEATURING THE BEETLES

SCRIPT
JANE ESPENSON

PENCILS
GEORGES JEANTY

INKS
DEXTER VINES

COLORS
MICHELLE MADSEN

LETTERING
RICHARD STARKINGS
& Comicraft's
JIMMY BETANCOURT

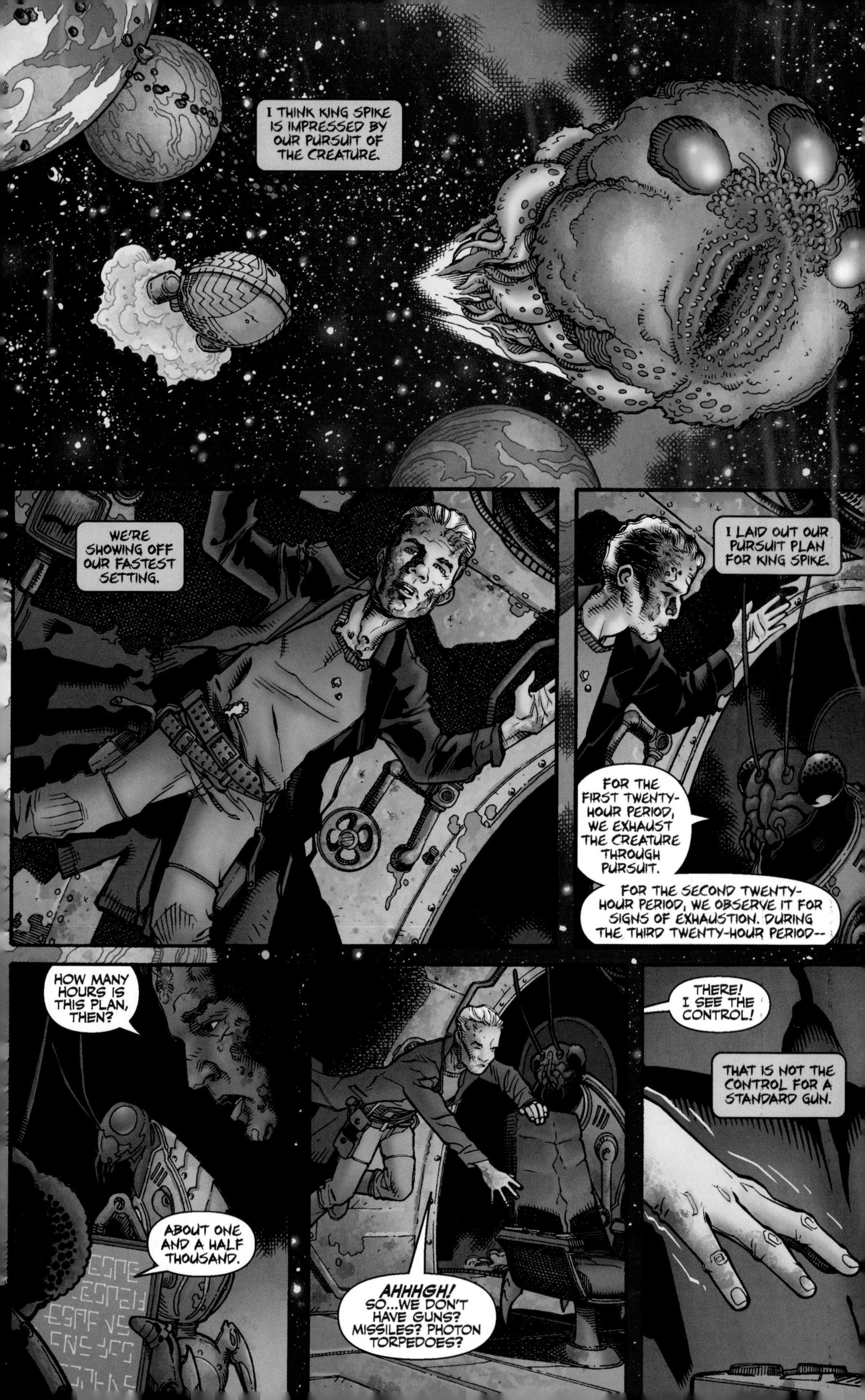
I THINK KING SPIKE IS IMPRESSED BY OUR PURSUIT OF THE CREATURE.
WE'RE SHOWING OFF OUR FASTEST SETTING.
I LAID OUT OUR PURSUIT PLAN FOR KING SPIKE.
FOR THE FIRST TWENTY-HOUR PERIOD, WE EXHAUST THE CREATURE THROUGH PURSUIT.
FOR THE SECOND TWENTY-HOUR PERIOD, WE OBSERVE IT FOR SIGNS OF EXHAUSTION. DURING THE THIRD TWENTY-HOUR PERIOD--
HOW MANY HOURS IS THIS PLAN, THEN?
ABOUT ONE AND A HALF THOUSAND.
AHHHGH! SO...WE DON'T HAVE GUNS? MISSILES? PHOTON TORPEDOES?
THERE! I SEE THE CONTROL!
THAT IS NOT THE CONTROL FOR A STANDARD GUN.

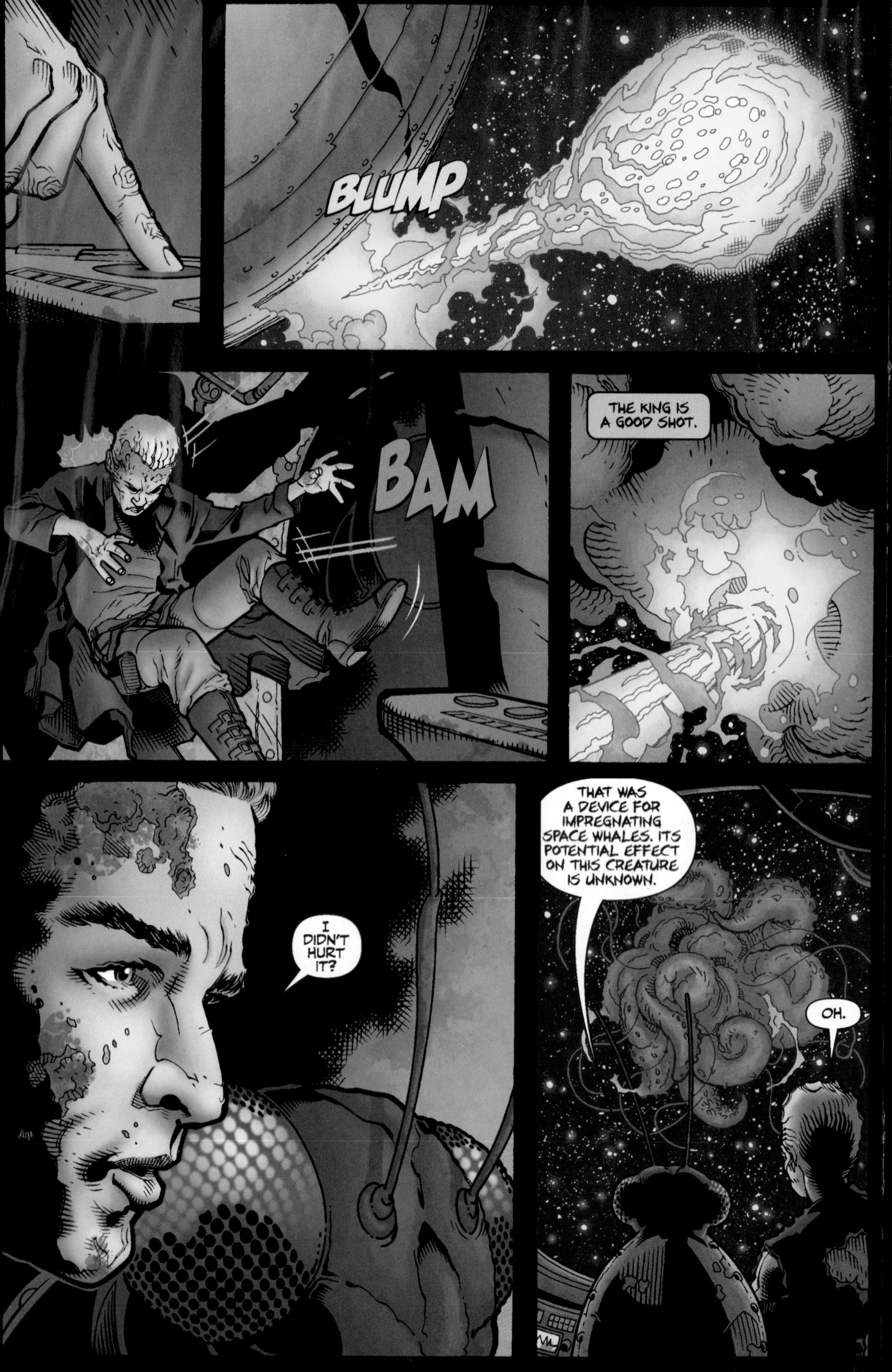
BLUMP
BAM
THE KING IS A GOOD SHOT.
I DIDN'T HURT IT?
THAT WAS A DEVICE FOR IMPREGNATING SPACE WHALES. ITS POTENTIAL EFFECT ON THIS CREATURE IS UNKNOWN.
OH.

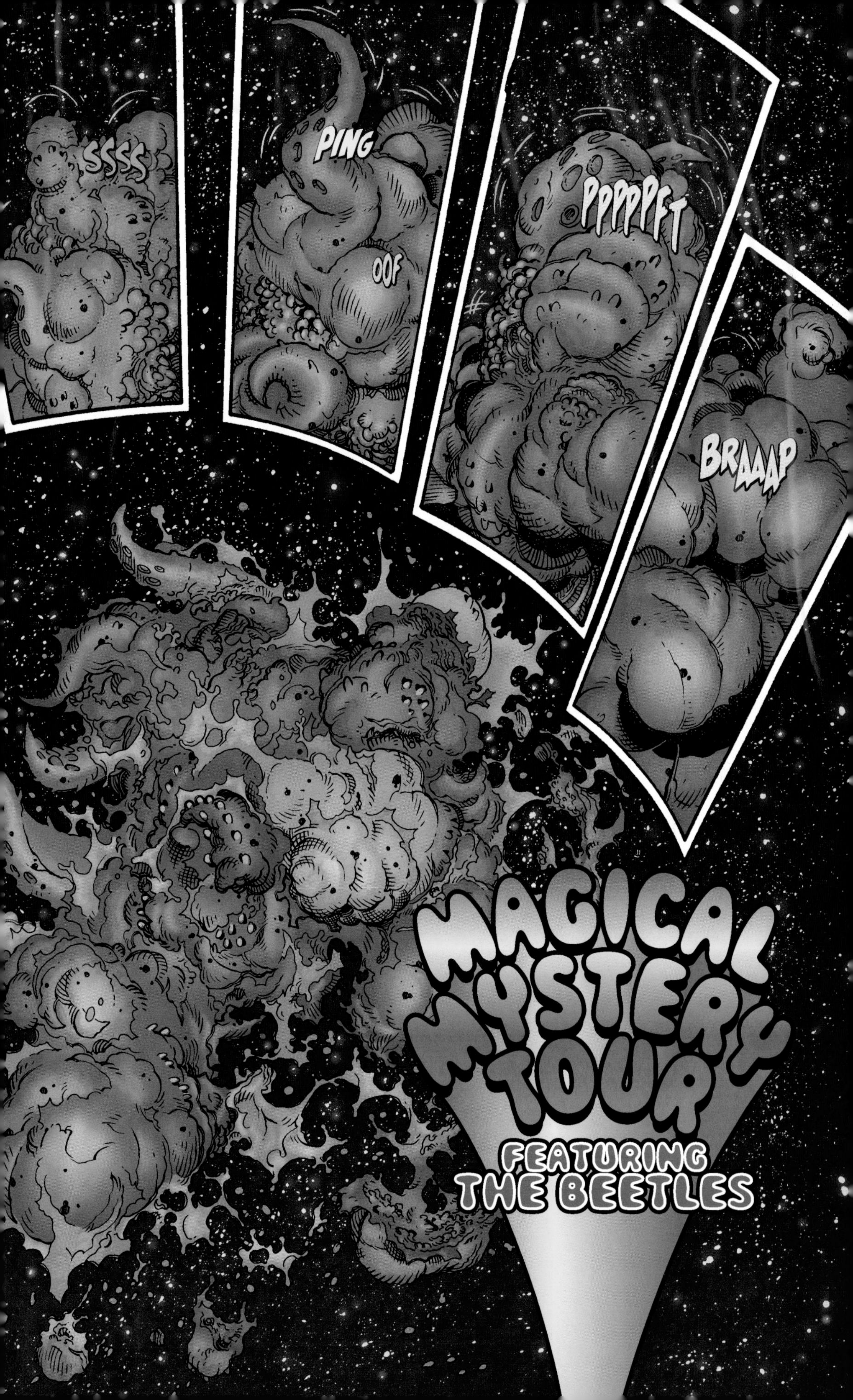
SSSS
PING
OOF
PPPPPFT
BRAAAP
MAGICAL MYSTERY TOUR
FEATURING THE BEETLES

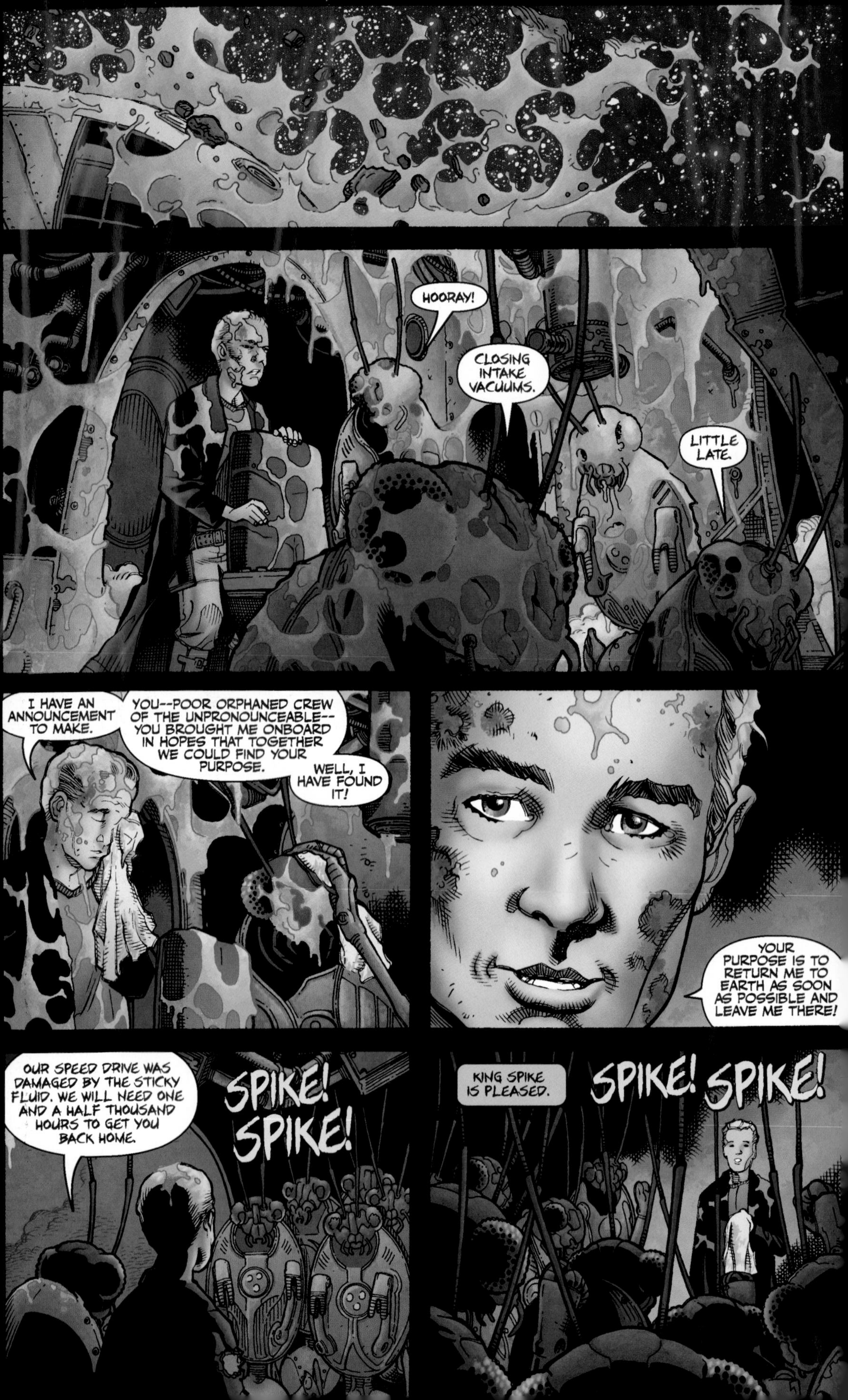
HOORAY!
CLOSING INTAKE VACUUMS.
LITTLE LATE.
I HAVE AN ANNOUNCEMENT TO MAKE.
YOU--POOR ORPHANED CREW OF THE UNPRONOUNCEABLE--YOU BROUGHT ME ONBOARD IN HOPES THAT TOGETHER WE COULD FIND YOUR PURPOSE.
WELL, I HAVE FOUND IT!
YOUR PURPOSE IS TO RETURN ME TO EARTH AS SOON AS POSSIBLE AND LEAVE ME THERE!
OUR SPEED DRIVE WAS DAMAGED BY THE STICKY FLUID. WE WILL NEED ONE AND A HALF THOUSAND HOURS TO GET YOU BACK HOME.
SPIKE! SPIKE!
KING SPIKE IS PLEASED.
SPIKE! SPIKE!

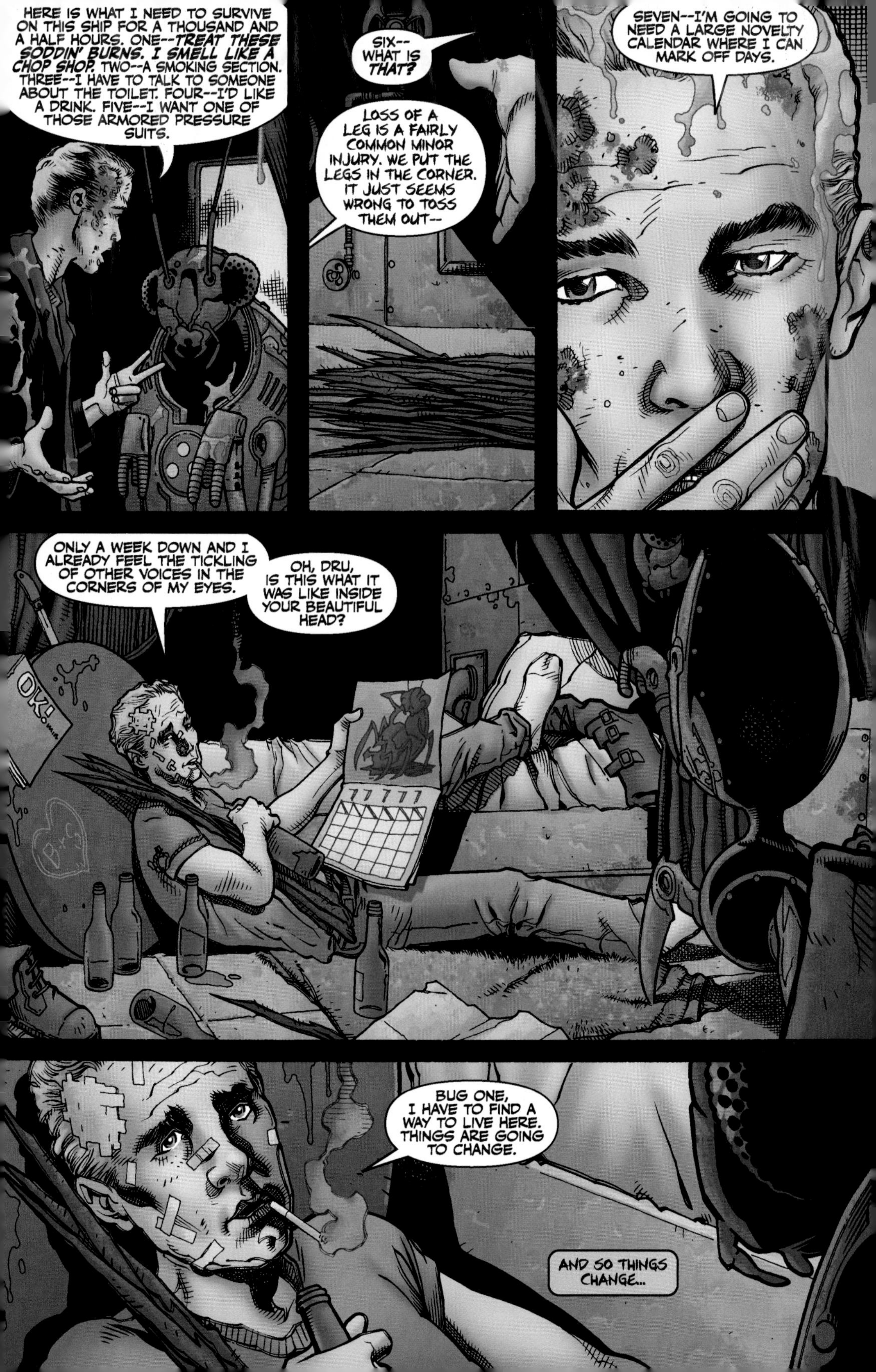
HERE IS WHAT I NEED TO SURVIVE ON THIS SHIP FOR A THOUSAND AND A HALF HOURS. ONE--TREAT THESE SODDIN' BURNS. I SMELL LIKE A CHOP SHOP. TWO--A SMOKING SECTION. THREE--I HAVE TO TALK TO SOMEONE ABOUT THE TOILET. FOUR--I'D LIKE A DRINK. FIVE--I WANT ONE OF THOSE ARMORED PRESSURE SUITS.
SIX-- WHAT IS THAT?
LOSS OF A LEG IS A FAIRLY COMMON MINOR INJURY. WE PUT THE LEGS IN THE CORNER. IT JUST SEEMS WRONG TO TOSS THEM OUT--
SEVEN--I'M GOING TO NEED A LARGE NOVELTY CALENDAR WHERE I CAN MARK OFF DAYS.
ONLY A WEEK DOWN AND I ALREADY FEEL THE TICKLING OF OTHER VOICES IN THE CORNERS OF MY EYES.
OH, DRU, IS THIS WHAT IT WAS LIKE INSIDE YOUR BEAUTIFUL HEAD?
OK!
BUG ONE, I HAVE TO FIND A WAY TO LIVE HERE. THINGS ARE GOING TO CHANGE.
AND SO THINGS CHANGE...

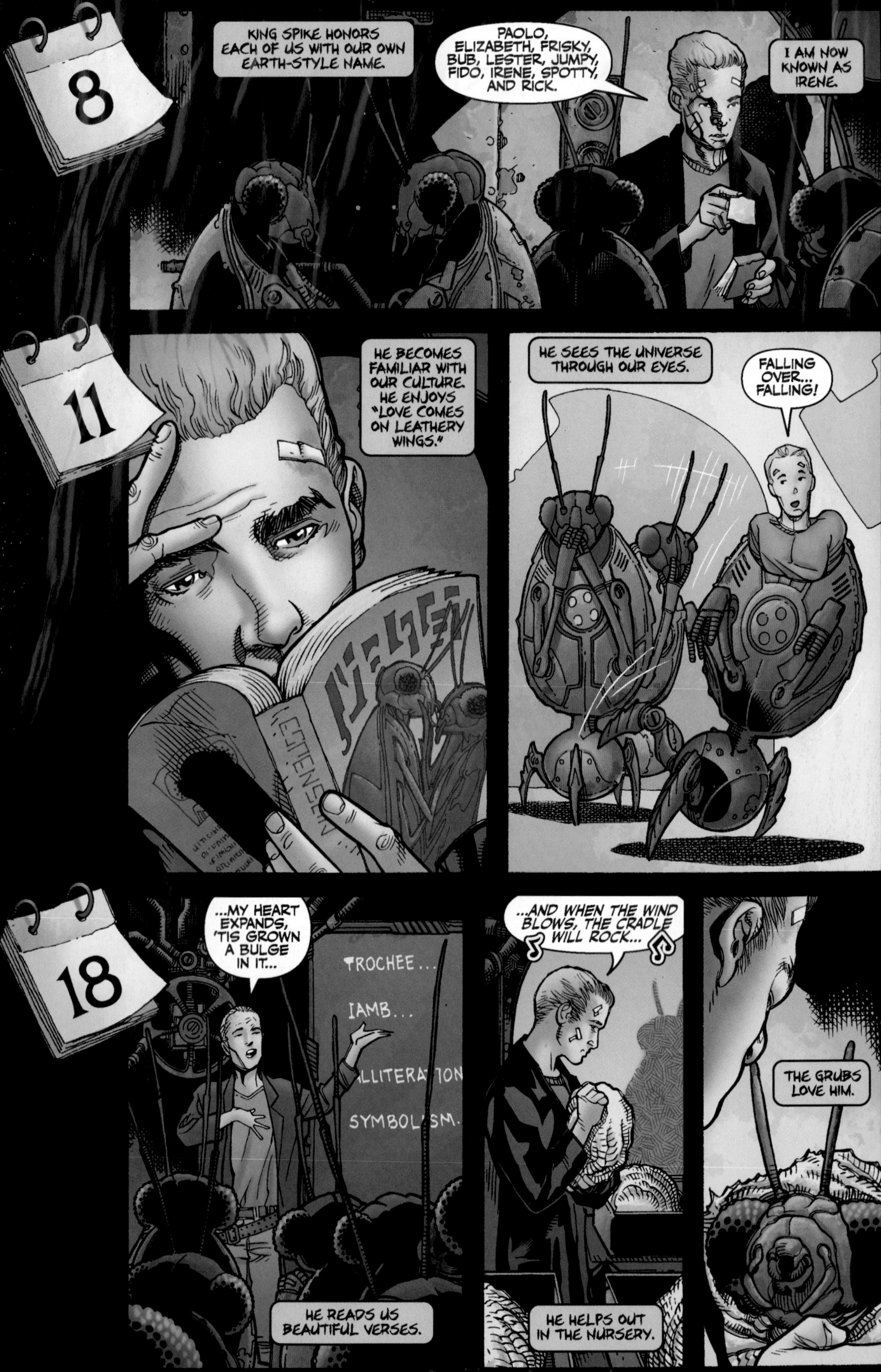

8
KING SPIKE HONORS EACH OF US WITH OUR OWN EARTH-STYLE NAME.
PAOLO, ELIZABETH, FRISKY, BUB, LESTER, JUMPY, FIDO, IRENE, SPOTTY, AND RICK.
I AM NOW KNOWN AS IRENE.
11
HE BECOMES FAMILIAR WITH OUR CULTURE. HE ENJOYS "LOVE COMES ON LEATHERY WINGS."
HE SEES THE UNIVERSE THROUGH OUR EYES.
FALLING OVER... FALLING!
18
...MY HEART EXPANDS, 'TIS GROWN A BULGE IN IT...
TROCHEE...
IAMB...
SYMBOLISM.
HE READS US BEAUTIFUL VERSES.
...AND WHEN THE WIND BLOWS, THE CRADLE WILL ROCK...
HE HELPS OUT IN THE NURSERY.
THE GRUBS LOVE HIM.

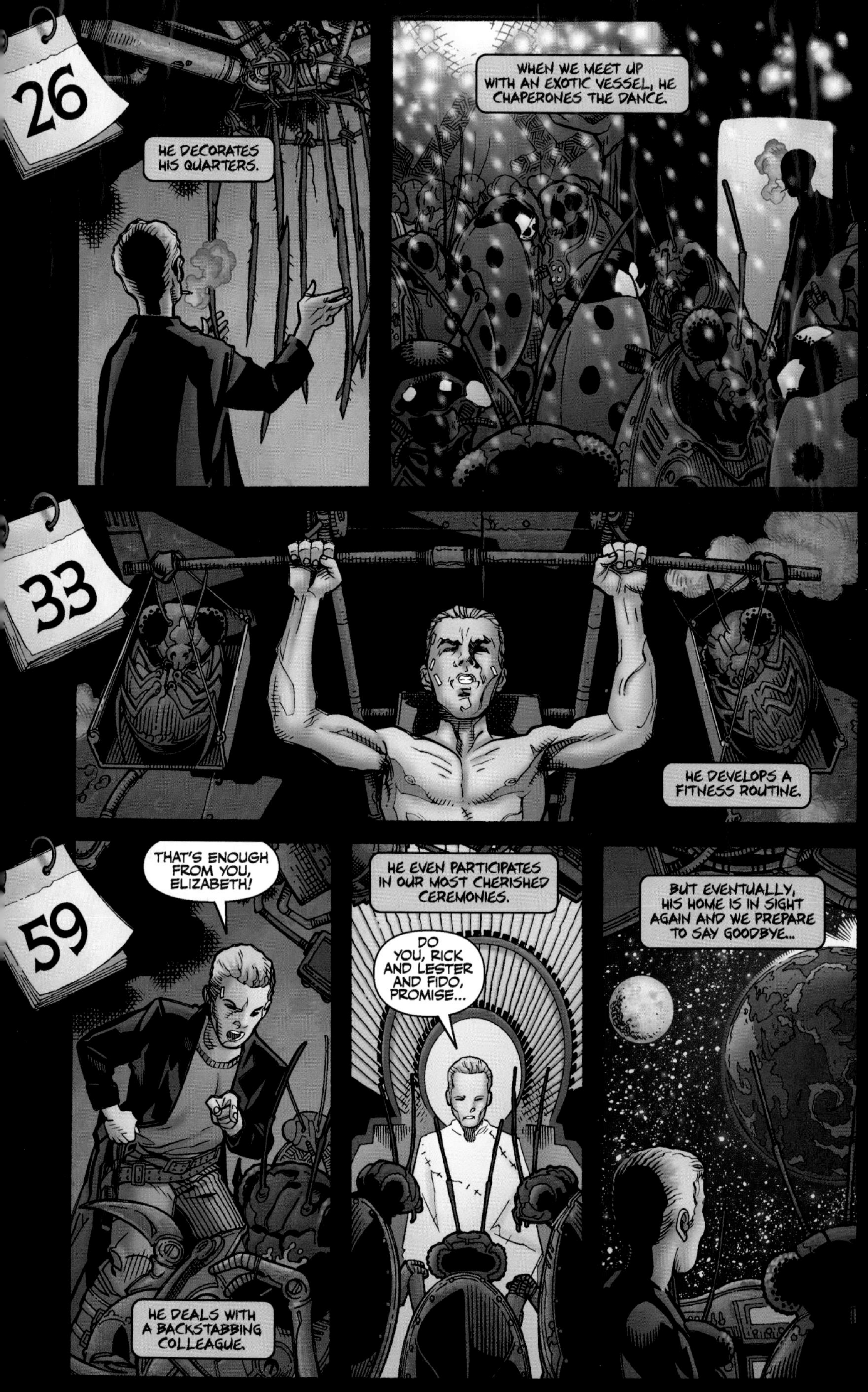
26
HE DECORATES HIS QUARTERS.
WHEN WE MEET UP WITH AN EXOTIC VESSEL, HE CHAPERONES THE DANCE.
33
HE DEVELOPS A FITNESS ROUTINE.
59
THAT'S ENOUGH FROM YOU, ELIZABETH!
HE DEALS WITH A BACKSTABBING COLLEAGUE.
HE EVEN PARTICIPATES IN OUR MOST CHERISHED CEREMONIES.
DO YOU, RICK AND LESTER AND FIDO, PROMISE...
BUT EVENTUALLY, HIS HOME IS IN SIGHT AGAIN AND WE PREPARE TO SAY GOODBYE...

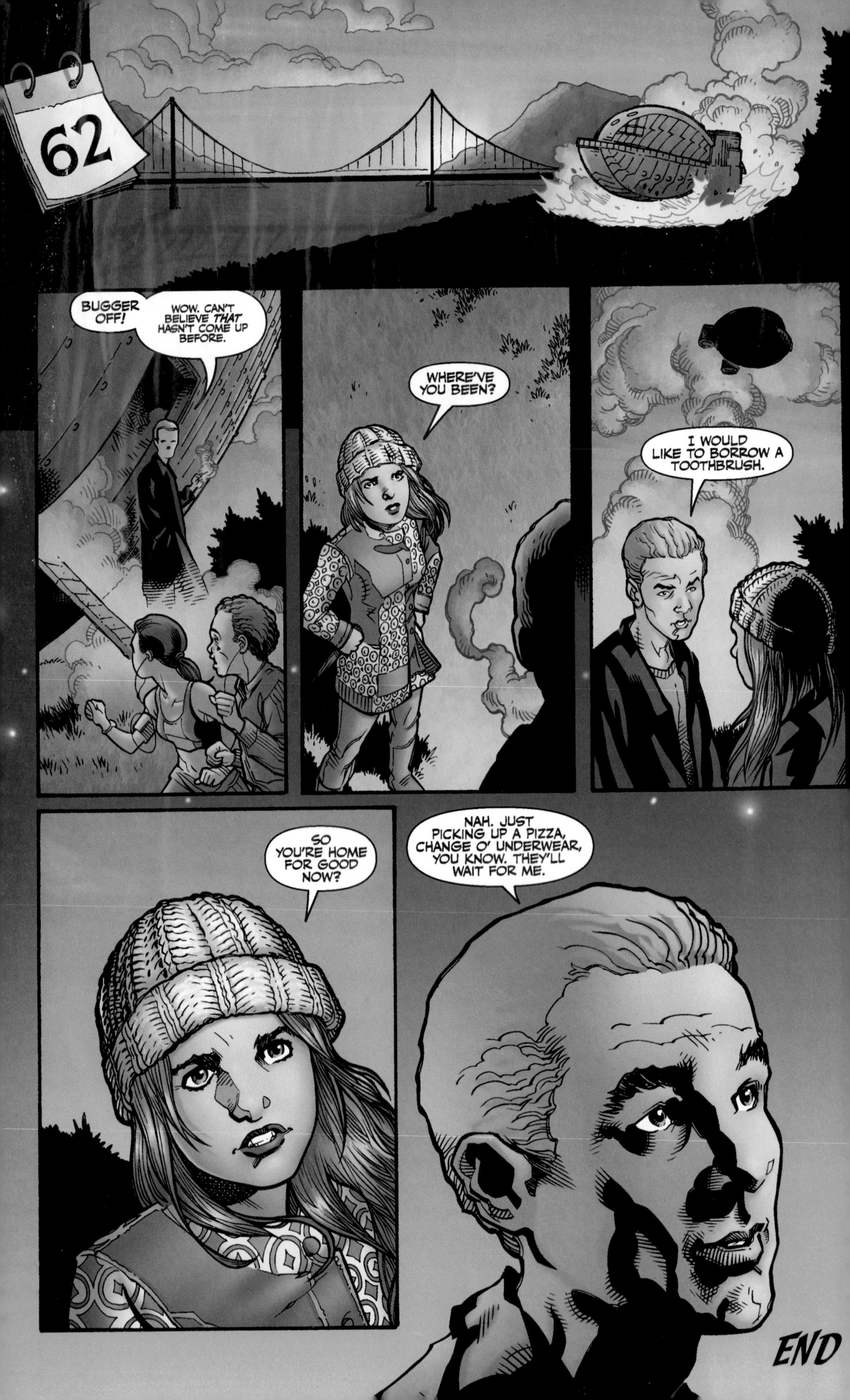
62
BUGGER OFF!
WOW. CAN'T BELIEVE *THAT* HASN'T COME UP BEFORE.
WHERE'VE YOU BEEN?
I WOULD LIKE TO BORROW A TOOTHBRUSH.
SO YOU'RE HOME FOR GOOD NOW?
NAH. JUST PICKING UP A PIZZA, CHANGE O' UNDERWEAR, YOU KNOW. THEY'LL WAIT FOR ME.
END